SPQR

10TH LEGION

BATTLE BORN

BY BEN SODEN

Published in the United Kingdom by:

Bellum Books

First printed 2015

ISBN 978-0-9932261-0-6

This book is dedicated to all the Fighting Men who have stood in the battle line alongside others in faraway lands. Men who became closer in ways more than any family ever could, those Men who marched, dug holes, sweated, laughed, fought, cried and bled in the dust together.

Those Men who for many years after the fighting is done still call each other by the name of 'Brother'.

Foreword

Dear Reader, I know it says 'Foreword' above this line. It could easily say 'warning' or perhaps 'mini autobiography', or even 'author's apology'! This foreword will be a mixture of all these things. Firstly, for all those historians, re-enactors and subject matter experts… I shall warn you in advance. I certainly do not pretend to know absolutely everything about the Roman army. In fact, unless you own a time machine or can actually speak to the dead in detail, I do not think anyone can say they know *exactly* what it was like to be marching in a cohort of Caesar's legions. Doubtless a good few will come across a detail or piece of minutiae that will cause an instant dislike to this book, but such is life! If it pleased everyone it would be banal and not worth reading.

For historical accuracy I researched as well as any man could. Often I would come across one source, then another contradicting the last, and so on. It seems the subject of actual 'boots on the ground' soldiering for the Roman army is partly a matter of personal interpretation by the writer. Of course, my bookshelf has Polybius, Plutarch, Caesar, Tacitus, Livy, etc., etc., and yes I have read many of the works of excellent modern academics on the subject of the Roman army that each have their own unique and varied interpretations. Further to this I joined various forums and asked for many opinions from historians and re-enactors whose opinions were very useful and numerous. So with a lot of subject matter material, general consensus on the unknown and a hefty amount of artistic license I began to write… and, gentle reader, I invoke the Goddess Clementia for you to be forgiving with this long-suffering author on his humble quest.

Technicalities — Certain aspects such as the ranking system I have kept simple and in a way that made the most sense for me. Each section has a section commander or senior legionary, because even the smallest units generally have an appointed leader, regardless if it's an official title or not, mostly due to accountability rather than command. In my opinion, the optios acted as platoon sergeants and the low- to middle-ranking centurions as the platoon commanders. The century was like an oversized platoon, the cohort a company and the legion a battalion. Yes, many say you simply cannot compare it to modern forces; well, the whole point of the book is to enjoy the many modern parallels that I personally see.

Other aspects of daily legionary life, the use of equipment, duties, dress, the sizes of artillery, etc., can all be argued about. However, in the modern infantry, I have seen with my own eyes fighting men use machine gun barrels as hammers, ammo tins as toilets or ovens, and wear sandbags on their feet when it was cold. Has anyone ever heard of a man trying to fit an army issue sock over his head when the biting midges of southern Scotland drove him mad? Probably not! But it is a true story nevertheless. Military men who live in the field for a long time are very adaptive and flexible creatures. The regulations that were usually written from someone's office chair often end up being rather vague guidelines more than rules. Caesar himself was known to be an unconventional commander. I have no doubt that some of the men serving under him were the same.

Timeline and perspective — I write with interludes and my narrative is not linear. My interlude chapters allow me to pad out the world and bring different perspectives into the frame. You will also notice I say 'we' in many sentences without actually explaining who the first-person character is. Well, that person is the 'unknown soldier'; he is nobody in the Legion, but then he is all of them. When I say 'we marched', 'we fought' and 'we sweated and shivered', it is because I felt the men needed a collective voice that united them — some unknown character who has also marched, fought, sweated and shivered. It is their voice as much as it is my own... It is the voice of the Soldier.

Terminology — I like to use different terms interchangeably. For instance I might say 'sword', then I might say 'gladius'. This is purely due to my own poetry within the sentence. I chose whatever sounded the most pleasing to me when read aloud. As for things such as place names, military ranks, roads and such, they are strictly Latinised. Also, for some of the military commands, I keep the best part of the shouted commands in Latin, because they have a wonderful music to them.

The Romans were masters of profanity; we can see it in everything from their graffiti to their poetry. So would the soldiers have sworn? I suspect, like the modern day soldier, that would be a resounding *yes!* Soldiers generally are filthy-minded and foul-mouthed creatures with a colourful vocabulary. Some might argue that my characters would not have said this or that in that particular way? But it is more about the spirit of the soldier rather than the accuracy of their vulgarities... After all, if it was 100% accurate the whole book would be in Latin, so I have used modern terminology to see you through.

So that is my warning to you. I apologise for any mistakes as they are mine alone. However, because this is the first book of several, I am happy for you to correspond with me directly in person if there are glaring issues that need addressing. It's exactly what second editions are for.

***

A little on me... Well, history has always fascinated me, particularly military history. Like most kids of my generation we would be running through the bushes playing WWII or Vietnam war games with juvenile attempts at German and Vietnamese accents that would have been hilariously offensive and incorrect. I can even vaguely remember the old black and white TV in our house showing grainy images from the Falklands War. As I grew, so did my appetite for the subject. I began with a huge pile of 'Victor' comics that I inherited somewhere and even read Homer's *Iliad* at the tender age of eleven just because there was fighting in it. I adored and loved every single war film and TV series I could watch and admittedly, TV shows like *Hogan's Heroes* and *'Allo 'Allo* left me a skewed perception of the horrors of war.

Deep into my teenage years I found that I would have history books, especially those on Romans, samurai or WWII soldiers, as my constant companion. It seemed I was destined for the military, but to what end? The British Army did not look particularly attractive at the time. Peacekeeping in the Balkans or driving around Northern Ireland in armoured land rovers did not seem interesting at all. My interest waned and almost diminished completely as I found the rave scene and college with its liberal sprinkling of creative substances. But my fledgling career with peace and dreams of wandering India looking for artistic inspiration did not last and came to an abrupt end on a fateful day. I was working part time on a construction site in Hatfield, England, next to a film set where they were filming part of the series *Band of Brothers* at the time. I distinctly remember an electrician walking past and telling us, "It's on the radio that a passenger plane has crashed into a building in New York". Shortly thereafter I took a phone call from a friend who was watching TV and said another plane had deliberately crashed. Apparently America was under attack! That was a Tuesday. By Friday I had smoked my last joint, given up on the idea of graphic design, had been into the Army recruiting office, filled out the papers and started running. It was all over the news and TV… War was coming and I wanted in.

The famous Infantry regiment the Royal Green Jackets was an easy choice for me. Firstly, due to a year in Army cadets under the same regiment… until I got asked to leave. (Myself and Darren K. were spotted at 05:00 coming out of the girls' tent on a field exercise… but that's another story.) Secondly, because of

Richard Sharpe. Yes, *the* 'Sharpe' of the 95th Rifles. I never wanted to be a Redcoat or jump out of planes, or wrestle crocodiles underwater. I wanted to be a Rifleman and on 13th December 2001 I was officially enlisted as one.

Basic training was eventful. I was in the winning section at Winchester barracks despite our platoon having an illegal 'fight club'. During 'Phase 2' in Catterick (or the second half of training for civilian types) I was one of only five Englishmen in an entirely Scottish training platoon. Men, corporals, the Sergeant... *all* Jocks and during the football World Cup, too! Never did an Englishman suffer so much prejudice... at least in the beginning.. By the end of Phase 2 training I was pronounced an 'Honorary Jock' and came out with a slight Scottish accent and a shitty little 'best field craft' award, probably just because my OCD with packing kit makes it look like I am squared away all the time. A month's leave, then a train down to Warminster to join the 2nd Battalion, Royal Green Jackets, where I soon learned that behind the professionalism, pomp, pageantry and outright media propaganda of the British Army lurks a very different world.

The Royal Green Jackets was notorious for more things than being the first British soldiers to wear green and use skirmishing tactics that we would recognise today. Certainly we were well known for our character and lack of correct dress code. I was once told by a Sgt Major from another regiment, "You lot are the scruffiest c*nts I have ever seen!" which we took as a compliment! Across the army we were known for more nefarious things, such as the highly publicised kidnap, rape and murder of a woman in Cyprus, and even driving an armoured vehicle into the office building of a C.O. who was 'disliked'. Yet at the same time we always outdid those around us, for a Rifleman was encouraged to think and act for himself rather than just wait for orders. Our antecedent regiments had accumulated a staggering amount of Victoria crosses. In real life we were more than just a *Sharpe* TV show and were swaggering fighters in the field, and much worse in the bars and pubs when drunk.

So in light of what infantry soldiers are like, has history left out a plethora of interesting characters? Will the colourful exploits of the Green Jackets be remembered through the mists of time or shall just the nobler aspects such as the volume of Victoria Cross winners remain? I believe this has happened to the Legionary. Certainly Julius Caesar and Mark Anthony are household names, even for those who know nothing of Rome. Those who studied Caesar's campaigns would recognise Sabinus, Cotta, Labienus and Cicero. Of course we also get little echoes of the fighting men like Considius, Crastinus, or the now more famous Pullo and Vorenus who have been further immortalised in the excellent HBO TV series *Rome*. But what of the tens of thousands of others? Were they all 'good, virtuous Roman patriots'? I seriously doubt it when you consider how many rough and tough, working class street kids would have enlisted back then... just like they do today.

History is written by the winners, we all know that. But it is also invariably and almost exclusively written by the officers, commanders, academics and/or the upper classes of the day. Would we know about Centurion Gaius Crastinus if Julius Caesar had not mentioned him? No, of course not. He would be another of the nameless masses that pushed his country's foreign policy forward at sword point.

It is also vital to remember that the winners who write these histories are biased. The enemy is, after all, an *'enemy'*; they are the bad guy! And so by default their own men are the 'good guys'. I have personally seen officers give eloquent TV interviews to the press that certainly did *not* give the full picture of what happened on the ground. Would ancient sources be any different? If anything, because of the lack of press coverage and because Caesar's account was to curry favour with the populace, he probably embellished even more than a modern commander might.

In both modern and ancient cases, did the author writing the histories have to smell the shit in the irrigation ditch in Afghanistan *or* in a ditch in ancient Gaul? Has he carried all that kit for many kilometres on a 45°C day for a minimal wage? Has he yawned at 03:00 on the never-ending guard and sentry duties? Has been crawled in the dirt and seen the bright red blood spill out of friends? Has he drunk, sworn, laughed and suffered like the men? Very few might have shared in some of the hardships… a great many of these authors certainly have not. That job is for the Rifleman, just as it was for the Legionary. And so we often find the voices of the silent masses being left out of the history books altogether in lieu of their commander's legacy. I know this to be true from my own experience.

So what kind of men would these nameless Roman soldiers be? In my experience, some of the most bizarre people you could ever possibly meet were in my battalion. I am certain those men in history were not much different to us. Probably worse in many ways! Certainly we did not make slaves of our enemies and were never given entire towns to pillage and plunder. I have read a few fictional books on the subject but the characters never seemed like 'real soldiers' to me. They all seem to be a standard, tame, inoffensive, two-dimensional cliché compared to the fighting men I have met over the years. So one day in the spring of 2013, I was sat in Afghanistan. Armed with my experience of the brave and bold and completely bat shit crazy, I sat down to write.

"Take me to the Brig...I want to see the real Marines"

General Lewis B. "Chesty" Puller - USMC

The words of "Chesty" Puller ring as true today as they probably would have done back then. This book is my humble attempt to bring a little colour to those forgotten faces and long silent voices. In my experience the biggest and best drunkards, perverts, brawlers, thieves, comedians, fighters, criminals, liars and especially warriors and friends I have ever met were in the army. No good soldier worth his salt is 'perfect'. I could not write a book about the biggest, strongest, fastest, fittest, Legionaries who get *all* the awards, promotions and girls, because this book is based on real people, not hero-worship, Hollywood films and brave, strong, patriotic 'superhero' characters with no vices who are just a little haunted from combat. Such people do not exist on the battlefield. They are a cliché written by men who have a romantic view of war and probably have never gone toe to toe with an enemy in combat alongside the mad, bad and dangerous.

Real Soldiers are far more interesting! You will find many of them are rogues that would be locked away if the army had not taken them! I know a fellow sniper in my battalion who is deadly with a rifle but absolutely dreadful with his fists when drunk, hence his lack of real teeth. I know a senior NCO who was jailed for international arms smuggling. I know a huge, violent man who went AWOL from our platoon to rob drug dealers and was recently jailed for flashing his penis to a shopkeeper before lifting him upside down and throwing him on the floor before he threatened to burn the place down if he did not get protection money. Another man was caught in the middle of the night drunkenly trying to steal a slot machine — not just breaking into it, but actually with the machine half out of the window of a recreation building. And do you know anyone who covered their stomach and penis in alcohol gel before lighting it as a joke, thus causing serious burns to themselves? No? Well, I do! He goes by the name Karl H. He suffered severe blisters and ended up sitting around mostly naked, covered in cream, in Iraq for weeks. Karl is a real person and the government gave that man an assault rifle.

Who are these lunatics, you might say? Well, they were all soldiers first and foremost, regardless of their colourful antics. Would the Roman Army have had the same? Or were they just the silent, orderly masses we are made to believe they are? "Chesty" Puller wanted to see the *real* Marines; I wanted to see some *real* Legionaries, and so my characters were born. People might say these characters are too fantastical to be real. Well, they are composites of many different people and all my characters would be pretty average for a Rifleman in the Royal Green Jackets! So now you know where I am coming from I shall leave you to it.

Lastly I would like to say a huge thank you to my Agnieszka for not only putting up with me for so many years but being a most excellent editor who stopped me from deleting the whole thing about sixty four thousand times. I would also like to thank my mother for constantly encouraging me to read as a kid. A word of thanks is definitely in order for the test audience who ranged from Arkansas to Austria with their valuable input and encouragement.

And finally a special thank you to all the fighting men, warriors and interesting characters I have known over the years, regardless if you were bayoneting Argentineans in the Falklands, racking up kills with sniper rifles, choking people out on the mats or getting half your limbs blown off and still cracking on with a smile! You are a rare breed that no-one will ever quite understand. History will always remember our commanders but *you* are the ones who stamped those names into the eternal stone of history! I salute every single one of you.

SPQR

Chapter 1

The sound rumbled and it was almost like it could felt more than heard, it was like thunder in the distance… at first. But as it got closer it changed and it became louder, harsher and more metallic, a hiss of metal on metal…

Clank, clank, clank, clank, clank…

"By all the Gods, I love that sound!" said the grinning, muscular Greek marching in our midst. "After all that suffering, here we are! No more training and ready for battle! Thousands of us! *Real* Roman soldiers on the march, eh!" he said looking around with a genuinely, enthusiastic happiness in his handsome face.

His comments immediately brought curses, some name calling and a snort of derision from those who marched around him in the formation as his powerful frame shifted side to side with a rolling gait that you might find on a sailor, although as far as we knew he was a merchant's son. He had not changed all that much through the last vigorous springtime months of basic training. Everyone else had got a little bigger and stronger but he looked much the same. He was already athletic and well-muscled when he turned up at the camp as a brand new *probatio[1]*. His recorded name was Kallias Ampelios, but we called this athletic Greek-turned-Roman citizen-turned-soldier

---

[1] a brand new recruit to the Roman army.

'Kratos[2] after he had taught a lesson to a much larger man who tried to fight him.

This fight had happened months ago when Kratos was on his way to the legion camp for the first time. Like all the other recruits with probatio status, he had originally hurried to stand in line with all the other eager, hopeful teenage men who had attended the initial recruitment phase called the *dilectus*[3]. After being physically inspected and passing the interview he was gruffly told that he had been successful by the recruiting officer. The clerk at the desk had scratched his name onto a tablet and gave him a token that he must present when reporting to the Legion camp for basic training and entry into the newly formed Legion.

Full of excitement and joy, he had returned home and said his goodbyes to his weeping family in the port city of Gades. They had not long arrived and the place never felt like it was home to him anyway. After a last hug from his father the young man left for the capital of the Roman province Hispania Ulterior. On his journey to Corduba he had walked along the damp tracks and roads in the countryside that were rutted from carts. He was wrapped warm for a winter journey but the weather had not closed in yet and Kratos thoroughly enjoyed the mild weather on his trip to his new home. He had made sure to stay off the main trade routes and meandered through the country and farmlands of southern Hispania so that he might enjoy his last few days of freedom. The reporting deadline was some weeks away, as many of the recruits had to come from far and wide, so he made use of the situation by travelling at a leisurely pace through small towns and villages and sleeping out in the open air or the many abandoned farms as he journeyed to reach the newly formed 10th Legion's winter training camp.

---

[2] Greek mythology, personification of strength and power.
[3] in the Roman army, official levy of soldiers for military service.

On one particular day he stopped at one of these small dreary towns to buy bread and fill his oil flask, and nothing more. Like everywhere in the province these days the tiny town was clearly not doing so well and its residents seemed suspicious of strangers. Kratos quickly purchased what he needed from the few grimy stalls in the market square and ignored the narrowed eyes of the young men on the street. He hurried and loaded his pack and once it was full with supplies for the rest of the journey, he left on the muddied, broken road out of the town with thoughts of looking for one of the many abandoned farm houses and barns he usually found on his way. The young man was on the open track near the town refuse pits and no more than two hundred yards from the gate when he heard the voice...

"Pssst! You there, Numidian!"

Kratos started at the sudden noise and froze as he looked around the empty road, dumbstruck. Did he really hear a voice? His ears heard nothing more than the buzz of a few flies from the nearby refuse pits. His eyes flicked to the remains of a ruined hut on the roadside that appeared empty and then glanced at a heap of stone rubble on the other side of the road.

"Stop peering around like an old woman looking for cock! You will give me away!"

There, next to the hut and low to the floor, he saw a pair of bright blue eyes with a tuft of red hair above them peeking out over the edge of a refuse pit.

The Greek blinked for a moment and cocking his head gave a wry look at this strange man hiding in the pit. Kratos quickly looked around to check there were no hidden knifemen or thugs looking to rob him, as these were dangerous times in the poorer parts of the province. After seeing they were indeed alone the Greek spat on the floor.

"Who are *you* calling Numidian? And why are you sifting through the rubbish, you filthy little beggar?" said Kratos, folding his thick arms with a challenging smile.

The bright blue eyes screwed up in annoyance, "I hope you get a wart on your cock, Numidian! Just tell me if the road is clear. Look, there, back towards the town... Can you see them?"

The red hair bobbed up and down in a rodent-like fashion as the eyes peered towards the town and Kratos could see a thin-faced young man of similar age with a sharp nose and cunning look that a fox would have envied. Kratos remembered the suspicious looks of the townspeople and that he had passed a bored looking town prefect who was listening to a small group of animated young men. One of these had a bloody nose and was very red faced; who could tell if it was from embarrassment or exertion? As Kratos walked past and out the gate, the group had all stopped talking and shot him a wary glance before they carried on the heated discussion. The man with the bloody nose seemed very angry and the prefect gave a nod, scratched his balls thoughtfully and grunted a few words before the group split up and headed back into town.

"I will *kill* the little shit when I find him!" came echoing through the empty street behind as Kratos walked on. Local trouble of some kind and it appeared Kratos had now found the 'trouble' they were probably looking for.

"Ah, yes, I met your friends. They said they were going to arm themselves to fight a 'mighty' warrior! I'm guessing that is you. So… what did you steal?"

The blue eyes looking at him narrowed and the head dropped out of sight. "I do not 'steal' anything! Apart from the hearts of the ladies, of course! The dice never lie! I cannot help that Lady

Fortuna[4] sucks my cock with vigour and she prefers to take a shit in their faces! Those fucking inbreds should know better than to attack a Roman Legionary!" came the indignant reply from the hole.

Kratos laughed "You! A Legionary! Ha, I'm sure the enemies of Rome will never venture into your rubbish pit through fear! Regardless, your friends have been scared away, so you can come out now, mighty Achilles."

The slim man climbed slowly and warily out of the pit, peering back towards the town. Despite being covered in mud and refuse, Kratos could see he was wearing a good winter tunic and what looked like a ripped half of an expensive toga with a well used traveller's pack slung on his slim shoulders. Just like most people he was taller than Kratos and thinner across the shoulders. Even so, a wiry strength could be seen through his clothing. After years of training and fighting Kratos looked at the man up and down as he did with everyone, as if he were an opponent in the ring. *I bet he can run a good distance,* Kratos thought as the lean stranger approached.

"Marcus Mammilius Felix, Soldier of the Senate and the People of Rome," said the freckle skinned man with a huge smile after one final, furtive peer over his shoulder. He then raised his hands like a lawyer about to address the court. "And who do I have before me? A dusty traveller who would think nothing less than offering food and refreshment to the Republic's finest! Marcus is my name but you may call me Felix... Yes, my name is well suited and lucky indeed, for a meaningful friendship with me can be auspicious and fruit-bearing if the lucky person in question attends the friendship as if it were his own beloved sick mother!"

---

[4] the Roman goddess of fortune and luck.

Kratos grinned at his theatrical companion and pointed back towards the gate. "What about them? Are your friends coming to lunch, too?"

Felix's eyes widened and he whipped round in alarm to see where Kratos had pointed before and turned back to the Greek with narrowed eyes. "Be wary, son of Numidia. You may speak my language but you are pushing your luck with this, Roman!" he said in an icy tone as he slipped one of his hands under the ruined toga.

"Peace, friend, we are ALL Roman citizens here."

Kratos tensed and noticed the hand of Felix, expecting a hidden weapon to appear. *This man IS trouble,* he thought taking a step backwards, wary of a sudden thrust from a blade. The mood had changed quickly and left Kratos feeling under his own cloak for his knife while he sought to placate the angry stranger.

"My name is Kallias Ampelios, probatio of the newly formed 10th Legion. I am on my way to the camp," he said in an amicable tone, holding up the military token he had been given by the official at the dilectus.

"Well, you are in the right company, my Numidian companion," Felix whipped a similar token out with a speed that made Kratos start. "When I am the Legion *Legatus*[5] I shall give you a promotion; until then, you may accompany a fine gentleman like me and I will install some good Roman manners into your sizable barbarian skull," said Felix in a lofty tone, reaching up to touch the head of his companion as if he was buying a marble statue.

Kratos smiled and swatted the hand away. "You seem to be more like a lowly actor than a 'fine gentleman' with the way you

---

[5] General in the Roman army, commander of a legion.

carry on! And I am a Roman citizen from Greece, my friend. We were masters of education, philosophy and manners while Rome was a stinky, little village! Besides, with your red hair you must be from Gaul? Or, judging by the smell, probably from Germania?" said Kratos, scratching his short black hair with a grin.

Felix stepped back with a look of irritation on his face. "Well YOU look a little too dark for a Greek. Perhaps you have a little Persian in you... or at least your great grandmother did?!"

Kratos smiled and shrugged off the insult, "Better a Persian than some drunken Gallic halfwit who..."

"THERE you are!!!" came a shout that startled the pair and cut off his sentence.

The three men had purposely approached from a blind spot behind the ruined hut and now stepped out into the road just yards away. The young man leading the group and swinging a short club was the bloody-nosed thug Kratos had seen near the town gate. He was looking much less red-faced and sported a savage grin now that he had caught up with Felix. One of his companions was a knife wielding, stringy-looking man that had a face a hardened criminal would be proud of; the other was a huge, ugly lumbering brute with a limp. His great head had a thatch of dirty hair over a scarred face that had the look of a man lacking in intelligence.

"Stand aside, Foreigner! That red-haired cocksucker is ours!" said the bloody-nosed leader, tapping the club on the open palm of his hand.

Kratos sighed. He was already slightly irritated with Felix and his Numidian comments, and now felt a surge of anger at the 'foreigner' remark that he always seemed to get in backward

Roman provinces, especially if far from the more diverse coastal areas. Involuntarily he placed his left foot slightly forward into a fighting stance. "Look, I know my skin is darker but I am just as much a Roman as you and...." He paused and muttered something as he shook his head to himself, then stepped forward, his voice bristling. "This man is my servant."

Felix uttered a short cry of dismay at that.

Kratos continued, "He will not be harmed by the likes of you. So I suggest you go back to that shit heap you call a town before I get any more angry than I already am."

The scrawny criminal spoke now in a weaselly, nasal voice. "Or what? What will you do, eh?"

He tried to sound tough but Kratos could see him eyeing the muscularity of the fearless, bronze-skinned Greek before him.

"Well if we all don't get our knives out and give each other a good slashing I KNOW I will beat all of you down with my bare hands, starting from the biggest all the way down to the scarecrow, and send you back to your shit heap a little worse for wear," said Kratos evenly with a casual shrug.

The skinny man looked sour at the scarecrow comment but fear flickered across his face. The large, lumbering man looked dumbly towards the leader who had the thoughtful look of a gambler. "Hand to hand, eh? You look strong... but Orbo here has won every fist fight in this town," he postured, jerking his thumb towards the brute. "What chance do you have?"

"Try him, fuck face!" jeered Felix. He had watched Kratos calmly deliver his threat of a beating and had noticed the muscular forearms and the squashed misshapen ears of the Greek that he knew were only gained through many years of fighting and wrestling. He now stood fearlessly offering to fight three thugs with an air of complete indifference proving there was more to his friend than meets the eye. Even with the Greek being so confident Felix looked towards the escape route on the road away from town just in case, and gathered his toga, tying it at the waist for mobility as he continued to taunt the three adversaries.

"This man was going to honour my family's name at our private games as a Gladiator! I paid dearly for him to travel here; if you want to see him fight, you must pay."

"Shut your fucking mouth, you lying cheat! We will beat both of you and have our money back and whatever else you both have on you!" said the leader with a look of hatred at Felix. "Hand to hand against the foreigner it is! If Orbo wins you are next, fox pelt!" he spat, waving the brute forward. Orbo stepped up with a savage grin, raising fists that looked like blocks of stone, his dim wits apparently only sparked by conflict.

"If it goes badly, get the kit and run. I do not want my pack stolen," Kratos whispered urgently as he dropped his belongings and quickly slipped the bracelet that his father gave him inside.

"Bollocks to that," hissed Felix, further winding the toga and looking at the bloody nosed leader. "If you go down I will jump in! Just get back up and get on the big bastard so I can punch that other fucker to the ground a second time!"

The hunched brute limped forward with a gurgling laugh that made him seem even more grotesque and stretched his hairy, ape-like arms wide, showing an impressive reach. Kratos circled, noting with satisfaction the other two men had stepped back and had even taken seats on some flat stones by the rubble pile. They were so engrossed in the coming spectacle they even seemed to be taking bets with each other. They had obviously watched their 'champion' in hand-to-hand fights many times before.

Good, thought Kratos. *A fair fight, I won't have to watch my back.* He saw the brute was at least a head and a half bigger than him and those long, powerful arms could cause problems if he rushed in punching and was seized by them. The tunic he was wearing was threadbare and stained by wine and Gods know what else down the front, his belt a simple cord. *Not much for leverage on the clothing,* Kratos thought. If he took hold of the tatty garment and tried to throw the man he might be left holding a piece of rag. The brute dragged his left leg slightly behind him. The knee was misshapen and the whole leg was considerably thinner and weak in muscularity: an ideal area to attack!

Kratos tested the speed of his approaching opponent as he darted in with two lightning-fast punches to the body that caused air to whoosh from Orbo's lungs. He skipped back out of danger with a swinging left hook aimed for the chin but that caught the much taller brute in the neck. Orbo swung a huge right fist the size of a ham that sailed through the air several feet from the retreating Kratos. Orbo's face squinted with confusion. This man had hurt his stomach and neck! Nobody attacked him first! Snarling, he lunged forward with surprising speed, clapping both hands together to trap this annoying little man. But he was gone!

Kratos slipped under the swinging arms and circled away, chuckling as he realised how slow the brute was. The Greek began to relax and enjoy the fight. He did a little skip before resuming his fighting stance, light on his toes. He then noticed Felix had too began to relax, sitting down next to the travel packs, and was happily eating bread... fresh bread that was clearly not taken from his own pack.

"Oi, look out! Stop staring at me, you stupid idiot!" Felix said, waving and spitting bread as the brute charged again.

This time a swinging punch came close and the forearm smacked into Kratos' mouth as he stepped in to roll under the punch. He spat blood. "Damn you, Felix! Stay out of my pack!" he said angrily, this time with his eyes back on the circling giant before him who grinned from landing the blow. Enough was enough! He charged in with a one-two combination to the body and followed with a scything right hand uppercut that hit the jaw perfectly. Kratos heard a sharp cracking sound as teeth and possibly bone were smashed and the giant staggered back with a howl. As soon as Orbo's weak leg was exposed, Kratos threw a powerful kick to the outside of the misshapen knee. The blade of his well-conditioned shin struck with the force of a solid oak club and the giant shrieked louder than the sickening crunch as the leg snapped inwards at an angle that it should not normally go.

As Orbo fell screaming to the ground, collapsing on top of his ruined leg, his huge, grasping hands locked onto his opponent's arm and dragged Kratos down so that he landed on top of Orbo with a thud. The ape-like arms desperately enveloped the Greek and squeezed. The howling brute was now in agony and fighting for his life. His last ditch effort would be crushing this hateful little man until he died. He had done it before and now he squeezed with all his might.

Kratos tensed his abdominal muscles to stop the air leaving him as Orbo's arms tightened around his torso. He looked down into the hideous face of the man underneath him; his jaw was slack and clearly broken, his mouth gurgled with blood and phlegm, his teeth a bloody ruin of yellow shards, his bloodshot eyes wide with terror and pain. Kratos began smashing his fist into the brute's face, holding the throat with his left hand and smashing down with the right. The hard punches caused the giant to wriggle frantically and his grip round the waist loosened. Kratos still straddled the man but dragged himself forward as he punched until he was sat on Orbo's chest. His adversary bucked and writhed, but Kratos had the benefits of perfect balance and powerful legs from years of training. The Greek maintained himself like a skilled rider on a wild unbroken horse and continued raining down blows with both fists.

The sounds were like a mallet hitting a piece of meat. A huge looping downward punch opened a bloody cut under the eye. Another made the nose crunch inwards with a sound like a broken eggshell. Kratos leaned forward and slammed powerful elbows into the thick, broad face of the brute, opening up fresh wounds. The blood soon covered his adversary's face, going into the eyes and running onto the dusty road.

The brute howled and thrashed his arms, trying to get this man off him. This was the moment Kratos had been waiting for. He grabbed one of the flailing arms by the wrist in a vice-like grip and spun his body, dropping off Orbo's chest with the arm firmly in his grasp. Kratos' powerful legs pushed across the body and neck of the giant and he lifted his hips, hyper extending Orbo's elbow joint. The arm was strong but the Greek's technique was perfect. He held the ogre's fist on his chest and made sure the thumb was pointing skywards, just like his old trainer had taught him, and pulled. He strained with all his might while pushing down with his legs across the neck and chest of Orbo and raising his hips, arching his pelvis where the elbow joint was being strained.

There was a dry, crunching sound as the ligaments gave way and the giant screamed again as his arm was bent to an unnatural angle. Kratos threw the limp, useless arm away and scrambled to his feet. The leering ogre that had faced him now rolled onto his side, nursing its ruined arm, whimpering and curling up into a ball. His deformed and now clearly broken leg was left trailing out at a sickening angle. "Peash, peash, mershy! 'Ave mershy on me," he babbled through his shattered mouth, his eyes rolling in a face that was a ghastly mess of open wounds and bright red blood.

Kratos spun round, ready for the rush of new opponents, only to see the man with the bloody nose standing agog in complete shock. The scrawny scarecrow man could be seen halfway to the gate, his spindly legs pumping like a racehorse's at full gallop.

"Well?" said Kratos, stepping forward, raising his bloodied fists to the new challenger. The man's eyes flickered from the whimpering mess on the ground, to Kratos, to a laughing Felix who was now lying on the road with the travel packs under his arms as if he were on a couch at a feast. Felix winked to the stunned leader as he crunched into an apple. The man gulped several times and mouthed a few silent words before he turned and sprinted away, following the skinny man who was long out of sight.

Felix hooted with laughter and sprang to his feet. He shook his fist in mock anger and shouted, "You better run, *cunnus*![6] That's what happens when you mess with Marcus Mammilius Felix!"

Kratos ran his tongue along the inside of his now swollen bottom lip. The teeth had cut the inside of the lip in a couple of places, but it was not bad at all. He turned and looked at Felix who was inspecting Orbo, now either unconscious or pretending to be so.

"By all the Gods! You have killed him! I have never seen such fighting! I saw the *pugilati*[7] in our town use their fists with the metal gloves before, but to do such a thing bare handed?! You snapped his arm, too! I have never seen wrestling of its kind!" Felix clapped his hands together in delight.

---

[6] Latin vulgarity: cunt
[7] Roman boxers who used hardened leather gloves with metal studs, sometimes fighting to the death.

"Never mind that," Kratos snapped, "you ARE a thief! I saw you going in my pack! Damn near had me knocked out because of it, too!"

"Peace, weary traveller," said Felix, showing his open palms. "I have no quarrel with you, Greek. Your bracelet is safe. My cunning nose and empty stomach led me to your pack. I just could not resist the fresh bread... as you cannot resist good companionship! Our friendship goes both ways, neh?"

Kratos narrowed his eyes. "Both ways? I save your skin AND you take my bread?"

Felix laughed. "Come now, let us hurry along the road and away before they find more people for you to fight." He shouldered his pack and held up the other to Kratos. "It's a little heavier from the wine flask I put in here, but if any man can shoulder the load, the mighty 'Kratos' can!"

"Kratos?' I told you already my name is Kallias Ampelios and I am a citizen of..."

"Hush now, Kratos... A name like 'Kallias' does not suit a Greek with strength and ability like yours. If you were taller I would call you 'Hercules', say 'fuck the Legion' and become your manager right now! It's a shame you are as short in height as my cock is long! Gods' fury, with my brains and your skills we could be off to astound the world! And yes, I know you're Greek, I saw the inscription on your bracelet and my patrician[8] upbringing has allowed me to learn Greek, of course," he said with a lofty air. "From now on you shall be 'Kratos', my bodyguard, paid in wine." He paused for a moment, scratching his red hair with a thoughtful look on his face as he looked at the well-defined muscle that could be seen under his companion's

---

[8] Patricians: the Roman aristocracy (upper class).

tunic "By the Gods, I COULD make a fortune from people paying to see you fight!" he said quietly in earnest.

Kratos spat another small glob of saliva and blood as he shouldered his pack and noticed a small crowd of six or seven males gathering near the town gate. The stringy scarecrow man could be seen amongst them, gesturing with his arms in an excited fashion. Kratos grimly noticed at least four of the men appeared to be carrying long clubs. "Let's go" he said as he began jogging down the road. "I am not fighting a whole town!"

Felix scooped up his own pack and trotted over to the stricken Orbo who was clearly pretending to be dead and kicked him hard in the back, causing a yelp that made Felix laugh with glee and give him another, even harder kick. "I agree, Kratos. I say fuck this shithole and let us look to the next town and our fortunes!" he said gaily as he set off with a languid stride that made running seem easy.

"Thanks for the wine," said Kratos as they ran side by side. The Greek checked over his shoulder, noting that the men were jogging slowly to the incapacitated brute who was now yelling back to them in anguish. "I thought you were trying to steal from me!"

Felix jogged easily next to him at first, then ran ahead in his long, effortless stride, shouting over his shoulder as he accelerated, "You are welcome to carry my wine for me. I figure if we both had to run you would carry the weight much better. Let's see if you can keep up!"

Kratos, irritated with his new companion, ran for more than a mile along the muddy road in silence. He was exceptionally fit and running at a fast pace but all the while he saw that Felix slowly pulled further and further away. The long stride of Felix was well suited for distance running and he irritated the Greek further by jumping over every muddy puddle in the track, neighing and whinnying like a horse.

The day was growing colder and the sky was a chilly bright blue over the scattered farms and orchards. Every time they passed some trees the winter birds would rise from the branches, cawing in protest at the running men. Eventually, now far ahead, Felix stopped next to a grove that offered good cover from the chilly breeze and somewhere to sit. The thin man immediately stretched out on the damp grass. Kratos jogged up to him and stopped, glancing behind to make sure they were not followed. "You have got *cac*[9] between your ears if you think I am YOUR mule! I AM going to drink the damn wine!" he said with his breath heaving before walking off to a good spot of dry bare earth under the trees a few yards from Felix. He threw his pack to the floor and sat down next to it. The sweat was running down his back and making him itch. He sat there panting to catch his breath and looked around the open countryside with its dreary, run-down olive groves. The track was empty ahead and most importantly behind. It appeared the local thugs had not set off in pursuit. Kratos, still irritated, looked sideways at his companion who now lay on his side in the damp grass. Felix was propping up his head with his hand and looking at the Greek with a huge beaming smile on his face.

"My dear Kratos... what is wrong?" said Felix soothingly as if talking to an angry child. The Greek shook his head and spat on the floor.

"You are a cheeky bastard and I can see why you have a fox pelt for a haircut! And stop calling me 'Kratos!'" he said gruffly, rummaging in his pack so he did not have to look at the grinning face of Felix. His lip had already swollen and he knew the little cut in the inside would leave one of those horrid little flaps of

---

[9] Latin vulgarity: shit.

skin that he would catch with his teeth all the time. He could almost hear the deep voice of his old trainer Theron back in the gymnasium in Greece.

"See! You should have slipped under that punch but you had the mind elsewhere… again!"

The Greek licked the inside of his cut lip, then smiled ruefully to himself until the voice of his red-haired companion brought him back to his current situation.

"Kratos my old friend! I agree, we shall both drink the wine and we shall rightly toast Bacchus and your victory," said Felix, springing to his feet effortlessly. He stood for a moment eyeing the Greek critically and adjusted his torn toga with utmost care and delicacy, even though the thing was virtually destroyed, stunk like a corpse and was covered in all manner of filth from the garbage pit. He shook his head at his sullen companion for a moment, then looked up piously and began to speak in a high pitched way he had heard the actors do on stage.

"Your wife Bassa always carries a baby by her side, Fabullus, and calls him her darling plaything.
I wonder why, since she isn't a nanny.
So, why then does she carry a baby?.... Because Bassa always farts!"[10]

Kratos looked at Felix who was stood still as a statue with his arms raised. The Greek's grim expression wavered for a moment then broke apart as he laughed at the absurd sight of his theatrical companion. "You ARE a strange one! Are you soft in the head or is it all on purpose? What spirits have cursed you, I wonder?" He looked skywards. "Apollo, am I safe to have some food with this maniac?"

---

[10] Martial - 'The Decoy Baby' IV.87

Felix elegantly half bowed and offered his palms like a priest. The bright blue eyes of the cunning man flashed as he arched his eyebrows and answered in a deep theatrical voice.

"Kratos, I may be an uninvited guest... but I *always* come impeccably dressed," he said, gently flicking an imaginary speck of dirt from his filthy, ruined toga.

SPQR

Chapter 2

Clank, clank, clank, clank, clank... The great snake of soldiers covered in metal and leather marched ever onwards, thousands of feet tramped rhythmically, sparks occasionally flying from the hobnails of the sandals intermittently striking stone and pebbles. During training we would mostly march on good flat Roman roads, but we could find ourselves on tracks and fields, labouring through sand which was hard on the legs if it was very fine but much easier when wet. Sometimes it was snow, which was not too bad as long as you were not in the vanguard making the trail. Sometimes it was wet, swampy lands where the grassy tufts would form small mounds that you could break an ankle on. Sometimes the grasslands were dry and you would be bitten by a myriad of small insects. Lately, during training it was thick muddy lanes, making you piss wet through and miserable down to your marrow. But it did not matter. You got used to it. It was the way of things. You just kept marching.

Today it was a dry, hard track through the low hills and farmlands of southern Hispania. The only thing that annoyed us was the great cloud of dust that the thousands of feet stirred up. It dried the throat until swallowing became a hardship. It had been many days since the springtime rains and we had complained, of course, but now it was the dust. On days like these, throughout the entire column, the inexperienced soldiers emptied their water skins and flasks much too quickly. Some of the smaller and weaker soldiers would eventually fall to the side, feet blistered or knees and backs hurting. Most of them would rise with a threat or a beating from the Centurion's stick; those who did not would be left there. They were lucky this was a training march as being left behind was a death sentence in hostile territory. The Legion could not stop. Would not stop. It was not a place for the weak, it wanted only the strong.

The deep thud of the footsteps was given further resonance by the millions of pieces of metal hitting each other. The slung helmet hanging on our chests tapped against the poles on our shoulder called the *furca* that carried most of our equipment. Our belts had suspended from them long, leather-studded strips to protect the groin called the *cingulum*. They clinked together in the way they were designed to do. These belts never left our waist, even when we were out of the camp and in the wine shops, inns and whore houses, as they proudly marked us out from mere civilians. The *gladius*[11] hanging on our hips clanked against the thigh along with the dagger on the other hip we called the *pugio*. Our *pila*, or javelins, of which every man was issued two, were tied to the furca and everything that hung from that banged against the shields strapped on our back. These shields, we called the *scutum,* were in the waterproof leather case that helps protect the wood from the elements. Noise also came from our chain mail shirts, coin purses, flasks, wooden stakes for the encampment, mess kits, shovels, wicker baskets for moving dirt, earth cutting tools and dozens of other items of military equipment. Every man was loaded down with enough kit to keep our Legion marching, fighting, eating and building camps for weeks. Everything seemed to add to the impressive crescendo. Occasionally we accidently clanked against each other, knocked off balance by a slippery stone or a slight trip in a pothole.

"Watch where you are going, you stupid fucking *cunnus*!" could be the hissed reply if you fell into someone and a few moments of raucous chattering would erupt where people would declare

---

[11] Latin: sword.

you had been secretly drinking wine or were too weak and effeminate to carry your kit, or that your mother had sex with a cripple while your father was out drinking. Sometimes one of these jokes might run for days, especially if someone foolishly reacted in a defensive fashion or became angry. Such was the nature of fighting men when they sensed a weakness or a gap in someone else's defences. It might even end in a full scale argument or actual physical violence until a passing centurion[12] beat you with their stick. One thing you would need to learn is to have thick skin... both for the punishments and the jokes.

Onward we marched, a great snake of military might making clouds of dust rise from the Iberian landscape. Travellers would move off the road and the impoverished farmers or their slaves would stop working in the fields to watch us pass. Grubby children would often run to the roadside to wave and chatter amongst themselves. More often than not young boys inspired by the spectacle would end up fighting with sticks before the column was out of sight. For many of the impressionable young farm boys seeing that huge, clanking column with thousands of soldiers marching along would fill them with dreams of battle and often bring them to the dilectus in later years. Why follow an ox with a plough when you can follow an Eagle with glory? Why stay out here where a single man alone cannot achieve much when you could be part of this huge column that can built a fort in several hours or bridge mighty rivers in days? Why be at the mercy of poor harvests and tax collectors when you can march and fight for your daily bread and coin?

Farms usually make good money but Hispania was crippled with debt these days, The disruptions from the Sertorian war had impoverished the province and despite a decade passing it had

---

[12] Officer in charge of a century but with many varying grades. Modern equivalent could be anything from brand new platoon commander through to a regimental Sgt Major or Company commander .

not fully recovered. A great many of the poor worked on the struggling farms and the dispossessed turned to banditry to escape poverty. We were children of these hard times. The governors and tax collectors would say the province was doing well, these were good times, we should be happy. But for the young growing up after the Sertorian war there was not much to look forward to. The lure of a steady career with the Legions was strong and the rewards numerous: adventure, steady pay, companionship and a life of prestige instead of begging or thievery that could end with your hands being cut off, or worse.

There was something else, though. We did not realise it at the start, but once you have joined the legion, there was something that developed without you even realising, something impossible to explain... One you marched under the Eagle and stood with men that you began to call 'brother' the life became so much more. You developed a sense of belonging, a fierce loyalty like a pack of wolves but all the more deadly in so many ways. Wolves worked together to kill, just as we did but wolves could not bridge rivers and scale the walls of cities. We deserved our reputation; it did not matter if it was the Numidians, Greeks, Cimbri, Teutones, Gauls, Celts. Pirates, Bandits or mighty Carthage? Tribes, armies or nations mattered little to us. We would fight and win! Even despite the hardships, there were times when we knew this was our home. We found comfort in the little tents and solace in that great clanking column. We found a family that was in many way closer than the ones we were born into. Marching with the Legion made us stronger, taller and better in our eyes and probably more fierce and arrogant in the eyes of others especially civilians... but that never bothered us! The great clanking column represented more than just the military power of Rome: it represented the strength of the brotherhood that bound us together.

If you were marching with us in the column today and looked to your front, you would see the backs of heads, a vast column with rows of heads next to furcae loaded with equipment. The heads all had cropped hair. Some were darker skinned, some lighter, some balding, others completely shaved; all were tanned by the sun. The heads swayed together like a ripe cornfield in the wind. They swayed in the rhythm of the march as if they were dancing to the low thunder of the thousands of feet hitting the ground in unison. It was hypnotic and restful in many ways. It was easy to lose your yourself in thought as you looked ahead, and many did. Looking forward over the heads you would see some of the standards adding their colour to the scene.

Each century that marched had the *signum* at the front. The long pole with its spear point underscored with metal plates, carried by the *signifer*, told all that we were the 2nd century. Bearing the signum was an important job usually left to an experienced man. Our signifer was a veteran called Marcus Attius, the son of a veteran who was already held in high regard as a swordsman. A good man for a job that required one hand on the standard, the other on your sword with only a small round shield, usually slung on your back, to protect yourself. The signum was the rally point for the century when we had to get into formation, or if we were to muster for a parade, or, in the worst case, when the fighting was not going well and a broken formation needed to reform.

On a larger scale, it was the same when our six centuries would gather round the *vexillum*, the square flag mounted atop a spear which marked us as the 6th Cohort. This standard was carried by a tough senior *vexillarius*. The man marching with this standard at the front of our cohort was from a veteran legion. He was older with a huge jagged horizontal scar across his top lip. This gave rise to his nickname, 'Two Smiles', which suited him as he never smiled at all and the only movement anyone saw on his face was an ugly sneer at all the young probatios when we arrived at camp for training.

"What a shower of shit! They look like a bunch of village idiots come to get us all fucking killed," he had said to an equally grizzled and disgusted looking centurion standing next to him. The grim centurion had nodded in agreement.

Far off at the front of the column at the head of the ten cohorts in the Legion was the most important and sacred standard of all. Sat atop its pole and glittering silver in the sunlight was the Eagle – the symbol and very soul of the Legion itself. It was more than the symbol of Roman power, it was the very anchor of our loyalty. Every man from the legatus all the way down to the newest recruit would pledge his honour and life to it. The Eagle would live on after the men who marched under it had died in battle or even old age. We carried it in each prayer, each sacrifice, even the image of it tattooed on our hands that we were allowed only once we had passed our final training. The Eagle embodied the sacred part of the brotherhood that bound us... something outsiders would never and could never understand.

"Gods, this dust is choking me," coughed a huge man called Borras. His fair face, already reddened by the weak springtime sun, became darker as he hacked and coughed until he spit. The big man shot a glance at the others with eyes teary from the coughing to make sure no one was laughing.

The stocky man marching next to him, who was missing an ear, looked at him. "You will get used to it," said Quintus Galba, smiling up at the big man. The crow's feet around the veteran's tired looking eyes made him look older when he smiled, and he generally smiled a lot. His round, weathered face with its brown eyes showed a wealth of experience under the bushy brown eyebrows. We were pleased to have this patient, knowledgeable veteran as the *decanus*[13] in charge of our section. Other tent groups were not so lucky and many had tyrants who often had the recruits punished and flogged for the slightest reason. He did not mind us talking in the ranks when we marched easy. Galba always said, "When you are in hostile lands you won't want to talk anyway. Morale is just as important as discipline." His wisdom had helped the whole section get through training and everyone under his command knew it.

"Some days," Galba continued, "we will have the wind coming in from the flank and the dust blows away from the face."

Felix piped up, "The Gods of nature shit in one hand and pour gold in the other, eh?" He squinted as he scanned the heavens as if he could find the exact god.

"There is enough shit in the army as it is, half of it on my feet," said Borras with disgust, looking down at the road covered in animal faeces.

Today our legion marched as rearguard with two other legions ahead of us. Each legion would have one mule per eight-man section, which was our basic unit, plus carts for the legion quartermasters, artillery section and officers' equipment. Each legion could have anything up to a thousand animals in the baggage train, and we had more than twice that amount ahead of us... all doing their foul business on our line of march.

"Don't worry, Borras, where else would you be paid 225 *denarii*[14] per year for walking through mule and ox shit? Many people in the big cities have to do it for free," said Kratos with a chuckle.

---

[13] Soldier in charge of an eight-man section, equivalent to modern section commander.
[14] Ancient Roman currency.

"*Gerrae!*[15] That's 225 denarii *before* expenses! After my food and equipment deductions I will only get half of that!" said Borras angrily. "I should have left when I was a probatio," he groaned.

Felix laughed. "Ha! Moaning like a cheap whore! And that's with us getting a pay rise! Mind you, with *your* food deduction, you will have to sack all of Asia to pay for it!"

"I wake in the morning to be kissed by the sun,
but what is this? casting its shade upon my hut?
'Tis but Borras and his massive gut,"

sang Felix in a falsetto voice and everyone in earshot laughed heartily. Borras sent the slim man a murderous look under his fair eyebrows and growled "Felix! I am seriously going to...."

Felix cut him off, "Peace, Borras, you and I shall be great friends one day, I can feel it in my marrow. By the Gods, we both have red in our hair so I'm sure we were twins who took to fighting in the womb. You stole all the food while I read the scrolls of the learned Greeks, and now on this earth we are two parts of the perfect man. All I need to do is sit on your shoulders and be the head with all the brains and wit while you can be my body... Apart from the cock, of course! As in this case, it looks like I stole the larger of the two!" he said, cackling with laughter.

The irritated Borras turned to look at him with a sneer. "You wish, little man! *Everything* on you is skinny and my prick is like the oak trees of my homeland!"

Felix snorted and continued looking pleased with himself, "Part of the oak tree, yes! Maybe a twig from the smallest branch!"

---

[15] Latin exclamation. Modern equivalent: 'Get the fuck outta here!'

"Well, it was big enough to send your mother to the *medicus*[16] and she has had many more cocks than mine!" Borras replied smartly, at which Kratos chuckled.

"Pssst! Noise down! Watch out!" came the hissed warnings from behind and everybody immediately stop their talking and all marched in silence. Two centurions trotted past on the right and we kept quiet until they were swallowed in the great plumes of dust that were made all the brighter by the rays of sun shining through them.

Felix complained and shifted his furca for the hundredth time. "Fucking thing!" he muttered, "I would rather pay for another mule to carry my kit!"

Galba saw him struggling and said, "Next time try to get a stick with better branches at the top so you can hang more things in different places. Or lash a smaller stick across in a T shape like you see some of the veterans do; that gives a better spread of the load. Also, it's best to make a pad from something. I use a folded piece of sheepskin, see?" He gestured to the fur under the upright pole of the furca. "Some people fold their *sagum*[17] under there, too, which helps."

Felix rattled his furca and muttered, "I don't know why we have these things while the Gods gave us mules!"

Galba gave one of his fatherly smiles that always made us feel a little stupid and replied with encouragement, "Don't worry, lads, you will all get used to it. These things are a symbol of changes that were pretty important to us," he continued. "In my grandfather's time the great Roman general Gaius Marius reformed and professionalised the Roman army like no other had done before. The rules for being a soldier used to be strict and

---

[16] Latin: physician, army medic.
[17] Roman army cloak.

39

favour those with land and money. Soldiers were only signed on to fight the war and then go home, and sometimes they often did a piss poor job because of it. But now any Roman citizen can join the army and make a career for themselves. Even with no wars we are still training and making ourselves ready to fight and win. Since old Marius made those changes it has been a good profession for the plebeian working classes like us," Galba said, nodding his head to all who marched around him. "The only thing with the Marian reforms was that we had to carry more kit ourselves and that's when the furca was born. A faster army with a smaller baggage train means *we* are the mules from now on!" he laughed. "That is no joke, either! Some of the older veterans are actually proud to call themselves one of 'Marius' Mules' and would never go back to slow, lumbering baggage trains."

Felix sniffed with a dour look. "Dragging round a bloody crucifix with half the army equipment in the world nailed to it is *not* something to be proud of! When I am rich enough I will have a solid gold cart full of whores pulled by elephants!" he stated grandly and nodded to Kratos. "And you, my Numidian friend, will march behind, clearing the street of elephant shit for my army of followers!"

Kratos grinned, "The whores won't be interested in your skinny little body! In fact, the elephants would rather use you as a twig to scratch their asses!"

Everyone laughed at that, including Felix. "Don't talk of such things with Borras around! His ass is the same size as an elephant's and he might get some funny ideas!" he grinned.

Borras replied, "Well, it just about says everything if you are staring at my ass all the time! I knew you were as bent as a Persian catamite!"

Kratos spat out the water he was drinking and laughed loudly. "Yep, he certainly does have a taste for..." he began, but Galba cut him off. "Shh! Noise down! Quiet, lads!" he hissed.

Centurion Falco stood to the left of the marching column with his feet apart, tapping his *vitis*[18] against his leg. His centurion's helmet with its fearsome transverse crest moved slightly as the piercing blue eyes in the bronzed face flicked about in a predatory way like that of a hawk taking in every little detail of the men of the 2nd Century who marched past him. He looked deceptively slender and was one of the smaller centurions, but he was a man of huge presence and lightning-quick with his blade. His piercing eyes caused fear enough yet his face was covered in numerous scars and his broken nose made him look even more hawkish. Despite his smaller frame he was all sinewy muscle covered in battle scars. He was a soldier of huge authority and every part of him looked like a man not to be messed with.

When we joined the Legion many months ago and began basic training, we were placed under the command of Centurion Falco. By that time we had been given the rank of *tirones,* meaning soldiers who had actually started training. Over the coming months, we would all see, hear and *and* feel the wrath of Falco in one way or another. In the seemingly endless, miserable days of shouting, running, drilling, and not getting much sleep, every *tiro* in the Century had at least once felt the sting of the vitis for crimes real or imagined or, as we were often told, just because we were lousy, stinking recruits here to fuck up anything admirable that already existed in the Roman army. Every man had seen Falco wrestle, box, run, march with his gear and drill with the biggest, smartest, meanest and fastest of all of the recruits and we knew why this man was a well decorated and

---

[18] Centurion's vine wood staff - a symbol of his rank, often used to administer discipline.

respected centurion. Any minor infraction during training would result in a one-on-one lesson being taught before the whole century and one of our section was the unfortunate demonstration man for such a lesson.

It was a cold, wintery day and the practice area outside the camp was churned up from the rains and the miserable occupants who marched out there to train. The cold and hungry recruits from the whole 6th Cohort were all working hard in the sword fighting lesson in the freezing drizzle. This particular lesson involved the inevitable warm-up jabbing and slicing at the tall posts called the *palos*. These bare wooden posts that were as tall as a man could be found near every Roman camp and many had come to hate them over the weeks and months. After our arms were warmed we took up the heavy wicker practice shields and were working on a technique known as the 'over and under', as the veterans called it. This was another variant of legionary sword fighting: going over the top of the scutum for the throat or looking to come under for the groin. It was all designed to cause the enemy a fatal blow in a usually lightly armoured area so he would bleed out in the quickest possible time. Many of us came with preconceived ideas of showy and glamorous swordplay, spinning around and fighting like gladiators, but under the tutelage of the centurions we learned the most simple and brutally effective methods were all we needed and this technique in the hands of a well drilled battlefront could turn the legionary cohort into a tireless and deadly meat grinder.

The tirones threw their efforts into the sword practice lesson just to stay warm more than anything. It was exhausting but it was either that or stand around and feel your toes freezing in the icy mud. For the love of the gods, do not try and tuck cold fingers under an armpit to warm yourself or you will feel the sting of the vitis which can cause agony on the back of a cold leg: something the centurions, who seemed impervious to the bitter cold, knew very well.

During one of the short rest breaks we crowded around the pot of warm *posca*[19] brought to us by a camp servant. A handsome young man called Aulus Vettianus Decius, with brown hair and eyes to match, was bragging about his veteran uncle teaching him everything and that he was basically as good as a veteran legionary himself. His bruised and battered companions were sullenly slurping down their warming drinks and did not disagree with his boasts. Even Felix, who would imagine himself the greatest of all skills, refused another bruising bout with the well defined, handsome swordsman after he beat him easily with the heavy wooden sword we practiced with. Designed to be heavier than a gladius, the *rudis* was intended to strengthen the arm but could cause some serious injuries and even break limbs during sparring. Decius had beaten everyone in our section and continued to talk big to the shivering group before him, not noticing the sudden looks of fear or some of the other students already standing upright and coming to *intente*[20]. Decius sipped his hot posca as he smilingly bragged to a sour-looking companion whose bloodied nose still dripped into the wet mud.

"Look, I am just saying... Trying to fight like a gladiator *is* bullshit. It's just showmanship! Uncle Haterus taught me real legionary skills when I was just a boy and now because I am so good with a sword, I am probably going to get promoted much quicker than all of you and..."

"INTEN....TE!" roared Centurion Falco who had stopped silently a yard behind the stunned Decius. The bellowed command made him drop his rudis and cup of posca in fright. Everyone who had not already done so snapped immediately to attention in the silence that followed the deafening command. Falco looked

---

[19] A soured wine/vinegar, mixed with water and herbs. Everyday drink of the Roman army.
[20] Position of standing at attention.

down thoughtfully at the muddied ground and circled the boastful man three or four times, then stopped right in front of the hapless Decius. The Centurion looked up and stood staring into his face for what seemed a long time, his icy blue eyes hooded under his dark eyebrows as the rain drops rolled along the rim of his centurion's helmet.

"Name?" Falco said flatly.

"Aulus Vettianus Decius, Centurion!" the shaken recruit replied in a quavering voice.

"Did I hear you saying you were as good as any veteran?" Falco growled in his gravelly voice, bending down to pick up the rudis that lay in the mud before handing it back to Decius. "Do you want to stay here in my Legion?"

"Yes, Centurion" said Decius smartly, then his face registered the mistake. "Erm... No Centurion, I... mean yes I..."

Falco cut him off. "Oh! So you *are* as good as a veteran, eh?" he said, raising an eyebrow and casually stepping back. He stood for a moment, eyeing the man up and down like he was buying a horse. Internally he was enjoying the little trap he had played so many times, asking a cheeky recruit two questions in the same sentence that required opposite answers. "Perhaps you might give me an exhibition of your skills?"

The eyes of Decius looked watery and a droplet of snot dangled from his nose as he stood surrounded by people but feeling very much alone under the icy glare of Falco. His legs could clearly be seen shaking and most of the other recruits who did not like his boasts had suddenly forgotten the cold wind and had very faint smiles on their lips as they flicked their eyes left and right to share a smile with a friend. Decius stammered in reply to the lithe, menacing centurion before him. "No... I mean, yes...

Centurion, I..." but before he could finish Falco whipped the vitis through the air cracking the faltering soldier on the face. Decius reeled from the blow which left a large red weal on the right cheek. He regained his balance and we could see the wound already oozing blood. The smirks instantly disappeared from the gathered century and every man stood still and silent before their fearsome commander.

"I asked for an exhibition of your skills. I did not ask you to mutter," said Falco with a snarl. He walked to the nearest student standing to intente and took a worn rudis from him in exchange for his vitis. Falco swung it a couple of times and quickly inspected around the top of the handgrip, making sure the tell-tale signs of fatigue were not in the wood. He did not want a rudis to break while he demonstrated a lesson.

"Listen in, you bunch of fucking morons!" said Falco, who took off his helmet and tossed it to another recruit. The man caught it with wide eyes and held it gingerly like it was his own newborn child. Falco looked around at the silent students. "This will be a demonstration of the biggest mistake *all* of you will make in your first few years of the Legion. I won't show you step by step, but see if you can spot it... Stand easy and close in, men, form a circle to enjoy the lesson and discuss the points quietly amongst yourselves." Falco flashed a grim smile and tossed his cloak to the man who held his vitis as the rest of the recruits formed a circle. With the dreaded attention being focused on poor Decius, we started talking in a low whisper that turned into chattering when we could see it was not another trick of Falco to make the group relax, then get punished for it.

The shivering Decius was still standing to intente under the cold grey skies as the circle of jabbering recruits formed the walls of a small, muddy arena around him. One of the tirones in front of his eye line grabbed his penis and winked at him in jest. Another bruised recruit that he had beaten in a training bout ran a finger over his throat and grinned as Decius stood there looking positively ill. The *optios*[21] and centurions from other centuries left their own students for a moment and came to watch, as did the odd decanus. Apparently, half of them were placing bets on each other over what was going to happen. "Ready yourself," said Falco as he swung the rudis smoothly and quickly, warming up his arm. Decius moved back and raised his own sword into the fighting stance but was still very pale and shaky. Falco shook his head and with a smile to the assembled century he ordered us to cheer our 'champion' to warm his fighting spirit, but the bragging of Decius had not won him many fans in the crowd and all he got was jeers and hoots, to which Decius gave a sickly smile in return.

Falco dropped his smile and with a nod ordered, "Attack!"

Decius, despite looking unsteady, bounded in with several well placed strikes to the head and neck area, which Falco parried. Decius tried going low, then high, to test for weaknesses, but the tough centurion was more experienced and much faster. Falco stayed in the pocket, fighting at close range, until he felt he had seen the best of Decius. He blocked, then threw a hard thrust into the thigh, right where the artery was. The blunted tip of the rudis would leave a huge bruise that would be there for some weeks later.

Decius gasped with pain as Falco circled away. *The boy is pretty good,* the centurion thought. Falco then snaked forward with lightning speed and feinted another groin blow which Decius tried to defend frantically. Falco batted away the defending sword and twisted his body, stepping in close to Decius. From right within the boastful man's guard he brought up the heavy, round pommel of the rudis and smacked Decius under the jaw.

---

[21] Optio: second in command of a century, roughly equivalent to a modern platoon sergeant

The young man staggered back but recovered and bounded in with another attack, swinging wildly with no strategy now, like an enraged Celt. His breathing was already becoming ragged and his eyes stung with sweat despite the cold.

Falco ducked under a wild swing and drove the sword hard into the stomach of his opponent. As Decius doubled over from the impact, Falco's right knee came up and smashed him clean in the nose. The boy went down with a splash like a sack of wheat and lay unmoving in the wet mud.

There was a cry of cheers and the centurions at the back immediately began arguing over who had won what bet. Surely it was the head wound blow that won the fight? But the last strike was to the stomach? The discussions about it would doubtless continue for some time after. Felix was having the same conversation with another of the young tirones and it looked like he had lost the bet, as the other man was shaking his head and could be heard protesting above the chattering, "Fuck off, Felix! A bet is a bet!" Falco smirked and remembered when HE had been on the end of his centurion's lesson. A painful one but something these 'boys' needed if they were going to be useful in battle.

"*INTEN... TE!*" Falco roared and everyone went silent and shot to the position of attention, immediately recognising that the fun was over. Falco strapped on his helmet with its transverse crest and said in his commanding, gravelly voice, "So... what were the mistakes? Raise your hands if you have an answer." Two dozen hands went up. Being so close to the end of basic training, we all thought we were sword experts by now and many wanted to show their knowledge to the centurion.

Falco pointed to the volunteer nearest him. "You?"

"He rushed in and..." the lanky fellow began and Falco shook his head, moving on.

"You?"

"He should have circled left when..." and again Falco shook his head and moved on and on shaking his head with each reply.

"He did not use his reach to..." said Kratos.

"He... he was, erm..." said a nervous looking blonde man with large ears.

"The laws of war dictate that he..." began Felix.

"SILENCE!" Falco roared and glared around. "All of you sacks of shit missed the mistake! The one mistake Decius made was that he thought he was better than anyone else here! Because no matter how good you think *you* are, there is always someone out there who will fuck up your day! No matter how much better you think your skills are, the man stood next to you in the formation *will* save your life!"

He glowered around at the assembled troops, making sure everyone was taking in what he was saying. The recruits were wisely hanging onto every word.

"Learn your trade, learn to soldier, learn to march, learn the formations and learn to fight. We are moving out in a few weeks to fight a war! The Lusitanian and Gallaecian tribes will send some of you to the underworld because you thought you were better and knew everything," he continued. "Well, I have news for you! Guess what, you stupid little bastards?! There are mules in the wagon train with more experience in Legion life than you have! So keep your fucking mouths shut and learn the how to soldier! Maybe in five or ten years, when you have marched enough, sweated enough and bled enough, we can talk about experience! It is not about who is 'best', it is about who is left because they worked together!"

He spun on his heel to leave and stopped near the moaning Decius who was starting to move. Falco pointed to two nearby recruits "You. You. Take this mouthy bastard to the medicus, and if he wakes on the way, tell him well done, he fought much better than most recruits at this stage." He nodded to the optio who was leading the sword training and walked off.

Everyone had remembered the sword lesson on the cold, grey wintery day and now in the dust and the bright sunshine of spring those men marched past Falco in perfect step, occasionally risking a glance at the fearsome centurion. Falco screwed his eyes up as he saw Decius remembering him by his face. He nodded to Galba as we marched past and then disappeared in the billowing dust to our rear.

Felix twisted his head slowly as we marched, checking that Falco had not followed. "Hey, Decius!" he called softly so the man one rank ahead could hear him. "Did you see the way Falco looked at you? I bet you hurt his knee with your nose and he is struggling to march with it!"

Decius sniffed and chose to ignore the comment. His nose was healing fine but it was at a different angle and one of his nostrils felt blocked all the time. He had not really managed to have a look at himself and hoped it did not look bad. Decius was used to the girls following him, admiring his looks. Now everything was ruined! He touched his misshapen nose. The medicus who fixed it did not do the best job, it seemed.

"It's a shame he can't hurt his knee on your mouth, Felix!" grunted Decius in reply and Borras laughed until a big gust of wind and dust left him coughing and squinting. The coating of dust was making his reddish blonde hair seem almost white.

"Arghhhhh!" came a sudden, sharp cry from the man marching next to Decius. "My leg! My leg!" The thin man who was as slim as Felix but much less tall or muscular hopped along for a moment before taking up his stride again, but this time with a very pronounced limp.

Kratos shook his head with a groan and rolled his eyes. "Here we go again."

"Legionary Marcus Rabirius Ignatius, what in the name of the Furies is the problem?" barked Galba in his official decanus voice which we heard mercifully little of. "What ailment do you have now?"

"No doubt another fucking imaginary one," said Felix with disgust. "He has been making sacrifices to *Laverna*[22] instead of *Angerona*[23]! Probably with someone else's money, too! And to think he argued that we all nicknamed him *'Ignavus*[24]'!"

"Decanus, I think my leg is broken" said Ignavus, trying to look back at Galba in the row behind. He limped and skewed into Decius who cursed and pushed him back across the file.

"It can't be broken, you idiot! You would not be able to stand," said Kratos wryly. We had learned from him that being an expert in hand to hand fighting means knowing a lot about injuries, even though this statement was clearly obvious to us all.

Borras, who marched right behind him, placed a large hand on the shield strapped to Ignavus back and kept it there, pushing him forward. "Don't you dare fall out of the march again," said Borras with a growl. "You will make the century look bad! And you do not want to face Falco again, do you?"

---

[22] Roman goddess of cheats, thieves and the underworld.
[23] Roman goddess who relieved people of pain and sorrow.
[24] Latin: idle, sluggish and cowardly.

Ignavus kept quiet but continued his limping and cursing. His furca was off balance and badly packed. Galba had shown us back in camp how to do it. "Remember, lads," he had said, "the way you pack your kit is important. Over time you will be able to tell a seasoned veteran by the way he loads his furca. It's not just about carrying things in a practical way, it's about looking the part, too! No one wants to march in a cohort that looks like a bag of shit! People might think we are reservists or auxiliaries instead of line infantry!" We had all listened apart from Ignavus who had bet on something for a guard duty and lost, so he had to do another shift. Borras had tried to show him at a later time after the guard shift finished, but he had groaned that he only wanted to sleep instead.

Galba looked at the limping Ignavus and said in a firm tone, "You all knew basic training would involve many, many miles of marching when you signed on at the dilectus. It does not matter that you dropped out on some of the training marches," he said, urging Ignavus on. "I told you, the back and legs will strengthen and the pains in the shins will become less and less over time. Just keep going." Ignavus looking at him pleadingly and Galba glared back "You *will* keep going!"

Everyone marched silently for a long while thinking about those moments where the shins felt like the bone inside was ready to burst and the soles of the feet burned like a fire and in many cases became a bloody, raw mess. We had all marched many miles and had been there, but most had silently dealt with the pain wondering if anyone else around them suffered and more often than not they did. But we kept going because the Eagle kept going… that's just the way it was. Even now, when it hurt we knew the pain would subside, the blisters would heal. If anything, we were more concerned for our pride and having other soldiers mock us, even though those who seemed to have no pride like Ignavus could often limp on like he did right now.

He did not share the same sentiment as many of his comrades, and everyone knew it.

He spat in the dirt as he shot a glance at the stoic face of Decius marching next to him with ease. He looked every part the soldier in comparison to Ignavus with his watery tearful eyes poking out of his thin face that looked ill underneath his bald shaved head. He should have run away, he thought, but where to? His debts had followed him everywhere and thievery was not working out very well. That last farmhouse still haunted him. She was beautiful... He did not realise anyone was home. He should have left with the items he stole but he wanted to touch her while she slept. It was her fault! She should not have cried out... She should have kept her mouth shut! His face stiffened and he noticed he had stopped limping. *Well, at least that brute behind me is helping a little,* he thought. *I don't want Falco's vitis across my back again!*

The humble vine stick was not only used as a badge of rank and for directing the movement of formations, but also heavily applied to 'encourage' those young ones in the new legion who fell out from the march. Nearly all would take the punishment and hobble onwards. In truth, it could be said, the vitis keep the whole damn army going! The odd few would cry and raise a hand in a plea for mercy to the centurions, but these men were proud professional warriors who had earned their scars and experience in combat. There was no mercy in them, because they had gotten the same treatment from their centurion, It wasn't cruel, it was just the way it was. Ignavus knew from several bitter experiences that pleading and begging for mercy with a centurion did not work. The theatrical limp now gone, he marched onwards lost in thought, not even noticing that Borras was not helping him anymore.

"Galba?" said Kratos quietly. "Umm... When will you be promoted to optio?"

Galba smiled and could see that the question was, "Why have you not been promoted?"

"Well, Kratos, you know about flogging and I also assume you know about *gradus deiectio*?"

Kratos paused for a moment. "Reduction in rank... why yes, of course... oh *cac*... Galba, sorry, I did not mean to pry and..." he said, looking sheepish.

"Don't worry yourself " laughed Galba, but his eyes showed a little sadness. "That is not a conversation for a nice day like this! Trust me, we shall have plenty of cold nights in our tent with nothing to talk about. I will bore you to death with it another time."

We marched on, each man to his own thoughts of food, rest or women for the most part. The day was growing warmer as the sun had passed its zenith. The sound of marching feet was hypnotic, the rhythm never changing. The only other movement from our military column was the occasional dispatch rider galloping past, going to the front or rear, and the occasional centurion walking back and forth up the line, saying a few words, occasionally reprimanding someone for being too loud or giving words of encouragement to those who looked like they were struggling. The centurions must have covered at least three times the distance we did with all the walking to and fro.

Suddenly a *cornu*[25] blared its braying command somewhere far to the front with the headquarters command group and the *cornicen* of each cohort echoed the command all the way down the column. The centurions immediately began to roar the command verbally.

---

[25] G-shaped Roman brass instrument used for communicating orders.

We recognised the voice of Centurion Falco somewhere from behind. "Second century... *CONSISTI...TE*[26]!" he cried, and we came to a halt on the next step. Our timing was much better these days. The first mock battles in training where we fought century against century, then cohort against cohort were messy affairs to begin with, but we learned the drill and learned the tactics. As with every lesson, anyone who did not learn fast enough felt the whack of a vitis or ran around the parade ground until they did!

"Second century... *OTIO...SE*[27]!" There was a collective sigh of relief as we stood easy and caused a cacophony of noise as the butt of every single one of the furcae hit the ground with scraping thuds. Often a tent mate would hold another man's grounded furca with his own while his comrade adjusted some clothing or stretched, simply because it was so difficult to pick up a fully loaded furca from the ground. Our first training marches were so strict that no one talked or moved without orders, even during the rests. Every man had stood in the columns with ranks six abreast trying to stretch off backs and legs while the centurions and optios stalked up and down trying to catch someone moving or talking. Finally, when half of the rest time was over, we were given the command to drink from our skins or flasks. Doubtless they would have like to deny us this pleasure but thirst can destroy an army better than iron swords. Now we were allowed some movement and felt lucky to have earned this privilege. The side of the road was full of legionaries who had fallen out to piss and sometimes more.

Felix stood at the side of the dusty road and looked back over his shoulder. "Pity there aren't some pretty farm girls around here to enjoy the cock show!" he said, grinning and nearly pissing on another man standing alongside.

---

[26] Halt!
[27] Stand easy!

"Shut your mouth, soldier," said Centurion Falco, walking past. "Finish your piss and fall back in line!"

Felix dropped his grin immediately. "Yes, sir!" came the prompt reply. Even the ever irrepressible Felix knew where the rules lay when it came to a man like Falco. The centurion stalked off. Even when he could be resting himself, the man kept moving amongst us, making sure no one was sitting down. Brand new legionaries were not afforded such luxuries until we had earned them and Falco was still not sure about the quality of these men.

"If you were allowed down, you might not get back up again," said Galba when asked about it. "In time when you are proven men with discipline you will get to sit down during the rest breaks."

"It's a stupid rule," muttered Ignavus, trying to adjust a sandal while holding his furca. He made sure his complaints were quiet enough for Galba not to hear.

"Well, at least this is the last rest stop before we get to camp," said Kratos cheerfully and everyone nodded in agreement. "Just think, this is the last training march before we go north to war!"

Borras scratched his chin that always seemed to have red stubble on it, even seconds after he'd shaved. "Kratos, they said that about the last march, and the three marches before that," he noted with a raised eyebrow.

"Maybe we won't even fight at all," said Ignavus, shuffling his feet.

"Snivelling wretch! Don't you worry, Achilles!" said Felix with a menacing sneer. "You will be fighting soon enough... with me!" he promised as he patted the gladius on his hip threateningly.

"Stow that *cac,* Felix," Galba growled in an angry voice. "I don't care if you dislike someone or think they are weak. I won't have talk like that in my section. You are brothers by oath, so take that poison elsewhere!" he spat, looking around him. He stood bristling in the midst of the silent section for a moment, then grunted in a quieter voice. "Trust me, you will all have more enemies than you want soon enough."

Felix fell silent as Borras and Kratos looked at each other thoughtfully; even the usually indifferent Decius looked quizzical. It was quite rare to see Galba angry.

The distant cornu split the silence and once more the command was carried down the column. There was a commotion as everybody quickly got back into the ranks now and ready to go. The experience was beginning to show and the centurions did not have to chase people into rank or dress the lines.

Falco nodded with satisfaction that all the men were in place and ready to march. "Second Century, listen in!" He looked forward along the line and could see the formations ahead begin to move.

The vexillum of the 6th Cohort dipped forwards and somewhere ahead Centurion Tanicus, the Head Centurion, or *Pilus Prior*[28], of the 6th Cohort, bellowed the command, "Stand ready!... *PROCEDI...TE*[29]!"

We all stepped off into the easy march as Centurion Tanicus roared the timing in a voice that Jupiter himself would have found deafening.

The Legion was going back to the camp and even though some of them suspected it, nobody knew at the time that this was

---

[28] Commander of the first century of each cohort.
[29] Forward!

indeed the last training march and the next one would see them advancing into enemy territory.

SPQR

Chapter 3

The man they called *Corvus*[30] rose from the ditch where he had slept. 'Man' was a generous tag to this boy who was barely old enough to join the army. But one look into his dark eyes that seemed to have no colour other than black told a different story. His frame was athletic but slight, his hair, long by Roman standards, was straight and black. His eyes were haunted by memories and his face was raked with monstrous scars that would make children weep and women shy away from him for the rest of his natural life. Those black eyes looked around in every direction as he furtively bounded up the bank onto the road. The sun was just setting and the great road, called the *Via Domitia,* that snaked through the province and linked Hispania with Rome was empty. Some merchant carts had gone rumbling past a while back but they were out of sight. If the merchants had stopped Corvus would probably reach their roadside camp at midnight. He knew this road and there was not a post house or inn for some miles. He shivered in the autumn air that cooled quickly once the weak rays of the sun set behind the hills of Transalpine Gaul. He gathered his ragged, tatty, nearly threadbare black cloak around him, slung his bow over one shoulder and began walking west. He used to go by the name Sextus Livius Decula but he had not heard that name in a while. The street children had called him Corvus and he preferred it... The other name was not his, not anymore. Sextus, that boy who

---

[30] Latin: crow.

had lived a happy life, was long gone and did not resemble the haunted young man that now walked westward along the road as silent as a cat.

Many years ago his father, Gnaeus, had sold off his small farm and loaded his family and belongings into several carts in the city of Mutina for the journey north. Corvus was young at the time but he could remember the journey to Narbo as exciting at first, then interesting, then utterly boring with many days spent in the cart playing with his sisters. Being cooped up for the whole journey eventually led to the children fighting. His mother, Claudia, would always protect her boy from his older sisters' spite. "You are cursed by night spirits!" Clarissa would say, teasing him for his dark hair and eyes, so different from the sisters' brown hair and fair looks. "He is a demon who has escaped from the underworld to torment us," Flavia would say until he cried or his mother shouted at them both. Despite the teasing it was altogether a happy time and it seemed as if things were only going to get better in Narbo... but they did not.

Narbo Martius Colonia was a relatively new town that benefitted from commerce coming to and from Hispania and all over Gaul. The Atax river was full of boats and barges while the Via Domitia had its endless traffic of dispatch riders, travellers and merchants carts rumbling east and west, all of them carrying goods that would end up all over the Republic. Learned Greeks came from Massilia, wild Celts would bring furs and Gaulish traders came down from the north with exotic goods that would even come from as far away as the legendary isles of Britannia. It seemed anyone with a business idea could prosper and thrive in this crossroads of commerce, and for several years Corvus' father did. Gnaeus had immediately rented a small shop and the next two floors above in a four story *insula*[31] on a busy street. He had inspected every inch of the building and was satisfied

---

[31] An apartment building in Ancient Rome, inhabited by the lower classes.

that is was well built, as some insulae have been known to collapse from poor workmanship. It was not in the best neighbourhood, but it was a good enough place to start.

The family began buying and selling and trading many different goods immediately, but Gnaeus knew the real money was in the local honey. Rosemary honey from Narbo collected a good price in Rome and he had a very good business plan to profit from this. He set up his hives on the lands of many agreeable farmers with a promise to give them a share of the goods and any resulting profits. With this plan he set up hives all around the surrounding areas and merely had to harvest the sticky gold. Despite a few harvests coming up short and even several hives going missing entirely he always made sure the farmers who were the guardians of the hives profited from his sales. Corvus could remember being out with his father one day when they were looking at a busy hive in the country. His father had said, "Look, son! They are *our* little soldiers!" as he stared at the tiny insects working away in unison.

At the end of the first full season the business had made a lot of money and with its storeroom full of the coveted and imperishable honey it was a life of leisure for the family. His sister, Clarissa, who was bright but very shy in nature and rarely left the house, would help school him. He often would go with his father to meet the farmers or accompany the slaves with the carts to collect the honey. His mother and Flavia would sell wares in the shops downstairs where he would help out, too. But as time passed, he noticed his father smiled a lot less and, despite the business doing well, he would always seem to be arguing with someone over money. A group of men would often come round and speak to his father in a threatening manner until some money was handed over and this had made Corvus worried.

Gnaeus used to tell his son, "It is just the nature of business. You must pay attention to these things. You will take over this one day!" But commerce and shop keeping was not in his blood, nor was beekeeping. Corvus loved the country, he loved being outdoors. He began to explore north beyond the farms until he was in the deep forests. There he found many snares set by the hunters in the area who seemed to be mostly old discharged soldiers. Corvus would occasionally steal a catch from these snares or follow a hunter into the distant shrubs to see what hunting grounds he was using and would set his own snares. As the months wore on he perfected the art of stalking and walking through the forest so no person would ever know he was there, even to the point that the wild animals and birds would start at how close he could get to them. When he was home he worked hard in the shop until he could afford his own bow to augment his homemade spear, and with this new hunting tool he began to stay away from home more and more. At first, his father complained about his son's taste for hunting, but when the young man started bringing home food, and more importantly furs that could be sold, he just let him be and looked forward to his return every few days.

As Corvus honed his hunting skills he became very adept in moving stealthily and would often follow others that he saw just for fun. He could even remember following a hunter to a farm where he took an absent man's wife right there out in the barn! Corvus had smiled getting closer and staring at her white breasts and tousled hair from only a few yards away. He listened to their conversation afterwards where she cursed her husband's lack of vigour and looked at the ex-soldier's tattooed hands as he touched her. He saw their private world and they had no idea. He had felt like a fox, a creature of stealth and cunning, and the feeling was good.

As the months turned into years, hunting the forest became his life and he never worked the shop or gathered the honey anymore. The family was doing well and had several slaves working for them to cover the workload so his parents did not mind if he stayed away so much. They knew he would be home as he always was with many hares and deer; even the odd fox or boar fell under his well placed arrows or spear. His father was most pleased to be selling the meat to the butchers. It was a welcome piece of additional trade with the furs and skins, which fetched a good price in the shop. Despite the continuing arguments his father had with some of the local men, the family lived well. That was the last time Corvus had felt happy.

One day the family's world fell apart. He was home when it happened. They had closed the shutters of the shop and were preparing dinner when the crash and the shouts came from downstairs."Help! Mother! Anyone! Help!"

Corvus had sprinted down from his room on the third floor to see his father in the back room of the shop. He lay in a mess of broken goods, face was pale and pasty and his hands clutching his chest while Clarissa knelt by him wringing her hands. Flavia and his mother also came running and they all cried out to the gods as they lifted Gnaeus up to the counter in the shop. Corvus remembered his mother Claudia collapsing on the floor, screaming with grief, and the way his father's eyes looked frantic as he silently mouthed a few words and then died right there before them. Little did they know that this was the death of happiness for the whole family and it was the beginning of the end for most of them.

***

"Well, today's the day, my dear!" said Milo, striding behind the shop counter and squeezing Claudia's breast. He grinned, showing his sharp-looking teeth in a mouth that stank of stale wine.

The red faced Claudia slapped his hand away. "You were paid five days ago," she hissed, "and my husband would not like seeing you touch me!" She said looking at the ruffians, her eyes were fierce but she was filled with dread. These men were known to carry out their threats and she had been counting the days until this one.

Milo and the squat, bald man accompanying him laughed heartily. He grabbed her round the waist and grinned, "Now, now! He won't mind! He has been in the afterlife for nearly a year now and you are months behind with your payments!" He grinned at his bald companion who was staring intently at Claudia's chest and licking his lips. Milo smoothly rubbed his chin and yawned. "My dear woman, you have been putting this day off for too long, but you knew it was coming as sure as winter." He leaned forward with a leer and his hand went straight between her legs. "It is now time to pay up, Venus!"

The enraged woman stiffened at the violation then slapped him with all her might. Milo's head snapped round, making his gold chain that all the higher level gang members liked to wear jump around his neck, his cheek immediately turning red. The sound was loud and shocked the woman, but she knew she had to stand her ground.

"Don't you ever touch me!" she hissed "If you do that again I will..." Milo cut her off with a roar of rage "YOU FUCKING *CUNNUS!*" he bellowed as he threw her against the wall. Jars of honey and wares fell from the shelves, smashing on the floor. "You don't EVER hit me, you whore!" said Milo, punching her clean in the face, and she collapsed into a heap amongst the broken earthenware.

"Mama!" screamed Clarissa as she raced down into the shop to investigate the noise. Her long hair and filmy *stola*[32] streamed behind her as she rushed to her mother. Milo immediately seized her by the hair and dragged her screaming onto the counter and began stuffing a cloth in her mouth to shut her up. "Fuck it! We will take this young *cunni* until payment and if it doesn't come we put her to work, eh, Glycon! The boss will be pleased."

Glycon licked his lips and nodded his fat, bald head. He looked around and grabbed some string from the counter and began to tie up the struggling Clarissa. When this was not enough he tore strips from her stola. As he expertly trussed his victim his eyes ran up and down the girl greedily. "Mmm, I hope the boss lets us have her after he is done! Shall I take her?" he said, looking at the taller thin man.

"Wait a moment... let me just tie this knot... Good! Take the little bitch," said Milo, tying a sack with practiced ease over Clarissa's head. "The old bitch had her chance, now her daughter will pay the debt!" Glycon nodded and the squat ugly man threw the muffled, screaming girl over his shoulder like a pig carcass and ran with surprising speed down the street.

Everyone in the busy street cleared the way and hurried to their business. Many turned their heads away in shame so they would not be witnesses to this abduction. They cursed themselves and said, 'What can I do? I cannot stand up to them'. They were disgusted and ashamed but remained silent, unmoving witnesses to the kidnapping. These two men and maybe three dozen more all worked for a man called Vespillo. He ran the only remaining criminal *collegium*[33] within Narbo. There had been three such organisations before, not to mention some criminally minded Gauls in the area, but a bitter gang war had raged for the best

---

[32] Traditional garment of Roman women - a long pleated dress.
[33] A form of Ancient Roman organised crime gang.

part of a year which left Vespillo and his men on top. The collegium made its fortunes from crooked dice, whores, murder, robbing people on the road and lately, fire insurance.

You would often see the crime boss in the forum or going out to dine with many bodyguards. His fat frame with his hair combed carefully to hide his baldness and the extravagant materials he used for his togas would normally have marked him out as a figure of fun. But this man could have anyone in town killed and get away with it. On several occasions he had even paid off or threatened the local magistrates and prefects, and was considered above the law.

Vespillo's headquarters was a cellar wine shop called the '*Lupum Antris*[34]'. The whole insula above it, that sat on a busy junction in the rough part of town, was filled with his bodyguards, pimps, whores and thieves. All around the ground floor were doorways leading to small rooms where the whores serviced travellers and locals alike. Plenty of people used the doors except one that led down a dim grimy stairway to the cellar. This door had a sign written on the wall either side of the doorway showing the head of a wolf with bloody fangs. No decent citizens of Narbo ever went in that door and down those stairs. Generally when normal citizens did, they never came back out again. This is where Glycon disappeared down into the darkness with his struggling bundle.

Corvus had been out hunting the forested hills around Narbo as usual, but this time he came home to find the shop ransacked, his household penniless, his mother with a broken nose and his sister abducted. Looting collegium thugs had arrived on Milo's orders and emptied the house of everything of value while the screaming Flavia and Claudia had barricaded themselves in a room on the upper level. A year's worth of honey lay smashed

---

[34] Latin: The Wolf's Lair.

on the floor, all the other shop wares were gone and most of the furniture was stolen or destroyed. To cause even deeper insult someone had swept the household Gods onto the floor and defecated on them.

A crude picture of a wolf's head had been scratched into the wall, its grinning mouth almost mocking Corvus. He stood staring at it, bristling with anger. He knew what that symbol meant, he knew who had done this and he knew where he would find them. He took up the black mourning cloak his father had used when his grandfather had died from the floor where it lay trampled amongst the broken furniture. It was the only garment left in the house but was good enough to hide his long knife underneath, he thought. He then went into the street and sold the brace of rabbits and the young fawn he had killed to first person who wanted them and gave the money to his family with promises to his weeping mother that he would return soon. She frantically told him it was not the collegium and begged him not to go, but his sister was missing and he had seen the grinning wolf's head. He knew had to do something. He pulled her hands from his wrists and, still shaking with rage, hurried down the debris littered stairs of the building he once called home. The young man was ignorant of the wailing of his pleading mother who clung to him and he shrugged off her hands from his clothes. Rushing out onto the street he made straight for the seedy part of town to find his sister and get his revenge.

He knew the gang and particularly Milo and Glycon. He had been helping the family pay for the extortionate fire insurance for the best part of the year. He had visited the local magistrate when the rate was increased three times in a month but no official would listen. He knew they would have his sister in the stinking basement they used for their headquarters. He double checked his razor sharp hunting knife was secured under his black cloak and headed for the Lupum Antris.

He remembered charging down the stairwell, a short but violent struggle and remembered there was blood. And screaming. Was it his own voice? He could recall waking in a rubbish pit with lightning bolts of pain shooting through his head. He was covered in blood and his eyes could barely open. He tried to stand up, but he vomited and the whole world went black, and he could not remember any more.

His mother and Flavia died in the fire along with the poor family who was renting the top floor. The fire was so great that it had collapsed the insula, not before Vespillo had bought it from the desperate landlord who watched the fire consuming his building while the gang leader stood idly by with his men and their fire fighting equipment. He coolly offered the landlord a cheap price that went down every few seconds until the frantic man said yes. Vespillo's men had been fighting the fire when the building collapsed, killing two of them. The fat crime boss was not amused by the incident. The men meant nothing but the building had a shop front facing a busy street and was one of the sturdier built insulae… or so he thought. The property would have made him a lot of money and maybe, if he put the rent high enough, would have paid for itself in a year! He told his men to leave the blaze and said to the former owner that the deal was off. The gang walked away and left the landlord weeping in front of the burning, ruined building.

Corvus had crawled from the rubbish pit and wandered the back streets of Narbo in a daze. The horrified citizens avoided this blood-caked spectre dressed in black who staggered feverish and sick until he found his way to the shrine of *Empanda*[35] next to the Temple of Saturn. The shocked priestess gave him food and helped knit the skin on his head back together. His lips, nose, cheeks and forehead would remain a patchwork of scars for life,

---

[35] In Roman mythology, goddess of asylum, charity and hospitality.

but they were not the only scars he carried. Those he carried inside were much deeper.

As hours and minutes became days and nights, he shook with a fever and sickness. His dreams were full of the last moments he spent in the Lupum Antris, seeing his sister naked and tied to a table as she was raped in the dingy, smoky cellar. The drunken brutes leered and sweated, and took turns over her as old painted whores laughed at his sister's whimpers for mercy. One of them cackled as she burned his weeping sister with an oil lamp. Milo spat in Corvus' face and turned his head to watch, telling him she would be chained to the wall for all to use, free of charge.

Clarissa had seen him before he slipped into the blackness. Poor Clarissa, the most quiet and gentle person he had ever known. Her eyes had met his and they pleaded with him but he could do nothing. They were the last thing he saw in the blackness as they began carving lines in his face. For the rest of his days he would never forget that look of horror and anguish in his sister's eyes but also the moment where she silently said goodbye to her little brother.

One morning before dawn his fever broke. Corvus woke in the darkness and in silence he left the temple, creeping past the sleeping priestess who had attended him. He went back and stood in the blackened ruins of his home where his family had been destroyed. At first he was still and silent, then he began to tremble, then he wept bitter tears. His whole life up to that point seemed to have died in the fire. He remembered all the times they laughed around the dining table, his sisters, his mother's ready laugh and his father's love of honey and commerce. All these sweet memories seemed to crackle and burn into blackness in his mind. He dropped to his knees and sobbed tears that stung the fresh wounds in his face. His fingers clutched at the charred remains of his home.

For a long time he wept bitterly, clutching at a fragment of pottery here or a burned timber there, and then holding his soot covered hands to his ruined face. Eventually he stopped. Exhausted and completely out of tears, he stared blankly into nothing as the wind ruffled his torn black cloak. Silently he sat with his wild black hair that had been caked in blood, his blackened face an agony of wounds and cuts. As the sun rose and the town came to life the townsfolk passed the wreckage and were taken aback at the sight. Men and women who went by stiffened and looked away, muttering to various gods to protect them before gossiping with friends about the unnerving sight. Even the street urchins who would torment the homeless or drunk and throw stones at them were scared of this man with the burning black eyes that stared out from the ruins. The shocked children ran to other streets to get their friends. "Come see the *Corvus*," they said and peered quickly around the broken and burned front walls, daring one another to speak to him... Some shouted to the Corvus but none dared approach and many had nightmares about him for a long time after.

He sat there for a whole day in the smoky ruins, not eating, not drinking, not speaking or moving until the sun dropped and night fell. He remained motionless in the darkness as the skinny alley cats slinked past, barely sensing him there. He sat listening to the wind and tuning his senses like he did before the hunt, except this time the wind was not blowing through the trees but moaning its lament through the piles of stone and timbers of his destroyed home that now looked like exposed ribs on a charred corpse. The man in black then stood up and moved silently down the dark streets.

***

The prefect stood at the entrance to the smoking ruin of the Lupum Antris trying to comprehend what he had seen when he first looked inside. The upper floors had collapsed from the fire but the ground floor and basement were still standing. His colleague Prisca came stumbling out of the cellar door holding a lamp with his scarf tied around his face.

"Gods! I have never seen anything like that before! You were not joking, Crito!" said the young man, looking very pale. Prisca had not long joined the *Vigiles Urbani*[36] but he had already witnessed many grim sights. Dead drunks in the sewers, dead gamblers and debtors, dead prostitutes. He had seen slaves being tortured in trials to admit the guilt of their masters, he had seen bloody things in the arena. But nothing like this.

Prefect Crito sighed and looked at his notes on the wax tablet. He had hated Vespillo but the man had 'helped' in the election of the local magistrate and had him in his pocket. Vespillo had come to him with an offering and Crito could either do his job and get fired or take the bribe and look the other way. Since that day he had never felt comfortable seeing Vespillo or his men walking the streets and saluting him with mock respect. That bastard Milo had made a point of personally giving a sweet pastry to his daughter and asking her to pass on his respects to her father, the prefect. He knew what the real message was: we can take anything precious to you at any time. "Well, they are all dead now!" he said aloud, vowing to never get involved with their type again.

"Sir?" said Prisca with a look of concern on his face. "Are you all right?"

"Of course," grunted Crito "Don't just stand there, man. Fetch the slaves with the carts so we can send them all on to the afterlife" he said. "Give me the lamp, I want to make a final check of the numbers."

---

[36] A type of early Roman police force.

Prisca hurried off through the watchmen who had sealed off this part of the street and ran towards the centre of town. Some of the large crowd that had gathered pressed him for answers him as he passed, "Are they all dead? Is that fat bastard gone? I hope they are rotting in Hades!"

It seems I am not the only one who is glad they are gone, thought Crito as he watched the townsfolk openly declaring their happiness at Vespillo's demise. He took a deep breath before walking down the stone steps into the pitch black cellar.

The scene in the cellar was horrifying. Crito lit another lamp, then another, more to comfort himself than to illuminate his way, but the light did not help. The flickering lamplight merely shone amongst the open wounds and intestines, and he could see now that entire floor was covered in blood. Corpses had been piled up by the other staircase that led into the building above. From the blood trails Crito could see that some of Vespillo's men must have been killed upstairs, then the bodies were dragged down and some decapitated. He peered into the darkness and found the heads piled in another corner, many with deep slashes across the face.

Milo was hanging upside down from a bracket on the wall and he had been castrated and half skinned alive, it seemed. There were signs of his bloodied arms thrashing against the wall and they had left a gruesome pattern like the corpse had wings made of blood growing from it. His face which had been left untouched had a look of absolute agony and terror transfixed upon it. Crito saw a lumpy looking head sat atop a dismembered body and thought he recognised Glycon. He too had been castrated and his penis was stuffed into his mouth. Vespillo had been tied naked to a table and castrated. His face was a pulpy mass with what appeared to be teeth marks imprinted on it. His mouth in particular was a blackened mess. Crito looked closer and could see that half-melted silver coins had apparently been stuffed in his mouth, possibly while he was still alive. His usually swollen abdomen look deflated from the thirty or more puncture wounds that oozed blood and the stinking contents of his stomach.

Crito blanched and made a quick count. Nineteen people, all dead! Some signs of fighting. But no one seen coming or going. He set down his lamp on the large table in the middle of the room next to a pile of cloth. "Surely a large rival gang would have been spotted by someone?" he said aloud to himself. "But all the rivals are dead. Trouble with some Gauls, perhaps? Strange..." He paused as he noticed the brown cloth on the table was, in fact, not in a pile but looked like it covered yet another body. Crito took a deep breath to prepare for the sight but when he pulled away the cloth, he jumped back with a start.

The face of a girl! Was she alive? He leaned forward to listen... No, she was dead. He removed the whole cloth and lit another lamp. The girl showed some signs of bruising but she had been washed and completely wrapped in white linen as if she were ready for cremation. Her face was beautiful and serene. Some dried flowers, a small jar and an arrow had been placed next to her. Crito could see a coin jutting from her lips that had been placed in her mouth to pay Charon the ferryman for taking her to the other side. She looked pale and perfect like a priestess of Vesta, and appeared to glow in this dank and grimy place. Suddenly the cellar felt very cold and Crito felt a shiver of fear, wondering if it might be a trick of the gods of the underworld. She clearly was not one of Vespillo's gang. What in the name of *Dis*[37] was she doing here? Who has washed her and prepared her so? He backed away from the pale girl, looking around in the gloom and feeling the unease rising inside him. He quickly retreated back up the stairs, almost tripping up the last few steps

---

[37] In Roman mythology, god of the Underworld; Pluto.

as if an unseen terror chased him out of the cellar. The prefect came out into the cold grey day and did not venture inside again.

Prefect Crito of the Vigiles Urbani of Narbo Martius Colonia wrote a report with a summary that Vespillo and the gang from the Lupum Antris had caused trouble with a rival gang from Tolosa, Massilia or perhaps Tarraco and had finally gotten too big for their boots. Twenty-seven bodies had been pulled from the wrecked building and most were recognised as either prostitutes, their customers or collegium gang members. All the gang members' bodies were thrown into a public cremation pit and burned. The few that were unlucky patrons of the prostitutes caught up in the attack were taken by friends or families for their own personal rites. No formal will was kept by Vespillo or any of his gang and no claimant had presented themselves, so the plot and the remnants of the Lupum Antris building were to be auctioned as a lot, the proceeds to be divided between the civic offices of the city minus a deduction for the cleanup operation and the gang's funeral costs. And officially that was the end of the criminal case.

However, the people of Narbo did not stop talking about it. In the forum and the bathhouse and wine shops and inns, everywhere rumours in the city ran wild. Witnesses began to speak out, saying they saw a black spirit furtively try the doors in the darkest watch of the night and, finding them locked, scale the walls. Some had seen the spirit shooting a bow and cutting throats in the building. Some said they had passed the monster the day it happened as it sat in the rubble of burnt buildings and passed down dark shadowy alleys. Some had seen this dark shadow on the roofs, some even said it had a shredded human face and it was the spirit of Nemesis coming for revenge.

Crito did not write all these wild rumours down, of course, and mostly dismissed it as typical townsfolk gossip. The story had become instant folklore in Narbo and people loved to chatter about it, spreading new and often fantastical slants on this strange incident amongst each other and with travellers from the road. Some swore to the Gods they spoke to the evil spirit and more than one said their used their own magic to curse Vespillo and took credit for it. A drunken man had run naked and screaming through the streets two nights ago. "It's the black spirit! It's the black spirit! Help me...HELP ME!" he had cried, causing chaos and panic in the city.

Crito poured himself another cup of wine in the light of his lamps and smirked. How stupid people could be! *They are such fools, ready to believe any amount of superstitious nonsense,* he thought. His sipped the wine, shifted his weight on the stool and shook his head. "Nothing but small town superstition by small minded people!" he said aloud with a sneer but his face turned thoughtful and sneer quickly faded.

His report also did not mention the one unknown body that was not thrown in the public cremation pit. The young girl in white linen had been brought out of the cellar of the Lupum Antris and immediately people wept and crowded around her. The young girl was taken from the prefect's clean-up slaves and was carried to a temple in the forum where further crowds gathered. Just as the stories of the evil spirit gathered pace so did the tale of the young girl that people called 'The Spirit of Our Lady *Justitia*[38]'. On her funeral day she had been carried on a litter outside to an open field and cremated on a huge pyre with lavish offerings. Her remains, along with the arrow, flowers and a jar that was found to contain honey, were sealed in a shrine not far from the city. In the end several thousand people had attended her funeral in full mourning. It said she was the embodiment of all the people who had suffered at the hands of Vespillo and his gang and indeed any who had suffered injustice. They thanked her, for she had brutally punished the collegium for their crimes. Indeed

---

[38] The Roman goddess of justice.

many visited her shrine to ask for forgiveness for crimes they had committed themselves. The priests and priestesses from every temple in town came with offerings, and a great many people stood weeping as they lit the fire under her. Crito the Prefect who found her was one of those who stood with tears rolling down his cheeks.

**

Corvus had travelled the road until he caught up with the travelling merchants. He kept looking behind, expecting to see men galloping after him, but they never came. The merchants were buying up all the leatherwork and metalwork supplies they could and heading for Corduba. The jolly leader of this group said, "The new *Praetor*[39] is raising a legion for war and that means a shrewd merchant who supplies that legion can come away rich!"

Corvus gave the few coins he had left and offered to catch fresh meat along the way if they let him travel with them, and the merchants agreed. They asked about the wounds on his face and wondered why he preferred to sleep in the back of the cart during the day. He told them that the best hunters hunt at night and the scars were from a wolf that had attacked him. The jolly mercantile captain had frowned at the scars and asked, "Well, I hope you killed that particular wolf and made it suffer for what it did!" At this Corvus nodded.

"I made it suffer." The jolly man looked soberly at him, examining his scars and opened his mouth to speak but closed it sensing that he should not talk of it further.

The young man travelled with the merchants and made small talk and gave a wry smile occasionally. Corvus was welcome for the prolific amount of wild game he caught for the men. He

---

[39] A middle-ranking elected official. Some were given charge of a province.

would sleep in the cart during the day and hunt from the merchants' camp at night or early mornings. He seemed like an indifferent and introverted young man whose scarred but blank face did not portray any emotion, but internally Corvus felt cursed. His sleep was filled with dreams of his sister and her anguish, but also with the horrors he inflicted. He remembered strangling the first sleeping thug he found and taking the man's knife to kill the next. He remembered clearing the building silently before going down to the cellar. He ambushed the remaining few who were barely conscious in a drunken stupor and kept them alive. He found his hunting knife, that had been tossed in a corner, and used it to open them up, he drank their blood and laughing, ate parts of them as they screamed. He had torn apart their bodies, using his knife, fingers and teeth to rend the flesh as he looked for their very souls to devour.

Ultimately he had been too late. Clarissa was dead; she was lying in a crumpled heap in the corner of the stinking cellar when he found her. After he had killed the entire gang and everyone else in the building, he carefully cleaned her and prepared her for the onward journey before he said goodbye. The man in black then took up a bow he found, a flask of water and some coins before he set the upper floors on fire. Corvus left as the flames began to flicker inside the building and walked on without a backward glance, his feet padding silently on the darkened road that led out of the town. He no longer cared where his path took him.

SPQR

Chapter 4

Centurion Falco walked briskly down the main street called the *Via Praetoria* away from the centre of the camp where the commander's tent stood in front of the parade square. This whole central area was known as the *praetorium*. The camp was divided so that it had two main, perpendicular streets running through the middle of it. The Via Praetoria came straight from the parade square to the main gate and the other main road, called the *Via Principalis*, cut across at the foot of the parade square at a right angle. These two roads led to the four gates of the camp and all met back at the praetorium. It did not matter if it were in a marching camp or a permanent winter quarter, this was generally the standard for every Roman fort.

Falco hurried near the main gate to speak to a fellow centurion over the matter of an outstanding bet. After a few moments of coins changing hands with his gap-toothed grinning friend, he walked off again in his quick stride, cursing his bad luck, this time turning down the perimeter road, called the *Via Sagularis*, just inside the ramparts. This was a broad, open space more than a street; it was designed to make sure all the tents were a safe distance from the sloping mound upon which the palisade walls were placed. A volley of fire arrows into a tent city like this could cause serious carnage and the open area made sure there was enough distance from the perimeter for any missiles to fall short. It also worked as an area for the baggage animals to stay, or the cohorts to form up in marching order, not to mention being a good space for training and keeping fit in more peaceful times. As Falco walked down the Sagularis he had many groups of soldiers running past him, wrestling and taking exercise.

The lithe centurion continued past the organised rows of back to back tents that were arranged into streets. The neat little lanes were full of soldiers enjoying their rest day or bustling back and forward on various tasks. Cook fires were tended by the men themselves or the slaves and servants who drove the mules in the baggage train. The bread for the evening meal was being baked and the soldiers ate yesterday's leftover ration cold. Many diced and shared jokes in the warm spring sunshine. As he turned up the street belonging to the 6th Cohort, he noted that the other centurions were already there and were briefing the decanii from each tent section.

"2nd Century... optiones, decanii and section leaders... on me!" Falco said gruffly, irritated that he was the last centurion there. Every decanus and senior legionary closed in around Falco with expectant faces. Was today going to be the day we went to war? Optio Leptis, who was the second in command of the century and the physically largest man in the gathering, quickly counted everyone, making sure a man from every tent section was present. He nodded to Falco as confirmation and called out to a legionary nearby. "You!" he said to the man who stiffened to intente immediately. "Fetch *Tesserarius*[40] Vibenius."

"Yes, Optio," said the man and he ran to fetch Vibenius, the tesserarius of the 2nd Century. His role was that of watch commander who issued the daily password. In battle he would take his place at the rear of the century with Optio Leptis and help dress the lines and deal with casualties. Vibenius was an intelligent, well-liked and honest man with no corruption in him, his skill in numbers and letters had him picking up a lot of the work of the Optio. Along with Leptis, he kept a tally of our pay

---

[40] Second in command to the *optio*; watch commander.

for us, as well as handling other matters from the legion clerks on our behalf.

The small, dark man who looked like an older brother of Kratos with less muscle came jogging up with his small satchel of wax tablets that he always seemed to wear. His sleep crumpled face blinked at Falco. "Sorry, Centurion, I was sleeping and..."

Falco cut him off, "It's not a problem, Vibenius. I would usually let you sleep, but both you and Leptis will need to administrate these points." Vibenius immediately opened a fresh wax tablet and prepared to write.

"Listen in! Pilus Prior Tanicus is standing in for the 6th Cohort in another meeting, because the tribune is ill. So there might be more information to come. That said, everyone is now confined to camp until we know what's going on," said Falco, looking around before adding, "Every tent section, report your exact number of men today to Vibenius and we shall go round up whoever is missing." He took a deep breath and scratched his chin "Secondly... everyone knows the centuries are short of numbers due to the harsh training marches causing desertions and injuries amongst the new Legionaries, so we will get other men folded in to make up the numbers."

There was a quiet groan at this, as people assumed we would be having non-trained, recruit volunteers joining us.

"It's not all bad, It's men who have had 'issues' in training and others coming back from the medicus," said Falco, reading our thoughts. "We are looking at getting all our sections up to eight men strong. The 10th Legion will be fully manned," he added. He looked skywards, recalling the other points. "Oh yes, despite being confined to camp we will not move before noon tomorrow, because we have a column of supplies coming in *and* because half the tribunes are missing from camp, having no doubt wandered off into the fields to read each other's poetry," he added with a smirk, showing his teeth.

Everyone sniggered at this. "Probably looking at each other's cocks as well, no doubt!" came a voice from the back, and Falco flashed a grin and nodded in that direction, then immediately carried on in his usual serious manner.

"Next... Vibenius," he said, nodding to the tesserarius, "there is iron and wood working to be done immediately. Can you round up the blacksmith and carpentry *immunes*[41] and have them form up outside the tents. Leptis, you march them up to the praetorium as soon as possible. Prefect Balbus wants them to get to work on the artillery."

Leptis and Vibenius nodded. The tesserarius excused himself to Falco as he said aloud to the whole group, "Everyone. Give me your section numbers as I come round for the immunes." The decanii all nodded in acknowledgment to Vibenius.

Falco looked around and saw one of the slaves who tended the mules sitting next to a nearby fire but obviously listening in. "You there! Get out of here, now!" he commanded, pointing at the scrawny young man who shot off immediately.

He looked about once more and then took off his helmet with its red crest and rubbed his forehead with his palm. "Listen in, men, it seems things are worse than we originally heard. The 8th Legion scouts have reported back with prisoners saying that every tribe of the Lusitani is part of the uprising and the tribes of the Gallaeci to the north are marching south to join them. They have burned most of the Romanised towns and trade posts. I even heard they sacrificed Roman citizens to their gods as customary preparations for war!" The group muttered with a few

---

[41] Soldiers who possessed specialist skills: engineers, blacksmiths, medics, carpenters, etc.

angrily shaking their heads. Falco continued with a savage gleam in his eye. "This could be a long, dirty fight, boys! These people have fought us before and they know how we work. They are skilled in ambush, hit and run and guerrilla tactics up in their hills. Make sure the men are ready, because we might end up staying up there for a long time," he said, looking around with a grim smile. "Right, off to your duties. Optio Leptis, remain".

The group split apart quickly, chattering amongst themselves, then going into their own tents and having any section members outside follow them in. The chatter sounded aggressive but positive and that was good. Falco hated to see soldiers who did not want to fight. You can hate the marching, hate the heat and the cold, hate the food, hate the officers and even the discipline. That's your right as a soldier, but when it came down to it, you had to be prepared to stand in that front line and fight like a warrior. Falco liked soldiers who looked forward to battle!

"So..." said Optio Leptis, "It's looking like tomorrow, then?" His round face with its rosy cheeks looked almost childlike and podgy despite having hardly any body fat. His frame was broad and strong from growing up on the farms outside Corduba. Falco had seen him wrestle and was surprised how this mild mannered man could get so aggressive when fighting. A good man to have around.

"Yes, tomorrow... or the day after," said Falco thoughtfully. "Listen, Leptis, we might have a problem with some of the replacements. I saw a few of them in the praetorium. Half of them are carrying injuries, I suspect a good deal of those dogs want to be discharged altogether and the others, well..." Falco looked away, shaking his head. "Our new chief has decided to show leniency to a few criminals here and there!"

Leptis' mouth dropped open. "You're joking! Civilian criminals or..."

"Pluto's cock, no! All military and just those who have dropped themselves in the *cac* recently." He nodded with a wry smile, "At least there are no malingerers or weak bastards. He has only kept those charged with drunkenness, fighting, rape or going absent. I heard some of them have committed all four of those charges!"

Leptis ran a thick farmer's hand over his stubbly brown hair and looked thoughtful. "Hmmm, well, it's not so bad. Glad they did not keep those who were thieves or were weak, or even worse, cowardly. We have about ten places that need filling in the century. I'm sure half of those will be snapped into shape come the battle. Those who do not prove to be so can find themselves in the vanguard, neh?"

"I would rather fight a campaign and not lose a single man, Leptis," said Falco, looking at him with his fierce blue eyes. "Every death under our signum is a bad thing."

Leptis shuffled his big feet and looked embarrassed. "Sorry, Falco, I didn't mean it like that? I was just trying to think of ways to help with the..." he stammered.

"*Gerrae!*" said Falco breaking, into a grin. "It's hard to believe you are like a bear in battle sometimes! Look at you, as meek as a new barmaid who spilled the wine!"

Leptis grinned sheepishly. He knew he was good in a fight but felt a little out of place with men like Falco. He was designed to be a centurion! Leptis was fond of saying during the dice games with other soldiers that Falco's mother must have had a painful birth because he doubtless came out as a newborn already wearing the helmet with the transverse crest, probably telling the nursemaid to stand to fucking intente before she could put him on the nipple.

"Well, better a bear in battle and a maid in camp than the other way around like some of the other bastards in the legion," Leptis said, nodding at the slim but formidable man before him. "Don't worry, Falco, I will get into the ribs of the decanii and get these criminal bastards onto our system, and if they do not toe the line I will crack their heads. We have a damn good century and I will do my best to keep it that way," he said, his round face becoming stern.

Falco smiled and his harsh features almost looked softer for a moment. "Well, we must expect these issues forming a new legion. But I know you will get the men ready. The army will take casualties in this war and there will be promotions. You will make centurion soon enough, Leptis, you just got to have a little more confidence in yourself... especially around Tanicus and the other senior centurions. My word only counts for so much when they ask for candidates and even though you impress me you also have to impress them!"

Leptis smiled and blushed with pride. "I will do my best and try not to let you down," he replied, thankful for the compliment.

Falco slapped his thigh with his vitis. "Right, then!" he said with a grin at the big man's embarrassment, "I'm off back to the praetorium. Watch things here for me and get those immunes moving for artillery construction." He turned on his heel, pulling his helmet on, and walked in his fast pace up the cohort street towards the Via Praetoria and then to the centre of camp.

Optio Leptis watched him go and the smile dropped from his face. He was very good at following Falco and helping command the century, but the thought of leading from the front as a centurion frightened him a little. It was not the fighting, just the responsibility that was the issue. Yes, the extra money and prestige was great but...

"I am not like you, Falco," he said quietly to himself, watching the formidable centurion stride away. "You were born for this."

Falco was one of those men that were proud professional warriors who earned their scars and experience in combat. Rome did not promote men to this role just because of age or some aptitude in letters and knowledge, or even being deadly with a sword. He could not bribe his way, kiss an ass to gain the rank or find a way to 'get in the back door'. Occasionally some fat, weak, out-of-shape 'bar fly' who had no combat experience got the promotion. They drank with their superiors and fawned over them, laughing at the right jokes in the wine shops, but they often came unstuck when the blast of war was ringing in their ears. Worst of all, good men sometimes paid with their lives because these people were inept and ill-suited for command. Centurions had to be the best and bravest of the group, and they mostly gained their rank through merit and the respect of their peers... just as it should be. All the way from the transverse crest on their helmets, to the round metal discs on their chests called *phalerae* which they were awarded for bravery, down to the humble but potent vitis, centurions were men to admire and emulate. These men were the iron backbone of the legion. Those who stood in front of them, be it our enemies taking up the sword of war or the newest recruit making mistakes during training, would find these hard professionals to be without mercy or pity. *Do I have that in me?* thought Leptis. *Will the men trust my orders in battle? Will I make the right choice of orders to give?*

"Leptis, are you all right?" Leptis blinked and turned to see Galba smiling at him.

"Yes, I'm fine," Leptis said, swallowing and coughing slightly. "Where are the immunes?"

"I have only Legionary Decius from my section. Trained as a blacksmith by his father," said Galba to the motionless Decius who stood trying to look indifferent to the clearly unwanted extra duty.

"Fall in with the others, Decius," said Leptis, motioning towards a small group of men who had come from the various tents and now stood around looking unimpressed with the prospect of additional work. Immunes could often get out of guard duties and some other camp tasks, but usually had to work hard when they were needed.

Felix poked his head out of the tent and whispered, "Have fun, Decius. We shall all miss you, including the dice!" he cackled and whipped his head back in as Decius kicked a piece of mud at him as he strode past.

"Form up, you lot!" growled Leptis and the group sparked into action.

"Listen in, and make sure you march well enough for nobody to cause me problems. Any bastard who doesn't look the part will get a boot in the ass. By the left... *procedi...TE*!," said Leptis, and the formation moved off down the street towards the Via Praetoria. Another section of immunes thirty metres ahead were led by a zealous Optio who bawled the step out just for the hell of it. Leptis' section naturally fell into the same marching rhythm and followed the lead section in step.

Saves me a job, thought Leptis as they wheeled onto the Via Praetoria. The main road was bustling with centurions, optiones and tesserarii coming and going, as well as many slaves, servants and traders carrying all manner of objects. Sections of immunes were marching towards the centre of the camp on the left side of the road, as was the rules. Three huge empty grain carts pulled by oxen lumbered past on the right, heading out of camp, after depositing their goods with the quartermaster. A mule driver and his team was being shouted at by one of the legionaries whose duty was to keep the traffic moving on the street. The hapless mule driver had wandered into the wrong lane and was upsetting the oncoming foot and horse traffic.

"Look around, you stupid prick! What makes you so special that you can drive your flea bitten nags on the wrong side of the street!?"

The muleteer apologised and desperately dragged his stubborn, braying mules with great difficulty into the left hand lane heading away from camp. Usually all the supply traffic and traders would only use the rear gate of the camp called the *Porta Decumana* but the camp was exceptionally busy due to the upcoming campaign. The extra traffic only seemed to increase the general state of tension.

"*Oculus dextrorsum… ADICI…TE!*" came from the overly-loud optio in front with his tiny section of immunes who whipped their heads round to the 'eyes right' command.

Cac, thought Leptis. "Bollocks to all officers!" he said aloud, to which his small section grinned. Leptis took a deep breath and bellowed out the same command for 'eyes right' even louder than his noisy counterpart out in front.

The officer in question was already well known to the soldiers for his arrogance despite only joining the Legion a short time ago at its formation. The young tribune with pale skin and slender limbs walked past on the right, dictating to a clerk who hurried behind him. The young man gave a salute back to Leptis with a clear look of irritation on his face that worsened when Leptis heard another marching section behind call 'eyes right' and then another! The tribune would walk through the entire camp, tiring his arm out returning the incessant salutes that were more a mockery than a mark of respect. Every section would take up the joke and carry it on. Such things were the symbol of solidarity amongst the lower ranks and would be used on trumped up patricians or unpopular officers whenever there was an opportunity. Leptis smiled and gave the 'eyes front' command quietly to his smiling section. He thought how things like that can cheer you up in the army, sticking one up the upper classes when they came to play war.

Leptis marched the section into the main parade square of the praetorium and followed the various other sections who were all halting the men outside the main quartermaster's tent where an ever growing detachment of immunes were gathering. The *praefectus castrorum*[42] was standing there with a camp clerk tallying up the numbers as they came in. This thickset, powerful man was the third in command of the legion after the Legatus, and Senior Military Tribune, of course. This role was usually exclusively filled by those that came up from the ranks and was one of the ranks that could be gained by a former *primus pilus*[43]. The praefectus castrorum was the most senior in time served and was in charge of supplies, equipment and camp maintenance, not to mention dictating the training regimes of the men themselves. But seeing as these men had generally lived their entire lives in the army they frequently get involved in everything else, too. This particular camp prefect already had a bad reputation for being overzealous in his role. He had already earned the reputation as a ball breaker and reputedly even had a centurion flogged occasionally. His nickname was 'Pug' because of his flat, bashed in features. Apparently, he had been quite a fighter back in the day both with weapons and bare hands, and it seemed he still engaged in such activity, as one of his eyes was bruised

---

[42] Camp prefect, third in command of the Legion, responsible for training , maintaining the camp's equipment and supplies.
[43] Commanding centurion of the first cohort and senior centurion of the entire Legion.

black. His face was permanently fixed with a look at disgust for everyone in the camp who was below him in rank. His barrel chest and thick forearms showed strength and he was covered in twenty or so scars which he had acquired in the East fighting with the great general Pompey Magnus.

Leptis saw him taking the parade he was to attend and he groaned inside as he marched his section to a halt on the end of the formation of soldiers who were already there. He quickly told his men to dress into the file that was three deep and more than ten long. Just as Leptis was about to hurriedly march away, the fat faced immune clerk who had a flabby stomach looked up from his writing tablet with an expression of irritation.

"Well, optio? What cohort? What century? And how many men did you bring?"

Leptis swore inside at this pen pushing legionary who had now caused Pug to stare at him! The fat little swine with the big drooping nose called Catalus was often known as 'Catulus[44]' around camp, which was an affectionate term for 'Pug's pet'. The pot bellied legionary clerk was always well fed and supplied. Indeed, many suspected of him having various dodgy deals and corruptions with Legion stores. His popularity, or lack of it, meant he only went to the wine shops and inns with his master Pug, where he could always be seen sycophantically laughing at his commanders jokes and fetching drinks for him.

"Optio Leptis, 2nd Century of the 6th Cohort with seven... erm no... eight men," Leptis stammered, looking at Pug who now stared back at him with nothing short of open hatred.

"Well, optio, what was it? Seven or eight?" said Pug in his deep bass voice. The praefectus castrorum put his balled fists on his hips and stood there in a basic civilian tunic with a simple belt.

---

[44] Latin: puppy.

The only standard military items he wore were his hobnailed sandals and the soldier's scarf knotted around his neck. He was at that rank where he could wear what the hell he liked around the camp and he knew it.

"Eight, sir," said Leptis making a quick tally of the men he had brought with him. The big man cursed that he did not even think to count and wondering why in the name of Dis did it really matter!

"Get out of my fucking sight and go buy an abacus with your next salary, you stupid *cunnus*!" said Pug, jerking a thumb away and wrinkling up his face as if someone had put a piece of cac in front of him instead of his dinner. Leptis saluted and marched off quickly, noting the grin on the face of Catulus and seeing that a following decanus had done the same thing with his section of immunes and was now getting the same treatment.

"Gods! What fucking bastards! The pair of them!" Leptis muttered quietly to himself as he marched away. "People like that find a home in the army."

SPQR

Chapter 5

Inside the tent was cluttered with equipment but comfortable and warm. The rest day was welcome and the 6th Cohort made the most of it. They had worked hard on camp fatigues earlier in the day and now they would not start their turn guarding the camp perimeter until the first watch of the next morning, so everyone was guaranteed to relax their legs and backs from yesterday's march. But despite this seemingly relaxing day, the goatskin tent that housed the section did not drown out the noise. The whole camp was much busier than normal and seemed to have a feeling of expectation lingering in the air. Galba could feel it and began sharpening his sword a second time that day, not through nerves on his part, he merely liked adding to the already keen edge. The scraping of the stone on the gladius made Borras look up.

"Do you think we will leave tomorrow?" said the big man, looking apprehensive.

Galba clicked his tongue. "Gods only know, Borras. Falco says we cannot move until all the supplies reach us but look at Caesar... How many times does that man change his mind and do something out of the ordinary? He is always in a rush and so are we because of it," Galba said in a matter-of-fact voice. "The 8th Legion has some of its cohorts still protecting the supplies coming in, and we usually don't move until we are all together."

"Hmmm, but like you say, he does things differently, eh," said Ignavus, picking his long nose.

"True enough," nodded Galba in agreement. "I guess we will have to wait and find out," he said looking down at his work at the whetstone.

Felix yawned from his cot in the corner at the back of the tent, clearly bored by the conversation. "Well, despite this old maidens' talk making me want to sleep I personally am wondering who shall be joining us for a grand feast this evening?" he said with an expansive sweep of his arm. He looked at the always bedraggled servant who sat on the floor opposite to Galba next to the tent door. "Ictis[45]! We will have guests tonight, so prepare the best, whatever the expense! Bollocks to rich old senatorial farts like Lucullus! I want people to say the name of Marcus Mammilius Felix when they think of extravagance!"

Borras snorted with laughter and shook his head, smiling. The section servant Ictis stopped sewing the garment he was mending and grinned his toothless grin as he often did. When questioned he said he could not remember his age or indeed where he came from although it was suspected he was at least forty. His weathered, simple features were offset by his industrious nature; he was rarely lacking in energy, his bowed legs carrying him at remarkable speeds. He smiled now, not because he understood the joke, but rather because he had slow wits. That said, the skinny little man with his hooked nose and bald head was efficient with administration and could erect tents, start fires, cook the food and set out our sleeping cots in record time and worked much harder than most camp servants – abilities which everybody in the section appreciated, especially Galba who had known him from his previous legion. Now Ictis sat there grinning at the staring Felix for many moments after the joke had passed.

---

[45] Latin: ferret.

"Well?" said Felix with exasperation. "What is for dinner, my dear Ictis?"

"Bread!" said Ictis. "And maybe something else!" he said, looking pleased.

"A goose!" Felix said with a gasp and a convincing look of genuine surprise on his face. "By the brazen beard of Jupiter! Ictis has brought a great golden goose to our feast!" he cried, clapping his hands together like an excited child.

Ictis screwed his face up and looked hurt. "No, not got a goose? Bread I says? You ask this before and I could not find it cheap, too much money for goose," he said, looking down into his lap in shame.

"Gods, give it a rest, Felix!" said Kratos on the cot next to Galba. "Every damned day you get him with the same poxy joke!" he said, defending the hapless servant. The Greek dropped the chainmail shirt he was attempting to modify and lay back with a yawn. Felix put his arms out in front of him and began stretching. He had promised Borras to teach him some grappling moves before they hit the baths. Even the idle Ignavus said he would like to try it, much to everyone's surprise.

"Still better than your shitty weak jokes, Numidian!" Felix said and he cocked his leg and farted as he lay back down. "Gods! It does not help that we are all confined here. All this waiting is not good! I was thinking of going downtown and spending a few coins seeing Orbiana! She knows how to suck the tension from my bones... and some other places too!" he cackled.

Borras looked unimpressed at Felix. Ignavus sniffed the air and pulled his tunic over his nose in disgust at the stink; everybody else ignored his laughter. It did not feel like a day for jokes. Felix sighed and heaved himself back up. "Well, as much as I am enjoying the general good humour in here, I'm off to 'check the perimeter' and make sure all of my dearest friends are safe," he said gesturing to his companions. Felix always said this when he went to run round the Via Sagularis. He had hustled some people and won several bets through racing men in the 1st Cohort. Felix was developing a reputation as a pretty good distance runner in the Legion and certainly many would not bet against him these days.

"Make sure you do some more of those exercises I showed you," said Kratos, eyeing Felix as he stripped down to just his underwear. "You need to work on building strength!" Felix had wiry muscles that had filled out over the months of training but he still looked quite thin despite his tremendous appetite. Active campaign could strip the fat from a man very quickly and Kratos was worried for him.

"My dear friend, I shall build muscle when you build some brains," said Felix in a soothing tone. "Even the runners of the Olympics in your homeland would agree that I have the body of a champion." With that he took a wide stance and adopted a pose he had seen in a statue once, which caused Borras to burst out laughing.

"You look like a bent stick with a rag wrapped around it!" the big man howled, rolling back onto his creaking cot. His mirth caused Galba and Kratos to grin with the infectious laughter and even the sullen Ignavus smirked.

Felix stood holding the heroic pose and slowly turned his head, his eyebrows raised with an almost comical look of disbelief at the laughing Borras who now had tears in his eyes. Galba and Kratos were now laughing too, and even Ictis was chuckling, more in spirit than in understanding.

"A pox on your fat fucking ass, you son of a Germanic goat!" said Felix angrily, striding past. "Ictis! Make sure this fat pig stays away from my goose!" he said to the confused servant as he stormed out of the tent and Ictis looked puzzled and called after him "We isn't got goose?" This caused Borras to laugh even harder now, almost falling off his cot as he howled.

The *buccina*[46] blared sounding the changing of the watch and Kratos stood up, laughing. He stripped down to his loincloth, revealing his muscular physique. Each muscle group was as defined as those on professional athletes or the statues you might see the masons carving for rich families. Some of the women amongst the camp followers were very taken by the Greek and he was never short of company in the wine shops. He turned to the still recovering Borras who wiped the tears from his eyes. "Let's go and get to it. We shall do a lap or two of camp to warm up, then begin working on those arm-locks I was telling you about. I think some of the lads from the 3rd Century want to join in, too."

The big man nodded and agreed, stripping down to his loincloth. His limbs were larger than Kratos' but less defined, his pale skin covered in a fuzz of golden reddish hair.

"Titans, the pair of you," said Galba. "One day you will have to show this old man how to fight," he said, glancing up from his needlework.

Kratos looked at him, wondering if he was being sarcastic. "We shall be on the Sagularis if you need us," he said, leaving the tent with Borras. Ignavus slinked after them, still wearing his tunic and feeling a little self conscious behind those two powerful men.

---

[46] C-shaped Roman brass instrument used for communicating orders.

Galba smiled to himself. *It's a good section*, he thought. *They are a touch loud but that is the price for having character. They will settle and hopefully become good fighters*, he mused as he looked at Ictis who was concentrating on his own needlework. "We will have the food for the next changing of the watch. Did you prepare everything as I said?"

Ictis looked up with a grin, pleased that he had been part of a secret plan. "Yes, sir, fish and beans are soaking for soup. Added onions and *garum*[47] for more fish flavours. Got salt and eggs is hidden with apples," he said, patting a sack under a nearby cot. "I took grain for normal bread and flasks for oil like normal dinner." He chuckled and pointed at a small bundle near the corner of the tent. "Wine for officers had one small jug swapped for cheaper kind and fresh posca is ready to drink, too."

Galba grinned back. Too many people would beat the slaves and servants of the baggage train, but he would have none of it. These men spent more time around the supplies and the baggage train than any other from the army. He had heard of muleteers stealing booty from soldiers' packs and always making sure they helped themselves whenever they got the chance, partly due to the ill treatment they received from the men they were there to serve. Galba made sure to inspire loyalty from Ictis and this man, simple as he seemed, was proud that he had been asked to come to the new legion and was already fiercely loyal to the section. Time and again he would prove to be a wonderful scrounger who had some level of shrewd cunning hidden inside him.

"Good work, Ictis," he said, smiling at the man. "The section will have a good feast tonight before we leave."

---

[47] Fermented fish sauce, very popular in Ancient Rome.

The bedraggled servant dropped his grin and frowned, "Bad time with war, sir! Sometimes, anyways? Bad in blood and bones but good in gold... Sometimes, anyways?" He said, thoughtfully scratching the side of his nose. "Ictis will go for firewood and see friends for more food." His face lit up. "Ictis has some good plan for trade! Can go now, sir?"

Galba nodded and replied sternly, "No stealing, Ictis! Make sure everything 'traded' will not cause any trouble!" He pointed his finger at the skinny man who wrung his hands.

"No, sir. Course not, sir. Never, sir! Always trade, always trade!" pleaded Ictis pitifully.

"Good," nodded Galba nodded with a wink "Off with you and make sure the beans soak well! I do not want to lose a tooth on them!"

Ictis grinned. "Yes, sir!" he replied and darted out of the tent. Galba smiled after him, knowing full well that Ictis would try and pinch anything and everything from the stores if he could. Anything to help the section was always welcome but stealing from the Army was not really 'stealing' in most soldiers' books. Miserly bastards like Pug loved to keep supplies stacked up idle rather than give them out... so why not take what should be issued! Of course the same could not be said for someone who stole from his fellow soldiers; this was an unforgivable crime that often meant a savage beating and being permanently ostracised by your peers or worse. Apart from cowardice, nothing was worse than being known as a thief in the Legion.

Galba sighed and lay back on his cot, his tattooed hands holding up the cloth so he could inspect his own neat needlework that rivalled any· tailor or dressmaker. *It* is *a good section*, he thought. Then he paused and said aloud to himself, "I wonder what these replacements will be like?" His face clouded over and the smile was gone. It would not be long before he had his answer.

***

As the sun had reached its zenith and the buccina had announced the change of the watch across the camp, Falco and the majority of the legion's centurions were stood to the side of the large, square headquarters tent which was full of all the command elements of the 8th, 9th and 10th Legions. A table had been thoughtfully placed out with some camp servants serving cups of warm posca to refresh the soldiers. The centurions of the 10th mixed with the various centurions from the 8th and 9th and chatted to old friends, but the relaxed atmosphere was not universal around them. The area near the entrance of the headquarters tent was filled with an endless stream of runners and clerks carrying orders and information from here to the nearby camps of the 8th and 9th Legion.

From the other side of the parade area, the praefectus castrorum would occasionally bawl out the name of a certain century of a certain cohort to a group of tesserarii and optiones standing close by and demand to see someone from that unit, no doubt absolutely furious over some small matter of blankets or a sack of grain that needed counting. Every time Falco looked around it seemed that Pug was shouting at someone outside his own tent for one thing or another. The artillery immunes could not be seen by Falco but he could hear them working in the area known as the *fabrica*[48]. The din of hammers and saws that manufactured the legion's heavy weapon systems competed with the shouts of Pug and the all general noise that filled the air. The whole centre of camp was a hive of activity with rumbling carts coming and going, soldiers and camp servants busying themselves with tasks and anyone with the rank to do so seeming to find any reason to

---

[48] A legion's workshop area and forges.

shout at someone. Falco smiled as he saw Vibenius hurrying along scribbling on his wax tablet with Leptis next to him counting on his fingers.

Gods, it's good to concentrate on the tactics instead of the administration, thought the centurion, remembering how he had hated his earlier ranks. *Fighting* is *the job*, he thought, smiling to himself as he turned towards the headquarters tent entrance. The flap opened and closed with the regular stream of clerks coming and going, carrying messages, often being directed by the headquarters adjutant officer who seemed to leave the tent every few moments to talk to a messenger in person or explain exact details to a clerk.

Falco sipped his posca and looked back toward the via praetoria and saw a group of the *speculatores* come trotting in on their horses. These covert soldiers were dressed in the manner of the Celts and many sported large moustaches or beards. Some of them would go on missions dressed as Roman citizens, merchants, freedmen, even occasionally disguised as slaves or travelling actors, depending on the task at hand. These men had the dangerous job of scouting occupied territory, spying and occasionally visiting locals chiefs, outspoken warriors, troublemakers and druids who were known to be against the rule of Rome. Their visits would be well planned and co-ordinated so the visit would often be somewhere secluded and in the dead of night to get rid of the 'problem'. Assassination, reconnaissance and subterfuge were meat and drink to them.

Falco recognized the leader trotting his muddied horse at the front as a former centurion from the 8th Legion. He knew this man had ancestral roots that went back to the Lusitanian war eighty years ago. His Celt-Iberian tribe had come south and were Romanized and settled into civilized society. The man had worked as a translator on the northern trade outposts but now his Celtic looks and the language that was passed down through his family made him a section commander for this special unit. He trotted at the head of six muddied cavalrymen. His unit was made up of convincing-looking Romans with a Celtic appearance that was so good they might even be Lusitanian allies. They all wore variants of the tight fitted goatskin trousers and boots, and woollen Celtic cloaks. All of them had facial hair of some kind and the former centurion had a blonde moustache that drooped at the edges. His beard was rough and unkempt. The deadly curved sword of the wild tribes hung easily at his hip.

Falco cursed his own darker looks and distant Carthaginian ancestry. He had tried out for the speculatores of the 8th Legion and passed their rigorous selection tests, but was ultimately let go for his inability to blend in. He knew these men were paid the rate of *duplicarius*[49] because of their dangerous work and, more importantly to Falco, were often involved at the deepest levels of military strategy. Their reports would usually decide how the legion would operate and all of them had the general's ear. He always swore if he went to a place where he could fit in he would immediately volunteer. Parthia or Egypt, perhaps maybe somewhere east or south? Did Scythians have dark hair and blue eyes?

He jealously watched the leader dismount as another trooper took his horse reins and trotted the animals away from the tent. The tall speculator spoke to the legionary on guard, then strode into the command tent, no doubt to impress Caesar with some snippet of vital information.

"Bollocks to him! All because of a blonde moustache!" said Falco aloud, spitting on the floor and cursing his luck.

---

[49] A pay grade in the Roman Army receiving double the basic pay.

"Falco! Still talking to yourself, you mad bastard!" said a deep voice behind him that he recognized. He turned around and saw a tough face with a sharp-toothed grin looking at him from under a transverse crest.

"Crastinus, you old dog!" said Falco, gripping the large man's outstretched hand and shaking it. "I should have smelled you coming!"

"Ha! You would have only recognized me because of your sister's perfume all over me!" Crastinus laughed. "Tell her to wash before she pleasures me next time!"

Falco looked thoughtful. "She did mention you... said that you were useless down there and gave you the perfume to aid your new life as a woman," he continued with a grin. "Now you can smell sweeter to any man who wanted to buy your ass".

Crastinus laughed and slapped him on the shoulder. "Well, Brother, she is not wrong about my cock, I wanted to get hard but she cranked me like a trainee catamite on the first day of the job! You should have taught her better!"

"Well, she is stronger than the average catamite and yours is so tiny you need a soft young *pullus*[50] with hands small enough to pull you off!" said Falco, waggling a little finger at Crastinus who hooted with laughter, his friendly brown eyes full of mirth.

"Gods, it's good to be back around old comrades, eh!" said Crastinus, giving him a punch on the arm. "I saw you training with your century the other week but we were marching out for formation drill so I could not stop. How are they? It looked like you had some good men?"

---

[50] Pullus - lit. young chick/animal; slang term for young male prostitute specialising in receptive intercourse.

"They are not too bad, to be honest," said Falco. Then, looking over his shoulder, he said in a lower voice, "There are a couple of centuries who are not up to standard. I guess that is the price of forming a new legion so quickly, neh?"

Crastinus nodded, his crest fluttering in the light breeze. "It's the same with the 1st Cohort," he said in agreement. "Yes, we do have a lot of the experienced men but those who transferred from the 9th Legion are always fighting with our lads from the old 8th."

Falco sighed, "To be expected, I suppose." He thought of the bitterness between his old legion, the 8th, and the legion that was recruited alongside it, the 9th. The rivalry was a couple of years old and was often the reason the legions were kept apart from each other. Since they were camped together there had been plenty of trouble in the local inns, wine shops and whorehouses and the parades for punishment were now happening daily.

"Always seems to be a drunkard or a brawler being flogged for trying to fight against another Legion," he said ruefully "Still, soon they will have reason to hate the 10th Legion, eh!" said Falco with a wink.

Crastinus grinned. "Absolutely! I am a fan of the new chief and proud to say I am one of Caesar's men! He is much better than old Pompey…what did he ever do for us? Fuck all, that's what!" said Crastinus with some bitterness. Everybody had joined the dilectus years ago with promises of going to the east to fight King Mithridates of Pontus, Cilician Pirates and the Kingdom of Armenia. It seemed they had a whole new world of adventure and riches coming to them and many had ended up being forgotten and left to guard against tribal incursions by Celts or the constant road building and repair duties in Hispania. This angry sentiment was very deep amongst many of these men.

"Well, judging from the shit storm that's happening up north it seems Caesar will definitely be taking us to war this time," grunted Falco, looking around at the camp that was a hive of activity. "Did you see anyone from the 8th?"

Crastinus nodded. "I took a drink with Commius and Murena, those bastards are still the same!" He said with a laugh. "Oh, I saw a couple of the old boys from the 3rd cohort and, remember that shithouse from the quartermasters with the limp? I saw him too and glared at the *cunnus*!" he paused for a moment, clicking his tongue. "I thought I saw Galba, too, marching in the ranks, but I could not tell?"

"If it was 2nd Century, 6th Cohort then yes… Galba is with me," said Falco with his icy blue eyes narrowing. "Did you hear about what happened?"

Crastinus' face clouded over. "I heard it was gradus deiectio all the way down to Legionary, then ten lashes and minor duties for six months," he continued. "All because of some little prick from Rome!"

Falco nodded in agreement. "It was a shitty business, all right! But he took it well and his back healed up nicely, luckily. Tanicus pulled a few strings to make him a decanus for the new guys in the 6th Cohort. I already pushed him for optio but the paperwork still has him marked down. Vibenius, my tesserarius, might find a way around it via the Legion clerks. But you know what it's like once you are on the shit list? You have to virtually kill yourself in battle to come off it! We shall just have to wait and see."

As he was speaking he saw the flap of the headquarters tent open and Pilus Prior Tanicus came striding out of the doorway. The squat, powerful man paused for a moment to look around the busy parade area, then strode over to the centurions of the 6th Cohort.

Crastinus spotted him coming. "Here is your Pilus Prior, I will be off. We will get a cup of something stronger when we can, eh?" he said, clasping Falco's hand before going back to his own unit.

"*Mars* and *Bellona*[51] protect you, Brother!" said Falco with a wink.

"You too, Brother... now I am not there to protect you!" said Crastinus laughing as he turned on his heel and walked away.

Pilus Prior Tanicus walked over with his quick military stride. His permanently tanned, balding head showed its stubble of iron grey hair that looked more silver in the sunlight. He was not particularly old, but a life of marching and fighting had leathered the skin and probably helped speed up his hair turning grey. His stout, muscular frame was a testimony to a long life of soldiering and many civilians his age would certainly envy his build. His forearms and face bore scars from a dozen battles and most of his skin bore the tattoos of Eagles, standards and symbols of luck and war that were popular amongst the soldiers. Tanicus was involved in the wars some years ago and had been in several savage battles advancing on hill forts and prepared enemy positions. The weathered face of this professional soldier was shrewd in thought, warm amongst friends and fearsome to the enemy. He stopped before the centurions who immediately gathered around.

"Listen in, 6th Cohort... Who is missing? Nobody? Good! Right, our tribune turned up. He was not 'ill', just in bed with his mistress and forgot the time," said Tanicus with a look of utter contempt. "Well, young Apollo is in there now and got his ass

---

[51] The Roman god and goddess of war.

chewed by the Chief himself, so it saves me having to say it in a less pleasant way," he said, tapping his leg with a worn vitis. "It looks like we are going to break camp in the morning and get moving north closer to the enemy. Some of our supply convoys have been attacked on the roads coming up from Hispalis, Gades and Corduba. It's nothing too serious and sounds like banditry levels have become elevated due to the conflict. We might have sporadic incidents from locals who are supportive of the Lusitanian cause. Either way, it is nothing I would say is a real military threat. The cohorts from the 8th legion have taken care of everything so far but they are spread far and wide, so we might be leaving without them and they will catch us up when we are staged deeper into the enemy territory."

He turned his head as one of the incoming *exploratorii* patrols came cantering onto the praetorium, mounted on some muddy and exhausted horses. This unit often worked alongside the speculatores, except they were the eyes and ears of the marching legions. These horsemen were specialists in long range military reconnaissance into enemy territory rather than actively talking to locals, finding enemy spies and insurgents in occupied territories. The job involved mapping possible routes of march, fording points for rivers and streams as well as enemy locations. They were more conspicuous than speculatores as some wore their standard Roman chainmail under the tribal cloaks, that would fool the distant onlooker. Falco spotted at least three of the riders wearing the Roman soldiers sandal as they relayed some important information to the headquarters adjutant officer who emerged from the tent to speak to them. Tanicus turned back to his assembled men and continued.

"The replacements..." he paused with a heavy sigh. "A clerk just told me they have been marched in and one of the tribunes has already deposited them around the Cohorts... In other words, we might have been shit on and find that they have left us the garbage!" he said, looking grim. "They probably have already been divided amongst your centuries but you need to place them in your sections if your optios have not already done it. Get the names and details in to your tesserarius and have them report to me by the change of the watch." He grunted and jerked his head back towards the command tent. "I best get back in there before they start to think that some soft ass tribune with bum fluff on his cheeks will run the 6th Cohort! Everybody, stay near your tents and I will come get you once I know the full picture." He sighed and scratched his head. "The sooner we get going the better, eh." And with that he turned and hurried back to the command tent for his briefing. Falco and the other centurions said farewell to friends and headed back through the chaos of the praetorium to the tents of the 6th cohort as the entire army bustled to and fro preparing for the coming fight.

**

"Decanus Galba? Can you come out here, please?" said Optio Leptis, poking his head through the tent door.

Galba sat up with a smile. "Of course," he replied.

Leptis was clearly above him in rank but always acted respectful to the veteran soldier. He left the tent and saw two legionaries, with shaved heads, standing at intente wearing their full uniform and carrying their full marching equipment. One was a thick-necked, hulking creature with powerful shoulders and piggy little eyes in a bruised, ugly face that had clearly recently seen a fistfight. His squashed nose looked like it had been used by a professional boxer in the past and the man looked every part the villain. The other legionary looked lean with pale skin and a face lined with horrific vertical scars that were much worse than any Galba had ever seen before. The lines were raked like a ploughed field and the tissue around the mouth had healed in such a way that the lips were a thin impassive line. His eyes were black, reptilian and pitiless, and quite frightening to look into. Anyone could clearly see that these scars were not from a conventional fight.

"These two men are for your section, Galba," barked Leptis in his best command voice which was impressive at times. "They have been flogged, particularly the big one. Both been jailed but they are erm?... physically better than some of the others. Two were limping and one was crying so I saved the most warlike looking for you," said the big optio with a smile which dropped to a scowl as he looked back at the two soldiers standing stiffly to intente. "The medicus has cleared them, all the flogging wounds are healed enough and they are ready to march and fight for the 6th Cohort."

Galba scratched the lumpy scar tissue where his left ear used to be and replied, "Thank you, optio. It appears Caesar was merciful to these men and understood that crime is commonplace in situations like this." Gesturing around, Galba continued. "With three whole legions being brought together in Roman territory there will always be fighting, stealing, women troubles, desertion and cheating at dice. At least in enemy territory you appreciate being in the camp and having your fellow soldiers around you. I am happy for these two to come to my section as they look like they will make good soldiers and probably earn rewards from Caesar himself," Galba said to Leptis but clearly for the benefit of the new arrivals. The big brute looked down with a filthy-toothed grin and the scarred fellow looked at the decanus, blinked, then seemed to stare off in the distance, lost in thought. Galba knew he had to get off on the right foot with these men who potentially might damage his section.

Leptis fidgeted and said, "Well, I shall leave you to it. The names have been logged with Vibenius and I shall brief Falco when he comes back."

Galba thanked the optio and watched him walk away until he turned back to the men. "Name... and crime?" he said curtly to the brute.

"Legionary Spurious Flavius Sertorius, or 'Saxum', Sir!" said the huge brute in a grating voice. "I was wrongly accused of insubordinate behaviour by Pug... sorry, I mean by the Praefectus Castrorum in the wine shop nearest the gate." He coughed and added, "Erm, so he swung a punch at me and I decides that I should knock some sense into him but he did not appreciate that I was only helping!" He said, shaking his head, "He punched me on the jaw a few times but could not knock me down no matter how much I encouraged him, and then he said I was stupid with a rock in my head, which is funny because my uncle gave me the name 'Saxum', which I got because I could use my head to bash holes in the..."

"Enough! I get your point," snapped Galba sternly with a little internal smile. There was not a man in the Legion that would pass up on the chance to punch Pug! "And what about you?" he said, looking at the man with the scars.

"Legionary Sextus Livius Decula Decanus. And my 'crime' was telling one of the clerks for the headquarters adjutant 'to go fuck himself' and that no one who sits in a warm headquarters tent and scribbles notes for a living can make fun of me. And if he does it again I will visit him in the darkest watch of the night and give him some scars of his own," said the man evenly and quietly without malice in a way that Galba found disturbing. He looked at the men in silence for a moment, weighing up the potential for trouble from these two that was balanced by their obvious amount of fighting spirit.

"Right... here it is..." said Galba with his hands on his hips. "I have a good section of men and we have become a good little family. You two scary bastards are welcome into this tent and I will do my part to ensure that you have all the knowledge and help to get you where you need to be. But as big as you think you are and as threatening as you think you are," he said, gesturing to both individually, "I *will* gut you both in the first skirmish and leave you to bleed if you walk in this tent thinking you are bigger than the section. I will bleed for these men and if you earn it I will bleed for you, too. Have I made myself clear?" They both nodded silently with thoughtful expressions on their faces.

"Stand easy, men, stow your kit next to the tent for now and get inside. Welcome to the 2nd of the 6th of the 10th," he said, smiling. "I hope you like fish soup."

SPQR

Chapter 6

The two men walked quickly up the expansive entrance road to the villa that was well outside Rome. The older man who walked ahead had strong features and short greying hair, despite being relatively young. He urged the younger and slightly better dressed slave to keep up. *I* am *keepng up,* fumed Bellus inwardly. *Gods, it's cold! I do not know how he deals with it,* he thought, hurrying behind the barefooted man, clutching his bag full of writing tablets and other instruments that the master bade him carry. A gust of wind rushed between the manicured trees that lined the road and tossed open Cato's simple travelling cloak. He shivered as it went down the front of his black toga that he wore in the old fashion, with no tunic underneath. *I must be getting old,* he thought as he gritted his teeth at the wind and kept walking towards the large walled compound of the mansion, noting with displeasure the decadent decorative plant pots and the very intricate bronze work on the inlaid front door.

"Open up! Marcus Porcius Cato, Senator of Rome, demands that you open the door," called Bellus, banging on the thick door. The viewing slot shot open and a beady eye looked them quickly up and down, then narrowed slightly just before the slot closed with a snap. Some moments later the door opened and a very tall, well dressed slave with refined, tanned features beckoned them in with an elegant sweep of the hand.

"Welcome to the residence of Senator Marcus Licinius Crassus. May I get you some refreshment while you wait, sir?" said the slave with a practiced eloquence.

Cato looked the slave up and down with a slight look of disgust. From his well made slippers and expensive blue tunic, all the way up to his immaculate, shaved head, this slave oozed confidence. His features and colour showed he was from Egypt, perhaps. Gods! Even his name tag hanging around his neck looked like it was engraved by a professional. Cato looked up at the tattoo above the slave's perfectly manicured eyebrows. "M.L.C," even that was obviously done with the steady hand of an artisan. He snorted and shook his head at the slave who stood by with a patient indifference to this scruffy man eyeing him like he was cattle.

"Tell Senator Crassus I am here and I will speak to him immediately," said Cato, pushing past this arrogant slave while taking off his cloak and tossing it to another slave standing by who immediately began to fold it with great care. The entranceway was warm and led to a greater inner atrium that was dark and lit with lamps.

Bellus shuffled his cold feet in his damp sandals. He could feel the warmth in the house and was glad to be inside. The clouds outside looked like rain for the whole five mile journey from Rome to one of the many villas belonging to Crassus. The rich senator had many to choose from and apparently this huge and beautifully styled villa was one of the smaller ones! Bellus bit his own lip in regret and, for a moment, looked with a pang of envy at the four other slaves who stood motionless in the entranceway. All of them were dressed in the same fine blue cloth and looked well fed and healthy. He looked forward to his Master having a meeting so he might be given food in the kitchens where the slaves ate. The food here must be good! The fires in the *hypocaust*[52] had long since been lit and the floor was warm to the touch. Looking along a sumptuous corridor to the adjacent rooms and further in the house, Bellus could see

---

[52] Roman underfloor heating.

beautifully crafted columns that held up the grand and elegant roof of the main atrium and the air was fragrant with what seemed to be the scent of burnt pine cones.

Cato walked along the corridor into the dimmed atrium and first looked up at the skylight which had been covered in a timber frame with tile work to block out the light and presumably the cold winter weather. He then looked down to the exquisitely detailed mosaics and the simple yet tasteful frescos lining the walls that glowed in the light from many lamps that added their acrid smell to the house. It was far too warm and stuffy for this particular guest. He stood and shook his head in disgust. "What a pretty house," said Cato aloud in a sarcastic voice that echoed through the atrium. "I feel like I'm in Asia."

"They can't afford houses like this in Asia, my friend," said Crassus in his deep voice. "*Salve*[53], Cato, this is an unexpected surprise." The older man glided forward like a spectre, his long robe barely moving. His lined face with its usually downward tilted mouth was smiling with a warmth that Cato knew was affected. He clasped hands with Cato and bade him follow to a dining room. "Callidus! Have wine and something simple brought in," he waved to the elegant slave who had opened the door. The man gave an almost imperceptible nod to another slave across the room, who left immediately. "I had the wooden cover built when the weather turned so cold," said Crassus, looking backwards at the atrium. "A novelty, I know, but it keeps it warm in here, neh?" he said smiling as they walked into a simply decorated dining room with a dozen couches and tables. Cato could see in the dim light that the walls were full of alcoves from which the busts of great philosophers and statesmen looked out at them. Their presence in a well lit banquet room would usually stir debates on history and politics,

---

[53] Latin greeting.

but today they peered out of the darkness like pale, disembodied heads.

"I did not come here to talk of mild weather or effeminate ways of keeping warm, Crassus," said Cato, looking around the room and noting all the simple finery that was still ostentatious by his own standards. "I was told you had not attended the Senate due to some ailment. I sent men to your various properties in Rome, yet I find you out here and you seem perfectly fine to me."

Crassus reclined on a couch and moved his long winter robes to cover his feet. His lined forehead furrowed even more as he saw Cato standing there with arms crossed, his accusation as well as the insult to Crassus' masculinity still lingering in the air.

"Yes, the fever has died down a little, but I am still feeling the effects of the herbs my doctor gave to me. He is a very talented Greek. Well worth the amount I pay him. Please do sit, Cato, we shall talk in comfort," Crassus said in a placating tone, but internally he was already extremely irritated with this uninvited and unwanted meeting.

Cato sat stiffly on the nearest couch and did not recline. The hem of his tatty black toga that was damp and splashed with mud from the road began to steam in the warm house. He tried not to enjoy the warm floor under his dirtied feet as he looked with barely concealed contempt at the 'fine' Roman sat across from him. He noted with a smirk that Crassus was looking at him with a similar gaze.

"So... Pompey Magnus celebrated *another* great Triumph in the streets of Rome, neh? Did you see the procession, Crassus? Rome's greatest general certainly is a prodigy. I swear he will rival Alexander one of these days," said Cato with what passed for a smile for him. Crassus narrowed his eyes slightly, wondering if the remark was sarcasm or a verbal attack against him for his own military shortcomings. The memory of Pompey snatching his triumph against the rebel Spartacus still stung him deeply and it angered him more that the common upstart Pompey had now celebrated his third triumph where Crassus had not a single one.

"Yes, the man does well enough. It was agreeable to see him win a victory of his own rather than steal it from another," said Crassus smoothly. "But surely, Cato, you have as much a reason to dislike Pompey as any man. You are against him politically and always have been. Did you not regard him as the 'Teenage Butcher' when he was working for the Tyrant Sulla? How many good Roman lives did he take from the Republic in the dictator's name?"

"He was called a butcher because he *was* one. As for the lives of good Romans, he probably took as many as you did when *you* worked for Sulla!" said Cato icily. As he leaned forward, his severe face and intense eyes seemed almost demonic under the flickering lamps.

Crassus shivered and looked to his slave who stood silently nearby. "Callidus, bring more light, then leave us."

The tall slave nodded demurely and quietly had the serving slaves lay the tables with a selection of simple dishes, both savoury and sweet. He personally poured the wine for these two very powerful and yet very different men. Once everything was laid out and extra lamps were adding their yellow glow to the scene, Callidus left with a last look to make sure everything was perfect. The tall slave padded away silently and closed the double doors, but remained just outside the entranceway.

Crassus smiled in the cheery glow of the lamps and leaned forward to take a small roasted songbird that was flavoured with herbs. He beckoned his guest do the same as he began to eat.

"So, Cato, I heard you will be endorsing Metellus as next year's Consul? I have good relations with the man. Please do let me know if you or he need any assistance with the campaign," said Crassus, chewing on the succulent flesh of the bird.

Cato inspected the food laid before them, it was not lavish by any standard but he did not want Crassus to see his hunger. He took a little bread and poured oil into a small bowl. He sniffed the wine, which did smell good, but wrinkled his nose just to irritate his wealthy host. *I will never give him the pleasure,* he thought as he replied.

"There are still men who do *not* need to pay bribes to earn their place in our Republic like the other rogues," he waggled a finger at Crassus. "Like your friend Gaius Julius Caesar! I heard he has finally escaped the money lenders and scurried off to Hispania, in the middle of the night, to take up his role as Praetor. Anyone would think he was scared of prosecution for his involvement in bribery within the Senate? I also heard your son Publius has gone with him. A very disagreeable company for a fine young Roman like him," he continued in a quieter voice but his eyes gleamed brighter in the lamplight. "It has also come to my attention that there are some inconsistencies with the investigation of the Catiline conspiracy..."

Crassus' eyes flickered up to Cato's over the wine cup as he drank. He knew full well that the ambitious Catilina was long dead, his rebel army crushed and his followers in Rome hunted down and executed for their plot to seize the power of the Senate. But the plot was still an important and touchy issue amongst the senators, as so many people had become involved or were whispered and talked about as suspects. Everybody knew that some of the conspirators had managed to deflect accusation and evade justice. Crassus was certain that Cato had listened to those who denounced Caesar and himself as a co-conspirators despite both men being instrumental in bringing the plot to the senate. He also would have likely invested some time and effort towards investigating the matter and preparing the prosecution. What did he find out? Did he have any new evidence?

"When such a plot comes to light," said Crassus with a sigh, "many people throw accusations like flower petals at a parade. I even heard *my* name was mentioned amongst the traitors. In these circumstances it seems many foolish mouths tend to open. I would like to think that only foolish ears would listen to them."

"Yes, your name was mentioned, but such is the price for being the richest man in Rome. There are many who would like to see you fall," Cato replied, brushing aside the 'foolish' comment as if he never heard it. "What concerns me is the poorer and more ambitious men that you are inclined to support. Caesar has bought, bribed and tricked his way through every political appointment he has ever had! He should be sat in the Mamertine prison awaiting execution like any other traitor!" Cato angrily banged his cup down on the table.

Crassus gave a wry smile. "Cato, my friend, surely all this anger is not because of what happened in the Senate House with Caesar so long ago?" he said with mock consideration, knowing that the incident had hugely embarrassed Cato. During a special session devoted to the Catiline conspiracy, Gaius Julius Caesar had stood in the Senate that was clamouring for blood and he alone announced that Catilina and the conspirators should be given a fair trial and shown clemency in an eloquent speech that changed many of the senators' minds and opinions. Cato, who led the bloodthirsty faction that demanded execution, rose to oppose this and charged Caesar with supporting the plot and being complicit with the traitors. During Cato's accusation someone had passed Caesar a note and, regardless of the indictment against him, he coolly sat reading it to himself with a smile on his face. Cato saw this and, thinking it was some evidence of a fresh intrigue, demanded the note be read aloud in front of the whole Senate. Caesar cheerfully agreed and offered the note to Cato with his own hand to be read aloud. The contents of which were a love letter from Servilia Caepionis, Caesar's mistress and Cato's half sister.

Cato clenched his fists and sat upright. "I do not *care* about the note or my half sister's devotion to that greasy haired whelp who dresses like an actor! Traitors *will* be punished and no amount of money OR intrigue will save them!" he hissed angrily. Crassus raised his eyebrows in alarm and was glad that he could see Callidus' feet in the light that flickered from under the door. Even as a boy Cato had offered to stab a dictator and general of Rome, such was his political zeal. Crassus looked at the furious face of Cato and wondered if he was going to physically attack him, and not just threaten him with some imminent legal action.

"Cato, I knew Lucius Catilina as well as you did. He borrowed money from me before, but who has not? If there is evidence then place it before me so I can defend myself. Also, I did not mention the note. I assumed you were talking of Caesar's defence speech of Catalina?" said Crassus pleasantly. Inside he was gratified that the note caused irritation every time it was mentioned.

Cato sipped his wine and took a deep breath, allowing himself a moment to regain his composure. His temper was notorious and very difficult to cool once heated. His eyes flicked up to his wealthy counterpart who was calmly examining his well groomed fingernails with a faint hint of a smile on his face. He knew Crassus was goading him and savouring his anger. Cato nodded to himself. He would not let Crassus anger him again during this meeting.

He took another sip of the delicious wine in the silence and spoke with a firm resolve, "All the evidence will be uncovered and the enemies of the Republic will be brought to justice. I hope you steer well clear, Crassus. True Roman justice is incorruptible and shall visit the doorstep of *every* traitor."

"By 'traitor' I assume you mean Caesar?" said Crassus, looking up thoughtfully.

"If the evidence is there.. it *will* be found, then I shall see he stands trial for it. I dare say he might have some interesting things to say about who his sponsors and allies are. He might even have evidence of other crimes from other senators who would be dictator," said Cato, closely examining his rich companion's impassive face.

Crassus shrugged. "Who knows what Caesar might say? He is a popular man in many circles. Certainly, I have paid some of his debts in the past, but that does not make me or any man a sponsor to treason. Otherwise you would need to execute half of the Senate," he said.

He could see that Cato was up to something and was clearly testing his reactions to certain statements. What was the cunning swine up to?

"Let us be frank, Cato, you don't have anything to gain by pursuing me. If there was any concrete evidence then you would not be here. You would simply speak against me in the Senate and have me seized for prosecution." Crassus sat up from the couch and leaned forward, speaking candidly, "I know you are not here for money, nor friendship either, so what do you want? Why are you here?"

"Well, if we are being 'honest'," said Cato, smirking, "Caesar is an embarrassment to the Senate and people of Rome. He is a fraud, a debtor. He is a ruthlessly ambitious man who rouses the rabbles with populist ideas that would upset the order of our

Republic and he conspires with the worst elements of our government. There is enough evidence to engage in litigation and I suspect that will happen when he returns from his provincial post. He will need money to protect himself and he *will* come to you," he said, nodding to Crassus. "I suggest you either distance yourself from him or you might find yourself dragged over the cliff with him."

Cato made a gesture, looking around the room. "You have everything you need, Crassus, more wealth than half the Republic put together. More comfort and luxury than half the Princes of the East. Sometimes I think you occupy yourself with politics only for recreation and the opportunity to make yourself even more wealthy. Yet as always your name gets mentioned in every whisper of insurrection against our fair and free Republic. I know you are wise enough to comprehend the fate of any man who would perceive themselves as King of Rome."

Cato leaned forward, his voice full of foreboding. "Slaves, gold and villas are much better than being thrown from the Tarpeian rock[54], neh? No, a traitor's death is too risky for you. But these young ambitious men who flock to you might see you as kingmaker and it would be most unwise to encourage their aspirations. Accomplices will receive death as easily as the traitors themselves… just ask Catilina and his friends," he said, taking a sip of wine and looking at Crassus whose face was a mask of polite attention but his eyes gleamed with a cat-like cunning in the lamplight.

Crassus smoothed a fold of his well-made robe, then leaned forward and gestured to one of the many dishes laid before them. "Have some nut pudding, Cato. I have a cook who specializes in nothing but desserts. She adds a little more honey than usual to

---

[54] A cliff in Rome from which criminals were thrown to their death as punishment.

the recipe and I find it perfect." He sat back, taking a piece with his spoon. "Mmm, delicious! Really, old friend, it is not a crime to eat such things."

Cato chewed slowly on a piece of bread and looked at the array of plates and dishes with indifference. "My dedication to the Republic is nourishment enough," he said gruffly gesturing around in contempt. "I do not need all this fine living to serve Rome."

"Wealth is a blessing of the Gods on our Republic. You should not seek litigation against our Lady Blessed Fortuna! *That* is one case where you should not look to prosecute, my friend!" said Crassus, laughing and taking another bite of the delicious pudding. "Your dedication to inflexibility will be the death of you, Cato!"

"And your unquenchable thirst for gold and riches will be yours," said Cato sternly, taking a sip of wine.

Both men looked at each other for a long time without speaking.

SPQR

Chapter 7

"Hey... *Hey!* Stand aside! Stand aside there! Move your fat ass, Borras! Keep your filthy hands off, Numidian! This is a feast of patricians, not a bunch of fucking Nubian savages ripping guts from a carcass! Move aside, you ugly bastards! Move, damn you!" said Felix with genuine anger. The tent had been emptied of the bulkier equipment and most of the cots to make room for the feast. Borras sat cross legged near the door and had been sniffing the air for about a quarter of a watch. Occasionally he would lean forward and lift up the tent flap to look outside and sit back with a muttered curse. His eyes looked over the items placed on the blanket that was spread on the floor: a dish full of boiled eggs, apples, a small heap of salt, plenty of oil. The only thing missing was some fish soup. And apparently that was nearly ready.

Felix placed down a large round army loaf that had been scored before baking to show eight equal wedges for distribution amongst the section. Kratos immediately reached to break it apart and received a sharp blow from the wooden spoon in Felix's hand. "What did I just say?" he said, pointing the spoon at the startled Greek who rubbed his head from the blow. "This is not the *Saturnalia*[55], my foreign friend! You will obey the rules or by the Gods you WILL feel the wrath of my spoon again!" He stared at Kratos as he swatted an imaginary fly away from the warm bread and went back out of the tent flap.

---

[55] Ancient Roman midwinter festival held to honour the god Saturn; festivities included a banquet.

"In the name of Vulcan! He is insufferable," said Decius, thoughtfully examining his finger, swollen from an accidental hammer blow at the forge.

"I heard that!" snapped Felix from outside the tent where he could be heard lecturing poor Ictis on the finesse of soup making.

"My uncle said this job is easier when you are tent mates with a good bunch," said Decius, touching his misshapen nose. "Just my luck I have fallen in with a cheap pantomime actor!" he said loudly, turning his face to the tent door.

The voice of Felix floated back through the goatskin fabric of the tent in a high pitched parody of Decius,

"I am so good with a sword... I will be promoted first... What's that? Oh no? Please Falco, not in the ass in front of the whole Legion!"

The whole section laughed and Decius shook his head with an unimpressed glance at the gathered men. "You bunch of dicks," he retorted and carried on examining the injured finger with a sour look on his face.

As the laughter died away, Ignavus shuffled and quickly reached for an apple, but the brute Saxum grabbed his skinny wrist in a flash. Ignavus looked outraged and tried to pull away, but the grinning Saxum squeezed until his victim winced and dropped the apple.

"Rules is rules, eh!" Saxum said with a glare in his piggy eyes.

Borras looked over at him threateningly. "I suggest you let go of his wrist, friend!" he rumbled. "You are new here and don't decide who eats or when!"

The tent went quiet and instantly became very tense. Even Corvus looked up from his corner as all eyes went to the two biggest men in the tent. Saxum gave a look of surprise and let go of Ignavus before giving a savage grin showing his broken and dirty teeth.

"Oh so you got some big balls eh? Well, for a Teutonic dog you talk a good fight! But you have not fought me yet, have you?" said Saxum, pushing away the hand of Ignavus and leaning towards Borras with a challenging leer.

Just as Borras was about to open his mouth in reply, Galba drew his gladius with a rasp as he sat forward on his cot and spoke, "I only draw this on special occasions. Tonight we are having a feast because we march to war tomorrow. We have been given our orders from Falco, everyone has bathed and made ready their kit and now it's time to relax." He paused, turning the highly sharpened gladius around to admire its keen and deadly edge and making sure everyone else could see it, too.

"Guess what? I *am* going to enjoy tonight as it might be the last night we have in comfort for a while. If anybody ruins this evening they will be thrown in chains and flogged in front of the whole damn Legion! So the pair of you... shut it!"

Galba's voice was quiet but full of intent as he stared at each antagonist in turn. Borras sat back and looked coldly at the brute Saxum who picked absently at his teeth with an unconcerned look, but obeying the decanus.

"Well!" said Kratos cheerfully, trying to break the tension. "I'm sure tempers are fraying waiting for our cooks to finish our meal!" he said, raising his voice to those outside.

"Cock!" came the instant reply from Felix through the tent wall. Then, after a few moments of muffled whispering, Ictis weakly

parroted it too, obviously egged on by the cackling Felix. "C...
C... Cock!".

Everyone laughed and the mood relaxed but Borras still gave
Saxum a scowling look which he returned with a leer. Galba saw
it and knew it would probably raise its head in the future.

"So, Decius," said Borras clearly, trying to forget about his
growling stomach and the irritating grin of Saxum. "Why all the
extra metalwork for the artillery train? I thought the 10th was
already fully equipped? Did you work on the weapons we saw
firing earlier?"

Decius had spent all day at the forge in the fabrica creating the
metal components for the artillery pieces. The immunes who
were carpenters made a similar effort with the framing and now
the legion boasted a surplus of the large *ballistae*[56] and the
similar in design, but smaller, scorpion bows. Earlier we had
watched the immunes of the artillery who actually operated the
units making a huge fuss over the calibrations as they test fired
them. The veterans shook their heads disdainfully at us gawking
at the impressive torsion-powered machines, although they
would have done the same once when they were young and new
to the Legion.

"We still have the normal compliment of one scorpion per
century," said Decius, still examining his damaged finger. "I
heard the spares are going to be used for sieges."

Saxum whooped. "I do not know what's going to be better,
seeing those ballistae throwing huge rocks at the enemy or
looting their town afterwards!" Everyone grinned to that.

"I saw those scorpion bows firing their bolts at the tree that must
have been two hundred yards away! Imagine it hitting a man!"

---

[56] Ancient Roman torsion-powered artillery.

said Kratos, smacking his fist into his open hand for emphasis. "Surely they would go through ten or fifteen of them?"

He looked up at the veteran Galba, who was clearly amused by our enthusiasm. "They can go through a couple of people," he conceded. "But the real strength is the range and accuracy. It is always good to bring down an enemy chief or champion before we clash with their main battle line," said Galba, tapping his nose in a conspiratorial manner. "Ruins their morale, eh!"

"I know what is ruining my morale," said Borras, crossing his arms over his large, powerful chest. "Waiting for this damn soup!"

As if on cue the tent flap opened and Felix came in holding a standard army cook pot, suspended by its handle, in each hand. Saxum whooped and punched the ground while Borras clapped his hands together. "Yes!" he drooled, looking at the pots.

Ignavus, who looked even more famished than usual, snatched up his bowl and spoon and sat hunched over, bobbing up and down like a vulture. Decius forgot about his swollen finger and reached forward for the bread. "About time," he grumbled.

Felix hissed at him in anger, "It's about time you learned manners, you oaf. Have we forgotten the Gods? Are we to become pigs at the trough by your command? Hands off the bread until the Gods are honoured!"

Decius opened his mouth to speak but saw that everyone's faces were hungry but solemn in agreement.

Felix placed the pots down and took up his place by the door. Ictis brought out the amphorae of wine he had 'acquired', which caused a murmur of appreciation. "Looks like the officers' wine?" said Kratos quietly and Ictis flashed a huge smile which Galba returned.

"No, tonight this is wine for the *real* soldiers, Kratos," he said grinning and scratching around his missing ear.

Felix took up a small bowl and offered it to Galba, who shook his head. "No, you make the offering. You put more work into this than me."

"Jupiter Optimus Maximus, being the father of Rome we ask your blessing on this feast as we prepare for war," said Felix, holding the bowl before him with both hands in a priestly manner. "For the feast itself we must thank *Bacchus*[57] for providing a humble wine for the simple men present. Personally I will probably find it tastes like swill compared to the good Falernian wines I am used to, but I am thankful nevertheless. These oafs would not appreciate a 'real' wine anyway," he said, looking up at the tent roof with a look of practiced virtue on his thin face. "Of course we must thank *Neptune*[58] for giving up one of his children from the sea for this delicious soup... and come to think of it, he needs thanking twice as two of his children went into the pot. There are actual pieces of meat from another fish I organised myself from a one eyed fisherman I met in town. Either way, we hope you don't get upset that we flavoured your children with parsley? A fine noble herb that can work well as their funerary garlands, if you ask me. Foolish Ictis wanted to use oregano, which might have fixed a sore throat but would have brought the wrath of all the Gods down on our heads and resurrected the little fishes into huge sea monsters that would have devoured the Legion whole!" he said as he spooned some of the soup into the bowl. Kratos smirked and Ignavus fidgeted while Ictis looked at Felix in open-mouthed wonder as if it was the *Pontifex Maximus*[59] blessing the entire Republic.

---

[57] Roman god of wine.
[58] Roman god of the sea.
[59] The high priest of the College of Pontiffs (Collegium Pontificum) in ancient Rome.

Borras, thinking the ceremony complete, reached forward, but Felix quickly grabbed his hand and tossed it backwards, continuing, "We also thank *Disciplina*[60] for giving us the strength to endure our training and observe the rules!" Irritated, he placed an egg in the bowl with the soup.

"How could we forget the goodness of *Ceres*[61] that keeps us in bread and Borras in belly," continued Felix in his most pious voice. Kratos giggled as Felix now added bread to the bowl slowly and deliberately.

Galba shifted forward and stared at the pots. The whole tent smelled like hot fish soup and Ignavus' stomach made a huge noise that seemed to speak for everyone in the group. Even the quiet Corvus had now moved into the circle with his bowl and spoon in hand.

Felix smirked, then his face hardened. "Mars and Bellona, we pour wine in your honour that you will keep the Eagle of the 10th proudly above its Legion. You will bring us victory in battle and see our enemies driven before us!" With that every man apart from Corvus and Borras raised their hands and looked up mouthing small prayers to the war gods in their own way. A soldier's prayer is always a serious matter. Felix took the wine from Ictis and poured some over the bread.

Felix looked around and said, "So now that the offerings are made..."

Before he could even finish, a huge rush of hands flew into the food and Felix leapt up, beating everybody on the hands with his soup ladle. "Hands off, you fucking barbarians!" he roared.

---

[60] Goddess of discipline.
[61] Goddess of agriculture and fertility.

Ignavus howled as the ladle smacked him on his knuckles. Decius blocked a strike with his empty bowl, Saxum scrambled backwards to get away from this red-haired demon and Galba rolled back on his cot, laughing heartily.

Felix knelt, holding the ladle like a weapon and turning in a half circle like a man surrounded by hungry wolves. "As I was saying, now that the offerings are made to all the Gods necessary we ask one last thing." he paused for a moment brandishing the ladle with raised eyebrows "*Aequitas*[62] look over us as we eat so everybody may get a good share!"

And with that he sat down with a gesture to the food and began to ladle the soup into the bowls as the group broke into conversation and laughter with hands diving in again. The bread was split and everyone made sure they gave a little for Ictis from their own share. He smilingly gathered his pieces and placed them on a cloth near the door. "I will take the food to the Gods now, sirs," he said, holding the offering bowl reverently as he crept out of the tent to take the bowl to the Legions' camp altar. When he got there he found a great many bowls and offerings and a great many soldiers coming and going to invoke the Gods for their last night of peace.

"So why are we marching late in the morning, Galba?" asked Borras back at the tent.

Galba chewed his bread that he had soaked in the delicious soup. "Probably to make sure everyone is rested. It gives time for the cohorts of the 8th Legion to get closer, too," he said, licking the savoury liquid from a finger. "The Lusitanians are sneaky bastards and have always used ambush as part of their tactics. We will have to be prepared for that in the near future."

---

[62] The Latin concept of justice or fairness.

"Well, I'm sure we will prevail!" stated Decius with pride. "We swore our oath under the Eagle! We are the Roman army and the best there is!"

Kratos winked. "It's a good job Falco is not around to hear you boasting! It would piss on your night if you went to the medicus again," he laughed into his wine as Decius sniffed and looked at him sourly.

"Regardless of your cow strength, Greek, I would still beat you with a sword... even left-handed!" Decius said with a smile, holding up his left hand and wiggling his fingers.

Kratos laughed and conceded in his disarming manner. "Yes, you probably would. The Gods blessed you with a good sword arm but not eyesight in the back of your head. '*Inten...te*'!" said Kratos in a rasping parody of Falco's voice. "Have some wine, Decius, so we may drink a toast to your swordsmanship!" said Kratos, offering a cup.

"Well, you know what they say about Greeks bearing gifts... but seeing as you're a Roman now I shall trust you," said Decius with a grin. Kratos sighed as he always did when they mentioned his heritage.

"Yes, I must admit with my appearance I was looked at a little more closely than some of the others in the dilectus! It was a close run thing," he said, laughing and telling his story from his recruitment day. The section was glad for this man and it would have been a shame for him to be turned away over a trivial matter such as a suspicious recruiting clerk wondering why a Greek was as far away as Hispania. Some rules were often passed by as long as the officers doing the inspecting saw some use to the army in the individual. He would have been checked for height and weight, which must have been a close thing for

Kratos, as he was probably just over the minimum height requirement.

"I grew some tall hair on my head and stretched my spine for the day," he laughingly told us when questioned on the matter that it seems he scraped though only by the smallest margin.

The other tests included eyesight and hearing, as well as writing ability to establish if the recruits had some grasp of literacy and numeracy. The armies of Rome required men of some education for certain posts like clerks and paymasters. There was also a need for men to oversee the delivery of the staggering amount of supplies even a single legion required. Every cartload was marked down and tallied by the quartermasters and their assistants. The logistics of our armies is the backbone of our strength.

The recruit would also be asked what trade skills he could bring to the legion and so become an immune. There was always room for recruits from certain professions, like Decius who was trained as a blacksmith. Others such as surveyors, wagon-makers, carpenters, engineers, masons and huntsmen like Corvus were also welcomed for their skills. Applicants from professions associated with women's occupations were less desirable to the army.

Most importantly of all, they rigorously checked to see your status as a citizen. Kratos had a written endorsement and all the necessary paperwork from a Roman patron who sent one of his freedmen there to testify for his legal status of citizen of Rome. This was a very formal check and your father or patron would have to swear an oath on Jupiter that you were indeed qualified. Some tried to sneak in and were harshly punished. Anyone who was a slave or a criminal caught in the Legion was executed.

The queue to join the Legion was long and many people had flocked to the Praetor's official residence on the days of the dilectus. It was an honour to join the Legion and for many of the lower classes it was an escape from a life of ignominy and toil. Many young men tried and many failed. They could be seen walking away in tears. Some were deemed too skinny, weak or with poor eyesight. Some of the rejected suffered afflictions of the mind or spirit and their 'loving fathers' had tried to sneak them into the Legion to be rid of them. Occasionally you might see a disgruntled father cursing and loading his imbecile son back onto the cart to return home with him. And rightly so. The Legion only wanted the strongest and best.

The feast in the tent went on into the dark hours and the section passed the time with laughter, jokes and stories, particularly from Felix who told tales from his days working for a local *lanista*[63] in the town of Mediolanum. Everybody doubted and often questioned the level of truth in these stories, but Felix always had an elaborate answer, so the section just enjoyed the stories nevertheless. The soup was delicious and went down well with much praise to Ictis who was flushed from wine and pride. Even the ever-quiet Corvus nodded to him with a word of thanks.

The wine had been mixed with water but still felt a little stronger than usual. The remainder of the food had been split between the group for the following day's meal and everyone stretched out and relaxed in the flickering light of some oil lamps that Ictis had lit in the centre of the tent. Decius and Kratos were quietly discussing fighting techniques and explaining various methods of footwork, both armed and unarmed, that could help each other. Ignavus had curled up and was sleeping under his cloak and Borras leaned back on a cot looking a little flushed. "That is some good wine," he said to no one in particular, looking around

---

[63] Owner of a gladiatorial troupe, responsible for their training.

with bleary eyes. Corvus sat in the corner sharpening his gladius while Saxum and Felix threw dice under a flickering lamp and made bets for each other's duties. Felix had lost a couple of games but had convinced Saxum otherwise.

"They call this 'the rule of the Trojans', my friend," said Felix, tapping his nose with a wink. "We play with 5 dice and if you throw a 2 and 4 together then you have to reroll until you get at least 3 sixes to wipe away the shame! And in the name of all the Achaeans who fought against Troy, make sure you do that within 3 rolls or you will lose the game like many a young Trojan maid lost her virginity on a pink Greek spear on one infamous night! Of course you could win the game with 1,2,3,4,5 but if you get all of those less one as a 6 then it's 2 games to me," continued Felix with a smile. "Of course that goes against the rule of throwing a 'Venus', but in this case it would be an 'Aphrodite' anyways, seeing as it's Greek rules. And if you throw all 1s then the 'dog', as we call it in Rome, is now called 'the phalanx', as it looks like the upright spears of Kratos' ancestors… and I mean the *real* spears and not their cocks!" he said with a laugh.

Saxum blinked his piggy eyes and scratched the back of his thick neck. "It all sounds a bit Greek to me! Can't we play something that we both fucking know? Like *Tropa*[64] or something simple where we can see who is winning," Saxum grumbled. All these numbers made his head hurt.

Felix looked very concerned and placed a hand on Saxum's thick shoulder. "Are you sure you want to quit while you are three games down?"

"Three games down! *Cac!* I was winning until you started changing the rules, you fucking red-haired thief!" protested

---

[64] A Roman dice game.

Saxum with outrage. "You have the cunning of a toothless old whore counting the money she stole from drunken customers!" He leaned forward and grabbed Felix's tunic while baring his filthy teeth. "Nobody steals from me and ever lives to tell the tale!"

Felix wrinkled his nose and looked down at the meaty fist that had grabbed his tunic. "My dear fellow, I will not be pawed at! Certainly not by someone who smells like you. I can see you are sore at losing and the fact is, I am generous with my friends who suffer defeat. I shall happily let you off the three duties you owe me." He looked over to Ictis and called to him in his most dramatic voice, "Ictis, bring us more wine to toast Saxum, a true Hero of the Republic!" Saxum looked suspicious and released the grip on the tunic.

"No more wine, it's all gone," said Ictis, looking forlorn as he sat by the tent doorway, peering inside the empty amphora.

"Never mind, we shall all toast myself at another time, neh? Felix the merciful! Beloved by all the Gods and benefactor to his friends," grinned Felix, internally glad he had swindled himself out of another loss. Three extra guard duties could ruin a man's week!

"So, Galba," said Felix, turning the conversation elsewhere before the duped man next to him had time to think. "These Lusitanian *cunni* are nothing to worry about, neh? A bunch of stupid savages in their mountain hovels that stink of sheep shit are no match for Rome's finest!"

Galba looked up and frowned, something he did not do often. "I do not know about any 'stupid savages' but I will tell you about the tribes that make up the Lusitani and Gallaeci. They were once called the fiercest fighters out of all the Celts in Hispania. They have fought against Rome many times before. The

132

Lusitanian war, nearly a hundred years ago, in which we had supposedly beaten them, lasted more than fifteen years and was a nasty affair, full of night attacks, broken truces, ambush and treachery. During that time they joined a mighty war chief called Viriatus who showed them how to fight, how to ambush our columns and how to run after we had formed up. Yes, we killed him and beat them, but they have clamoured for total independence ever since and always look to rebellion. Why, you only need to look at ten years ago when they fought in the Sertorian War, where they and some of the Gallaeci joined with the rebel general Sertorius to fight against Rome. He was a great man and a skillful commander who knew how to lead an army, I certainly admire him, despite what our politician's today say about him? Sertorius taught them about *our* battle tactics and the best way to beat us. These people have helped to give Pompey Magnus a black eye not so long ago plus are experts in guerrilla warfare and ambushes; they certainly like to fight. I would say it's been in their blood for hundreds of years, going back before the time when they served in the armies of Hannibal of Carthage."

Galba sighed and continued, "Remember, lads, it's their ground. They know the way around their forests and hills better than us. How many Romans do you think have died in Lusitanian ambushes through the ages? I only hope that Caesar is half the commander the centurions think he might be *and* the Lusitanians we face now are all young, prideful men who have forgotten the lessons of history. " He looked up at Felix. "Don't forget how hard they will fight! They *know* what will happen to them if they lose… women, children, homes… all lost. How would you fight if that was the cost of defeat?"

Everyone had listened to the knowledgeable decanus and now looked thoughtful, including Felix. For a moment the only sound was the scrape of a blade on a sharpening stone as Corvus honed the edge on his long hunting knife and the murmuring of Ignavus as he lay sleeping, curled up under his cloak.

"If they are like us, then each one of them will fight for his life and family like an evil spirit from Hades," said Corvus flatly in the silence. His black eyes glittered and seemed almost reptilian in the flickering light as he looked across the faces of every man in the tent. "But then who is to say how violent our souls can be? We can show them that terror has a face and it marches under our Eagle." And with that he turned back to sharpening his blade. The scraping noise seemed overly loud in the silence.

Kratos coughed. "Well, we shall do our duty as soldiers, I guess," said the Greek in an uneasy tone, clearly trying to break the silence. Everyone felt chilled by the words that came from Corvus.

Galba slapped his thigh. "We will show them how real soldiers fight, that's for sure. Just remember the training, listen to the commands and stay in formation. If we do that we could all come home with a few coins and a slave or two to sell!" said Galba with a grin, trying to lighten the mood a little.

But the mood did not lift; it seemed stricken with a nervous gloom. The feast was over and the flickering lamps now showed some concerned and thoughtful faces as the young soldiers prepared to sleep. The tent was devoid of speech as each man settled into his cloak. Galba had fallen asleep almost immediately but many lay awake for a long time until the final lamp sputtered, then went out. The only noise was the quiet snoring of Ignavus and the scrape of Corvus' blade on the stone.

Chapter 8

Numerius Pomponius Bubo whimpered as the simple wooden door creaked open again. Just like before, the four armed warriors stooped to enter the hut to choose another person from the bedraggled group. The older woman started screaming again, even though she had a bloody mouth from a vicious punch she received last time they came. Bubo sat on the dirty earthen floor in the remains of his torn green toga and concentrated on his tied hands in front of him. *Please take someone else... please take someone else... please take someone else*, he frantically thought to himself.

A large Celtiberian warrior with a drooping brown moustache cursed and, with a look of irritation on his face, gestured at the screaming woman before grabbing her by the hair and dragging her shrieking from the hut. Bubo had recognised her as a rich woman he had seen in Portus Cale. She had her body slave argue with him about the price of a bracelet he was selling to her... The miserly old cow! She did not realise what he had to go through to get the bracelet! She did not have to deal with these Celtic blacksmiths who were so haughty and prideful it was almost like they did not want to sell their work at all! He had seen many like her coming up north to the Roman trading posts at Conimbriga and Portus Cale to see some of the wild Celts and buy their famous jewellery. Bubo had always made good money from the likes of her when he took his stock back to the civilised cities along the southern coast of the Roman province of Hispania Ulterior.

God's mercy! He should have seen this coming... The attitude of the Lusitanians had gotten much worse these past few months. They were already sullen and now they would mutter and glare at the Romans with almost open hatred. Bubo had noticed the sense of foreboding in the air and looked to hire extra bodyguards for the return journey south in case of trouble on the road. He never expected to be caught up in a full scale rebellion. He always just assumed they were arrogant savages who did not understand that Rome had beaten them in past wars! Bubo thought it childish of them that they needed to play the big warrior man with their swords on their hips and that ultimately they would settle into a civilised life where money and commerce would prevail. But they didn't!

Why did these savages have an uprising? Why did they hunt down every Roman... even a poor merchant? Why did they burn Portus Cale? Why didn't he leave while he could!? Bubo raised his podgy hands, "Jupiter Optimus Maximus, please have blessed *Clementia*[65] look down and show her favour upon me! PLEASE!"

He rocked back and forth with the tears rolling down his fat, dirty cheeks; the clean lines through the dirt showed that he had cried a lot. His curly hair that was long by Roman standards was usually oiled and delicately brushed into tiers like the style his favourite actors wore. Now it was full of dried mud and stuck out in all directions. His face was tear-streaked and dirty, his fine green toga hung in shreds and his bare feet were caked in mud up to the shins. He would have looked comical in any other situation, but the four other people left in the hut did not laugh. They were silent or weeping themselves. One man lay unconscious and was bound much more securely than the others. He had tried to fight back and had been struck down. The man

---

[65] In Roman mythology, the goddess of forgiveness and mercy.

had several scars and a sturdy frame. He looked like a soldier to Bubo but now he lay silent and unconscious. Was he dead?

The deafening beating of drums and the chanting began again and jerked Bubo out of his prayers, making him wring his hands again. He dried his eyes with the remains of his gaudy green toga and looked around quickly once more. The circular building was low and the stonework was solid, as was the thatch. The dried shit and straw showed it as a place where sheep or goats were kept, perhaps. The door was simple but he could see figures outside on guard.

I need a sharp rock to free my hands, he thought, looking around, but the earthen floor was hard packed and the stone walls finished with dung that had dried like cement. In desperation he stood up and hurriedly tried to tear a hole in the dense dried thatch, but the thick branches woven inside made it impossible for his soft, fat little hands that were only used to counting coins or lifting wine cups. Outside the rich woman shrieked loudly over the sound of the drumming and chanting. The noise made Bubo sit down in fright and he started crying again.

Turicacus stood silently, watching the tatty-robed druid stamping his bare feet and inciting the crowd into a frenzy. The drums began their din and the crowd chanted the name of the Lusitanian god of war, *Cariocecus*, over and over. The hysterical Roman woman had been dragged into the open area before the shrine. She had noticed the fresh blood on the muddy floor and seen the boar and bull statues either side of the shrine doorway. Her screams became frantic when she saw the pile of severed hands before the boar statue and the stack of heads before the bull. She was held in place with long pieces rope lashed around each wrist and three men on either side pulled until her arms were stretched out. Despite feeling like her arms were being torn from their sockets she desperately lashed out her legs, shrieking, but such was the tension on the ropes that she bobbed in the air and nearly flipped over backwards.

"Hold her feet!" shouted Vordeco the druid over the noise of the chanting crowd. One of his assistants got down behind the woman and held her ankles in a tight grip that kept her feet on the already bloody floor. The priest stepped forward and tore away what remained of her fine, but now ragged, stola. She writhed naked with her drooping breasts swinging in an almost comical fashion. Her eyes were wide in terror and the screams from her bloodied mouth were loud, even with the din of several hundred members of the Turodi tribe who were packed into the central plaza of the hill fort. Some of the warriors had their sons on their shoulders and many had climbed onto the thatched roofs of surrounding huts to get a better view of the sacrifice being made in the centre of the chanting, stamping throng of people.

Vordeco held up his bloodied knife with both hands to the sky.

"*Cariocecus!... Cariocecus!*" he shouted with his painted face turned skywards. "We offer you flesh and blood so you may guide us to victory!"

He brought the knife down and took a firm grip of the handle as he stepped towards the woman. He paused, looking at her maddened face, then slashed sideways with terrific speed across the woman's sagging abdomen. The man holding the ankles scuttled away behind her and the men holding the ropes waited for a moment until her intestines dropped to the ground with a slapping noise before they let go.

Vordeco sprung back and waved his arms at the crowd, who fell silent. He paced back and forth, observing the woman, as it was customary to predict the future battles by the way the sacrificial victim fell to the ground and the appearance of their intestines. The woman looked down and shrieked piteously once more;

then her eyes rolled back in her head as she fainted, the sight of her innards hanging from her torso too much to bear. The woman fell backwards, completely straight, and hit the floor like a statue, lying there unmoving as Vordeco knelt before the stinking pile of viscera now strung over her naked legs and feet.

He looked sideways to Turicacus, the war chief of the Turodi tribe. The large and powerful dark-haired man with his long moustaches stood at the front of the crowd with his muscular arms crossed over his wide chest. He gave a barely discernible nod to the priest who noticed and immediately switched his eyes back to the pile of intestines. Vordeco stood up in the silence, threw his arms in the air and yelled to the sky. The drummers sitting inside the small shrine immediately pounded the drums to echo his cry and the crowd, full of zeal, needed no invitation to join in the rejoicing. After several moments of building the exhilaration Vordeco nodded to the drummers who stopped and he hushed the crowd.

"My friends! My people! Mighty Cariocecus gave us a clear sign in this Roman! She fell backwards, stone dead in fear! The Romans fear a warrior in our midst! It is the will of the God of War that we have the mighty TURICACUS to lead us to VICTORY!"

A huge cheer went up and Turicacus unsheathed his sword, holding it aloft as he walked into the open space in the middle of the crowd. He made a point of glaring at some of the tribal elders who stood in the front. These men had doubted his ability to lead the tribal contingent and he gave a hard stare at the group who favoured his rival Cernovis. No doubt that fool had got them to speak up for him by empty promises of gold! Well, it was Turicacus who had come back with the war band from Portus Cale, it was he who come back with prisoners and loot for the tribe. And it was he who would lead these men in the new war against Rome. He waved his sword in the air and roared a battle cry "TURODI!!!" to which the warriors roared back, either stamping their feet or clashing their swords on their shields.

Turicacus grinned and pulled the much smaller druid into an embrace. "Make sure our War God keeps saying the right things!" he growled into Vordeco's ear as the crowd roared its approval all around them. He stepped away from the druid and shot him a smile that was laced with a warning that Vordeco understood.

He nodded and gestured to the crowd to quiet down. "This woman also sent another sign. She lay on her back like a Roman whore! It shows they are nothing but immoral animals! WE are people of honour and WE WILL prevail!"

The crowd greeted this with more cheers and Vordeco nodded to his assistants who cut off the woman's right hand. The druid placed it before the stone boar and quickly did the same with her head, stacking it on the growing pile before the bull. Four of the men who held the ropes left to get another victim from a nearby hut while the lifeless corpse was dragged away to be tossed off the cliffs.

"Turicacus! Messengers!" came the shout from behind and Turicacus waved the two strangers forward through the lane that had opened in the crowd as the rope men returned with a fat Roman wearing the remains of a shiny green toga. Two Lusitanian messengers ran past the pitiful Roman who was babbling and wriggling on the floor as the four rope holders struggled to drag him. The toga ripped clean off and the crowd laughed at the fat, white, naked body and unfortunate endowments of this man. The warriors in the crowd smirked and made various comments about Roman courage or small genitalia as a child ran up and kicked him hard before darting back into the crowd. The fat, naked man squealed like a pig and clung on to a cursing warrior's leg. The brawny Lusitanian angrily beat at him with his fists, causing a loud squeak of pain with each punch, much to the delight of the crowd.

"Hail, Turicacus," said the older man with a completely bald head. "I am Virax of the Narbasi tribe and this is my son, Frovidus," he said, gesturing to the younger man who looked exactly like his father but with youth and hair to his advantage. "We have ridden here to ask you to summon all the men of your tribe. Also, if you are able, can you send men out on fast horses to call for any more of your neighbours to attend the meeting and bring all their warriors, too? The tribes are gathering into a great army."

The bald man paused and his bushy beard split with a white toothed grin at the fat, naked Roman as he was dragged screeching past them. A group of children mimicked the noises he made and tried to drag one of their smaller lame friends who ran off through the throng of people to avoid the torment.

"You were saying, Virax? Where is this meeting?" said Turicacus loudly above the noise of the crowd. The war chief flashed a droll smile as all six rope men bound the wrists of the fat Roman and dragged him squealing onto the blood soaked patch of muddy ground in front of the shrine.

Virax blinked and shook his bald head. "Sorry! Of course. The meeting will be back at Portus Cale, as most of the warriors are still in the area burning the Roman farms. The Lusitani elders will gather with all the chiefs and ask everyone present to elect an overall War Chief to lead the fight. Not a task to be envied. Many Gallaecians tribes are coming south and all the old blood feuds means the bickering has already started..."

Virax sighed and shook his head before continuing. "Also, some are saying we should face the Romans in open battle and others talk of defending their own hill forts. Of course, the experienced are saying we should draw them into ambush like we did in the Sertorian War, but it seems many are too young to remember how to fight the Romans properly, and sacking a few towns and killing merchants has got their blood up. But as we both know, killing a few townsfolk is *not* like fighting Legions," he said gravely and even the comical sight of the naked Roman being stretched out on the ropes with half a dozen extra helpers trying to keep him upright did not make him smile.

He turned back to Turicacus. "The new Roman governor has three Legions and is said to be marching within the next few days. So it might be worth sending a fast horseman ahead to Portus Cale in case the situation changes before your war band gets there," he said in a louder voice to counteract the rising drums and noise of the crowd. "That is all I have for you, my friend," he shouted as drums boomed and the druid held aloft his knife roaring, "*Cariocecus!... Cariocecus!*" The crowd stamped their feet and chanted with him.

"Thank you for the message," shouted Turicacus leaning closer to the man. "I shall have some men ride to the Lusitani tribes to the south and the Gallaeci to the north of us immediately." He gestured to a younger warrior of his own tribe, "Get these men food and drink and somewhere to sleep for the night."

The young warrior nodded and led away the tired messengers.

One of the larger men in the tribe now stood grinning behind the fat Roman, holding him upright by the head. The assistant who crouched behind, holding the podgy ankles, cursed as the victim's urine ran freely down the legs onto his hands. Even with six men either side and the brawny warrior holding him up by the neck, the fat Roman still sagged towards the ground.

The War Chief Turicacus was lost in thought and did not even notice the beating drums and chanting crowd, the flash of the sacrificial knife, the innards falling out or the fat Roman lying there screaming as he clutched his intestines, trying to stuff them back into the gaping hole in his sizable belly. Vordeco did not cut deep enough to spill the blood near the spine and now this Roman was scratching around on the floor, screaming and fighting with the assistant who had moved to cut off the head.

He'd better make a good prophecy from a bad sacrifice, thought Turicacus with irritation, but his thoughts immediately turned back to the war. *Open battle with Roman Legions is suicidal and everyone knows it,* he thought to himself. He looked around at the young warriors in the tribe, their faces full of zeal and hatred, and he hoped they would keep some discipline in battle.

If only we had another commander like Sertorius! he mused. Despite being Roman, the man knew how to fight our way. More importantly he ignored the petty blood feuds and united the squabbling chiefs to lead the Celtiberians to many a victory. Turicacus smiled as he remembered his old commander but that smile vanished as quickly as it came. If it wasn't for the cowards who assassinated him, the whole of Hispania might have been freed of Roman rule. But Sertorius was long dead and many of the veteran warriors who fought with him had stepped aside for younger and less experienced warriors to fight. He hoped the elders would choose a War Chief who knew how to ambush, otherwise this war might end very quickly. "Then it might be us being sacrificed to their Gods," he murmured to himself as Vordeco shouted to the crowd something about "leading the fatted pigs to the slaughter".

The last three victims from the hut were killed in the same manner as all the others. The fourth victim was an unconscious, trussed man who had killed three Lusitanians fighting back in an ambush and was indeed a tattooed veteran of the Legions. The man, who had been working as a bodyguard for a merchant, was now dead, much to the druid's dismay. Vordeco wanted to save him until last so the people could gloat over the ex-soldier, watch him fight and struggle, but the man never woke from the blow he had received on the head. His lifeless body was tossed off the cliff with the others and left to the dogs and other creatures of the wilds.

All the warriors of the Turodi tribe came to the shrine and made personal offerings and prayers before the altar of Cariocecus. The wealthier ones then donned their coats of mail and finely worked helmets while the rest made do with whatever weapons they had. The whole tribe revelled in the recent black eye it had given Rome and even those who would normally shy from battle made simple spears or took their hunting bows to war. The Turodi war band, now confident of victory, marched off with Turicacus leading the men of quality. The rest followed in their loose family groups or with like-minded companions full of boastful pride and ready for the coming fight.

SPQR

Chapter 9

"Make sure it's secured properly!" barked the young tribune to the *Aquilifer*[66] of the 8th Legion. "Yes, Sir," replied the veteran man smartly, but his thoughts were saying something completely different. "Of course I will, you stupid little shit!" he growled inwardly as the young, inexperienced officer walked off. When the tribune was out of earshot he muttered to a legionary who stood nearby guarding the rostrum, "A pox on that fresh-faced little *cunnus* telling me how to do my job!" This heavily tattooed soldier with many scars had been the bearer of his Legion's eagle for more than two years now and he knew, better than any upstart with his first flush of chin hair, the prestige and importance of his role.

The whole army was marching into the empty camp behind him as he fixed the Eagle of the 8th into its designated socket on the large wooden rostrum that had been built for the commander's address to the army. He looked up and made sure the wings were aligned with those of the Eagle of the 9th Legion that stood alongside. Once the pole was secure, out of habit, he said a small prayer to Fortuna that the sacred Eagle would not fall in any circumstance, be it wind, tempest or an enemy attack. It was not unusual for him ask for divine protection, as this standard was not a mere item of battlefield recognition. The Eagle is the very soul of the Legion; any slight to this sacrosanct object can mean eternal shame and dishonour for the men who march under it.

---

[66] A standard-bearer or signifer in the Roman army who was entrusted to hold the legion's most prized symbol, the aquila (eagle).

The loss of an Eagle could result in the worst punishment of all for a legion. This was known as 'Decimation' and it had a dreadful collective effect on the unit. The unfortunate legion selected for this punishment was divided into groups of ten with each group drawing lots and the soldier, regardless of rank, on whom the lot fell was beaten or stoned to death by his friends. The remaining soldiers were given rations of barley instead of wheat and forced to sleep outside the Roman encampment with the blood of their own brothers on their hands. If you were not so lucky to be punished so, you might find your legion being disbanded forever in shame. The Aquilifer knew all of this and understood it better than most, as he was the man with the place of honour to bear the Eagle of his Legion and, if necessary, to die protecting it.

The young tribune walked into the command tent that was empty apart from a pale, slender man of medium height with receding, thinning hair who was being attended by a slave. He halted and snapped a sharp salute. "That's the last cohort formed up, sir," he said, standing to intente. The pale-complexioned commander ignored the slave securing the straps of the polished breastplate and turned his cunning face with its refined, elegant nose to the tribune. He gave a very faint smile and looked at him with his dark, piercing eyes that seemed almost black.

"Very good, tribune. I will be out shortly. You may take up your position," came the reply. The tribune saluted and left the tent. Gaius Julius Caesar stood alone as his slave adjusted the final strap and waited for several long moments to allow for dramatic effect. He knew he could not rush out there following a tribune while the dust was still settling from the last cohort he had heard marching in. It might lessen his own prestige and authority, which would ruin the power of his oration to the men.

He listened for noise and was pleased to hear none of the marching or bawled commands he had heard previously. He wanted no movement or noise whatsoever and every eye on the doorway of his tent. He knew the massed instruments would sound his arrival and had already made sure the twenty best musicians had been chosen from across the legions to herald his presence on this particularly important day.

He enjoyed feeling his heart thump under the breastplate in nervous excitement. Looking down, he checked his immaculate uniform and made the slave adjust his scarlet red cloak. After a leisurely sip of lemon water he took three deep breaths and walked out into the bright, sunlit day.

The sound of the buccina and cornu split the air and the final note doubled the commanding roars of each Primus Pilus. The commander was greeted with a momentary thunder of noise as the entire army stood to intente. Gaius Julius Caesar walked forward up the steps onto the rostrum that had been covered in red cloth and was mounted with the Eagles of the three legions present... *his* three legions! They perched proudly atop their poles behind him with their outstretched wings glittering silver in the sun. Apart from his now empty headquarters tent, the camp had been completely cleared and he even made the baggage train form up outside the camp walls, under guard by the allied auxilia horsemen, so no braying mules would interrupt this special day. He stood alone with his sharp black eyes looking over a sea of legionary helmets. He tried to look across as many faces as possible and much more than ten thousand faces looked back. With expectation in the air he gave a slight smile and nod, and raised his hands to speak.

"Soldiers!" he shouted, pitching his words higher for impact. "Brave soldiers of the Republic, we stand here today on the eve of a great conflict." He paused and paced along the rostrum and pointed northwards. "I do not have time for a fine, noble speech like you would expect from a man from the Senate house. Because these people are far from fine and noble," he spat. "Out there lie a barbaric enemy! An enemy who has taken Roman civilians and made them into slaves! They have sacrificed women and children to their evil, outlandish gods! They have burned towns and plundered wealth! *Our* towns and *our* wealth!" He paused and saw anger on some faces.

Good, he thought.

"Well? Shall we teach them a lesson?" he shouted and received some scattered cheers as the men were still stood silent at intente as discipline required.

He cursed internally that he had not had them stood at ease and continued, "I cannot hear you, soldiers! Do you want revenge? Shall we take *THEIR* women! *THEIR* gold?" he shouted forcefully and got thunderous shouts back as the ranks became swept up in his enthusiasm.

Relieved for this reaction, he continued, "For every drop of Roman blood we shall take a river in return! These tribes of the Lusitani and Gallaeci are little more than savages! Our mistake in history was to fight them to gain peace… This time we *WILL* seek their total destruction!"

The Legions before him roared their approval and he allowed the hubbub of noise as the centurions in the middle ranks shouted back what he knew the rear ranks would barely hear, if at all. Amid the scattered cheers he unsheathed his gladius and pointed it to the men he recognised.

"What say you, Legionary Gellius? A man like yourself would surely like to earn a slave or two in this war!"

The veteran legionary saluted smartly and shouted, "Yes, Sir! Only if you can promise me a pick of the pretty ones!"

To which Caesar laughed, "Good answer, Soldier! I shall try to make sure you lead the assault on the richest town we find!" At this, the veteran saluted and grinned. Caesar smiled and walked back along the rostrum.

"You there, Centurion Asina! How many enemies will you kill?"

The square-jawed Centurion grinned and shouted back, "There will be more than enough bodies to fill an ox cart, Sir!"

There were cheers and laughter, at which Caesar joined in. "We shall leave the bodies and fill that cart with gold instead!" he shouted in reply, which gained more cheers.

"What about you, Legionary Pictor? I saw you running like the wind during training. Will you charge the enemy as fast?"

The tall legionary near the front flushed red and stammered, "Yes, Sir... I will, Sir... I shall..."

A voice from an unseen witty legionary behind him shouted loudly, "He will run well for you, Caesar! Or he will get my *pilum*[67] jabbed in his ass!"

Most of the army that heard broke into laughter. Caesar smiled and looked at the poor legionary who stood there with a bright red face. "Don't worry, Legionary Pictor. I am sure you could outrun anybody's pilum! Will you join me on the march?" he said, giving him a warm look and a second chance at speaking.

"Yes, Sir!" shouted the flushed Pictor with a salute.

Caesar walked back to the centre of the rostrum with his heart beating hard in excitement. He exulted in the moment. All the times he had addressed the Senate or spoke in defense of the accused at the law courts paled in comparison to this. He did not

[67] Javelin.

need his finely polished speech that came easily to him when he stood in front of the patricians, equestrians or any of the upper classes. Here he could relax and speak from the heart, because he was addressing an army... HIS own army! The assembled soldiers before him were his and he knew it. The nerves had melted away and he knew at this moment these men would follow him anywhere, even to Rome and the Consul's chair, if he ordered it.

He looked over the faces of the tribunes who were assembled next to the rostrum and noted several looks of disgust at the cheering and lack of discipline. Caesar sighed and thought how many patricians did not know how to speak to the working classes. He mentally made a note of who had sour expressions. *I will talk to those little fools later,* he thought.

He stood in the centre of the rostrum with his sword unsheathed and set his face with a look of grim determination. A hush fell over the assembled troops as they gazed up at their commander who looked every part of the warrior. The breeze picked up a little and his red cloak fluttered behind him, mirroring the flapping vexillum that stood in front of every cohort.

"Brothers... *My* Brothers!" he shouted as loud as he could. "We march against a savage enemy with strange Gods! We march with the blessing of Jupiter Optimus Maximus over our heads and the strength of Mars *Ultor*[68] in our sword arms! We march to utterly destroy them! We march for gold, we march for honour and we march for the glory of the Rome!"

Crying out, he trailed the last word and raised his gladius in the air. Caesar exulted as his final words were greeted with another thunderous roar. These men were now on fire as Caesar had wanted them. He stood for a moment feeling the energy of the

---

[68] Latin: avenger.

massed ranks, ready to do battle for him, savouring the sound that made his spine tingle. Then, with a savage grin of exhilaration at the deafening noise, he turned his head and nodded a signal to a smiling military tribune who immediately had the gathered instruments call the men to intente as he descended from the rostrum.

Many soldiers were still cheering as they came to intente and immediately the 8th legion musicians blew the signal to advance. The huge body of soldiers came to life as orders were shouted and the great massed ranks began to move. The Aquilifer of the 8th Legion, who would be marching in the vanguard, hurriedly took up his Eagle and ran to his position as the front with the command group as it passed out of the gates. The sky to the north was beginning to darken with a coming storm which could be heard rumbling in the distance and the air was starting to feel thick and heavy. With the braying commands of the musical instruments and a great cloud of dust, the army began to march out onto the road. The locals stood to the side, looking at the spectacle of the Legions on the march. Various Lusitanian spies who had camped a small distance from the Roman camp knew this was the moment they had waited for. They had watched the baggage train form up outside the camp and heard the cheers of the soldiers. As the men mounted their horses they saw the vanguard legion march out of the gate in it neat orderly rows. The riders nodded to each other before they galloped off to warn their fellow countrymen, just as Caesar knew they would. With the thundering sound of thousands of feet hitting the floor. The Roman legions, headed by their glittering eagles, were marching north to war.

SPQR

Chapter 10

The rain dripped down the side of Borras' helmet and went down his already damp tunic. He cursed and adjusted his scarf which every soldier wore to protect the neck from the constant chafe of the chain mail shirt. He stood watching the trees across the open field that was dotted with shrubs and bushes while behind him, in the grove, the felling party cut down suitable trees for the new bridge over the swollen river. The rain had started on the day they marched from the camp in Scalabis and had continued intermittently ever since. The enemy had disappeared into the hills and forests to the north and east with the advance of the legions, leaving only ruined villages, farms and trade outposts.

The big man hawked and spat into the undergrowth and looked across the open field all the way to the tree line once more. The distant vegetation and the rolling hills behind looked grey from the falling rain and coupled with the leaden clouds that filled the sky the whole scene looked colourless and miserable to him. Borras sighed and looked at Corvus who stood a few yards away, leaning comfortably on a tree, seemingly uncaring about the weather. His glittering black eyes appeared almost catlike as he scanned the area ahead of them.

"So," sniffed Borras, scratching the red stubble on his wet chin, "you come from Narbo, eh? I went through there once," he said, looking at his silent companion who gave a slight nod to acknowledge the comment but added nothing more.

Damn him thought Borras, *even Saxum or Ignavus would be a better comrade for picket duty!*

The large man shrugged, adjusted his scarf again and looked rearward as he heard someone moving through the undergrowth. Galba ducked under a drooping wet branch as he approached. "Salve, comrades, how's things?" he said, blowing his nose on his fingers and flicking the mucus into the long, wet grass.

"Well, I'm piss wet down to my marrow, I have not made a single brass *quadrans*[69] in plunder, my nerves are feeling shot through with all this silence, waiting for a damn ambush that never seems to come, and I'm stood here so engineers can build a bridge when there is a perfectly good one back in the place we marched from! How are you, Decanus?" Borras said glumly.

Galba smiled his warm smile and punched the big man on the arm. "*Gerrae!* Sounds like you have finally settled into army life! I knew I could rely on you to cheer me up, you big Teuton ox!" He gestured to the tree line that was several hundred yards away. "Think yourself lucky, lads, you are standing here looking at the countryside while the 8th Legion are building our joint camp for the night and all we need to do is chop some wood and throw a few logs across that little stream. Isn't that right, Corvus?" he grinned, nodding his head towards the swollen, flooded river off to the left. The scarred and silent man nodded politely but his eyes stayed locked on the trees opposite.

"That is all well and good, Galba, but my nerves are still shot! Where are all these Lusitanians, eh? The only thing we have seen is a couple of tiny, miserable hill forts that the 8th Legion assaulted and they barely captured a prisoner per section! All we seem to do is demolish empty farm houses, tear up crops and

---

[69] Literally meaning "a quarter", one of the lowest-valued Roman coins in production.

snatch a few livestock. When will they attack?" said Borras, spitting on the floor again.

Galba frowned, drawing his bushy eyebrows together. "Don't wish to meet them too much, lad! They are out there, make no mistake. We have been watched since we left Scalabis and they are gauging what we are about. That's why Caesar is marching a slow and deliberate pace for now to let them think we cannot go more than ten miles a day. He will lure them into battle sure enough. I have seen a good few patricians who want to play soldiers, but all the centurions are already saying he is different!" Galba smiled again as the rain dripped from his nose. "He will bait the traps and they will come to us... these people like to pick off stragglers and Caesar will be ready for them."

All three men stood silently for a while, looking at the distant tree line. For a moment the only noise above the patter of the rain was the hollow thump of axes on the trees to their rear. Borras took a deep breath and sniffed as he looked at Galba. "So why are we out here miles from the rest of the army? Are we the bait?" he said quietly, grimacing at the thought.

Galba looked up at him and smiled, but this time with no warmth. "Just watch the trees, Borras, and remember to fall back if you see anything. We have our full cohort here, the 5th Cohort is eight hundred yards down the river preparing another bridge site, and the rest of the legion is a mile to the rear. We are in a good enough position." With that he nodded and returned to the felling the party who were now working the logs under the direction of the carpentry immunes and a detachment of bridge builders from the engineers.

Galba walked past the oval shields that still had their leather covers on to protect them from the rain. They had been placed in formation, all facing the direction the enemy might come from. The work party would simply have to run into their place in their own century. He was glad to see that all the shields were placed so the cohort would form up into a tight rectangle with two centuries on each side and one on each end. Pilus Prior Tanicus knew what he was doing and took no chances with an enemy who was famous for ambushes. The whole cohort had pickets watching out in every direction while the rest of the men worked in a clearing within a good sized piece of woodland on a slight rise next to the brown, muddy river.

The centre of the clearing was now filled with logs that were being worked on ready for the bridge. Several ox carts had also been brought full of tools and ropes for the project. The open grassland around was dotted with similar groups of trees and bushes in various sizes and Galba liked being in a little cover away from the open ground and the eerily abandoned farms. He felt less exposed and had an uncrossable river protecting an entire flank. *Yes, it was a good choice of ground by Tanicus*, he thought as he walked over to the leader of the 6th cohort who was now directing the efforts of the men along with a senior engineer.

"Decanus Galba reporting, Pilus Prior!" he said, snapping a smart salute to the stocky senior centurion.

Tanicus looked at him with a wink. "Cut the shit, Galba! Send your report!" he said in a friendly voice.

"Pickets from the 2nd Century report no change," said Galba with a smile. "I have the hunter on there from my section and he can spot a flea on a fly's arse from a mile away."

Tanicus grunted. "Good! The face on him is ugly enough to scare away the Medusa! So we should not be troubled on that flank at least," he said with a white-toothed grin. "Take the lads some posca to warm them if needs be. We will rotate the other pickets, but keep his eyes on the forest. We probably could do with the big Teuton when we have to drive in the piles for the bridge and lay the logs, but the hunter is more use to us on watch."

Galba nodded and left to return to the 2nd century as the tesserarii or decanii of the other sentries came back from their own picket check.

Kratos and Decius were sawing a log together and cursing as the rain mixed with the sawdust and jammed the blade every time it bit into the wood. Felix was expertly hacking pieces from the end of another log that would become a sharpened pile for the bridge. He sang gently to himself and despite the miserable weather he worked as if he was on his own piece of farmland building a bed for a beautiful new wife. Galba smiled when he heard Felix's song was about a fat Nubian prostitute with particularly saggy breasts.

Ignavus was hacking away feebly at a piece of timber he was trying to split while Saxum carried a monstrous log over to the group from the felling site. The mighty feat of strength was having its effects on the big man. His ugly face was nearly purple and his thick, muscular legs shook as he took quick tiny steps. "Move... Ignavus... Fucking... Move... *Cunnus*..." he puffed and, staggering, he dropped the log off his shoulder and nearly crushed Ignavus, who yelped and sprang away like a cat on hot coals from the huge timber that crashed down where he had just stood.

"You filthy fucking swine! You nearly killed me with that log!" he hissed with his head bobbing like an angry vulture. Saxum grinned and balled his ham-like fists to eyes like a weeping child.

"Poor little baby wants to cry! You should get the shit out of your ears and the cock out of your ass! I warned you, didn't I? I can't help it that your brain is fucked and you struggle with simple commands! Besides, it's not like you were doing any proper work," he gestured to Ignavus' log that showed virtually no signs of toil. "You have hardly made a mark! You work on logs like a cheap whore giving a backrub!" he said, grinning.

Ignavus went red with fury, jumped on the log and began hacking into it furiously but with little real effect. Felix looked over and laughed. "Ho, Saxum! You should throw trees at him every time! It's the only way to get him to work... even if it is rather pathetic!" he added as he took another graceful swing, cleaving more wood from his own log.

"Well, if this drunken shit sack can do it better, let's see him try!" spat Ignavus, moving away from the log and eyeing Saxum who did not take insults easily.

Saxum's piggy eyes widened. "Shit sack, am I?!" he yelled "You little *cunnus*, I will tear you limb from limb, *after* I split this log like Hercules!"

He quickly grabbed an axe and with a howl of anger he jumped on the wet log which had no purchase for his studded army sandals. The howl tailed off as his feet slipped and Saxum landed awkwardly on his back with a grunt of pain. The brute lay prostrate over the log, wheezing breathlessly with the wind knocked out of him. "Ignavus... you... *cunnus...*"

Felix doubled up with hysterical laughter while Ignavus gave a wicked smile and sprang over the helpless Saxum with an axe raised. "I wonder if you doubt the strength of my arm NOW, you shit sack!" he said with an evil cackle.

"Legionary, I assume you are about to help your comrade to his feet?" said Centurion Falco smoothly as he silently appeared next to Ignavus, raising his vitis until it touched the thin man's nose.

Ignavus' eyes crossed as they looked foolishly at the vitis. His angry red face became very pale almost instantly. "Centurion... I..." he stuttered.

"Back to work, all of you!" Falco hissed. "Any man who takes a weapon to another in my century will be crucified! And if we are in field conditions I will personally nail you up out here for the Lusitanians to find!" he said, looking around.

The section wisely said no more and immediately carried on working in silence. Saxum eyed the centurion and quickly pulled out a small brown leather pouch that he wore on a string around his neck. He brought it right up to his lips and he whispered to it before quickly stuffing it back down under the chainmail and tunic he wore. No one but the ever curious Felix had asked what was inside the strange bag, to which Saxum had gone bright red and crossly told him to go fuck himself with his own cock. The subject had not come up again but all were curious to know what made the savage Saxum so sensitive.

Galba had trotted over just as Falco gave this warning to his section. The centurion gestured the decanus over to a place near the trees and out of earshot.

"I swear, your tent section must be from a prison for the those with the mania!" he said, shaking his head with a grin. "Would you like me to split them up, Galba? I think the 5th Century has some pretty tame characters in it. We could move one or two and they would cool down quite well," said Falco.

Galba shook his head and furrowed his bushy eyebrows. "There are some future centurions in this section, brother. Yes, they are a rowdy bunch of little shits, but combat will settle them, I hope.

If that doesn't then a good flogging will, neh? It worked for us," he said, looking at the section thoughtfully.

Falco smiled. "Well, let me know if you change your mind," he said, turning to the sound of approaching cavalry. A group of muddied riders had entered their small wood and had stopped next to the Pilus Prior. He saw it was the cavalry detachment of the 6th Cohort who had been out to satellite around the position half a mile or so away. These men would make sure no one got close enough to surprise the pickets. Falco eagerly jogged over to hear the *decurion*[70] report to the Pilus Prior.

"Decurion Cimber," said Tanicus with a grin, "seeing you is either good or bad. Tell me the rest of 10th Legion is engaged with the enemy and we are to march off in support!"

The dark, athletic man of noble birth pulled his helmet off and wiped the rain from his face. "*Salve,* Tanicus! We might see battle but could be on our own," he reported quickly with a hard face. "We just saw several hundred horsemen moving down from the north east." The black-haired cavalryman leaned forward in the saddle and patted the horse's neck. "Our little *turma* of thirty men cannot match three hundred, even as good as we are! I expect some of your pickets will see them soon. The trees will stop a charge but we might get pinned by the river. I have sent my two fastest men back to warn the Legion," he said, sitting up comfortably on the horse.

Tanicus nodded as he heard the report and, as if on cue, a Legionary came running from the riverside picket. "Pilus Prior! Pilus Prior!" cried the young man, making the entire cohort stop working and look up with worried faces. The man sprinted up breathlessly, pointing back to the river, his eyes wide with terror. "I saw... I saw... the enemy!"

---

[70] Roman cavalry officer in command of a squadron, or *turma*, of cavalrymen.

"SOLDIER! Stop panicking! Stand to fucking attention when you talk to me! And give your report like a Legionary of the 10th, not some young girl who is about to get butt fucked for the first time!" growled Pilus Prior Tanicus, swelling with anger at the show of cowardice from the panicking man.

"Yes, Pilus Prior!" The flustered Legionary snapped to intente and reported. "Legionary Columella of the 2nd Century reporting from the riverside picket. We saw movement in the forest on the other side of the river. It looked… it looked like thousands of warriors!" said the shaking man with a salute.

Tanicus nodded and grunted, looking around at the waiting centurions who had gathered for the cavalrymen's report. "Falco, that's in front of your sector. Go to the river, verify what you can see and give an accurate estimation of numbers. 'Thousands' to an un-blooded recruit could be a shepherd girl taking a lamb for a walk," he said, looking sourly at the young legionary who was visibly shaking.

Falco pointed to him. "Columella! On me. Let's go!" he barked and ran off with his easy stride, the terrified legionary following behind.

As they left, Borras ran up and gave a quick salute. "Pilus Prior! Legionary Gaius Borras, 2nd Century, reporting lots of cavalry sighted to the north east moving south around us, Sir!"

"Very good, Borras," nodded Tanicus. "Back to your post."

He turned to the nearest centurion. "Have the men stood to, with as little noise as possible! They might not know we are here just yet." The short centurion nodded his helmet with the transverse crest and ran off to carry out the order.

Pilus Prior Tanicus turned back to the cavalry commander. "Cimber, it looks like the horsemen could be a screen for infantry. If they are on the opposite bank they might be moving on this side, too. The boys are all fresh and un-blooded, so I am not going to wait around to be surrounded. Send some men down river to the 5th Cohort and tell them we have contact with the enemy who are in force and we are pulling back to the rest of the Legion immediately!"

The cavalry commander nodded and picked out two men who quickly manoeuvred their horses through the trees and galloped off to the southwest, towards the 5th Cohort.

Falco jogged back from the river, looking grim. "Well, it certainly isn't a shepherd girl! I saw at least a few hundred lurking in the trees on the opposite bank. They look like they are heading down river and the nosey bastards kept coming out to have a look at us. One of the cheeky bastards grinned at me. They know we are here!"

Tanicus grunted and nodded. "Cimber, send more riders to the Legion and tell them we *are* on the way back, and could be facing infantry and cavalry on this side of the river with many enemies on the other side! We will bear south to meet up with the 5th Cohort and get away from this river. These shit-kicking locals might know of a crossable point on the river that our scouts missed and we are not staying around to find out."

Decurion Cimber nodded and relayed the commands. Two more riders immediately galloped off into the rain. The whole cohort was now alive as centurions and optios strode around, hissing to the men to form up. The legionaries nervously scrambled into their respective positions in the central clearing. There was a slight hubbub of noise and a clatter of equipment as the soldiers abandoned the engineering works, quickly dumping their tools into the ox carts and rushing to take up their weapons. The air felt thick and suffocating. The noise of the worried soldiers arming themselves was only broken now by centurions and optios grunting words of command to dress the lines and keeping discipline. The gravity of the situation was not lost on the men as they stood in the rectangular defensive formation with each man holding his scutum in his left hand and his two pilae in his right, ready for action.

Tanicus called the rest of the centurions in and gave them his orders. "Right! Cimber's boys will spread out all around us and give us any warning of an ambush," he said and the cavalry commander nodded. "The Cohort will move in the formation it's in now and with any attack we can go firm in all-round defence with the trailing century just doing an about turn. Tell the men they will throw one pilum but keep the other and use it as a spear if the cavalry make a move on us." The gathered centurions nodded. "We will bear south and hopefully can link up with the 5th Cohort as they withdraw from their own bridging site. Any questions? No? Good! Prepare to move!"

The centurions hurried back to their centuries as the pickets began withdrawing. Suddenly, there was a cry from the picket to the north, near the river bank. There was a clash of steel, then a scream followed by crashing undergrowth. A single legionary burst through the bushes, without his helmet or shield, running at a full sprint with blood dripping from a wound on his sword arm. "ENEMY CONTACT!" he screamed with a wild look on his face as twenty or more Lusitanian warriors surged out of the greenery after him with many dozens, perhaps hundreds more following behind.

Pilus Prior Tanicus, standing next to the Vexillarius 'Two Smiles', swore violently. He had no time to give full orders. "LISTEN IN THE 6th! *GLADIUM STRINGE! AD ACIEM!*[71]" he roared as the front men in each century hurriedly positioned themselves off with space to fight. The musicians blew the

---

[71] Latin: Draw swords! Form battle lines!

command and the blast of the horns seemed to cause a little moment of panic as pilae were dropped or passed back in confusion, but the urgency of the situation took precedence. Every man in the front rank drew his gladius and fell into battle formation. The lines of soldiers behind them all took hold of the weapon harness of the man in front, ready to begin the bloody business of battle.

"Cimber! Ride and report our situation!" shouted Tanicus. "We will hold here until the Legion comes back for us OR until we can make a fighting withdrawal to the 5th Cohort!"

The cavalryman nodded and the remainder of his group spurred their horses into a gallop through the trees out into the open fields. The last thing Tanicus saw was the small group being pursued across the open ground by a much larger group of Lusitanian cavalry. "Sons of Dis!" he spat. This was not his first ambush, but he hated surprises at the best of times!

The bloody sentry had made it back and crashed through the ranks of the 2nd Century. The wounded soldier making his report to Pilus Prior Tanicus just as all the other sentries from the north and eastern flanks came running in with similar information. Warriors… many hundreds, possibly thousands of them! As this information was being passed, the Lusitanian warriors that had plunged through the bushes stopped fifty yards short of the Roman formation and began to swarm and surge in through the undergrowth, filling the large clearing and quickly surrounding the lone cohort. One group caught two of the pickets running back and clashed with them. One legionary fell screaming to the ground with a spear through the stomach while the other battled to get back to the cohort. He made it back to the formation but lost several fingers in the process and had a huge wound in the leg. His companion was not so lucky.

The vicious and wild-looking warriors gnashed their teeth in fury and impaled the screaming Legionary again and again. The body was soon hacked to pieces and his severed head sailed through the air into the formation of grim faced Roman soldiers. The warriors whooped and beckoned to the rear, calling everyone to come and join the slaughter of the trapped unit.

Many of the Lusitanians were dressed in the leather trousers and cloaks typical of their fashion and this group seemed to be of the same tribe, as they had similar patterned cloaks. There were many warriors who were wearing fine mail armour and good quality ornate helmets. They also carried the deadly curved sword of the region. Some wielded fine iron spears and beautifully worked oval shields while others literally had no more than a simple, fire-hardened wooden spear and knife. The soldiers of the 6th Cohort noted grimly that a great many were carrying captured Roman military arms and armour. Some looked quite old in design, but others were virtually brand new.

The Lusitanians chanted and whooped and stamped their feet on the ground. Those with shields bashed their weapons against them in unison, creating a pulsing rhythm of clashing metal and war chants that was terrifying to hear.

Pilus Prior Tanicus saw an opportunity as the enemy on all sides waited until their numbers and courage were sufficient to charge. "LISTEN IN THE 6th! REAR RANKS ONLY… *PILA TOLLITE*![72]"

With that the men in the rear ranks took up their pilae into a throwing position. They would not be able to get a run up like in training. *But it's better than nothing,* thought Tanicus.

---

[72] Latin: Ready javelins!

"*PILA… IACITE!*[73]" came the command and with a roar from the Roman soldiers a shower of iron tipped javelins flew into the first rank of enemy warriors. Without the proper run up some of them did not have enough momentum and were swatted away with shields, but many others found their mark as men fell screaming to the floor with wounds. The Lusitani gave a roar and charged the front rank of legionaries who stood holding their scutum up with the deadly gladius low to the side, ready to do its grim work. The momentum of the charge was not slowed by another volley of hurtling javelins from the rear ranks of the 6th cohort. And despite many hitting their target and leaving more men on the ground writhing in agony, the Lusitanian warriors thundered forwards in fury.

"Shit! Shit! Shit! Shit!" said Ignavus, his eyes wide with terror as he clutched Saxum's harness. The large man in front stiffened and readied himself for impact from the roaring wave of approaching adversaries. Felix looked grim standing next to him with Decius stood behind, bracing him for the clash with the enemy. One large muscular warrior, whose bare arms were covered in curious tattoos of animals and plants, charged straight for Felix. The powerful man jumped with a tremendous kick at the long scutum that smashed into Felix's shoulder and his knee at the same time from the force of the powerful blow. The warrior brought his curved sword scything down as Felix sagged onto one knee under his raised scutum and stabbed reflexively under the bottom rim and upwards into the muscular warrior's groin. The swinging sword clanged harmlessly off Felix's shield boss and the warrior sprang back, coming to a standstill with a surprised look on his face. His long blonde moustaches framed his open mouth as he looked down at the thick jet of dark blood that sprayed from his thigh.

---

[73] Latin: Throw javelins!

165

Decius heaved the shaken Felix to his feet, and the stunned man plunged his gladius through the warrior's open mouth, giving him an even more shocked expression. The point cracked through the back of the skull and the man dropped dead like a stone.

As Felix dispatched his first opponent, Saxum brought his sword down with a mighty stroke on the head of a charging warrior that split the skull neatly to the neck. "HA! You *cunnus*! That is what happens when..." He was cut short when he raised his shield to defend against a jabbing spear from another charging man. Behind him Ignavus looked more steely-eyed now but continued muttering "Shit! Shit! Shit!" over and over until Galba leaned across and punched him hard in the chest.

"Shut it! Calm down!" he shouted to Ignavus, who went quiet but kept gulping and looked like he was trying to swallow a frog as he desperately held onto the harness of the battling Saxum, who was cursing and swearing with every stroke and jab of his gladius.

Centurion Falco had already dispatched his third enemy and could see warriors were starting to shy away from his part of the line. The pile of bodies in front of him contained two warriors in good armour so this must have discouraged those with just simple wooden spears from trying their luck with this tough veteran. He raised his shield as a stone whizzed towards him from the back of the seething mob of yelling Lusitanians. Someone obviously thought it was safer to throw things from a distance. He looked at Kratos next to him with Galba at his back. The Greek had killed one and bravely battled another but his face was ashen and his eyes wide with shock.

The 2nd Century were doing well. The enemy's furious initial assault had been blunted against the disciplined wall of Romans, who now began their well-drilled technique of destroying the enemy by having a superior armed and armoured rotating front line. The ground was becoming slick with viscera and blood as the wounded lay screaming in agony.

Falco could already see those at the back of the Lusitanian horde looking uneasy. The lithe Centurion wanted to get everyone with some blood on the sword, so he shot a quick look back at Optio Leptis, who strode back and forth, marshalling the rear rank and seeing to the casualties. Falco met his eye, gave him a nod and blew twice on the wooden whistle he wore around his neck to signal the first rotation. Instantly, the men fighting on the front rank lashed out with extra vigour to give themselves enough room to change over with the man standing behind.

Saxum kicked a fellow as large as himself in the stomach and the great bear-like man fell back with a roar. He then turned sideways and moved down the gap in the files as they had been taught. Ignavus stepped forward and took his place in the front line. The scrawny man stood yelling and stabbing furiously at the big bear who looked more scared of this skinny, wild-eyed maniac than he did of the lumbering Saxum.

Felix hobbled rearwards through the ranks and took up his position at the back, assuming his place as the last man in the file. The whole front line of the 2nd was spread pretty thin, so he was only the fifth man from the front. Still, that meant a good few moments of rest, which would be needed, he thought as he forlornly inspected his rapidly swelling knee.

"Fucked, is it?" yelled Saxum, peering down with his piggy eyes. "I saw you stick him through the gullet! Ha! That will stop him sucking on stolen Roman tits forever!" he gurgled with laughter that Felix did not appreciate or share.

"It feels pretty fucked," Felix replied with a sad look, poking gingerly at the swollen joint. "What say you, Kratos? Is the bone broken? Will it mend? Kratos!?" he shouted to the ashen-faced Greek who was staring towards the yelling enemy who now had retreated a little.

Kratos glanced over quickly at the knee, blinked a few times, then looked back at the tribal warriors as they surged forwards with another roaring charge. "Looks bad, but if you can stand on it, then it's not broken. It will swell more and hurt for a week or so, then afterwards we will have to see if the sinews inside the joint can heal."

The Greek turned his head to look around and noticed that the whole 6th Cohort was now surrounded and being charged on every side. He looked and could not see Borras or Corvus. He saw the Optio of the 3rd Century rush to the front of his own formation, which meant a centurion had already been killed or wounded.

Pilus Prior Tanicus now stalked around the open space in the centre of the cohort. His gladius dripped with blood and his face had either been splashed with gore or he was wounded himself. He quickly walked around the back of the centuries, speaking a few words to the optios, assessing the few injured from the first charge or patting an occasional Legionary on the back. "Keep at them, boys! These shit-eating dogs won't beat this cohort!" he bellowed over the din of battle. Like a good Pilus Prior he was everywhere at once and seemed to be totally in control and without fear. Everyone knew this was not an act. This broad, tough and scarred veteran soldier had been in this situation before.

Falco's whistle sounded again and gave way to the sound of clattering shield on shield as the bloody men from the front side-stepped through the tight gaps in the files. Galba came to the back, took his place on the end of the file and calmly sipped from a small water skin. Ignavus came back and stood white as

chalk with his teeth chattering and wild look in his eyes. "Fu...
fu... fucking Lusi... Lusita... nians!" he stuttered as Decius
came back oozing blood from under the cheek piece of his
helmet and around his mouth. Optio Leptis was striding up and
down the lines, always with one eye on Centurion Falco and
another on the men to make sure no one ran away or to tend to
any issue. He spotted the blood oozing from Decius and stalked
over.

"Legionary Decius, how bad is that wound?" he said firmly but
with genuine concern in his big round face.

"It's fine, Optio," Decius replied with a lisp, drooling blood as
he spoke. "One of those filthy shits tried to shtick me with a
shpear but it deflected off inshide the cheek piesh of the helmet,"
he said, picking at his blood-soaked cheek. Leptis nodded, happy
with the reply, as he looked again at Falco before walking off
down the rest of the battle line, searching for casualties in a
worse state.

"I hope you got the *cunnus*?" shouted Galba with a wink to the
injured Decius.

The air above the Romans was now becoming pierced with
arcing projectiles from the swarming tribesmen. One of the oxen
harnessed to a cart was hit by several arrows and became
maddened with pain. The frantic, bellowing creature had its
throat cut by an optio before it could charge and destroy the
cohesion of the formation that surrounded it. A native javelin
sailed overhead and stuck in the ground next to the vexillarius
'Two Smiles', who stood next to a cart with the musicians and
the cohort vexillum planted in the ground at the centre of the
formation. The scarred veteran looked dourly at the javelin for a
moment before yanking it free from the ground and sending it
flying back in the direction it came from. He dusted his tattooed
hands off and spat on the floor angrily. It even seemed like the

wolf skin that adorned his helmet was angry at the impertinent enemy for trying a shot at him.

The centurions' whistles sounded over and over as the battle wore on. The piles of bodies with their scattered limbs, strewn intestines and gore began to grow in front of our ranks. Everybody now had a reddened blade and the wet, muddy floor was streaked with small rivers of blood that attracted hungry flies in the humid air. Each century had wounded men lying behind it inside the formation, some moaning with pain, some lying very pale and still, some never to move again. The cohort had drifted into an almost circular formation which we had practiced and drilled in basic training before. The *orbis*[74] formation was always meant for a unit fighting to the death or a unit completely surrounded and waiting for reinforcement.

The Lusitanian warriors would charge and fight furiously, losing more men each time, and then fall back to build up their courage and reorganise while their missile troops kept harrying us with stones, javelins and arrows. At one point a curious group of warriors dressed in the same fine armour pushed their way to the front and shouted accusations at the Romans before charging. They died all the same, screaming and clutching wounds that spurted thick, dark arterial blood, their eyes a mixture of agony and pure hatred.

The whistle sounded again and this time Centurion Falco took a break with Galba, Ignavus and Decius as they made their change to the back for the third time. Optio Leptis had pushed forward and would fill Falco's slot for a short while. The agile centurion had darted back through the ranks and was now standing, covered in the blood of more than ten enemies, studying his good Hispanic-made gladius. He shook his head at a large knick in the blade and glanced back every few moments to make sure

---

[74] Latin: circle.

Leptis was still on his feet. The centurion looked barely out of breath as he walked over to the signifer Marcus Attius and shared a joke with the man, making a thrusting motion with his gladius and telling a story about a hilarious death, no doubt. The veteran guarding the signum of the 2nd Century burst out laughing and added to the joke, which made Falco chuckle in turn.

"How can they laugh like that?!" yelled Kratos over the clashing noise of battle. His face shone with moisture; despite the fact that the rain had stopped the air was humid and sticky. The stench of battle was nauseating and the Greek took a large gulp from the flask in Felix's outstretched hand. "Urgh... What's in that? Unmixed wine?"

Felix snatched the flask back. "Thought you might need something stronger than water or posca right now! I know I fucking do!" he shouted with a wild look on his face. The dried blood caked around his eyes and made him look like he was wearing a mask. He winced and hobbled on his knee that was swollen like a ball.

Falco stalked past, dressing the lines, as always with one eye on Leptis. He said a few words to the four wounded men of the century and counted the files, noticing the numbers were short.

"We are missing three men," Falco said into Galba's ear, "unless they lie dead in the front ranks."

Galba frowned and shook his head. "Borras and Corvus were still at their picket post when they jumped us. I can't say about the other sections, but those two are missing from mine."

Falco nodded grimly and stalked back through the file to replace the optio. The Lusitanian warriors facing the 2nd Century had retreated to the tree line at the river less than a bow shot away and reorganised themselves into their own disciplined formation. This shield wall was now steadily advancing while men behind were firing arrows, and throwing rocks and javelins with renewed vigour until a rain of missiles clattered on Roman shields. A few arrows and stones from slings were reaching far over the heads of the centuries and into the backs of the opposite ranks of the circular formation. All around the cohort the last men in the files turned their shields inwards while the poor wounded dragged themselves behind whatever logs that had been cut for the bridge, under the carts or any available cover they could find.

"Wonderful!" muttered Felix sourly. "Our mouths have been stuffed with cock and now we shall have one in the arse, too!"

Suddenly, in the distance, a cornu split the air and the hail of missiles lessened. Pilus Prior Tanicus recognised it immediately and, ignoring the sporadic projectiles still flying into the formation, leapt up onto a nearby ox cart and looked rearwards through a gap in the trees, across the open ground. There, in the grey humid distance, he could see the shimmering Eagle of the 10th Legion in front of many cohorts advancing in the broad version of the *triplex acies*[75].

Tanicus gave a snarling grin. "You beautiful bastards!" he said aloud to himself and looked around, noticing that many of the tribesmen had seen the Roman reinforcements, too. The Lusitanian warriors closest to the advancing legion immediately began to break and scatter. Those warriors closest to the river and those facing the 2nd Century in particular were still advancing behind their shield wall and did not notice the powerful Roman reinforcements or the warning cries of their comrades as they began to break and run.

---

[75] The chequerboard-style triple battle line employed by Roman legions. Usually with 4 cohorts leading then two lines of 3 cohorts in reserve.

Tanicus ran to the vexillum at the centre of the formation and took a deep breath. "LISTEN IN THE 6TH COHORT! *PARA...TI*!" he bellowed the 'stand by' order and noticed all the optios had heard the command and echoed it to the embattled front ranks and centurions locked in combat. Tanicus nodded as he turned to the *aeneators*[76] who carried the cohort's instruments. They had maintained their position next to 'Two Smiles' who was still guarding the cohort standard with a look of grim indifference to the battle happening around him.

"Let's see if you lot together can sound the 'Charge' louder than I can shout it!" he called to all the musicians with a smile.

The aeneators grinned back and answered as a man, "Yes, Pilus Prior!"

The senior man amongst them gave a short count, then the massed instruments all split the air with their braying call as Tanicus roared the order to charge.

"PERCUTE!"

The readied cohort roared with one voice and charged in every direction away from the orbis like ripples from a stone thrown into a pool of still water. Those legionaries whose enemy had already begun to flee the oncoming reinforcements wheeled left or right to pin the remainder of the warriors against the torrential river.

With the command to charge, the 2nd Century stormed towards the shocked enemy, advancing behind their shield wall. Saxum sprinted ahead with surprising power and agility as he put his scutum to his shoulder and broke through the battle line with the force of a battering ram pushed by elephants. His speed and

---

[76] Roman military signaller using wind instruments. Some were given the status of immunes.

momentum was such that he knocked down five men and tripped forward head over heels, clattering deep into the surprised enemy formation. He lay on his back, lashing out with his sword, shield and feet in desperation and fury.

"Don't you fucking DARE, you bastards!" he roared as he dodged and swatted at a multitude of downward thrusts.

The rest of the 2nd crashed into the enemy line and it sagged for a moment, then broke completely. The Lusitanian warriors could now see they were being outflanked and many ran and dove straight into the swift-flowing, muddy waters of the swollen river. One warrior fell in as he was desperately tugging off his mail shirt and never surfaced again. Another fell and was trampled into the mud by the dozens of panicked men running over him. Some dropped to their knees and begged for mercy, but were brutally cut down regardless.

"Don't kill them all!" shouted Centurion Falco as Felix and another legionary were about to stab the same kneeling man. Within moments it was over. Every Lusitanian that was still alive was being tied and corralled together in groups. The broken faces of the defeated warriors were a great contrast to the legionaries who exulted in the victory, their first victory. The captives now had a lifetime of slavery to look forward to.

The soldiers that surrounded them clapped each other on the shoulders and kissed the pommels of their swords or lifted their eyes up to thank the gods. Several legionaries wept from the emotion of it all and many dropped to their knees in exhaustion. This was the kind of tiredness that only your first battle can give.

It was during this time that a cry came from the river. One large, muscular warrior was cornered with his back to the river, holding his wicked, curved sword. A dead legionary lay at his feet as blood ran freely from several wounds on his shoulders where the legionary had been stabbing at his neck. His drooping brown moustaches and beard were caked in thick, bright blood than ran from a nose that had been broken from a blow from a Roman scutum. His noble features were framed by his long hair that was pulled into a braid. He stood clad in brown goatskin trousers and boots and nothing more. His arms were covered in tattoos that looked like creeper and ivy winding around them and his face was a picture of fury. A multitude of savagely grinning Legionaries of the 2nd surrounded him like hungry wolves.

"He won't fight! He will try and escape by jumping in the river, I bet one guard duty," said Felix who had several men agree to the bet immediately.

"Surrender!" said Falco, stepping forward and gesturing to the man to lay down his sword. The warrior, who was more than a head taller than the slender Falco, spat on the floor and hissed a reply in his native dialect, leaping forward to attack. The bloodied but nimble centurion was much too fast. He stepped forward, ducking a wild, scything blow, and plunged the gladius so deep in the warrior's hairy, muscular chest that the point split the spine with a sharp crunch and poked out of his back. The furious man's face winced and he stood still for a moment before he silently slid to the ground and his life blood gushed thick and dark from the wound as Falco withdrew his gladius.

"Well, that is one prisoner we won't be interrogating!" he said smoothly with a wink to the watching legionaries who were always impressed by their centurion's skill.

"Damn! He ish good!" said Decius with envy as he drooled blood from a wounded cheek. "Better than your luck, Felixsh!" he said wryly to his hobbling companion.

"*Cac*! Fortune fucks me in the ass again," grumbled Felix as several other grinning legionaries patted him on the back and reminded him of the bet he just lost.

"And your ass is always grateful," mumbled a huge soldier covered in mud and blood who stood close by with a lost expression, his eyes gleaming white against the grime on his face.

"Very funny, friend, a lout your size must have come from a mother who.... Wait! Borras?" said Felix, peering at the filthy, bloodied man. "Is that you? We thought you were caught out in the open?"

The big man sniffed and looked around again. "Oh, I was... I was... I went back like ordered and Corvus had gone! I was on my own," he wiped his nose on his wrist. "I heard the shout but when I tried to run I fell in a ditch full of mud and then some of those bastards had got between me and the Cohort, so I had to fight my way back. I have been fighting with the 5th Century as they were the first ones I came to. I cannot find my shield and... sorry, I..."

Galba patted the big man's arm consolingly. "Don't worry, lad, you did well to fight your way back and pox on the shield. You were on picket and we were ambushed from along the river bank. If you get flogged for that I will stand there and take it myself!"

"2nd Century, listen up!" shouted Falco. "There is still work to be done! We are abandoning the bridging works and will use the ox carts to load up the enemy weapons and take our dead and wounded to camp! All section leaders, account for your men and let Vibenius know!" He turned to the tesserarius who had his nose broken when he was hit in the face with a stone. His eyes looked swollen and were already beginning to blacken.

"Leptis is dealing with the casualties, Get a figure of the dead and wounded for me straight away and get the numbers in to Pilus Prior Tanicus," said Falco to the squinting Vibenius who nodded in acknowledgment.

The rest of the 10th Legion had spread out and secured the entire area. They had captured more than two hundred prisoners, adding to the several hundred caught by the rest of the 6th Cohort. Every medicus of the legion was tending the casualties and the cohort had suffered twenty three dead with many more wounded. Luckily the pickets had spotted the creeping advance of the enemy who potentially could have annihilated the soldiers as they worked on the bridge. Tanicus nodded to himself thinking it was not too bad at all, considering there were many hundreds of dead Lusitanians lying scattered about. But still, this was a bittersweet victory for the mostly young and inexperienced soldiers, as it was the first time friends and comrades had fallen in action.

The four dead men from the 2nd Century were carefully laid together and the initial fierce joy of plundering enemy torques and bracelets was soon lost. The century became very quiet in the dank, humid clearing. We all knew these men, we had joined them at the dilectus and then trained and marched with them and now they lay there, unmoving, their skin waxy and pale, their Army career over before it had barely even begun. Two of the slain were from the same section and some of that tent group stood crying without shame. Those tears felt infectious for the whole century.

One grieving man was on his knees and sobbed uncontrollably as he held the hand of a corpse that had been stabbed through the throat by a spear. Everybody knew the dead man was like his brother and his weeping section stood with pale faces and wrung their hands until Falco strode over and coldly ordered them to get the body onto a cart. The ashen-faced soldiers stood still, unhearing, until he barked the command again. He turned round, pointing at the men of the century who stood idly watching this lamentable scene and coldly issued orders to send them about their business. "Move the wounded, secure prisoners, gather the enemy weapons and be quick about it!" No one knew it then, many even quietly cursed Falco, but in time we would realise that discipline must take first place and having a task to finish does help take away the pain.

Galba turned to Borras. "Shall we go find Corvus?" he said quietly and the big man nodded with a sombre look.

The veteran soldier turned to his men. "Felix, Ignavus, get plundering for the section. We will share the spoils later. Saxum, help lift the wounded into carts. The rest, follow Borras," said Galba and as he turned to walk away they saw no other than Corvus, looking relatively clean and unmarked, walking towards them and carrying a large bundle over his shoulder.

Galba stood with his legs apart and spat cold words of angry astonishment, "You're alive? And without a scratch? So! You ran from your post? Worst of all, you left Borras! You abandoned a member of the section! Do you know the punishment for desertion?"

Corvus stopped in front of the section and came to intente before the bristling soldier. "I saw two men sneaking towards another of our picket posts, so I came up behind them and killed them. Then there was a great shout and the enemy was everywhere, so I stripped a native cloak off one of the dead men and hid in the bushes for a while, figuring how to get back. I saw Borras hack his way through a sea of enemies, but I am not his size. am I? So I hid," he said in a matter-of-fact tone.

"You *hid* in the bushes?" said Galba, trembling with anger. "You abandoned a Brother in a fight, then hid like a coward?!"

"Galba, please, let me finish," said Corvus. "Once the Cohort was surrounded I was stuck out there. I killed another for his helm and sword, and moved around doing the best I can. I killed eight or nine warriors, plus some archers and slingers who attacked from a distance. Also, I think I came across the chief of this tribe," he said, gesturing around to the mounds of dead Lusitanians with indifference. "Well, chief or not, I think he was important. He was surrounded by a group of warriors in similar armour and was barking orders, so I assumed he was. He walked over and took a piss in the bush I was hiding in, so I dragged him in and slit his throat and plundered what I could from him before his bodyguards realised he was gone. They saw his body and went into a fury. The last I saw of them they were charging off to attack the cohort. I have his helmet here, if you don't believe me."

He placed down his bundle made from a native cloak and kneeled to open it. The section all closed in to see some beautifully wrought golden torques of Celtic design. There were also bracelets and a few daggers that would fetch a great price, and an ornate helmet worked with gold inlay that had been crafted by a very skilled metal worker indeed. Curiously, the treasure was bloodied and smeared from being mixed up with a dozen or so severed hands.

Decius leaned down and picked up a hand with a look of curious disgust before staring at Corvus with a questioning look on his face. The scarred man looked at him evenly and shrugged.

"I cut the right hands off so I could prove to you how many I killed. I can show you where the bodies of them all lie if you like, unless they moved them," said Corvus as he stood up. His reptilian eyes betrayed no emotion and looked on with complete indifference.

The shocked Galba looked at the pile of hands and plunder and then back up to Corvus before looking around the section who were all equally amazed.

Ignavus whistled. "Fuck me! That's a good haul!" he croaked, his beady eyes shining as much as the gold laid out before him.

"Everyone shall have a share," said Corvus evenly.

Galba nodded. "Well, I am happy to be wrong! I swear on the Eagle this isn't the work of a coward," he said, looking at the scarred man. "Truly, I have never seen anyone do anything like that outside of the formation."

Corvus shrugged. "I was caught out and just made the best of a bad situation," he said in his hollow voice. "If I tried to come back I would be dead... and no use to anyone"

Galba nodded thoughtfully. "Well, I am just glad you are on our side, both of you!" he said, turning to Borras. "Right, everyone! Toss those hands away and stow the loot. Let's get these weapons loaded and get back to camp! I don't know about you but I have had enough of this shitty clearing," he said with a tired smile.

The cohort worked quickly and efficiently. Every medicus dealt with the casualties according to the priority of the wounds. The weapons and plunder was gathered as the numbers were tallied by the tesserarii. Everything was a picture of military efficiency, but Falco knew this was a big shock for many of the men. He looked towards the ox carts where the gathered wounded men moaned in agony. One screamed as his life blood ebbed from him; his frantic eyes rolled as death approached. A veteran medicus shrugged and moved on to a man who could be saved — a friend from the same section — as the dying man held him and wept quietly while the thick blood ran between the wounded man's muddied fingers. Another soldier who was a closer friend could not bear to watch. He was crying as he busied himself picking up Lusitanian weapons, casting looks back as the desperate cries became little more than faint whimpers, then silence. Many of the century ceased work and went quiet as this man breathed his last. His friend who could not watch sank to his knees and sobbed uncontrollably, his anguish seeming loud in the solemn air. Even Ignavus had stopped rifling the undergarments of a rich-looking warrior and seemed to have water in his eyes.

Falco shook his head as he looked at the miserable men. He knew they would deal with this better next time. The first time you lose a brother in the century is always a shock. He remembered a time like this when he was a young legionary. They had been protecting a trade outpost in northern Hispania and his small patrol was ambushed by Celt-Iberian bandits. His face softened as he thought of how he had wept so bitterly. *Even so, they must carry on,* he thought. He stalked around, quietly ordering the men back to work. He did not disturb the man on his knees; it was best to leave him be for a moment.

Vibenius called to the centurion from behind the carts where he stood with the optios tallying the dead and wounded. During a short discussion over the numbers, Falco spotted Borras and Corvus.

"I thought they were the missing men from the picket," he said with a nod in their direction.

"Not exactly sure what happened to them, Falco, I saw the big one wandering around looking for his scutum," said Vibenius, trying to clear his bloody nose. The lean centurion spat and called them over. The two hurried over and went immediately to intente.

181

"So, you did not fight with the 2nd. Where is your shield? You know its offense to lose it" he said to Borras whose muddied face stiffened with fear at the question.

"There was... Erm... No excuse!" said Borras, looking off into the distance with a sinking heart.

Falco turned his head to Corvus. "And you? Leaving the designated picket area?"

Corvus looked ahead and seemed to sigh a little. "No excuse," he said with a resigned voice.

The centurion spat on the floor again and eyed them both critically. "Well, nothing can be done right now. We shall wait until a rest day to see what punishment you will receive! Discipline is discipline and we must keep to the rules at all times."

He ordered them back to work and had Vibenius write down a reminder. He would get the full story about these two if he had to ask every man in the Cohort. *But not today,* he thought, looking around. He was satisfied all the enemy weapons were nearly loaded. The wounded were already moving out, groaning on their rumbling carts. His satisfaction diminished somewhat when he saw two of his legionaries who were stood admiring a fine looking dagger and not working.

"What do you think this is? Fucking market day with many fine wares to look at? Get back to work!"

Yes, he would punish them if there was an infraction of the rules, discipline is discipline. But not today. Today was punishment enough.

SPQR

Chapter 11

Decius walked slowly back through the temporary marching camp to the tent street of the 6th Cohort on uneasy legs, feeling nauseous. His wounded cheek had become infected and now felt like it was on fire. The medicus had given him a hot drink of strong herbs to numb the pain and they made him feel sick to the stomach. It had been more than ten days since the battle on the riverbank where the spear tip had run along the inside of the cheek piece of his helmet, slicing his cheek all the way to the jaw line. Later that day after the skirmish when he had removed his helmet the whole cheek fell open, exposing his teeth in a ghastly grin.

Kratos saw him coming and went to greet him. "*Salve,* Decius. You are looking much better. I told you it would get infected! By Apollo! A drunken dressmaker must have done that needlework!" he said, inspecting the rough stitching on the swollen, livid cheek with a critical eye. "What did the Medicus give you? Hmm, perhaps we should get you some yarrow to speed up the healing," said the Greek thoughtfully.

"Fuck knows what they gave me," muttered Decius weakly, holding out a small pouch of herbs to Kratos who immediately took some out and smelled them. The Greek looked annoyingly healthy to Decius; his own wounds so far had been minor, a slash to the arm and a gash on the shin where an enemy weapon had cut through his leather greave. But even this was just from a man who fell forwards dead as they took a small fortified village a few days ago.

"Are you cleared for action?" said Kratos with a sceptical look at the ugly facial wound.

Decius nodded and winced a little as he opened his mouth to speak. "I checked myself out of there," he mumbled painfully. "It stinks, it's full of malingerers and there is no plunder to be won sat around in the medicus' tent."

The Greek nodded with his white-toothed smile. "That's true! Mind you, all the pus and rot in there still smells better than Felix's farts!" he laughed.

Decius nodded but did not share the mirth as he winced from a sharp stab in pain. Kratos gave a quick, sympathetic smile and beckoned him into the section tent.

"Look who is here!" said Kratos, guiding the shaky Decius through the doorway. Galba greeted him warmly and Borras made him comfortable on a cot. The mood in the tent had picked up from the long, hard days of chasing the enemy since that first hard skirmish.

It turned out that every part of the army had been engaged on the day of the riverbank battle by various groups of Lusitani and Gallaeci warriors. The 8th Legion had been attacked by the main force as they built the camp and, luckily for them, the defensive rampart was mostly completed. The enemy had tried to entice the 8th Legion into an ambush all day using a great herd of animals in the distance to tempt the Romans with plunder, but the disciplined Legion had its orders and did not take the bait as they carried on working on the fortifications. The impatient Lusitani were now convinced the Romans were probably aware of the large force in waiting and were scared of them, frantically working so they could hide in their camp. The young and inexperienced had clamoured to assault the Romans before the works were finished and the war chief had foolishly relented.

The great war band, unaware of modern tactics, had surged into a gap in the unfinished palisade. The Lusitanians became packed in the small bottleneck where those at the front sought to escape from the disciplined Roman battle line, and those at the rear only shoved more forwards into the breach. The end result was a catastrophe and cost the lives of several thousands of their warriors.

The 9th Legion had been on a search and destroy mission for 'bandits' and came back loaded with plunder and prisoners after sacking several small, undefended tribal forts, one after another. The forts were offered terms as per Caesar's orders, but they would not surrender.

The 10th Legion had the least luck in terms of plunder. Several cohorts fought actions, but it was mostly against individual tribes who were converging with the large main force attacking the 8th Legion's camp. There was one engagement of note that was being talked about by the whole army. Everyone knew the story of the 6th Cohort and how they had been surrounded and trapped against a flooded river, yet managed to hold formation and cut down the best part of nearly a thousand warriors. Since all the shattering defeats on that day the enemy had tried running and hiding, moving from town to hill fort to village with the legions in hot pursuit. And now the greatest part of their army were cornered in one of the largest hill forts in the region! Some of the speculatores had estimated that the lone hilltop fortress had as many as twenty thousand warriors crammed inside, with countless amounts of women and children who all flooded in to avoid the burning, pillaging legions as they laid waste to the countryside.

"In the name of Apollo! What a big difference a little time makes!" said Kratos with a grin. "Felix finally has make his legs thicker. Well, one of them, anyway! Decius was the prettiest in the section and now looks like the Cerberus has bitten his face!

Ignavus has killed the biggest man in Hispania and Corvus said more than three words," he said, looking around with a smile. Felix looked at him sourly and gingerly bent his knee that was still a little swollen. He had come off the medicus' lists only four days ago where he, along with Decius, had followed the legions lying on top of a baggage cart with the other minor wounded.

"It's a pity your wit was not wounded in battle, Numidian. Ah! Of course. You do not possess any that could have been injured in the first place!" he said with a dour look. "You are just pleased because you have burned a few farms and fucked a few native girls without me!" His bright, blue eyes narrowed into slits. "I bet you have hidden away a little plunder for yourself!"

Kratos looked at the surly Felix, then sighed as he sat down next to Decius who was poking at his swollen cheek. "Do not worry, brother. The wound will heal and as a section we already have a good amount of plunder that Caesar is letting us keep!" He laughed, "Ahhh, the fights have been easy and life *is* good!"

"You were not saying that at the battle on the riverbank, were you, Kratos?" said Ignavus with a sneer. The bold comment surprised everyone, especially the Greek, who lost his grin instantly. The scrawny man had been drinking plundered wine since this morning and was looking flushed and red in the face.

"I seem to remember that *you* did not enjoy the situation, either, you little weasel!" growled Felix. "Keep your fucking thoughts to yourself, drunkard, or you will get a big toe in your ass!" he said, raising a bony foot for emphasis and staring hard at the villainous face of Ignavus who glared angrily back.

The blushing Kratos mumbled, "Well, I think we were all scared, more or less?"

"Yeah, shut it, Ignavus!" said Borras as he sat sharpening his blade. "How many farms and villages have we destroyed since then? We have been chasing and marching and burning for bloody ages! And now they have stopped running we don't have to march after them! I want to enjoy the little bit of rest we have before we start building siege works!" He leaned forward and glared at the scrawny man who sucked at his wine skin. "If you are so tough I look forward to seeing you when you storm a fortress with twenty thousand warriors inside it! In fact, I will stand behind you holding your harness so I can push you through the gate first!"

Ignavus' eyes widened a little and he took another big swig of the sour wine. Corvus chuckled in the corner of the tent and everyone looked at this rare sight.

"Yes, it is going to be a hard fight. There might be more room in this tent soon... but less space in Hades!" he said with a grotesque smile that chilled even heartless beasts like Saxum. The big brute shivered and screwed his piggy eyes up at Corvus.

"Sons of Dis! I reckon you do it purpose! Like the Gods have put you here to make me shit myself!" said the big brute, scowling at the scarred man.

Corvus shrugged and looked back at the sandal he was adjusting. "Once you accept the journey, it becomes easier to live with."

Saxum opened his mouth to say something but closed it, fished out his curious leather pouch from around his neck. He held it close to his lips and whispered indiscernibly to it as his beady eyes looked at the mysterious figure in the corner.

The tent was uncomfortable when Corvus spoke, and luckily he spoke very little. The buccina sounded the change of the watch at noon. In the quiet, tense atmosphere the signal startled everyone and all except for Corvus reached for weapons before smirking at each other's fright as they relaxed again.

There had been several moments where the Legion was 'stood ready' because Lusitanians were seen coming out from the fortress that was much less than a quarter of a mile distant, but the movement was mostly just small cavalry squadrons or individuals trying to get messages out to the Lusitanian tribes who did not come or the Gallaecian warriors who had already begun to retreat homeward to their mountainous lands in the north to avoid the unstoppable Legions. All of the desperate messengers had been captured so far. Caesar did not want to let them get away and the three Legions were all camped individually around the enemy position with small cavalry and auxiliary forts dotted in between to cut off any escape. A major breakout would only see the Lusitanians fighting three legions from various approaches in a most disadvantageous way for themselves. He had sent a tribune with a message to the fortress ordering them to surrender and as a whole people agree to being settled on the plains of lower Lusitania under Roman law so that they might finally give up being the hardy hill folk they were and become productive Romanised farmers. Of course, the commander knew they would never agree — something which Caesar did not want anyway. Victory through battle looks much better for a man who would be Consul in the Senate one day. So with his mind inexorably fixed on battle he called for a 'rest day' and began to formulate a plan for the assault of the fortress.

Back in the tent, as the signal for the change of the watch faded, Felix coughed away the embarrassment he felt for jumping at the sound of the buccina and called to Ictis in his most pleasant voice. "Ictis, my sweet! What is for lunch?"

"Food," came the reply from outside the tent. "Got food, haven't I?"

The section all laughed and Felix punched his cot in mock frustration that might have been genuine. "I know it's poxy food! What *kind* of food have you got?"

There was a slight pause and then Ictis replied hesitantly, "Erm? Tasty food? Yeah, tasty food!" And with that the section erupted into laughter and Felix threw his hands in the air with a look of utter disbelief.

"Juno's *cunnus*! I am like Socrates amongst Syrians!" he groaned in a pained voice before sinking back onto the cot after casting a disgusted look at the section who were laughing at his theatrical exasperation.

Galba walked through the tent flap. "Juno's *cunnus* indeed!" he said quickly. "Borras and Corvus, you need to be in uniform, full parade dress including plumes on your helmets. I will be back in a few moments to get you," he said, walking back out. The tent went quiet as Corvus and particularly Borras looked a little stunned. The rest of the section looked at them sympathetically. They could not believe that the 'desertion' from the picket post and the lost scutum at the river battle was going to be punished after all.

"Oh... It looks like bacon and something else," came the voice of Galba from outside.

"Yeah, tasty!" said Ictis in agreement.

Borras started getting into his full uniform and Kratos immediately got up to help. Corvus followed suit and the limping Felix helped him, too. Saxum scratched his balls and belched. "This is bollocks, this! In the shit for a flippin' scutum and for moving a bit from a picket? Maybe Tanicus will flog you himself and go easy, eh?" he said, trying to sound optimistic.

"The discipline is getting serious round here!" muttered Ignavus, tapping his long nose. "I heard about those two Legionaries who had their noses cut off for raping a Lusitanian woman. I mean, that happens half the time we storm a place anyway!" he said angrily.

"Yes, but the tribe had surrendered to Caesar, who promised them clemency," said Kratos over his shoulder as he helped with Borras' armour. "Our chief loves us, all right, but we have to obey the rules he sets."

Ignavus looked unconvinced. "Yeah, 'our' chief gets rich from all the towns and hill forts that surrender to him! And we only get to keep the plunder from the ones we take by force. *That's* why he sends Speculatores and Lusitanian traitors ahead to convince them to surrender so we miss out on the women and riches!"

Felix snorted. "You whine like an actor having his leg hairs plucked! Go outside and look over the rampart! That fort must be over a quarter of a mile long and just as wide! And it's packed full with half the tribes of the entire region. Just think how many people will have gold and valuables with them? How many will be women, eh?" he said with a grin.

Ignavus picked his nose and retorted, "I don't think it's *that* big. And besides, what if they *do* surrender to Caesar? We get bugger all! Did not think of that, did you, Socrates?!"

Decius groaned as he opened his mouth and winced as he aggravated his swollen cheek. "He has a point. We won't get *cac*," he croaked. "And if all the warriors they have left are trapped here, like people are saying? It might be the end of the campaign?"

The section was quiet as each man weighed up the risk versus the reward of attacking such a large hill fort that could make them very rich indeed, IF the defenders did not surrender to Caesar. These sombre thoughts were interrupted by Galba poking his head in the tent flap. "Ready, you two? Let's go! Outside with you!"

Borras took a deep breath and was patted on the shoulder by Kratos, who gave him a sympathetic smile of encouragement. He went out of the tent looking every bit the condemned man, followed by Corvus who looked uncaring as always. Centurion Falco stood waiting outside, glaring at them. He was in full uniform with the *phalerae*[77] on his chest polished to a high sheen and wearing several *armillae*[78] awarded for acts of bravery. These items were hugely important and endowed a great deal of pride and respect to those who earned them. If you were a brave fighter you might be awarded a variety of decorations for bravery, including the *hasta pura*, which was a miniature spear. Phalerae were large, medal-like bronze or silver discs worn on the chest harness, armillae were bracelets worn on the wrist or elbow, and torques were worn round the neck, or pinned on the chest. The highest awards were the *coronae*, or Crowns, which Caesar himself had won, as a nineteen year old officer, during the storming of Mytilene. The crowns varied, depending on the act of valour, and were made from simple materials like oak leaves or grass. However despite the humble components of the award this accolade would seal your status in the Legion forever as a 'good man'.

Most of the Centurions were 'good men' in terms of decorations. It cannot be said that *all* were good men in terms of virtue, as some had too much a fondness for wine, young boys, dice, corruption, punishment of lower ranks or rape, which would

---

[77] Roman army medals.
[78] Bracelets awarded as military decorations.

overtake military discipline, but all certainly were good fighters. Some, like Falco, were clearly better than others.

Corvus and Borras came to intente in front of the fearsome Centurion. He looked down and, gesturing to the gladius each man wore, growled, "Take those off! You won't be needing them where you are going."

Both men unbuckled the belt that held the weapon in place, then removed the sling they wore over their shoulders that carried the gladius and handed them silently to Galba, who stood beside them. Falco looked over their uniforms and picked up several things with them. "You scruffy bastards will ruin your big day!" he said sourly. Finally, he grunted, "Let's get this over with." Falco ordered the men to turn and march off. Borras gave a quick, desperate look to Galba, who looked away, shaking his head. Then the big man marched off towards the centre of the camp with Corvus behind him while Falco marched crisply next to them, shouting out the step.

SPQR

Chapter 12

"What are your thoughts, Publius?" said Caesar, looking across the large map table to the young man. Publius Licinius Crassus felt an instant surge of panic from the scrutiny and paused as the tent went silent and more than thirty pairs of eyes looked at him. He rubbed his smooth chin and took a moment to calm himself as he weighed his answer carefully in the manner the academy had taught him when he had learned rhetorical theory and public debate. It simply would not do to blurt out an answer and he desperately wanted to impress Caesar, grateful for the opportunity to express his military knowledge. He had listened to some of the senior military commanders opinions of a long, protracted siege and starving out the Lusitanians. There was much talk of surrounding the fortress with siege works, using ditches, ramparts and a palisade to link all three legion camps and the smaller cavalry camps that were dotted in the spaces between. Publius did not agree with them. Part of him felt Caesar did not agree, either. The young man looked at the map table with its small model of the hill fort and the three legion camps spread around it, and cleared his throat to speak.

"Well, Sir, I think a long and well-engineered siege is a bad idea. Yes, we shall undoubtedly lose much less manpower than a direct assault, but we shall also lose the initiative. This advance is gathering momentum and we have them on the back foot. Also to pause for a long drawn out siege would be reinforcing our reputation of pragmatic fighters without audacity, and your entire campaign so far has been about showing them we are different to the Legions they have faced in the past."

Publius took a breath and continued. "Furthermore I think to accept parley and surrender from them would be an unwise decision. These people have fought and rebelled too many times before. You have the majority of their warrior caste trapped and to a disadvantage. You could cut off what is left of their fighting spirit right here and now," he said, looking up at the commander.

"Yes, it could be to your own detriment, Caesar, because your army would take a huge amount of plunder from this siege, but conversely you would most likely find every single fortress left in the region capitulating to your terms. I'm sure if added together they would all give ample remuneration, not to mention the external factors like the glory of winning the battle rather than taking their surrender. Politically, this would look much better when reported back in Rome."

He coughed and looked around, ignoring the hints of contempt in some of the gathered men's faces before continuing, "The enemy has been on the run, so offering battle in the open will not yield results, for they will refuse. Starvation cannot be achieved without extensive siege works that would require our entire manpower and we have heard from our spies that this fortress is well stocked. Also, as I said before, a siege could potentially rob us of the initiative and leave our supply routes vulnerable. If we hold for much longer I suspect they will want to flee and probably will attempt a breakout in the darkest watch of the night. If they succeed they might once more revert to hit and run tactics, which could prove disastrous for us, Sir. So with all the factors taken into account I would say the best way to proceed is to take the hill by force! You should… I mean I would begin the assault immediately."

Caesar nodded and smiled at the young man, pleased to see the boy understood all the military necessities and the politics behind them. "Very good, Publius. I agree with you at the strategic level… But what of the tactical level? If we were to

194

attack? What do you think would be best to see our standards victorious over the fortress?" said Caesar in a questioning tone with a raised eyebrow.

It was hot and there was barely room to breathe in the command tent. The large map table in the centre was surrounded by the legates from each of the three legions along their respective Primus Pilus, all the military tribunes, junior tribunes, various other centurions of skill or merit and a whole host of scribes and clerks that sat around the desks that lined the walls of the tent. Publius wiped the perspiration from his brow and noticed that everybody was listening to him; even many of the clerks and scribes had stopped their scribbling to overhear his answer. He cleared his throat and resumed.

"Well, the fortress is accessible by three sides with the main gates being north and south. I would draw up the 9th Legion on the northern side and the 8th Legion along the eastern wall with the 10th on the south. As they are already camped in those positions, it makes sense to do so. I would use the bulk of the cavalry to cover the cliffs and down to the river on the western flank in case the enemy try to descend down some unseen path. The rest of the cavalry I would have in a loose cordon several miles out to get any word of enemy relief forces that might hinder the assault phase of the operation," said Publius, looking at Caesar and feeling those black eyes boring into him as if he was trying to read his thoughts.

The young Crassus continued. "I would launch the 9th and 10th at the same time from the north and south, respectively, which the enemy *should* suspect as a feint, especially if they initially went in at a slower pace. Then I would have the 8th launch a fast, clamouring 'main attack' on the eastern side, which would be the real feint. This should distract the defenders on all sides and perhaps even the odds for the 10th to get ladders on the walls, maybe even bring something to bear on the gate," he said, nodding thoughtfully.

Caesar smiled and looked around at some of the unconvinced faces. "We are of one mind, young man. Well, gentlemen? Does anyone have any nagging doubts about the plan from young Publius?" said the general, addressing the gathered commanders.

"Sir! I think it's best to make sure the vanguard is those with the most experience... So why does the junior 10th Legion in particular get this honour, young sir?" said the grizzled Primus Pilus of the 8th Legion with his tattooed, muscular arms folded defensively in front of him.

Publius looked at the fearsome man and felt a little surge of anger at this upstart plebeian with his thinly veiled insult on experience. No doubt he had clubbed some people over the head in the past but had he studied the campaigns of Alexander? Or Scipio? Or Marius? Probably not! Publius took a deep breath and looked the weathered Primus Pilus in the face, wondering if this oaf could even spell.

"Well, Centurion, all the other Legions have had considerably more plunder from this conflict. Also, this is the Legion that Caesar has personally raised. It is where Caesar has stayed and marched for the duration of this war. Honour dictates that they shall be the tip of the sword that will cut the Lusitanian snake in two!" retorted the young man with a look of resolve on his face that belied his years.

The Primus Pilus sniffed and shook his head slightly, but flashed a glance at Caesar, who smiled but narrowed his eyes at him and gave a barely perceptible shake of the head. The veteran coughed and scratched his chin restlessly. The Legatus of the 8th, seeing his senior enlisted man flag, took up the man's cause.

"What about the artillery? And what about the gate? Does the young 'general' have a plan for that? Or are we supposed to scale the walls like children climbing trees?" said the man in a smooth, patronising voice that made Caesar narrow his eyes further.

Publius held his gaze for a few moments, then replied, "Yes, of course. There are multiple options. The artillery could be massed with the 10th. I had the idea when I saw the artillery being transported on carts. I would have the engineer immunes put to work immediately on building mobile mantlets or galleries across the entire army as per the standard procedure for a siege. However, seeing as we have some of the smaller ballistae, I suggest the galleries for the 10th will be used to covertly transport the artillery closer to the walls without giving away the location of our main assault. The other legions will keep their scorpions and siege equipment to position them in support to the feints to the north and east."

The assembled men of military experience grumbled and looked at each other, disagreeing with this plan that went against the standard use of artillery and galleries. Caesar spoke, cutting them off immediately.

"Balbus? Feasibility of the plan?" he said, looking at his chief engineer and old friend from Rome, Lucius Cornelius Balbus.

"It certainly is innovative and unconventional. In terms of feasibility, it could work," said *Praefectus fabrum*[79] Balbus thoughtfully. "The 10th legion does have the most level and sloping approach with the least amount of rocks, so we could get the ballistae in position much quicker and easier on this side. Gods, we might even get close enough to put multiple volleys

---

[79] Officer in charge of engineers and artisans.

into that gate? It looked pretty weak from a distance," mused the veteran officer from the Sertorian war.

"Knowing these people as I do, they tend to hinge all their luck on holding a fortress, but keeping the gate free to sally out and attack or to flee in the night? The idea of moving ballistae up so quickly without screens or siege works is novel but dangerous," he continued. "*If* you could guarantee the following cohorts were close enough to protect my artillery in case of a surprise attack from the fort then we could do it and then get through the gate in record time. However, I would insist we have a battering ram following in reserve in case the ballistae fail and the gate is stronger than we think."

A tall Roman of the speculatores with a long moustache who stood easily in his Lusitanian tribal attire cleared his throat to speak. "Sir, that gate *is* weak. I rode through it four days ago and the whole thing is secured by a single wooden bar that looked as weathered as the gate itself. They had no pilings to the rear to shore it up and the planks on the front are half rotten." He smoothed his moustache thoughtfully, "Of course, it might have been reinforced since then. We could send up a couple of men immediately as messengers offering a parley just to get a view at it. But as of four days ago it was not blocked from the rear or reinforced. Several well aimed barrages from the ballistae might break it open and you could get a foothold inside with a cohort of two. It might save a few lives instead of all the men attacking the walls with ladders." he said in contemplatively.

The legatus from the 8th Legion interrupted, "I think that gate will fall easily enough with the battering ram! We should build works and proceed with a ramp to overcome the wall, and use ladders for all the flanking attacks. Do all this and the men will take the walls easily enough." He turned to look at Publius. "Using galleries to move artillery? My dear boy, why don't we stick to the rules of war that Rome has perfected over hundreds of years," he said in a fatherly but utterly patronizing tone which caused some of the senior men to nod.

"Agreed!" said Pug with a hard stare at the young Crassus. "Young master, it's best we stick with what we know!" The Praefectus Castrorum jammed his thick thumbs into his belt and stood looking pleased with himself.

Caesar sighed, clearly full of irritation. "Gentlemen! We are dealing with an enemy who has perfected fighting against us for hundreds of years!" countered Caesar with an icy stare at the objecting Legatus and then Pug. "I have neither the time nor the inclination for extensive siege works! We have them like fish in a pond and I am more concerned a timely siege will result in breakouts or harrying attacks from other tribal units. I want that fortress taken in the next two days and it is time for some fresh thoughts and ideas!" He turned to Publius Crassus and nodded, "Well done indeed, young man. I was planning on sending my 10th in first anyway, but you have some novel ideas for the deployment of artillery that we shall try tomorrow."

The General took a deep breath and leaned forward on the map table. Caesar spoke and now his voice was full of command.

"So, here it is! First things first. I want to know how strong the gate is!" he said, turning to the commander of the speculatores. "Go immediately to offer terms at the front gate and make sure it has not been blocked to the rear. Tell them anything, just to distract from our real reason. Hmmm... Ah, yes! Tell them I *will* meet with them tomorrow in person!" said Caesar with a wicked grin.

The lean speculator leader grinned back and snapped a smart salute. "I will go immediately, Sir!" he said before hurrying out of the tent, calling for his horse.

Caesar looked around the remaining assembled men. "So, we shall wait several moments and *if* the gate still is as it was, *all* Legions will attack in the manner which Publius described. The ballistae will try and open the gate and I shall have the 1st Cohort of the 10th ready to charge in the breach while the rest of the Legion takes to the ladders. The rest of the army may take to the walls *only* when the Eagle of the 10th is inside." He paused for a moment before continuing "We will have a ram for the gates north and south and if all else fails I want a ladder every few yards along that wall with our soldiers storming the place. I want that place to fall!" he stated with authority.

Caesar looked around the group, his dark eyes flashing from face to face. "So, let us get to work. Have all the ballistae transported here to the 10th in the dead of night. I want increased pickets through the dark hours to warn of any breakout *and* to cover the movement of artillery."

Caesar turned to the cavalry commander, "Have your men and some of the auxiliary cavalry light torches and ride around the foot of the western cliffs throughout the night to create a little diversion. Everybody else, get all the men with the skills necessary building these galleries that will carry a ballista."

He turned to the chief engineer. "Balbus, my friend, get to work on a design immediately. Oh, and I would like to see the first one as soon as it's built," Caesar added, looking at the Praefectus fabrum who scratched his big nose and nodded, "Yes, of course."

Outside the buccina sounded the change of the watch at noon. Caesar looked across the assembled command group."You all know your roles and places in the assault. We shall form up before daybreak tomorrow and begin the assault on my command. Legates? Go to your sectors, listen to the best experienced centurions and prepare your assault by escalade.

200

Plan your attack according to your ground and send me the dispositions of your Cohorts by the end of this watch. I will look over your reports, then finalise signals and timings for you. Expect riders in your respective camps within two watches with final confirmation orders. Make sure you send back a receipt for the orders and any final issues. I shall go and make a private offering to the Gods, then I shall be in my tent attending to administration matters until the next change of the watch."

Caesar paused and looked around at the expectant faces before giving a determined smile to the group. "Gentlemen, we have work to do, but by this time tomorrow we shall have glory to massage our aching muscles. Let us get to work and may Venus, Mars and Bellona watch over us," he said and the whole group nodded before it broke up into noisy conversation. The tribunes took orders from the legates and then turned to the clerks and scribes who started scribbling official orders furiously. The whole tent became a hubbub of activity and planning with timings and placements of formations being discussed as legates and military tribunes and Senior centurions all pointed and discussed tactics over the map.

Gaius Julius Caesar walked around the table to Publius Licinius Crassus and gripped the young man on the shoulder, giving him a huge smile. "Well done, young man. Some of our present company can be too prideful to admit they like a bold idea that can often seem like a roll of the dice. But I am not! Let's away to refresh ourselves, neh?" said Caesar, gesturing to his *lictors*[80] to follow him out of the noisy command tent to his own private quarters next door. There were a few in the tent who heard their commander's stinging remark and shot looks of envy at the back of the young man who followed Caesar out of the tent door.

---

[80] Official attendants and bodyguards of Roman officials.

SPQR

Chapter 13

A small group of soldiers in full parade kit marched away, leaving Pilus Prior Tanicus standing alone in the open area of the praetorium before Caesar's personal tent. He stood tight-lipped with his tattooed legs splayed as Centurion Falco marched forward with the two men from the section. The lithe Centurion ordered them to halt and left them stood to intente. He walked over to the Pilus Prior and snapped a salute whilst reporting.

"Centurion Falco of the 2nd Century reporting with the two chosen men!" he barked in his gravelly voice.

Pilus Prior Tanicus grunted and returned a casual salute. He tapped his vitis against his knee. The cohort had begun to recognise this gesture as a symbol of growing impatience or anger in the stalwart senior centurion. He stepped close to Falco and muttered a few words. Both men looked over to the other side of the praetorium where the 7th Cohort were formed up. Three large carts were lined up in front of the assembled cohort and they could see a man tied to each. Their arms were bound to the high sides of the cart whilst their legs were tied to the bottom of a wheel. They were naked down to the loincloth and each man had a centurion behind him holding a whip. The Pilus Prior of the 7th shouted the number and the flogging began. The sound of the lash travelled across the plaza and one man started crying out in pain from the third blow onwards.

Borras stood still to intente, facing the tent, and could not see what his two commanders were looking at but he had seen the men being tied as he was marched toward the praetorium. The sound of the lash followed by the agonised cries travelled well enough and Borras felt the sweat trickle from under his helmet rim. He remembered the scars across his father's back and the way his father would rather punch an unruly slave in the timber yards than give them the lash. The large man would tell him that it stole honour from men and was only worthy of beasts.

"Now I am the foreman, I would rather break the nose than give them that pain and the dishonour that goes with it," he remembered his father saying in his native Germanic tongue.

Borras listened to the sharp crack of the whips followed by cries of pain and began to shake. He listened to the Pilus Prior talking quietly to Falco and heard *Missio ignominiosa*[81] mentioned several times before Tanicus jerked his thumb in the direction of the flogging that had reached fifteen lashes now. Borras did not even notice the screaming man had passed out and was now silent.

Missio ignominiosa? For whom? Surely losing a scutum won't see me discharged from the Legion in dishonour? Will I be flogged and *given the Missio ignominiosa?* Borras wondered. He would rather fight a hundred enemies than be dishonoured! Borras said a prayer to his native god under his breath until he felt a small surge of calm and looked ahead, determined to endure what he must, even though he still felt sick to his stomach in fear and worry.

Pilus Prior Tanicus adjusted some of his phalerae and the torque around his neck that he had won by killing many warriors in another battle long ago. He said something to Falco who looked

---

[81] Latin: dishonourable discharge.

him up and down and nodded. Then he turned and stamped off towards Caesar's tent as Falco fell in behind the two men. The lictors standing guard outside the tent bade Tanicus enter and he went in through the doorway.

Moments later he walked out and bellowed, even though the distance was only a few yards, "Listen in! Detachment from the 2nd Century, 6th Cohort, stand ready... *PROCEDI...TE*!"

The lictors held open the flaps of the doorway and the men marched stiffly forward with Falco quietly calling the step.

"Listen for the halt!" he hissed.

The men marched through the doorway and stopped before the desk of the commander of the army, Gaius Julius Caesar. Centurion Falco moved to the left of Borras and Corvus as Tanicus moved to the right. All stood to intente and Pilus Prior Tanicus gave a crisp salute to the slim man behind the desk who had in front of him a small plate of bread and cheese.

"Sir, Pilus Prior Tanicus of the 6th Cohort, 10th Legion reporting with Legionary Borras and Legionary Decula from the 2nd Century commanded by Centurion Falco, Sir!"

Gaius Julius Caesar raised his hand in an elegant, relaxed gesture. "Stand easy, all of you. Such heroes deserve to relax a little, neh!" he said, looking at the young man who sat on a chair next to the desk eating an apple. "What say you, Publius? The Legionaries from the 10th certainly are fearsome to look upon, neh? I swear some of them look like they would have bested Diomedes at the siege of Troy!" said the Commander with genuine warmth in his voice.

"They do look rather fearsome," conceded Publius, looking quite shocked at the face of Corvus.

"Now then, a good tale often needs a drop of wine to speed it on the way. Dolus! Bring some wine! A cup for these brave men and their invincible commanders."

A short, podgy slave who had been speedily writing at a small desk to the rear of the tent immediately got up and went out of a side door into another room. He came back with a tray of cups brimming with good wine, which he offered to each of the assembled men.

"Anything else, *Dominus*[82]?" he said to Caesar with his thick Greek accent and the Commander shook his head as he picked up his own cup from his desk.

"To Venus, Mars and Bellona," said Caesar, raising his cup.

The assembled soldiers echoed the toast and drank before placing their cups back on the tray of the waiting Dolus who looked exasperated at their obvious awkwardness.

Caesar's intense black eyes flickered over all of them and settled on Borras. "So, tell me what happened, soldier? Unfortunately, I arrived with the rest of the 10th Legion after you had slaughtered half of the tribe! Your centurion and Pilus Prior said in their reports that you both were on the picket line and ended up being cut off in the ambush."

"Yes, Sir... We were, Sir... But we were keeping watch, honest, Sir! They did not come from our sector, see, and kind of got in around us! I did not mean to lose the scutum but they surrounded us and by the time I realised I had to fight my way back. Everything happened so fast, Sir!" said Borras, his voice faltering. Tanicus coughed and shot the big man a look of irritation.

---

[82] Latin: master.

"Sir, Legionary Borras was on the assigned picket post when the Cohort was ambushed. I personally saw him fight his way through the enemy force where he killed more than six men in less time than it takes to drain a cup of wine. He then joined the nearest century where he cut down even more men. He spent that time rotating through the front line, fighting without a shield... And considering how we were hard pressed and the nature of the fight, Sir, that was a feat in itself," said Pilus Prior Tanicus in his deep voice.

Caesar's black, shining eyes widened as he heard the story and he punched his own palm with a savage grin on his face. "Very good! I knew you were the right man for the 10th Legion, Tanicus! It seems wherever you command the men become heroes!" he said to the stout commander of the 6th Cohort who gave a wry smile and thumped his chest with a salute.

"Thank you, Sir! I try my best."

Caesar turned his gaze upwards to Borras with an impressed look. "So all of this happened in your very first contact with the enemy, Legionary Borras?" he asked.

Borras nodded. "Erm... Yes, Sir! First time, Sir."

"Astonishing! And what of you?" said Caesar, turning to the impassive face of Corvus. "I heard your story is just as impressive."

Corvus relayed the events to his delighted commander with aplomb, completely forgetting about killing the chief.

"Now, Legionary Decula," said Caesar with a grin, "are you being modest? I heard you killed someone important in the battle."

Corvus nodded. "There was one warrior who looked important, Sir, but I took his life because I was more irritated that he pissed on the bush I was hiding in," said the scarred man in a matter-of-fact voice and Caesar laughed, lifting his cup.

"Fearsome! Truly fearsome!" he said, taking a sip of wine. "I think you certainly have strength and skill in abundance in your unit, Centurion Falco," said Caesar, turning to him.

"Yes, Sir! They will honour the Legion in time, Sir!" said Falco in his abrupt, gravelly voice.

The Commander stood up from his seat and everyone stiffened to intente as he walked around the front of the desk, gesturing to Dolus. The Greek slave scurried to the back of the tent that was an array of shelving covered in neat piles of scrolls and came back carrying another small tray.

"Men, I think all of you have honoured the Legion already and brought honour to me," said Caesar with a serious look at each of them. Dolus stood ready with the tray next to the commander and from it Caesar took a golden armilla which he quickly twisted onto Borras' arm.

"Legionary, for your bravery. The Senate and the people of Rome salute you." Caesar offered his hand and Borras gave him a firm handshake. "What do your friends call you?" said Caesar to the stunned man.

"Erm… just Borras, Sir," said the large man with an awkward smile. Caesar gripped his hand tight with a deceptive strength. As he looked up his glittering eyes bored into Borras.

"Will you fight hard for me tomorrow, Borras? I need your strength!" he said in a quiet voice full of purpose.

Borras' large chest swelled with pride. "Yes, Sir!" he said with a flushed grin.

Caesar nodded with a smile and then moved in front of Corvus before taking another armilla from the tray and fastening it on the arm of the impassive man.

"Legionary, for the single-handed killing of a chieftain of our enemies. The Senate and people of Rome salute you." He offered his hand to Corvus, who took it. "What do they call you, soldier?" said Caesar, politely ignoring the deep lines of scars and studying a pair of dark eyes that matched his own in intensity.

"Corvus, Sir," came the flat reply. Caesar could feel the strength in the hand as he gave it a squeeze.

"I need your cunning, Corvus. Will you fight for me as you have done before?" said the Commander.

"Yes, Sir," said Corvus without any trace of emotion in the black, glittering eyes that mirrored those of the man before him.

Caesar released his grip and walked back behind his desk. He stood beaming at the four men in front of him.

"Well, I am very proud of this Legion, because it *is* mine. I called the dilectus and I had it raised, but now more than that I can see it is clearly blessed by all the Gods of war!" he said with a grin. "Your performance at the river bank has made the 10th the talk of the army and I assure you that forthcoming operations will seal your reputation for ever. I am sorry we cannot call the assembly to award the bravest amongst us in public, but there is much to do and, more importantly, after many long days of hard work I want you all rested. Resting up and then winning the battle is more important than the pomp and pageantry of patrician ceremonies, eh!" said Caesar with a smile before he continued. "Pilus Prior Tanicus, have your optio sent to me immediately as I would like to reward the four finest from the 6th Cohort. Each of you before me shall have two hundred and fifty denarii placed into your accounts from my own official spoils!" Caesar finished with a nod.

"Thank you, Sir!" rumbled Tanicus, snapping up a stiff salute. Caesar returned a relaxed salute and sat down. "That will be all," he said, taking up a piece of bread and motioning to the lictors to open the tent flaps.

Tanicus quickly and quietly grunted the commands and the four men saluted before they crisply turned about face and marched out of the tent. The following lictors closed the flaps behind them, leaving Caesar alone with his two companions.

"What say you, Publius? Fine specimens, neh?"

The young man nodded his head and looked thoughtful. Caesar saw this.

"What is it? You have something to say?"

"Sorry, Sir! Yes, they are fearsome, especially the one with the scars. But it's not that. It's just you mentioned there is no time to parade, and yet there have been men from three different cohorts paraded for punishments. Surely you could have publicly endorsed the men on the square instead of using it for punishments and gained more popularity," said the young Publius, looking quizzically at the older man.

Caesar laughed, "My young friend, now I believe you have entered into a discussion on a factor that was not and never will be explained in any manuals of war! Public parades for punishment serve a great purpose, especially in a newly raised legion. Each cohort will feel the sting of the lash as dishonour is collective in the legion — this part you surely already know.

Those centuries and the few men who were found lagging will strive a little further in the next battle." He gave the young man a sly grin. "I dare say you suspect some of these soldiers are already thinking me a tyrant. Well, what you will learn is that giving these men a day's rest instead of marching them up for a parade will gain me much more popularity! Especially when a number of soldiers wandering the tents now have new awards pinned to them. News of the decorations will spread because camp gossip spreads like fire in dry grass. Borras, Corvus and the fifteen others awarded today will show off their prizes and brag about a year's wage that they earned in a single day. All the others will strive to receive the same. Because I called a few men in quietly to reward them, everybody immediately thinks there are more people being rewarded than there actually are. Now every person who is seen marching to my tent could be a hero and others will get jealous, spread the rumour and exert themselves in battle. Soldiers expect a flogging and may grumble about the discipline but they positively hunger for gold and rewards," he said smoothly.

Publius' grave face lightened for a moment and he smiled back. "That's very clever!" he said, nodding with enthusiasm. "They will hear of the awards for bravery but cannot be sure of the numbers because you have not held an official parade. So in their eyes the number will seem greater! You are using the lower class love of gossip and wealth in a tactical way!"

Caesar smiled at his young companion's enthusiasm and took another sip of wine. "I am indeed! And if this strategy fails then I am pleased to announce the idea was from Dolus!" he said, laughing and looking at the Greek who stopped scribbling on the tablet he was writing on. The portly little slave, without looking at his master, heaved a huge sigh and shook his head in disgust as he carried on with his work, pretending not to notice the remark. His impudent actions only made Caesar laugh harder.

210

Chapter 14

The mood inside the camp on the evening before the battle was full of expectation. The gathered men of the 10th Legion watched the priests lead a bull, a ram and a boar around the outer perimeter of the camp before guiding them to the praetorium. In the light of the setting sun many of the soldiers solemnly watched the animals that were wreathed with garlands sacrificed in a ceremony that purified and protected all within the camp. Offerings were placed at the altar before the Legion's Eagle as two of the great birds circled high above. Many saw this and the priests were quick to say that omens were good.

The men were satisfied and at peace with the Gods but many, despite virtually all of them having known the chaos of battle by now, were not at peace with themselves and did not sleep soundly that night. Many took to busying themselves with various tasks while sitting around the fires and talking quietly amongst friends. Wills were rewritten and handed in to the tesserarii and optios for safekeeping. Others sharpened weapons that already had a sharp edge. A few bold souls loaded their belts with leather thongs to tie the hands of prisoners and some boasted about the numbers they would kill. Their remarks always received jeers and raised eyebrows or calls for wagers. Indeed, quite a few made the odd bet over it.

Only the veterans seemed relaxed. They walked amongst their own sections and centuries, giving a few words of encouragement to those with nervous faces or sat discussing plans to gather the most plunder from the fortress once inside.

Many disliked the nerves or boasts of the younger legionaries in their sections and sat around talking with old friends before they retired to sleep, telling them they would see them after the battle. The younger and less experienced soldiers sat up alone or in groups with their thoughts. Even with the combat experience of the recent days and weeks this was more than just the largest battle many had ever faced — it was the storming of a well-prepared and well-defended fortress full of enemy warriors. Fear walked the lanes of the camp that night and found many hearts to creep into. It was in this atmosphere that the veterans, the brave and uncaring snored fitfully while others fidgeted in restless sleep and more than a few never even slept at all.

No instruments were sounded for the reveille and in silence the army was woken in the dark by centurions and optios hurrying from tent to tent. In nervous anticipation of what was to come every man armed and armoured himself quickly and quietly in the chilly gloom. Friends helped each other tighten straps on chainmail shirts and secure kit, oaths were sworn and lucky charms were kissed or grasped one last time before falling into their cohorts on the sagularis, ready to move out. With mouths hastily stuffed full of bread and with quiet, minimal orders the legions were marched silently into place before dawn.

In the dim light the rumbling galleries for the siege had been drawn up in front of each legion, as was the proper form. But those of the 10th were larger and particularly ingenious. Praefectus Fabrum Balbus had the ballistae lying flat inside the galleries, supported by several sturdy poles. These would be removed and the ballistae would be eased to the floor as the gallery rolled onwards. The artillery immunes, along with many auxiliaries, had been tasked to push the heavy galleries until their weapons system could be removed for action. Each ballista would be set up within range of the gate to get maximum surprise and effect.

The whole 10th Legion was drawn up in a narrow version of the *duplex acies*[83] formation with the first row of cohorts being the 7th, 3rd, the 2nd on the left, the 1st going for the gate and the 6th being the furthest to the right.

The Lusitanian hill fort had a squat stone gateway but the rest of the fortifications were a thick wooden palisade with a deep ditch before it. The rough road to the main gateway once had various huts and outbuildings dotted along it, but they were now charred, smouldering ruins as the Lusitani had burnt them to provide no cover for the advancing enemy.

The fortress was just a hulking black silhouette in the darkness as the legions stood silently in the gloom. After what seemed like an age the sky began to redden and then the blacks and greys of night turned into the colours of day as the sky turned pink with a hint of blue shining through it. The day was becoming clear and the air was cool as men shivered or fidgeted, and now there was a constant low murmur of noise: a man clearing his throat, a whisper between friends, someone adjusting their helmet, another bending down to fix a greave or a sandal. The soft morning breeze swept over the stationary army, making the horsehair plumes attached to the helmets gently wave like the vexillum at the head of each cohort.

'Two Smiles' looked up at his own standard, then back at the sea of faces behind him in the dim morning light. Some looked pale and fearful, but he saw many looking grim with determination. He even noted several were grinning in anxious excitement. He turned back to face the hill fort again and was glad the low light hid his own rare smile of content. Every little movement now seemed to be full of nervous anticipation.

---

[83] Two chequerboard-style lines consisting of 5 cohorts in each line.

The rising hill before them with its deep ditch and steep bank topped with the tall, spiked palisade was a good few hundred feet away, but it felt much closer. Many Lusitanians could now be seen on the walls here and there. One ran along the wall and disappeared as another yelled something in alarm. More and more shapes began to appear on the walls as the pink sky turned light blue and the sun split the horizon, lighting up the millions of droplets of dew on the fields and the glittering, silent rows of soldiers in full battle array that stood in perfectly disciplined ranks upon them.

An auxiliary cavalry formation made of tribes who had long since submitted to Rome and now supplied her with warriors swept past to the rear and galloped off to the western flank to augment the forces watching the craggy cliff face. The auxiliary skirmishers checked and rechecked their bows and slings while they chattered away in Greek and other curious languages.

The sections from the 10th Cohort who had been drafted to push the secret weapons made some last checks on the galleries to make sure they could roll up the gentle slope. From a distance these looked like the galleries the rest of the army was using. They had skins on the roof that the servants were now soaking with a little water to help with the ruse so the enemy would suspect they were prepared to get close to the walls. One of the artillery immunes shouted at a servant who carried the buckets to be careful. If the water soaked the torsion springs the artillery piece could be rendered useless.

The galleries were a good decoy; however, on closer inspection the wheels were much larger than normal to allow for the weapons system inside. They would be pushed forwards but all channelled towards the gate and would deposit their contents a ballista shot away from their target. The first shot they would each fire could be crucial and the crews knew it. Even now in the stillness Praefectus Fabrum Balbus galloped back and forth to speak with the artillery immunes with each gallery, making sure every team was ready for action.

Pilus Prior Tanicus walked between the ranks, speaking to each of the centurions, checking the wall ladders were ready for escalade, encouraging those who looked like they needed it and laughing with those who looked in good spirits. All the while he kept repeating the legion's motto as he stumped through the ranks of the cohort on his strong, tattooed legs.

"Remember, boys! We are the 10th Legion. If it's standing up, cut it down! If it's lying down, stamp it flat!"

He grinned savagely as he said it and you knew that this man would attack the fortress alone if asked. More than just a soldier, he was a warrior. In time we came to realise that the fearless presence of men like him in battle was beyond priceless.

As the centurions swaggered proudly through their own unit the breeze made the vexillum of each cohort flutter. The embroidered Fighting Bull of Hispania, the symbol of the 10th Legion, shone proudly in the early morning light.

"This is *cac,* this!" grunted a fidgeting Saxum. "That shitty fort is a fat whore ready for the fucking and here we stand with our dicks going limp! Why ain't we attacking, eh?" he muttered with a sour expression on his ugly face. Felix spat on the floor and looked around quickly.

"Caesar is not here. I bet he is having some discussions about the surrender of the town," he said anxiously, spitting on the floor again. "There is far too much spoil in there to hand over to the likes of you!" he gestured towards Saxum, wrinkling his nose as if from a bad smell.

"What do you mean?" said Saxum, squinting his piggy eyes under the rim of his helmet. "I am a respectable gentleman in the company of you shithouses!" he said with a leering grin.

Felix sighed and examined his dirty fingernails. "My dear fellow, *you* are the shithouse! All day nothing but bad sounds and worse smells emanate from you! It's amazing that you cause no ill effect on me nor cause the property price in our section to plummet, for if I were a building I would be the temple of Jupiter Capitolinus in Rome!" he said with a lofty air.

"More like a rickety old shed full of used up whores with nowt but disease in their *cunni*!" scoffed Saxum. "Look at your spindly legs! Any temple with columns like that would fall down when a priest tried to crack a quiet fart!" he said with a sneer.

Borras sniggered and Felix looked around at him. "Oh, another great shithouse in agreement! By the well-used *cunnus* of the chief Vestal Virgin, there is a surprise!" he said in a loud voice that set Centurion Falco stalking through the ranks.

"Shut your mouths and watch your front," he snapped with his hawkish eyes glaring across the section, particularly at Felix who wore his most innocent face.

A cornu split the silence and its cry announced the arrival of Caesar alone on horseback. The Primus Pilus bellowed the whole Legion to intente, which everybody did crisply and with a good show of discipline. Caesar immediately asked him to stand the men at ease as he trotted to the front of the formation on his horse. His scarlet cloak hung easily and his breastplate was polished to a high sheen. The slim commander trotted along between the front rank and artillery units with an air of complete relaxation, offering morning wishes and using his extraordinary memory to call on men by name. His easy manner and open affection to the lowest ranks made even gruff bastards like 'Two

Smiles' nod and say, "He is all right... for an officer!" The lone commander returned to the front and centre of the 10th and began to address the Legion in his loud, oratorical voice.

"Brothers! *My* soldiers of the 10th Legion!" he cried. "I have offered these people terms of surrender, I offered to save the lives and freedom of the men, women and children," he paused and let the news spread to the back of the gathered formations.

Nobody dared to move or say a word but a collective wave of disappointment swept through the men. There were a couple of brave shouts of discontent from the back, which had the centurions glaring through the ranks to spot the culprits. You could almost taste the anger and disgruntlement in the air... just as Caesar intended.

The general paused for a moment, looking at the sea of angry faces before he drew his gladius and held it aloft, pointing to the fortress. "I bade them come down from the fortress and pile up their arms in peace... But... *They refused*!" he shouted in well-acted anger. "They spat in the faces of the envoys and said to them, 'Roman soldiers will *never* capture this hill!' They *laughed* as they said it!"

The assembled legion sparked into life at this and many voices shouted in anger and happiness that the assault might still happen. "Let us attack them, Caesar!" came a loud cry from the ranks that had the centurions whipping their heads round to identify the bold individual.

Gaius Julius Caesar laughed and said something to the group of mounted officers who had galloped up behind him at the signal of the drawn gladius. The men listened intently and nodded in agreement with their commander. Several galloped off to the northeast where everybody could see in the distance the left flank of the 8th Legion formed up, ready to advance on the eastern side of the hill fortress. Caesar turned back to the 10th.

"I think I shall take your advice! We shall put an end to the barbaric Lusitanians once and for all! Then we shall march north, rooting out their foul friends, the Gallaeci, destroying every such fortress until we reach the ocean! These swine are ready for the roasting!" he shouted, gesturing to the stronghold behind him. "What say you? Shall we light the fire?"

Every man that heard him roared their approval while those at the back or on the flanks waited for parts of the speech to be shouted back. Caesar smiled and enjoyed the scattered cheers and the expectant, bloodthirsty faces of his men looking up at him.

Within several moments the distant noise of the massed instruments of the 9th Legion blared from the north and was echoed by a huge battle cry that went up, out of sight, from behind the fortress. Caesar turned with a grin to the distant noise, then looked back at the expectant faces of the 10th and raised his gladius into the air once more.

"Soldiers of the 10th Legion! The fortress is my gift to you! Don't you want it?" he yelled and the army shouted back that it did!

He continued, his face a picture of fury. "*My* soldiers, *my* comrades! *My* brothers! Don't let those dogs stop you! *If it's standing up, cut it down. If it's lying down, stamp it flat!*" cried Caesar, swinging his sword in the air.

The Legion roared its approval and every man began picking up their shields, scaling ladders, others even drawing their gladius in excitement. The pairs of artillery immunes who were in charge of the scorpion bows lifted their weapon system onto their shoulders and prepared to move forward. Every Pilus Prior bellowed to his respective cohort to stand ready. All eyes followed their general as he rode to the command group on the right flank. Caesar pointed his gladius to the officer of the musicians and nodded the signal with a savage grin.

The massed instruments of the legion blasted its clarion call to advance and every centurion bellowed the command on the last note with perfect timing..."*PROCEDI...TE!*" The men of the 10th Legion roared a mighty battle cry as they tramped forward in long, narrow formations, chainmail and weapons causing a hiss of metal on metal. Thousands of feet hitting the ground in unison made a noise deeper than battle drums and the crescendo was amplified by the rumbling galleries as the Legion marched inexorably forward with the glittering Eagle of the 10th at its head.

"By the Gods, my fucking balls feel bigger than ballista stones!" yelled Felix excitedly above the din. "I feel like Achilles storming the walls of Troy!"

Borras laughed nervously, "Don't say that, you idiot! He did not get into Troy using a ladder!"

"Yeah!" muttered Ignavus over the din. "And he bloody well died when he got inside, too!" he added nervously.

Many faces looked left and right to friends and comrades. Savage grins were exchanged. Some faces were pale and staring straight ahead; others looked grim and determined. The 'Clank, clank, clank, clank' with the matching hiss of metal on metal sounded much louder than before. This was what it was to be in a Legion marching in full battle array!

The fortress walls were thick with Lusitanians who had previously stood unmoved, watching the spectacle of the formed

219

up Romans. They now began to shout and mill about with the signal to advance. Many rushed off and others appeared in their place.

The auxiliary slingers and archers picked up their small wickerwork mantlets and ran forward ahead of the scorpion bow teams who jogged along with their much heavier equipment to set up in the designated areas. The scorpions were concentrated in groups so the cohort formations could march between them unhindered. Once deployed, all missile troops began to pepper the palisades with stone, lead shot, bolts and arrows. The Lusitanians fired back arrows and a few javelins came arcing down to skewer some of the lightly armoured auxiliary soldiers. The screams could be heard before the 10th had covered half the ground in its orderly marching step.

Ignavus stuttered a prayer. "G... G... Gods! p... p... protect us!" he said, looking up at the looming hill fortress that seemed larger with every step.

Kratos looked a little pale as he turned to swear at him. "*They* will need the Gods today! Not us! Today we will win!" he said with a look of grim resolve on his face.

He was third from the front and in charge of holding the ladder firm at the foot of the wall. Every soldier marched the deliberately slower pace up the gentle slope of the hill. No pilum was in hand today, just the scutum and the other hand empty to climb the ladder. Centurion Falco's gravelly voice shouted out, "You know what's coming, boys! Don't forget your place in the *testudo*[84] when it's called!"

---

[84] Latin: tortoise. Formation where interlocking shields were used to protect the soldiers from the top and sides.

The sun was fully above the horizon when the cornu and *tuba*[85] of the 8th Legion announced their advance, causing a slight reprieve in the enemy fire from the battlements of the southern wall. The Lusitanians on the palisade ran up and down in panic, many pointing to the east. One warrior stood on the gatehouse, yelling and gesturing down to the advancing Romans as a well placed bolt from a scorpion bow punched clean through his stomach, sending him screaming backwards from the gatehouse. The two immunes who served the weapon grinned and laughed as they rapidly began winding back the torsion mechanism for the next bolt.

The scorpion team next to them saw the shot and jealously looked to better them by shooting at a group of warriors on the palisade wall. The bolt soared on its arcing trajectory and slammed through one warrior while punching the man behind off the back of the rampart and out of sight. The rest of the Lusitanians ducked for cover as the artillery immunes grinned and one of them quickly scratched another two marks on the legs that supported the artillery piece. These deadly, accurate weapons began to take their toll and many of the enemy on the walls hunkered down behind the palisade. The galleries had rumbled up to the scorpion positions and were now beginning to dispatch their contents. A great many immunes crowded and heaved as the large and fearsome-looking ballistae were beginning to be quickly erected, much to the alarm of the Lusitanians.

A man screamed from the front of the 6th Cohort as an arrow struck him in the thigh. Many more arrows began to flash down through the morning sunlight, probably directed from someone on the wall. They were firing skywards from the dead ground behind the palisade and the soldiers of the 10th were now in range of this deadly rain from above.

---

[85] Straight trumpet.

"Listen in the 6th Cohort!" roared Primus Pilus Tanicus. "*TESTUDO!*"

With a great drumming of shields the centuries closed their ranks and advanced up the hill in six compact, armoured blocks. As they did so, the Lusitanians gave a roar and, ignoring the incoming fire, sprang up to man every inch of the wall with archers, slingers and warriors throwing rocks.

"Close that fucking gap!" shouted Galba as Kratos struggled with his scutum overhead. He had seen through the gap in the shields up at the looming barrier of the palisade.

"They are all over the walls!" yelled the Greek with an ashen face.

The rain of missiles intensified and the clatter of impacts became deafening. The distinctive thud of the scorpion bows and ballistae from behind us could no longer be heard, even though the artillerymen were frantically trying to clear the palisades of defenders. A man in the front rank of the advancing century tripped and fell flat on his face as the man behind stepped on his back. He lay cursing on top of his shield but knew he could do nothing as the formation trampled over him. The century could not stop, being so close to the defensive rampart and in the killing area. Once the formation had passed the trampled soldier scrambled to his feet and, under his shield, he ran to join the back of the testudo with nothing more wrong with him than injured pride, sending a quick thanks to the Gods.

The century crested the final slight rise, then descended into the defensive ditch. Gaps instantly appeared in the formation and screams of the wounded could be heard over the rattle of incoming missiles. The slope was steep and the grass was still damp as men slipped and the testudo began to come apart under a vicious hail of enemy fire. Arrows, javelins and rocks rained down as wounded men fell to the floor crying out for mothers and the Gods. Someone frantically yelled, "We are trapped!"

Falco, leading from the front, heard the desperate cry despite the rattle of missiles hitting the shields. He spun round and immediately punched the frightened man viciously in the face.

"LADDERS FOWARD, YOU *CUNNI*!" roared the Centurion in anger. "CLOSE IN, SHIELDS TOGETHER! Get those fucking ladders on the wall NOW!"

The warlike soldiers hurried with the task while the frightened ones jumped as discipline kicked in. The ladders were dragged through the formation and began sliding up the wooden palisade. The deadly and accurate fire from the scorpions was making itself felt as a Lusitanian warrior dropped onto the testudo and crashed through the shield roof. Saxum stared in disbelief at the screaming man who had appeared before him. Decius began to kick at him.

"He is still alive! He is still alive!" he yelled, fumbling for his gladius that was still sheathed as he held his scutum aloft.

Saxum whipped out his pugio as the crazed warrior grabbed his legs, frothing blood at the mouth. He stabbed him hard in the head but the blade skittered off the skull, peeling a large flap of skin and partially severing an ear. The dying warrior screamed and thrashed about as multiple men began to stamp and stab in alarm. Decius finally plunged the tip of his gladius in the warrior's throat and his blood joined the rest that was beginning to pool in the ditch.

"Fucking horny bastard was trying to fuck me leg!" said Saxum with his gurgling laugh, his piggy eyes gleaming wildly.

"I hope they die a little easier than that one!" said Decius, his face covered in a sheen of sweat.

"What is the fucking delay?" shouted Felix with a worried look on his sharp face. "We are standing in pretty much the worst place in the world here and gentlemen like me prefer more refined pleasures than dying in some shitty ditch!"

A great crash and shouts of alarm came from the left as a volley from the massed ballistae punched holes in the gate, smashing the wooden beam that locked the barricade. The Lusitanians inside had not sealed up the gate or blocked it from the rear, preferring to keep it accessible to sally forth and attack the Romans. Now the aged wooden gate splintered and sagged under the concentrated artillery fire. A huge, well formed testudo from the 1st Cohort now raced to the weakened gate and the defenders in that sector became panicked, trying to shore up the splintering broken doors.

"LET'S GO! UP THE LADDERS!" came the shout from Falco as four of the century's ladders were now against the wall. The scorpion bows now concentrated all their fire on the areas at the top of the ladders to clears a path for the troops about to scale the defences.

Borras climbed behind another man, looking at the frantic face of Kratos through the rungs as he strained and pulled the ladder back towards the wall. One of the defenders on the palisade above pushed with a pitchfork high above him, trying to topple it. The orderly testudo had seemingly gone to chaos in the steep ditch, but the century had formed up in some sort of cohesive unit, each man instinctively finding a place in the formation without commands.

Borras got to the top of the ladder as the body of the first legionary sailed screaming back down into the ditch. Centurion Falco and another soldier had scaled the top of the vertical log fortification and were already on the earthen rampart side by side with a huge throng of warriors hacking and slashing at them. Borras yelled a desperate war cry and jumped into the men, using his scutum as a ram. The huge man smashed the crowd backwards on the eight foot wide rampart and gave room for two more legionaries who sprung off the ladders down onto the hard-packed mud.

A tough veteran from the 2nd century stabbed into the neck of a broad warrior and the Lusitanian fell gurgling to the floor, choking on his own blood. Corvus nimbly hopped down off the ladder and stood by him, followed by another man, then another. Decius now joined the fray and soon the century had a foothold with three men facing either way and the men at their backs fresh from the ladders facing their shield towards the town as a hail of missiles flew up from the seething mass of enemy below.

The split formation began advancing down the walls as others hurried up the ladders to reinforce the foothold they had gained on the palisade. Decius stabbed several times with deadly accuracy over his shield at a warrior with a bald head and strange tattoo markings on his neck. The man parried every blow with his small buckler and hacked a vicious blow in return that split a huge notch in the top of Decius' scutum, missing his face by a hair's breadth. The man was clearly well trained and was looking for a counter strike. Falco, who was now atop the wall and commanding the advancing lines, gave the signal for the change.

Behind Decius, Felix was holding his harness strap and shouted "Change!" echoing the centurion's command.

The thin man grinned as he took the front. "I will kill this bastard! Just watch!" he said and lunged forward with a vicious low strike that the warrior countered with a blow to the helmet of Felix that made his ears ring.

"You filthy *cunnus*!" howled Felix in anger and aimed a high blow that was a feint while he smashed his scutum downwards, the bottom rim smashing the foot of the warrior who jumped back with a cry of pain. Felix grinned and stabbed forward for the kill as a scorpion bolt flashed past and tore through the bald warrior, leaving a gaping wound sideways through his chest, jutting broken ribs and gore. The man sank to the floor and died almost instantly as Felix swore and yelled over the ramparts in the direction of the scorpion gunners, shaking his gladius at them in a rage, "TOO CLOSE! *TOO* FUCKING CLOSE, YOU DUMB SHITS! I swear on Bellona that..." Felix was cut off as stone cracked him on the back of the helmet and he staggered from the blow, nearly falling off the ramparts altogether.

Galba grabbed the stunned Felix and shoved him forward angrily. "Shut it! Face the enemy or you will get worse from me!"

The veteran now looked down at the scene in the fortress. The 1st Cohort had broken through the gate and was engaged in vicious fighting as they pushed past the defences and into the settlement. The narrow lanes and streets between the round stone houses with their pointed thatched roofs were packed tightly with warriors, women and children all surging back and forth, mingled together. Many were fighting, many were throwing anything that came to hand, many were screaming and crying out, while others were desperately trying to escape. A group of women had mounted the thatched roof of one of the houses and bared their breasts, screaming to the Lusitanian warriors in desperation to inspire them. They knew the fate of the vanquished; they knew what the Romans would do to them.

Some of the huts began to smoulder as fires broke out and hundreds were fleeing to the western cliffs or the north gates which were now engaged by the advancing 9th Legion. Borras looked at the young warrior he was fighting whose eyes flicked down to the Roman soldiers pouring in through the shattered gate. The Lusitanian glanced back at Borras and suddenly jumped over the palisade wall into the outside ditch, clearly preferring his chances getting past the auxilia and cavalry. The other cohorts were swarming the walls and many Romans were now jumping down from the rampart to fight amongst the streets inside the fortress.

Falco checked the sector was clear on the wall and jumped down to join the furious fighting inside the settlement. "2nd CENTURY... FORM UP ON ME!" he roared in his gravelly voice and men began jumping down to form a loose battle line in the muddy space between the rampart and the huts. Lusitanians now began to attack in vicious desperation. Women, children and the elderly stood at the back throwing rocks and some even pushed forward with the men folk to fight the Romans as their battle lines were forming up.

Pilus Prior Tanicus was now striding back and forth in the mud, indifferent to the swarm of projectiles sailing through the air, barking commands to dress the line. His 6th Cohort was flanked on its right by the fortress wall and now linked on its left flank with the 1st Cohort who had secured the gate. He grinned as he glanced up at the ancient stone gateway and saw the aquilifer climb up with a small bodyguard of legionaries. The glittering Eagle of the 10th now stood aloft the ruined gateway. The walls were taken. The gate was ours!

The soldiers still outside who were crowding the bottoms of the packed ladders now abandoned them and sprinted along the defensive ditches to gain access through the ruined gate. The men that streamed under the gateway were spreading left and right to reinforce the growing battle line of the 10th Legion that now stretched along the entire southern wall of the fortress. The continuous front of legionaries began its grisly work of slaughtering the enemy people.

Pilus Prior Tanicus gave the word and instruments of the cohort blared the advance into the smoky air. The formation moved forward inch by inch, killing everything in its path. Ignavus looked forward along the line and saw he was three places from the front. He nearly lost his grip on the harness he was holding as the man in front shifted forward... A legionary had fallen. Now he was only two places behind, he thought, stepping over the muddied corpse of a tribal woman. The Lusitanian warriors were screaming blood-curdling war cries and battering themselves against the impenetrable wall of Roman shields as the ground became thick with bodies and sticky with blood like a ploughed field on a rainy day.

"These goat fuckers will have reason to scream soon enough!" shouted Saxum, standing in the rank to the left, his deep voice nearly drowned by a shrill shriek from the front as someone received a mortal blow. Ignavus glanced up at the big man, who smirked as if his comment had caused the scream.

Saxum looked down with an ugly grin. "Told you so!"

The centurion's whistle sounded and the clatter of shields overtook the sound of battle as the front rank of legionaries filed back for a well earned rest. Then the noise of battle rose again as the Celtiberian warriors faced a fresh, grim-faced legionary. The smell of leather, sweat and iron was becoming mixed with the usual stink of battle, the stink they never mention in the glorious poems and the stories in books. It's the same smell that you have in a slaughterhouse, the stink of shit and blood.

Decius stepped forward and kicked something, but managed to keep hold of the man in front by the harness as he began his work stabbing over the shield at a tall and thin-looking Iberian with a wicked face. Looking down at what nearly tripped him, he saw a wounded man looking up at him — no, just a boy, no more than fourteen perhaps. He looked small, curled up in the thick mud. The first flush of beard darkened the chin of a pale face that was devoid of colour like all dying men have. The boy clutched his intestines into the gaping wound at his belly and was buffeted by the feet of the man fighting in front. One hand grasped weakly at the leg of Decius and the watery eyes pleaded... but there was no time for mercy. As Falco had told them in basic training, such mercy can be rewarded by a dagger to the groin as you pass the enemy by!

Decius gritted his teeth and stamped as hard as he could on the boy's neck. Crack! The boy screamed as his jaw broke open and blood and teeth slid from his ruined face into the muddy morass. *Cac*! The damn kid had moved and caused more harm to himself! Cursing, he gave another stamp that broke the boy's neck like a dry twig. Decius instantly felt sickened, but he remembered what his uncle Haterus had told him about such things. It was the nature of battle and he would get used to it. *There is no time for mercy,* he thought. *Remember the Legion motto: "If it's standing up, cut it down. If it's lying down, stamp it flat!"*

The clear sky was now streaked with plumes as many huts began to billow smoke from the thatched roofs that had caught fire. The roars and screams and clashes of steel reached a blood-curdling crescendo. Lusitanian men, women and children now tried to get out of the ring of steel and jumped from the palisade on every side. Many even flung themselves from the cliffs to their deaths to escape the bloodthirsty horde of Romans.

One group of well-armed warriors roared a battle cry, charged the 1st Cohort and died fighting bravely to the last man. This marked the last real resistance as the surviving Lusitanians began to throw away their weapons and drop to their knees in surrender. Now the 10th Legion lost its cohesion and the formations broke apart. The scene was like something from Hades as men ran forward, whooping and snatching gold and silver torques from warriors, collecting prisoners or dragging women off into huts.

Galba anxiously shouted to the section, "Remember the plan! Remember the plan!"

The men that heard him ran forward to collect prisoners for booty. Kratos shuddered when he saw a legionary of the 1st Cohort corner a woman with her small child. The soldier, covered in mud and blood, stepped forward and kicked the child hard in the chest. The small boy flew backwards into a wall and fell lifeless to the floor like a doll as his mother screamed in horror. The legionary from the 1st looked at Kratos with a gap-toothed grin and winked as three other soldiers dragged the woman into a hut that had a smouldering roof.

The Greek paled and moved on, finding more kneeling men and ordering them to their feet. Most of the section were collecting prisoners and herding them to a place, designated by Galba, at the earthen palisade wall where the shields had been quickly dumped. Decius agreed to take the first watch. Nearby, Ignavus was wrestling with a large Lusitanian woman much bigger than him who responded by punching him viciously in the groin. She sprang up and ran off into the chaos, spitting oaths as Ignavus chased her, yelling into the smoke, "Come back, you stupid whore! You are mine now, you bitch!"

Decius shook his head with a grin and turned back the prisoners he was guarding. They stood in a scooped-out muddy hollow in the rampart wall and were staring up with shock and fear. His facial wound was throbbing and it felt like the stitch had opened again. Borras came trotting back, herding a man and woman with what appeared to be their three children. All were ashen-faced and crying.

"Salve, Decius! I have a whole family here! That's more money in the pot, eh!" said Borras with a serious look on his face as the screams of rape and murder caused a fearful din from behind.

Decius shoved them into the hollow in the rampart and grunted, "Good, go get some more!"

The big man nodded and paused for a moment, looking a little ashen-faced himself. "It's... erm... pretty hellish, isn't it?" he said, jerking his head to the chaos around them. Without waiting for a reply he ran off, back into the smoky chaos.

Decius looked back at the fifteen or so prisoners the section had already collected. One or two pretty girls and a few strong men would fetch a good price, he thought. All stood shocked and shivering in the shin-deep muddy water as they watched the grisly scene that unfolded behind the blood-spattered soldier guarding them. They were broken. They knew at least here with this Roman they might remain alive. To escape back into the smoky maw of theft, rape and murder could mean much, much worse. The captive children cried and wailed as loudly as the women, while most of the men stood weeping silent tears of shame and anguish as they realised the true price of defeat. Some just stared blankly in shock as the world they once knew disappeared into blood and flame. Each face was a picture of total misery.

Saxum appeared out of the smoke, whistling a jaunty tune and pushing before him a naked young girl who had clearly been laying on her back in the mud. He shoved her into the hollow with a splash and she kneeled in the filthy water where she fell, sobbing. Saxum's ugly face was red from exertion and he grinned with his filthy teeth at Decius.

"Well, mate, I will stand guard if you want to go find the booty with the rest of the lads. I just had mine and I need a rest!

Hopefully we can sell the little *cunni* before they realise she is pregnant with a Legionary baby!" he gurgled with laughter as Decius nodded and sprinted off through the chaos towards the central plaza of the fortress.

The night before, Galba had spoken to them in earnest about this assault and how they might get rich if they were smart and disciplined. He said the chiefs of such places liked to bury their gold under the flat stones that made the floor for their halls and so it was agreed that the section would meet there after they had collected some prisoners first, just to ensure they would have some initial plunder for the section before going prospecting for more elusive prizes to find.

Decius had raced through the chaos and now arrived in the long chieftain's hut in the centre of the fortress plateau to find perhaps ten or more small groups tearing the place apart. It seems Galba's knowledge about the treasure was widespread. Groups of soldiers were prying at stones from the low walls or lifting flagstones from the floors, jabbing at the sloping thatch of the roof and ransacking every item in the large hall. Decius grimly noted that a few men from the 9th Legion were already there, which meant the soldiers of the 8th would not be far behind.

"Decius! *Decius*! Over here!" came the shout and Decius turned to see Felix, Galba and Corvus standing in the central fire pit in the great hall. A bucket of water had doused the fire and the men stood with their filthy hands prying at a large flat stone in the pit. A dozen soldiers were fighting and squabbling at the other end of the hall over some treasure that had been found under some piles of clothes. Two in particular were accusing each other of stealing another's share and engaged in a furious fist fight. Other small groups where busy smashing open jars or wicker baskets and rooting through the straw piled in a corner. One soldier was energetically thrusting away at a Lusitanian woman who screeched and clawed at his face as he lay between her legs on a filthy make-shift bed. Another grinning soldier grabbed her arms as he waited for his turn. A large group from the 9th Legion were torturing an old maid who was shrieking in her native tongue.

"Where is the gold, you old bitch?" one of legionaries snarled as he jabbed at her with his pugio.

She pointed wildly with her free hand and jabbered away in her shrill voice as her eyes rolled madly in her wrinkled face. One of the soldiers who held her arms looked confused.

"*Cac*! Go find an auxilia who can speak her language!" he said.

Another agreed. "Yeah! She is probably telling us where the loot is and we need to get to it before anyone else does!" he said, spitting on the floor.

Galba looked over at the men and carried on pushing a wooden pole under the flat stone he was trying to lift. Felix had stopped to look at the shrieking woman and the growing group of soldiers that were now convinced the jabbering prisoner knew where some hidden booty was deposited in the town.

"Back to work, Felix," puffed Galba, straining from exertion. "I'm not sure of everything she said but I'm sure she said she is only a farmer's wife who was hiding in here with her pig."

The flagstone lifted clear and Decius and Felix held it as Galba slid the pole under the stone even further.

"Where is all the muscle from the section?" said Corvus with exasperation. "Where is Kratos, Borras or Saxum when you need them?" he sighed as he clawed at the heavy stone.

Decius, Felix and Galba gave an almighty push on the thick wooden pole and the stone lifted up with a wet sucking sound.

Immediately there was a glitter in the sooty sludge. Felix opened his mouth to shout and Galba immediately clapped a filthy hand over his mouth.

"Quiet, you fool!" he hissed. "Do you want us to get robbed?"

He removed his hand and Felix spat out a glob of muddy soot from his mouth. The group stood looking as the black water in the fire pit oozed and covered the glinting gold they had found in the recess under the stone. Borras came puffing into the hall and looked at the group who stood motionless in the chaos of pillage and destruction around them.

"Looks like the 8th boys are over the walls! There is still sporadic fighting going on, so watch out! I nearly ran into a load of armed Lusitanians on my way here. We have fifteen or twenty prisoners for the section, though, and… Eh?" He stopped talking and frowned at the silent men with a look of confusion on his sooty face. "What's happening here? You lot look like you have seen the Gorgon!"

Corvus gave a hint of a wry smile. "We have found some of the chief's treasure. It's in the hole under the water right there," he said with aplomb, pointing down into the filthy black water as Borras followed his hand with a dumbfounded expression. As the large man bent down to reach for the hole, Felix grabbed his helmet by the cheek piece, pulling him back upright.

"*Not* with the rest of the army looking, you big oaf!" he hissed with a hard stare. Borras glanced over at the group of soldiers who were torturing the old woman and noticed that one of the legionaries, a young and very handsome man, was looking back at them with suspicion.

Felix sighed and rubbed his grimy hands over his face until it was black with soot. "Get it all out as soon as I have them distracted!" he said quickly to Galba, then shouted with anger, "*I told you so!* Stupid shits digging in the fire pit! You have wasted my time!" He angrily spun away from the open-mouthed Galba and walked over the to the group holding the old woman against a large timber column that supported the roof.

"What's this here? Stand aside there! Let me at the old bitch!" growled Felix, barging his way to the front. "Stinky old bag smells like she shit herself! Or she was eating it for breakfast!" he said with a cackle, pulling his gladius from its sheath.

"What's it got to do with you? This is *our* prisoner!" said the blood-caked legionary who was holding one of her frail arms in its tatty sleeve.

Felix sighed and offered a muttered prayer to the heavens. "So you must be the scholar of this merry little band!" he said, gesturing to the group of soldiers standing around the old woman. "Do you want to find out what she is saying or not?" he asked with a sigh.

"*Gerrae!* A fine friend you are, offering to translate! Why would you help us?" muttered a decanus from the 9th Legion with a look of suspicion on his leathery face.

Felix rolled his eyes. "Well, my services are not for free, chum! How about ten percent of the hidden treasure she is gabbling on about?" he said casually, examining the point of his blood-stained gladius.

The veteran decanus looked around and noticed that more and more soldiers were now furiously breaking everything they could and looking everywhere for loot. His group of soldiers from the 9th fidgeted with anxiety, very aware that all around them in the chaos the entire army was gathering plunder while they were not. The handsome soldier who had noticed Felix moments before darted his eyes back to group at the fire pit and then to Felix who was energetically chewing on a dirty nail with indifference to their plight.

"I don't trust him!" he said, narrowing his brown eyes in his youthful face.

Another soldier in the section, a squat, lumpy man, sighed with impatience. "Ruso! You are always suspicious!" He then turned to the veteran decanus, who still looked thoughtful. "Come on, Sextius, we are wasting time here!"

"Fine, fine! Ten percent for you. Just tell us what she is saying!" said the leather-faced decanus with a scowl.

"Let her go!" said Felix as he leaned forward and poked her bony chest, growling a few words at the woman who stopped struggling and stared at him for a moment before she jabbered back in her incomprehensible language. Felix nodded and pointed out of the main doorway of the hut, speaking quickly, imitating the words and sounds he had heard her say. The woman alternatively nodded and shook her head as she looked confused at this black-faced antagonist who spoke to her in a garbled language as he poked her in the chest and threatened her with his sword. She tried to explain that she was hiding in here as it seemed the safest place, and that she was just a farmer's wife who had been selling a pig in the town when the warriors locked the gates and said the Romans were arriving. She heard him say 'pig' and 'selling' and 'gates' and 'farm' in her language, but the rest was garbled. Why did he say 'wine' and 'whore' and 'hello' and 'how much' in her language? Did he want to buy a woman?

He keeps pointing to the door! Can I be set free? she thought.

She followed his hand again with her eyes and nodded frantically as he pointed at the door. She sobbed a few more words and whimpered, looking at the crowd of hard-faced killers that surrounded her.

Felix nodded and turned to leave. The veteran instantly grabbed his shoulder.

"Whoa there, friend! Where are you going?"

Felix looked blankly at the hand that grabbed him, then at the decanus.

"She said she was the chieftain's cook and knows the hut furthest in the north-western corner has the chief's treasure hidden under the dirt inside, close to his escape route down the cliffs. I am going to get my share before he gets away with it!" he said angrily.

The leather-faced section commander smiled wickedly. "How about you wait here, friend! We will bring your share," he said, stepping back a pace and aggressively lifting his gladius to waist level. The section of soldiers followed suit, fanning away from Felix and raising their swords as they grinned at the duped soldier whose mouth dropped open in shock.

"You traitorous dogs! You are swindling me!" yelled Felix, springing backwards and bringing his gladius up, ready to fight.

"Don't even think about it, you scrawny shit! One more dead legionary won't be missed on a day like this," grinned a huge, ugly soldier in the group as he raised his bloody gladius. The man's toothless grin and ugly face made even Saxum look like Apollo in comparison.

The leather-faced decanus chuckled and told two of his section to grab the woman. The whole group began walking backwards out of the hall, laughing at this furious soldier with the dirty, black face who swore and cursed as he began hacking a table to pieces in frustration. Once they were all out of the doorway only the handsome legionary called Ruso lingered for a moment, watching the enraged Felix with narrowed eyes before he turned and ran off into the smoke.

"You filthy fucking swine! I will get revenge! Nobody steals from Titus of the 8th Legion!" shouted Felix, hacking chips from the stout table he was attacking in rage. "You greedy bastards! Fucking 9th Legion goats, each man of you congealed in the rancid womb of a filthy whore! I will kill you all. *No one* does this to the 8th Legion! Just you wait! I will find all your mothers and get a male donkey from the baggage train and I will…"

"Well done!" said Corvus with a crooked, joyless smile as he walked up to the raging Felix, holding a flaming brand in his hand. "They have all gone running off and the rest of our section is away with the loot. I did not know that you spoke the Celtic languages."

Felix glanced at the door and dropped his act with a smile. "I barely speak a word of it. But I can sound like I do! Well, hopefully they will get what they deserve… fuck all!" he said, laughing merrily as he whipped out his penis and urinated into the sooty puddle of the fire pit.

Corvus cocked his head. "Oh! Well, you sure did sound convincing. You had me fooled," he said as he pushed the brand behind a beam near the sloping roof. The thick, dry thatched roof of the chieftain's hut that had probably stood for much more than a hundred years smouldered for a few moments, then caught alight.

Corvus looked at the sloping roof with all the soot-darkened human skulls fixed to the heavy beams alongside many animal skulls and wondered if they were defeated enemies, friends or relatives. He noticed the empty hooks where weapons once hung and thought how many feasts had happened in this place. He sighed as he realised this tribe's history had died that day and the burning of this hall was like their cremation. He looked back to the burning brand and nodded as he saw the flames begin to spread.

"I feel sorry for 'Titus of the 8th Legion'. I suspect they will want revenge when they realise they have been swindled," said the scarred man thoughtfully.

"A fine lesson in the arts of trickery *and* negotiation, my dear Corvus," said Felix, looking pleased with himself as he shook off the drips of urine and put his penis away. "As for any 'Titus' in the 8th Legion, well, there must be five hundred men who answer to that name! However, I could be caught. Even with shit all over my face, I seriously doubt any of those five hundred are as handsome as me!" he said with smile, touching his own face in admiration.

"Shall we go?" said Corvus, looking around the smoke-filled hall at the small groups of ransacking soldiers who were still desperately lifting slabs or sifting through the litter of straw, broken jars and furniture, looking for gold. The flames of the fire that Corvus had started were now licking up the roof and soon the whole building would be ablaze.

Felix nodded. "Yes, we should get back before Saxum rapes all our prisoners… or Borras eats them!" His blackened face split open as he laughed uproariously at his own joke. The pair walked out of the ruined hall with one merrily whistling and the other quietly observing all around him.

The scene outside was of utter chaos as they headed back towards the southern wall through the shattered, smoke-filled fortress. The troops of every Legion had run amok through the settlement. The more prudent soldiers had herded together groups of prisoners who sat huddled together, clutching each other silently as other, less disciplined soldiers dragged women of all ages off into huts for pleasure. One small hut used as a barn for pigs was merrily ablaze and the porcine occupants battered themselves against the sturdy door and squealed in the most blood-curdling way as they burned to death.

Travelling through the twisting lanes between the huts shrouded in fog-like smoke, Felix and Corvus came upon another group of soldiers who had found some native wine and salted pork. They were laughing and feasting at a long table they had dragged from a hut and piled high with food. The men sat comfortably at the benches as if they were friends enjoying hospitality at another's house. The scene was all the more bizarre as there were at least ten dead bodies scattered in the mud around the table and a nearby hut was on fire. Two small children who were the last living occupants of that home now sat crying as they rocked back and forth, looking at the corpses of their parents that lay in the doorway. One of the children wailed piteously as she stroked the hair of a woman that must have been her mother. The neck of the corpse gaped from a huge wound and her lifeblood had formed a large, dark pool on the muddy ground. Their parents had defended the hut to the death and now they lay still with singed hair and scorched skin as they slowly caught fire, their unseeing eyes luckily not witnessing the macabre scene of the bloodied soldiers feasting on their food before they sold their children to the slave traders who were attracted to the legions like flies to shit.

Felix recognised a man from the 10th at the table and stopped to slap him on the back with a whispered joke in the flushed man's ear while his other hand deftly stole the cup of another man who was busy eating a huge piece of ham. Felix emptied the cup in several quick gulps and grabbed some bread from the table as he bid them farewell with a belch before jogging to catch up with Corvus who walked on impassively through the white haze of acrid smoke. The scarred man had his gladius drawn and was alert but seemingly ambivalent to the screams and cries and burning huts all around him. Felix belched again even louder and added to the noise with a fart which made him laugh uproariously once more.

"Well, my silent friend," he said, winking to Corvus as he stuffed some bread in his mouth, "if this isn't a great day to be a soldier of the Republic then I am not hung like Hercules!"

They choked a little in the billowing smoke of a nearby hut and nearly fell over a dead Lusitanian warrior lying face down in the bloody mud. Felix paused to look at the dead man before reaching down and quickly yanking a thin but finely worked golden torque from the still-warm neck.

"There is so much gold we are tripping over it!" he laughed to Corvus who nodded impassively. In this merry mood Felix broke into song as they walked through the chaotic scene.

"Load the strings of the musicians ... and fill the cups with wine,
Banish sobriety until morning ... for we are here to dine,
No talk of Scipios or Ciceros ... just delicious whores divine,
I hope you drink until you puke ... then all the whores are MINE!"

With that he skipped and danced as if playing an imaginary lyre at a festival.

"Laaa la la la, Laaa da da dee, Laaa la la la," he sang, dancing ahead through the bloody sludge of mud, hacked up bodies and burning huts like a demonic satyr. Corvus grinned a small but rare and genuine grin. *It is a good day to be a soldier,* he thought.

SPQR

Chapter 15

Vala sighed as she quickly gutted the fish, more by memory than sight. The wickerwork of the tiny pier was uncomfortable; lately it seemed she was having to pile more furs and blankets under her bottom. Behind her the small wickerwork, mud-daubed hut on the shore of the huge lake was silent as her grandson had finally cried himself to sleep.

"Peace and quiet at last," she said aloud with a sigh. A couple of ducks splashed and noisily rose from the nearby reeds, quacking in protest at some unseen disturbance. Their wings flapped in the chilly, springtime air.

Vala sighed again. "So much for a quiet life!" she chuckled, finishing the fish and tossing it in a basket before reaching for another one.

This morning's catch was good and her sons had taken most of the bigger fish down to the marketplace where they would fetch a decent price. The old woman shifted to get more comfortable against an upright wooden post that made one of the piles for the tiny, rickety pier. She looked at the squashed, curled toes on her bare, leathery feet that did not like to walk much these days. They always ached, especially in the cold, and although the pain subsided in the late morning sunshine, it did not fool her. They felt good now but as soon as she stood to walk she would feel the pain that hurt so much she needed sticks to move even a short distance.

She peered down at her feet and scowled at the thought of travel. Journeys used to be fun, but not anymore. Vala was very cross with the talk of this new journey coming up. She was not looking forward to it at all! She had nagged her sons to put her in the hand cart and wheel her into the village to talk to the local chief. She had even offered the gold coin she had kept for emergencies so they could hire a cart to take her to the fortress to speak to the warlord. Who do they think they are, planning to make people move because they did not like living near to the tribes of Germania? Such nonsense! The warriors of her day fought them! Not ran off like frightened lambs!

She angrily gutted the next fish and in her haste slipped with her knife and cut her thumb. Vala's rheumy eyes blinked as the blood oozed from the cut. It was not deep, but it hurt.

"This is all Orgetorix's fault!" she said aloud to herself and sucked on the thumb, spitting out the bloody fish flavour before sucking on it again. Her glob of spit caused a ripple in the lake and some fish flashed to that point, expecting a small morsel like they did every day. She smirked at her greedy guests and enjoyed making them wait.

Ah, the lake is so beautiful, she thought, trying to ignore the injury and cheer her mood. Her rheumy eyes gazed over its smooth surface that reflected the distant snow-capped mountains. The lake was already higher from the melting snow that seemed to have thawed earlier this year. She smiled fondly at the mountains. She had not been able to see them for many years, but she remembered them and knew they were there. The usual winds that buffeted the lake had gone and in the still air the sun felt warm. It reminded Vala of those days in her youth, fishing and swimming with her long dead husband. She remembered her own athletic body when she danced at the festivals and all the men had admired her. She remembered how it was her dancing that attracted her husband, she remembered making love in the forest and even out in the boat sometimes because 'mama' was back in the hut looking after the children. Now she was 'mama' and a burden to everyone.

Not long now, she thought, peering once more at her gnarled feet. The pain in her back caused her to shift once more and she wiggled her crooked toes with a wince, taking the thumb from her mouth. It throbbed and the blood still oozed from the slice in her leathery skin.

"The sooner it's over, the better!" she exclaimed, picking up the fish and trying to ignore the throbbing pain. She would speak to her sons when they returned. She did not want to leave the lake. It would not matter if she was the last Helvetian left in the entire valley. She would like the peace and quiet! Besides, they wouldn't be able to take the boat and she could still fish.

Maybe if they left me plenty of firewood I could see out the next winter, she thought pragmatically, sucking on one of the few teeth she had left. That might be a plan.

They had been stockpiling dried fish, wheat and barley for some time now. Everybody had obeyed the orders coming down from the fortress and sowed every inch of land, even sending men with carts to the east and south to purchase more. Vala had laughed incredulously when they told her.

"Mama, we are serious," said her son Duni, his weathered face a picture of concern. "All the chiefs have agreed and the whole tribe will move to fertile bottomlands in Gaul."

Vala had argued long and bitterly. "This is *our* home! I have never been out of sight of this lake! We cannot leave just like that! Do you think we will find empty land? If the land is so good there, why is it empty? Do you trust Orgetorix *or* any of the swine he has around him? Who does he think he is, making the whole tribe walk to Gaul for the promise of land no one has ever seen? Will the Gauls want us going through their lands! Does anyone trust the Aedui tribe that he calls 'friends'? Who is to say they won't try and make slaves of us when we leave?" She had pointed at her eldest son and called him weak. "You are foolish! Your father never would have left this lake that has fed us our whole lives just for some rotten chief's dream!"

Duni had angrily argued that he was the head of the family now and she would go where he ordered. The bitter arguing had finally died down into an uneasy peace before life continued as normal, but Vala sulked any time the migration was mentioned. She had pleaded the children were too small or she was too old, the chiefs were wrong, the outcome uncertain, and she felt Duni agreed on many points, just like most of the village neighbours did. But Orgetorix had spread many rumours of the savage warriors coming from Germania and everyone was scared to be left alone. She pointed out that if the savage Germanians *did* come it would be just when they were planting crops and storing extra food. Surely they would come for rich pickings? Yet they still hadn't arrived.

It must be one winter since the migration talk started. Or was it two? she thought. *And soon we shall leave our home, all because of some chief's plan that makes no sense.*

The chiefs had even accused Orgetorix of some sort of corruption and brought him to trial. All the warriors had armed and it looked like civil war, but despite Orgetorix evading his trial and execution he still died, in odd circumstances in the end. Poisoned? Or even suicide, some said?

Vala thought this would be the end of the stupid migration idea but regardless of the death of Orgetorix the whole tribe still was preparing to move. She thought it would blow over as they had said they were moving at this time or that time, and now after so many full moons had passed, seasons even, it was here, the migration. Vala screwed up her lined face in disgust.

Maybe this silly plan will be forgotten once they actually try and make people leave, she thought, nodding to herself.

"Gods! A pox on Orgetorix! May the dark spirits torment him forever!" she snarled, spitting into the lake and tossing the last cleaned fish into the basket.

The old woman picked the last pieces of fish guts from the wooden board between her outstretched legs and tossed them into the lake, causing ripples in the calm waters. Vala felt so tired of all this worry. She was worried for the migration, worried for her children and grandchildren, worried for her own future. Ambitious chiefs often drag tribes into war; she knew this from the gossip overheard from the villagers who spoke to the travelling traders who talked of lands and peoples she had never heard of or seen. Germanians? Romans? Gauls? Pah! Some things are best left as they are. Be happy with what you have... like the lake!

She wearily rearranged the fur and the blankets so she could lie on her side, the sun warming the bedraggled, woollen dress. Vala farted contentedly in the new, comfortable position and blinked lazily at the shimmering waters that were all a blur these days.

"Why leave this paradise?" she murmured as she felt sleep coming over her. "I shall not go," she continued. "Damn Orgetorix. I am glad he is dead. They will... regret..."

She nodded off and slept soundly in the sunshine while the various creatures of the lake nibbled on the gift of the fish guts that they enjoyed every day. What the little creatures did not realise was this was the last time they would ever receive them as all across the Helvetian lands hundreds of thousands of people loaded their possessions into carts, burned their huts and began to move south.

Chapter 16

Borras stopped the mule pulling the little cart and stepped off the road under the cover of a large tree. The rain hissed noisily and made the paving stones of the abandoned road reflect the grey of the sky above. The large man shivered as the cold wind bit into him. He was glad for the woollen *braccae*[86] and socks that he wore under his army sandals. They kept some of the chill out on miserable days like this, even when they were wet. The mule hung its head out on the road under the grey sky and flicked its tail in annoyance at the water that dripped from its coat. The small, two-wheeled cart was full of supplies for the soldiers working on the road detail, some water, grain, onions and a few mouldy looking carrots… and nothing else.

"I should never have joined," sighed the big man, looking at the eagle tattoo on his hand for a moment before squeezing the excess water from the bottom of his drenched and threadbare sagum. He looked right and then left along the empty expanse of the neat and well built road that cut through the bleak countryside which still looked wintry despite it being spring. There were many scattered pieces of woodland and some farms in the distant hills, but this land was quite open and not well populated these days. The road cut straight through the landscape from Ilerda to Osca and Borras could remember patrolling along it before, back in the late summer of last year… before all the trouble!

---

[86] Early form of trousers adopted from the Celts.

He wiped his face and tightened the scarf around his neck before walking back into the rain. Why did he join again? He could not remember any more. He knew it was partly due to his father being a freedman with a 'funny accent'. As a child he had heard the snickering and laughter of the other children in the town. He'd had several fights with people who said he was not a 'proper' Roman and merely the son of a slave. His frame had soon outgrown these taunts and in the end he was left alone. Very few dared say it to his face, but he knew the insults continued behind his back. That's why he joined. At least he remembered that was one of the reasons. Or was it because he did not want a dead-end job in the timber yard? The big man shook his head as he touched the wounds on his shoulders that had been deep gouges but were now almost healed. He really could not remember any more.

"Piss on everything!" he said aloud and the mule eyed him with a disapproving gaze. The big man smirked and tugged on the reins. "You *would* look like that, wouldn't you? I guess even Roman mules do not like Teutons!" he said as they continued up the road.

He spat as he passed one of the curious sticks that had been dug into the dirt next to the road. The pole was perhaps half as tall as a man with a strip of white cloth tied to its head. It had been placed there by the *Architecti* officer in charge of the road maintenance team who had ridden down this road, identifying all the faults that needed fixing. Subsidence, vandalism, even theft of the stones that made their way into local farm houses — they all needed correcting.

Road repair duty was a common task that would normally fall on any soldiers based in a province. Usually they would have marched from the camp and returned for good meals and warm beds or, if the work site was too distant, stayed in small, temporary camps and billets. They would have rotated through the duty and had down time, of course, interspersed with seemingly endless guard duties. But in this case the more remote and dangerous parts were given as punishment and the detachment had to stay there. Some officer of the 10th had no doubt lined his pockets with coin from the magistrates of Tarraco or Ilerda, or probably both, just to ensure the road was worked on over winter.

A miserable duty at the best of times was made worse by the time of year and the location. The town of Osca had been the stronghold of the rebel Sertorius and many in the area still had resentment towards any armies controlled by Rome. The local townsfolk were Romanized for the most part, but the countryside still had many who spoke the Celtiberian language of the Ilergetes tribe and wore the local dress. The further north you went the more these people resembled the Lusitanians and Gallaeci in their dress and manner. Borras remembered some of the shrines with the heaped up heads and hands he had seen during operations in Lusitania.

And they say the tribes of Germania are savage, mused Borras as he plodded along with the mule.

The war in Lusitania seemed a long way off, he thought. Those heady days marching with Caesar and destroying all before us, taking plunder and gold! The campaign had gone extremely well and the 10[th,] Legion, despite being a junior legion, had acquitted itself most admirably. The Lusitanians had been crushed in several open engagements and a great many sieges. The tattered remnants of the tribal armies then escaped to islands of the coast. Caesar had ordered warships from Gades to row northwards to support the army and after several attempts the islands were cleared. The army then continued northwards into the lands of the Gallaeci who had retreated to their wild and hilly territory, not expecting the Romans to come after them as they hid in their hill forts. They were wrong. Caesar was as merciless in command as the men who fought for him.

"What a year that was, eh, Marius!" said Borras to the plodding mule beside him.

His marching companion seemed to nod his head as he walked and Borras smiled a wistful smile. It was a good year — joining the legion, a fast-tracked basic training and straight into summer operations that only saw victory and plunder. The enemy stopped being vicious warriors and became string after string of subdued slaves, all chained together, heading south to be sold. The cities of Gades, Corduba and Carthago Nova had boomed from the trade and the wiser legionaries had finished the campaign with the same amount of coin that would normally have taken many years to make. Borras and the whole tent section under the wise tutelage of Galba had done this and made much more money in spoils than most other sections, even despite the Lusitanians being a relatively poor people compared to the Gauls or those out in the eastern provinces near Parthia.

By autumn time the conflict was winding down and another legion supplied cohorts that stayed for ongoing minor pacification. Caesar was hailed as *Imperator* and was eager to leave for Rome, where he might request a triumph and increase his glory. The 10th marched to Corduba and winter quarters loaded with gold and slaves. There was plenty of fanciful talk amongst the army of going to Rome for a triumph, but for the most part the men wanted a decent winter camp to rest up and enjoy the drink and whores with the fat coin pouches they all now wore. Once word arrived that Caesar had abandoned the request for a triumph so he could be Consul, the army resigned itself to a pleasant life in the now quiet province. Corduba had been comfortable for winter quarters. It had been a quiet time until the next summer when some of the cohorts were detached up to Tarraco and then it all went horribly wrong!

"A 'theatrical company'! I knew it! I fucking *knew* it! Should have never got involved!" he said aloud, angrily tugging at the mule's reins in frustration.

"Are you all right, soldier?" came a voice next to him.

Borras spun around to face the sound, whipping open his cloak and half drawing the gladius in alarm. A toothless old man half his size, wearing a travelling cloak with a pointed hood stood leaning on his staff, looking at him as if he was peculiar. He wore a set of stout leather boots of Celtic design and some patterned woollen braccae on his own legs. Borras scowled at the man for surprising him and quickly whipped his head around, checking the empty landscape and road.

"I'm fine, old man," he grunted, sliding the gladius back into its sheath. "You should not creep up on people!"

"I am hardly in any condition to 'creep'," retorted the old traveller. "Besides, you must be going slow. I saw you leave the way station back on the Cinga river ages ago when I stopped for some food! Anyone must be slow for me to catch up!" he said with a snort, peering up at the much larger legionary.

"Look, old man! You best watch your tongue or..." Borras began, only to be cut off.

"*You* best fix this bloody road, you young bugger!" said the old man defiantly, lifting his chin with a another sniff. "I walk this road once a month to get my medicine from Ilerda and you lazy little shits lounge about poking pebbles when you are not causing trouble in the towns! Oh yes, I have heard! Bah, you lot today! No discipline!" said the old man with an angry wave of his hand and set off at a surprising pace in the direction Borras was going.

The big soldier stood open-mouthed for a moment as the old man hurried ahead, muttering to himself in the rain as his stick clicked on the road. Borras sighed, watching the old man depart, and pulled on the reins. "Come on, Marius," he said to the mule. "Let's get going." And onward they plodded in silence through the grey drizzle.

**

The thud of the *dolabra*[87] and the scrape of tools on stone and the rain were the only sounds that Galba could hear and he was thankful. If he had to break up another fight he would kill someone! He sat in the tent looking out through the open flap at the section working on the road. The cold grey day with its constant drizzle that seemed to soak everything through had made the mood even more sour of late.

Saxum dug in sullen silence, squinting through his swollen black eyes at Decius whose enlarged split lip jutted out of an angry face as he shovelled the fresh piled earth to the side of the road. Ignavus hobbled on a swollen knee, carrying pitifully small amounts of gravel that would provide the foundation for the repaired section of the road. Kratos shovelled the gravel into the ditch that Saxum had dug, his face a mass of lumps and bruises as if he had rolled down a cliff or been used as a punch bag by a boxer. Corvus winced as he made himself more comfortable under the small leather awning near the tent that protected the cook fire. The scarred man stirred a cauldron of bubbling gruel with one hand while the other arm was tightly swathed in bandage. He carried it very gingerly. The medicus said it was not broken, but Kratos had examined it and said the bones could have been cracked in his forearm.

---

[87] Roman army entrenching tool; equivalent to a large pickaxe / mattock.

The three other soldiers on the punishment duties were from the 7th Cohort and they worked a stone's throw away in silence after their last battle with Saxum. They were finishing the pavement on another nearby patch of the road and like all present were only wearing their tunics and belts over their braccae. Nearly all wore woollen socks and scarves. Their weapons were placed nearby under their shields in the leather covers to keep them out of the rain and stop the rust. They were positioned within easy reach in case the bandits tried their luck again, but the danger at the moment was internal rather than external. The mood was foul, the men cold and hungry after a long winter of working on the accursed road. Their tunics had gone from a clean light grey to a grimy dark brownish-grey and were now augmented by local clothes or any rags and tatters they could find. All were muddy, unshaven and they did not look very soldierly. Certainly their hairy faces looked much thinner than they did a few months ago. They were miserable and the incessant rains had made things much worse over the last few days.

Saxum stood up and stretched, leering across at the sullen men from the 7th working silently in the grey drizzle. The big man screwed up his eyes and spat as he glared at the largest in the group, an older looking veteran with a squat, powerful neck and shoulders.

"Oi! Shit breath! Oi! Cassius! Hey, you pig necked *cunnus*, I am talking to you and…"

He stopped, spat on the ground and began digging again as he saw Galba spring out of the tent and advance on him with his club in his hand.

"Shut your fucking mouth, Saxum, and keep digging!" the decanus hissed. "Do you want another flogging, you stupid shit?"

Saxum sniffed as the rain dripped off his nose and gently scratched his back. The wounds had mostly healed but they were now really itchy. He remembered how much he had howled in pain. That was his third flogging and he knew he did not want to go through that ever again.

Galba turned and shook his head at the exasperated section of soldiers who had deployed from another tent nearby. The detachment had the duty of guarding the punishment detail for ten days at a time and were eagerly waiting for their own replacements to get off the detestable road. They all wore full uniform and were armed, but they too had cudgels and clubs that had to be deployed on the unruly section, much more than once! At least two of the guards suffered black eyes and some had a missing tooth here and there from battling with Saxum. They muttered curses before going back to their dice in the sodden tent, where they sat and glared out from the open flap at the punishment detachment working on the road.

Galba turned and went back to his stool in the tent doorway. He was glad of the trees on this section of the road because they lessened the wind a little. He ducked under the open flap of the waterlogged tent and heaved a huge sigh as he sat on his stool once more. He looked down at his muddy woollen socks and noticed how one of his toes was poking through the tatty material. He gave another sigh and listened to the patter of the rain on the tent that was broken only by the clack and scrape of tools on stone and dirt.

What a mess, he thought.

Once more the army had screwed him over. Yes, this time due to his own bloody section rather than some officer, but such seemed to be the life. What was it Felix had said? "The Gods shit in one hand and pour gold in the other"? Galba could not quite remember. He grimaced and knitted his bushy eyebrows together. The red, misshapen remains of his severed ear glowed pink in the cold air.

"Felix!" he spat. "That little swine!"

As if on cue, the silence was broken by a high-pitched voice wafting through the trees on the opposite side of the road.

Oh what is it that I see? ... Ta daaa

Oh there are none as sweet as me ... Ta daaa

The prettiest under the heavenly skies ...

Or is this mirror telling drunken lies? ...

Every man wished to open my thighs ...

Decius immediately ceased work, threw his shovel on the floor with a clattering noise and looked at Galba with disgust on his alarmingly thin face.

"At *least* tell him to stop fucking singing!" he cried in dismay as Felix emerged from the undergrowth, strolling merrily along and carrying a wicker basket.

Despite being dressed in wet, muddy rags and looking as skinny as skeleton, Felix's grin was still as sharp as ever. His face was still bright pink from the burns that were now healing nicely. His mop of red hair was beyond the patchy, burnt stubble and starting to grow back in. He winked at the angry section with the eye that was not swollen from the last fistfight with Decius and walked straight up to Galba, uncovering his wicker basket that was clearly not full of the gravel that he was supposed to collect.

"Salve, Galba!" said Felix solemnly, giving an immaculate salute with one hand. "In honour of yourself and our most esteemed company I have not brought gravel but a gift from the forest spirits who, in their infinite wisdom, said to me that gravel was not edible or useful, no matter how many times you send me for it!"

He reached into the basket, lifted a plump dead chicken and held it high in the air, looking up at it as if it were indeed something holy. "This cunning, brown feathered beast sacrificed himself and four other comrades so that we might dine tonight on something more than gruel... *if* those who wish to dine are thankful to the blessed priest of the forest in whose tender care they landed!" he said with a look over his shoulder at all the famished men who stared at the chicken like hungry wolves.

Galba shifted himself off the tiny stool into the drizzle and looked inside the basket at the freshly killed chickens and then into the pink, smiling face of Felix who was stood smartly to intente.

"'Plunder', Felix? Have you not caused trouble enough?" he said with more than a hint of angry exasperation in his voice.

The antics of this red-haired devil seemed endless and no amount of flogging or punishment duties seemed to make his spirit flag. Felix looked at the decanus and sighed. He bent down and began poking holes in the mud. He repeatedly made five small ones in a formation, then the same pattern again and again. He took a twig and made small marks next to the holes, working deftly while Galba bent down to look.

"What in the name of Dis are you doing? If this is some other nonsense, Felix, I am too tired to..."

He trailed off as he realised he was looking at a very authentic-looking set of fox tracks.

Corvus left the bubbling cauldron and joined them, nodding at Felix's handiwork. "Pretty good, they look convincing enough," he said in his blank voice.

Felix stood up with a tired look on his thin face. "Look, Galba," he said, pinching the bridge of his nose. "The farm is a long way off. I sneaked over in the dead ground, unseen by anyone, and left a chicken bloodied up with a lot of feathers everywhere. The only evidence I left were some fox tracks like the ones you see here. If you want, I can take the chickens back and dump them, *or* we can all eat well?" He jerked his head towards the guards who were busy with the dice. "I even got one for the praetorians! No one is left out, eh?" he said with an expectant look at Galba.

Kratos walked over to look in the basket. His eyes peered out of his lumpy face with distrust at Felix, but widened when he saw the chickens. Ignavus limped over and licked his lips at the sight. Felix smirked, reaching into the bottom of the basket, and held out two eggs to Ignavus, who instinctively recoiled but stopped and gulped with a famished look on his face at what Felix held in his hand.

"What say you, anyone? You, Ignavus?" said Felix smoothly, looking around at his company. "Are we 'friends' again?"

Everyone apart from Decius and Saxum, who angrily worked on the road in silence, was now standing around Felix and looking at his gifts, trying to weigh up the anger and outrage they still felt against the gnawing hunger in the bellies.

"I... Erm..." Ignavus fidgeted and looked back at Decius whose eyes bored into him. His hand reached, then dropped, then reached again for the eggs as Felix smiled warmly at him. Saxum coughed pointedly as Ignavus reached once more and he looked worriedly at the brute who had threatened to kill him when Felix tried to buy him off with some bread several days

258

before. Corvus sighed and reached for the eggs with his good arm.

"Fine by me, Felix, I think it better to eat than be angry," he said with indifference as Saxum swore and Decius cried out. Corvus shot them both a look, went back to the bubbling gruel and prepared another pot to boil the eggs. Ignavus looked longingly after Corvus and back to Felix with eyes a hungry puppy would envy. Felix sighed and reached into the basket, pulling out another two eggs and offered them to Ignavus, who snatched them greedily this time and then scurried under the makeshift shelter with Corvus.

"You little shit!" shouted Saxum, throwing his dolabra to the ground and stalking over. The guards in the tent leapt up and advanced with their clubs raised. "You never fucking learn, do you?" snarled the decanus in charge as the men readied themselves. Saxum had finally learned he would never beat the six men at once, no matter how many times he tried. The brute howled furiously and dropped to his knees, punching the mud in frustration.

"Here you are, brothers!" said Felix cheerfully, handing a chicken to the surprised guards who were still eyeing the angry Saxum warily. "Courtesy of Legionary Marcus Mammilius Felix, 2nd of the 6th of the 10th! A feast fit for Roman heroes, neh?" he said with a wink.

The guards nodded and murmured their thanks as they took the chicken and returned to their tent, smiling. It was not the first bribe that Felix had bestowed on the detachment and his corruptions had guaranteed their support. They had more than once saved him from the fury of the section.

Galba felt his belly grumble. He too was on half rations as punishment, but Tanicus had told the guards to help him out from time to time with a piece of bread or some bacon here and there. But he *was* famished and the chickens looked plump and delicious. He sighed as he watched Felix give another to Cassius, the leader of the three punished men of the 7th Cohort, and said he would accept a half of the cooked breast and they could split the rest between them. Felix had lived with these three for the duration of the punishment and, like the guards, these too were his unofficial bodyguards. Galba spat on the floor and shook his head. It seemed that no matter what happened Felix would always come out on top and it was time to move on from the incident.

"Fine. Let's all eat!" he said with a finality in his voice. "But I swear to the Gods of the underworld that if you cause a situation like that again, Felix, I *will* kill you!"

Felix grinned and placed the basket on the ground. Saxum, already howling and punching the mud, heard the announcement and went into a fit on the muddy floor. He rolled on the ground, beating it with his fists and kicking out with his legs like a furious child. Decius shook his head at Galba as he threw down his shovel in disgust. He sat down in the rain with his back turned to the section.

"PEACE!" cried Felix, looking to embrace Galba who pushed him away, shaking his head.

"I *am* serious, Felix!" said Galba quietly. "I *will* kill you if you try and drag me into any criminal enterprise like that again!"

He stared at Felix who still smiled, but his cunning eyes registered the sincerity in the veteran soldier before him. The two men looked at each other for a moment, both clearly understanding the threat. Galba nodded and reached down for a chicken that he began plucking immediately. Felix turned to look at Kratos and broke into a smile.

"There he is, the pride of Greece, my old friend! Like Leonidas himself! Only twice as mighty," he said, beating his fist on his own chest.

Kratos scowled at him, then looked down at the remaining chickens, one of which he took and moved into the poor cover of the makeshift awning which was constructed from half of a ripped leather tent. Ignavus limped about energetically, collecting dried firewood from the sleeping tents, as Corvus fashioned some sticks to spit the chickens. Felix hurried under the cover, pulled some dirty mushrooms and herbs from the basket, and busied himself plucking a bird and merrily telling Ignavus about a delicious recipe for Numidian chicken that involved nuts. Ignavus was now frying a mess of eggs and gruel in a pan, barely paying attention to Felix. Both of their slender frames had suffered on half rations. His eyes were locked on the mess in the pan and he nodded and agreed without even listening. He was so hungry! Felix hooted with laughter and held up the chicken to kiss it on the beak.

"What say you, Decius?" he called laughingly to the sulking man who still sat with his back to the section. "Did you hear Ignavus agree that 'he loves nuts in his mouth'?"

Decius ignored him and Felix continued, "Just like old times!"

He winked to Kratos who glowered from his lumpy face as Felix jogged over to the guards' tent. Kratos looked at Galba who had moved his tiny stool under the shelter to enjoy the warmth of the cook fire.

"The bastard is insane," said Kratos, looking towards Felix who stood outside the guard tent sharing a loud joke with the occupants and now seemed merry as they prepared their own chicken for dinner. "Borras won't like this," said Kratos, bitterly shaking his head.

"Borras loves chicken and what choice do we have?" sighed Galba, smoothing his bushy eyebrows. "I am tired of being cold, hungry and angry. We are all in this together, and if you let it, the army tends to shit on people more than reward them. We have been shit on, but it is time to move on. Besides, one more month and we shall be back in barracks on normal pay, normal rations and off punishment duty," he said with a sigh.

"Maybe so," said Kratos with a sniff, "but you are lucky to keep your rank, Galba, and none of us will get a promotion now for years because of this. And perhaps worst of all, we shall never have money or riches like we did before! We should have never got involved in his plan!" he groaned.

"Yes, but we did," said Corvus, looking evenly at him. "We all thought we could make money and no one cared if it was illegal. Like Galba said, it's time to move on," he said quietly, gutting one of the plucked chickens with his razor sharp hunting knife.

Galba looked absently at Saxum, who now lay covered in mud, sobbing face down on the ground, then over at Decius who sat on the road. Then he stared into the fire. *Yes, we should never have got involved!* he thought to himself, remembering the entire bizarre affair.

After the conquest of the Gallaeci and Lusitani the army had marched to Corduba with Caesar at its head. The great column had kept many of its slaves in tow and the merchants and dealers came from cities as far away as Gaul to buy up all the stock. The sales of slaves and the fine Celtic metalwork were so lucrative that there was not a man in the 10th Legion who did not have a fat bag of coins on his hip and much more deposited with the legion clerks.

At the end of the journey the city of Corduba certainly looked forward to this influx of wealth. The local brothels and wine shops of the city had anticipated the incoming victorious legion by stockpiling food and drink. Indeed, many a trade sprang up almost overnight to cater for the garrison. Wine, women and song were not the only thing in demand as many of the men commissioned local artisans to fabricate items for them and the city's blacksmiths, leatherworkers and tailors turned out high quality military equipment for the soldiers who replaced and augmented their kit.

Caesar had guaranteed himself loyalty and affection from the men of the 10th by accompanying them on the march south from the defeated lands of the Gallaeci and Lusitani. All along the route he would take the time to periodically march alongside the men and share their fires in the evening, impressing all by seemingly knowing everyone by name. At the journey's end, Caesar, who was ever the showman, called a parade of the army and gave a moving, heartfelt farewell speech that left many in the assembled 10th Legion in tears and swearing everlasting loyalty to their commander.

Once he made his tearful farewell he left, heading east through the rest of Hispania on to Gallia Narbonensis and the Alpine passes that led to Italy. The 10th Legion moved into its upgraded permanent camp and the usual sacrifices were made, letters sent to the relatives of the deceased, last will and testaments honoured, Legion equipment reconditioned and stored away and myriad other post-campaign administration tasks completed. Then the men could officially begin taking leave amidst normal duties.

The 8th Legion had been assigned ongoing pacification in Lusitania, while most of the 9th and 10th were assigned to normal army training and other peacetime tasks such as irrigation projects and road building duties. Several detached cohorts began to go various places in the province, but generally everyone settled comfortably into winter quarters. Everything was quiet and army life was as enjoyable as it could be.

With the new year the news had arrived in camp that Caesar had become Consul and many of the soldiers were pleased for him. Others were very disgruntled, of course. There were those who said he had only become Consul off the back of the soldiers' blood and sweat. They muttered if he had any respect for the men at all he should have forgotten the consular election and called for a triumph in Rome for the victorious army, so each man could see the capital and march proudly through its streets, enjoying the adulation of all. The chatter soon quietened, apart from the occasional grumblings over the matter, but such is life in the army. Within every tent section there is a politician or at least a rabble-rousing malcontent.

As the winter became spring and turned into summer, many soldiers of the Hispania legions had become regular customers to the inns, wine shops and brothels of not only Corduba, but everywhere from Gades to Tarraco, as cohorts worked on various projects far and wide in the province. It was just after summer in the city of Tarraco that several cohorts of the 10th had officially outstayed their welcome. One of these cohorts was the 6th and, in particular, a section of men who caused a bizarre chain of events that would be remembered in that area for a long, long time.

SPQR

Chapter 17

Felix, typically, had been the first of anyone from the cohort to make contacts within the gangs and criminal underworld of 'Little Athens'. He had got drunk, gambled and fraternised with all the worst ruffians since arriving for road building duties around the city of Tarraco. Little Athens was a shanty town of tents and rough buildings that had been constructed by a band of enterprising Greeks who were locals but also citizens and traders from the free city of Emporiae and even as far away as Massilia. The nightlife of this already notorious part of town had attracted soldiers like Felix for the wine and whores that helped the men relax after their shifts of working out on the roads. The business-minded locals had constructed the extra attractions to augment the local facilities so they could make even more money from the visiting troops.

Their visit coincided with the influx of many people coming for the annual *Ludi Romani*[88] Festival which Tarraco hosted at the end of every summer. The festival alone attracted throngs of people from towns and villages far and wide, also with several cohorts stationed in the city it was indeed a time of plenty for pimps, vendors and sellers. Every effort was made to profit from the abundant wealth that was on offer.

One warm, autumnal morning Felix found himself free of guard duty and striding along the busy streets wearing his military sandals and tunic. His hob-nailed footwear struck the worn

---

[88] Lit. "The Roman Games", a festival lasting from about September 5 to September 19.

stones in a manner that pleased him greatly. His cingulum clinked proudly from his belt, adding to the noise. The sound alone went ahead of the striding man, causing civilians to move aside. He walked past two soldiers who were dressed in full kit and nodded to them cheerfully. One raised his eyebrows in acknowledgment and looked down quickly to make sure Felix was not carrying anything more than a pugio as per the town rules. The two soldiers posted outside the large wine shop glanced at the pack Felix carried on his shoulder, but settled, leaning back against the wall, looking anything but happy with the duty as they listened to merry, drunken laughter coming from within the building.

The officer in charge of Tarraco at the time happened to be the infamous Pug, who had come up from Corduba to enjoy the Ludi. The Praefectus Castrorum had ordered two centuries to take turns in augmenting the local town prefects over the approaching festival period. With this extra force policing the city, discipline was as relaxed as it could be and with Pug in charge it would not get any more liberal. Luckily, Pug stayed content with the whorehouse nearest the camp and, ever the hypocrite, tended to binge on the wine offered there, despite being staunchly against other soldiers drinking.

Felix walked around the corner, happily whistling to himself and pleasantly returning the wishes of good morning to the townsfolk. The traders who manned the many market stalls along the bustling streets offered him trinkets from all the ports of the Mediterranean and the painted whores who stood in the doorways called out that they had never seen such a handsome man — something they said to everyone who passed, of course. Felix laughed in good spirits and replied to a large-breasted, dark-eyed prostitute.

"Not now, Venus! Bigger things than your tits are afoot!" he said with a wink and merrily walked on until he turned down a dark, deserted alley in the poorer part of town near Tarraco's bustling quayside. The yells and catcalls of the sailors and all those who worked on the docks unloading the ships echoed down the narrow, filthy street that snaked between the towering insulae. Felix hummed and looked at several doorways in the gloom before he hopped over some dog shit and then stopped at a door with a crude picture of a penis drawn on it with chalk.

"*Open up!* In the name of the Republic! Open this door in the name of Imperator Felix, I say!" he yelled at the top of his voice while banging on the door with his fist.

He heard muffled swearing as someone slid the bolts before opening the door. A wild-eyed man with a beard glared at him from under a shock of matted black hair.

"Quiet, you stupid bastard! I am supposed to be hiding here!"

Felix pushed past the short, thickset man and walked into the dingy, one room apartment. The insula was of poor construction and there was a great crack in the ceiling that usually did not bode well in a building such as this. Felix looked at the filthy straw bed on the floor and the table with its heap of rancid-looking leftovers, and wrinkled his nose at the smell.

"Really, Zeno, you should not have not gone to all this trouble! And such a breakfast you have bestowed on me! Surely this is meant for a woman you are trying to seduce?" he said sarcastically, sitting down on a stool.

He took out his pugio and prodded the rotten food away in disgust until he made some space on the table. Then he carefully took off his soldier's scarf and laid it down as a napkin. Felix solemnly took his small vinegar flask and some bread from the knapsack and laid it on the scarf while his agitated friend stood in the doorway, looking up and down the street nervously.

"Were you followed?" he said with one hand on the curved dagger he wore on the back of his belt.

Felix took a swig of the posca in his flask and belched before biting into the bread.

Zeno turned to him. "Felix! Were you followed?" he hissed angrily.

Felix stopped chewing the mouthful of bread and raised an eyebrow in disapproval at his companion. He pushed the bread into the side of his mouth until his cheek bulged.

"I was only followed by the prefects who are looking for you," he said earnestly. "They said you were worth the hundred-denarii reward," he added, nodding. Then his face went serious.

"Or was it a mere one hundred quadrans? Hmm, that is *not* very much for turning you in?" he said, shaking his head with feigned disappointment.

Zeno glowered at Felix, then noticed the chalk penis on his wooden door and his mouth dropped open in astonishment.

"What in the… Did *you* fucking do this?" he said angrily to Felix, who grinned with bread falling from his mouth.

"I was as drunk as a priest of Saturn the other night and needed to remember which flea-bitten shithole you showed me, didn't I?" he said, laughing, as his bedraggled companion spat on the chalk and rubbed it with his hand, cursing when it proved difficult to remove.

Felix sighed at Zeno's lack of mirth and took another swig of posca before he reached into the knapsack and brought out an apple which he placed on the table.

"So, shall we get on with this?" said Felix, now irritated with the worrying of his companion.

Zeno tried another frantic scrub to at least break up the penis shape and sighed in defeat, closing the door. Felix blinked in the low light and wrinkled his nose in disgust as the smell of his scruffy companion assaulted his nostrils as he walked past.

"Before we do anything, open that window!" he demanded, gesturing to the tiny opening in the wall above the bed. "And light a lamp! I can't see anything in here!"

Finally, with two sputtering oil lamps on the table, Felix looked at the wild-haired Zeno and nodded.

"So, now we are sober and alone. Tell me the whole thing again," he said seriously, his thin face looking fox-like under the smoky flicker of the lamps.

Zeno leaned forwards and took a deep breath before speaking conspiratorially. "So, here it is. Several members of the Scipio family get on their own ship from Rome and come here every year for the full fifteen days of the Ludi Romani Festival. They do this because old Scipio Africanus came here back in the days of the wars with Carthage and did the same..."

Felix interrupted, "My dear fellow, I am well versed in history and not as stupid as you look."

"Carry on, on to the point... the money!" he prompted, looking at Zeno expectantly.

The thief scowled and continued. "So, as I was saying, he was here for the games once so now the Scipio ancestors come and have a little holiday away from Rome to stay in the private villa next to the magistrate's compound. As for the money! They bring a chest of gold the likes of which you have never seen! It is stuffed full of cups and jewels and especially sacks of coins! Maybe thirty or forty sacks bigger than a man's fist! Of course they are the patrons of the games so they like to make a big show with the prizes," said the grinning thief, throwing his arms wide before continuing.

"All the charioteers, gladiators, dancers, poets, actors, boxers and everyone involved in the Ludi that wins a laurel does not get their prize money until the big ceremony at the end, right? So the games start with the usual stupid ceremony and that's when I first saw the chest of gold. They carry it out and it sits at the feet of the presiding patricians and all the other rich bastards from Rome! But they do not give *all* of this out. It's merely a show of the Scipio wealth, because they take the chest back with them still two thirds full. So we get the chest and swap all the sacks without anyone noticing! We can leave a few cups and gems on top so it all looks fine."

Zeno nodded enthusiastically at Felix. "Anyways, me and the boys looked at all the angles and we have three options. They have a strong room on the ship and the Scipios have a detachment of soldiers — at least a century. So I reckon the ship is a no-go. During the day the chest gets escorted out into the open to wherever the day's events are and gets plopped down right by the feet of the Scipios with maybe twenty or so guards around it at all times, so that is also a no-go," said Zeno, shaking his head. He then leaned forward with a cunning look on his face and continued in hushed tones, even though the two men were completely alone in the shabby dwelling.

"At night they lock the chest in the villa, which also has another strong room with three locks, and that is guaranteed because one of my boys is a right good-looking bastard, see? Young Apollo is fucking one of the magistrate's gossipy slaves. So, I need some good fighting men to cover me while I work on the locks and..."

"Why?" interrupted Felix, who had been looking thoughtfully at the bread he was chewing.

Zeno stopped and looked at him blankly. "Why what? What do you mean?"

Felix looked up with irritation on his face. "Why is it a 'no-go' at the day's events?"

"It's perfect!" he muttered to himself.

"Eh? My friend," said Zeno in a patronising tone as he scratched his bearded chin, "take it from me: the middle of a packed arena is *not* the place to steal something *and* get away with it!"

Felix looked once more at the bread and took another small bite. His mind was working overtime as it considered all the possibilities. He did not even hear Zeno talking about the time it takes to break locks open and how they would get into the villa.

"A packed Arena *is* the best place *if* we can cause some chaos! We create a diversion!" said Felix, sitting bolt upright. "But more importantly than that, we have people at that prize-winning festival near the chest as we cause a diversion so big that it becomes a riot!" He slammed the bread down on the table so hard it made Zeno jump.

"You… you can't… the middle of the day? What about the…?"

Felix snorted and mimicked his voice.

"You can't, you can't! Meh, meh, meh. Zeno, the famous thief of Massilia, eh? I can see how your bold plans have acquired all this finery!" he said contemptuously, gesturing around the filthy hovel. "Look, we are *not* getting into a patrician villa with a strong room that is next to the magistrate's compound. It's a festival! They will be feasting and awake until all hours, they

271

have extra guests staying with them, there will be slaves scurrying back and forth with booze and food!" He paused to glare at the thief.

"It is not a case of *if* but *when* we are spotted! Imagine how quickly the guards can be roused! The prefect's office is right there! The centurion in command of the soldiers policing the town will be there. I have been on duty and walked around the walls of the place myself," Felix continued with a nod. "We *will* be spotted and we will never be able to fight it out of there. Then we are caught and crucified, thanks to your shitty plan. However, if we create complete chaos in a packed arena of thousands we can simply make the switch, or if the riot is bad enough we just scoop up the whole chest! If we are caught we say we were trying to defend the gold as good soldiers of the Republic, and hand it back over."

The worried Zeno picked at his teeth and wrinkled his leathery forehead. "I don't see how we could start a riot or how we could get close to the winners' podium," he muttered.

Felix sighed and replied with a wink at his thoughtful companion, "That's because *you* are not a showman!"

He banged his fist on the table and laughed uproariously as the furtive Zeno jumped. Standing up, he pulled out some coins and tossed them on the table.

"Get a Roman-style haircut and have a shave. Also, get a nice, dignified toga! Something a Roman of substance would wear. We are now businessmen and event organisers! Find out who the most corrupt magistrate is here and we will throw him a party. I want to know who the games organiser is, too, and any corrupt bastards all the way from the Scipios down to the man who cleans the shit in the animal cages in the Arena. Get a good crew together as well. We need thieves, muscles and some whores and pickpockets who can keep their ears open. I will come back tomorrow at the same time to get you for our first strategy meeting... but somewhere else," he said quickly, looking around in disdain. "I won't spend another moment in this dump!" he said, stuffing the breakfast items into his knapsack as he stood to leave. Felix strode out of the door, knotting his soldier's scarf about his neck and a confused Zeno shut it quickly behind him.

As he walked merrily down the alley, Felix suddenly stopped, cursing aloud, "By the sweet *cunnus* of Venus! Now I have thought of it, it would be rude *not* to do it!"

He searched and found a suitable piece of chalky stone before he padded quietly back to Zeno's hideout and gently traced a fresh outline on the drawing of the erect penis that had been scrawled on the wooden door and crept off, laughing to himself.

***

"Eh?" Saxum squinted as he tried to understand what he had just heard. "You want all of us to take our annual leave at the same time and enter the bloody Ludi Romani... as *contestants*? I was going back to Narbo to fuck whores so how the fuck am I gonna win a prize for poetry or dancin', eh?" He scowled in confusion at Felix across the big wooden table in the comfortable tavern called 'Scipio's Sword'.

The establishment looked like it had been renamed due to its freshly painted sign on the wall outside, perhaps just for the duration of the upcoming festival or to tempt wealthy soldiers inside. Regardless, it was generally considered a much more respectable inn that was known for its good food and did not cater for the drunks or entertain prostitution. Ignavus and Saxum had grumbled mightily when Felix had the whole section follow him there to a business lunch. And now the big fool was irritating him further.

"Listen, my philosophical friend, as much as I appreciate the artistic talents of the section, I think we best play to our strengths and enter the sporting events," he said gently to the still squinting Saxum. "*You* could enter the gladiator matches, the beast hunts or the boxing," he said with a flourish. "Same as you, Decius," he nodded to him. "You could surely best anyone with a sword in the Arena. And you, Kratos! Boxing or wrestling? Easily done, neh? And the same for you, Borras!" he said to the thoughtful group.

Saxum squinted again and vigorously scratched his ugly head. He opened and closed his mouth a couple of times before speaking ."But… Why? What's the point?" he said, still gripped with confusion.

"Gods below!" exclaimed Felix, pinching the bridge of his nose in exasperation. "Why do you think? The glory of winning in an athletic pursuit of excellence, the glory of gaining honour for the 10th Legion, oh and, erm… of course… *money*!" he cried, banging the table with a fist and causing several of the inn patrons to look across at the group of soldiers.

Saxum nodded at Felix but still looked confused.

"Yeah… but we already have money, Felix, a *lot* of money!" said Borras, nibbling on a delicious roasted songbird with savoury stuffing. It was the same kind that he had seen rich people eat, and it was good.

Saxum pointed at Borras agreement. "Yeah, see? We are loaded down with denarii!" he nodded. "Why do we need more?" he asked.

Felix sighed and bit into a piece of cheese. He savoured the delicious taste as everyone ate their expensive lunch. Last night's revelry after another week working on the roads had taken its toll and the section was quietly enjoying eating their vicious hangovers away.

"Saxum! What is better?" asked Felix, raising one hand and forming a circle with his thumb and forefinger. "One whore? Or five whores?" he said, taking his other finger and pushing through the hole several times in the universal sign for intercourse.

"Six whores!" said Ignavus quickly and the section chuckled.

"Please, Ignavus," said Felix in a pained voice. "The adults are speaking!" he said, looking down his nose at him and turning to Saxum again while the laughing Borras choked on his roasted bird.

"Five whores, obviously!" said Saxum, irritated with the questions. "What the fuck are you on about, you sneaky red fox? I don't get it! My head feels like a donkey has kicked it! Let me enjoy my meal," he said angrily and took another bite from his huge pile of *tagenitai*[89] that was covered in honey.

It seemed many of the hung-over section agreed with a nod and continued eating in silence. Felix ignored the want for quiet and eloquently explained how much prize money was on offer. He cunningly talked of each man's attributes, playing to their vanities, describing how each man might win not only the money but the fame of a sporting hero! Famous gladiators and charioteers from Rome were now spoken about by everyone who read the new invention of Caesar's called the *'Acta Diurna'*. These printed 'newspapers' were full of lines of script relaying events in politics and births and marriages, yes, but more importantly to the plebeian class, on the back page they listed the results and scores from the sporting events. Such widely distributed publicity was causing already famous gladiators,

---

[89] Pancakes.

boxers and charioteers to become heroes known throughout the Republic! Felix speculated that these newspapers would soon be everywhere.

"And who knows," he whispered conspiratorially, "who might hear about the famous boxing, gladiator, charioteer group from Tarraco that won half the laurels! Do you think Saxum the Brave would ever need to pay for a woman again? Or Kratos the mighty could not be employed at any Gymnasium around the Republic to train anyone with coin to pay? Same for Decius the Skilful? Corvus, the Killer of Beasts! And Borras the Bear!" he said with a wink to the section, who were looking more and more interested by the moment.

"What about me?" said Ignavus, looking hurt, and the table cackled at his sorrowful face.

"You can massage my aching muscles after I win a great fight in the Arena!" said Saxum, standing up and grabbing his groin. "You can start massaging here and only use your mouth!" he gurgled with laughter.

Felix smirked and placated Ignavus, who glowered at Saxum and the chuckling section around him. "We shall need more than winning physiques and attitudes, Ignavus. We shall need our opponents losing their wills to win! I need a shrewd and cunning man watching the betting action and perhaps getting access to the other contestants… particularly their food! It would be a shame for an opposing wrestler to get the shits and us to get rich because of it, eh!" he said with a wink and the section all mused on how life would be if they were indeed rich and famous. Only Galba, who had been eating silently, looked at Felix with narrowed eyes.

"'Influence the outcome', Felix? People getting the shits? You mean cheat! And even with you admitting to cheating, why do I feel there is more to this than meets the eye," said the veteran suspiciously. "I don't want any trouble! They are already sending punishment detachments up into the hills on road repair duties for the winter. We are heading back to a comfy winter quarters in Corduba after the Ludi. Let's not ruin a good thing!" he said, looking at the shocked and overly-innocent face of Felix.

"Decanus! I would *never...*" he protested.

Galba raised his hand to silence him, "I have seen that look before, Felix! Just don't enter a foot race and then poison everyone else or something?! I know what you are like!"

Felix's face changed into an even more shocked version that made Kratos snigger.

Galba grinned. "Yeah, yeah! Spare me the act. So, Felix? You have the whole section here and if it's easy and safe enough to double our coin, what needs to be done?"

Felix took out a wax tablet and spoke hurriedly. "Well, seeing as we split everything evenly, I say we go into this evenly! I will need an initial investment of roughly half of all the plunder you have left right now and according to my calculations," he said, showing the wax tablet covered in various scribbles and numbers, "you will make at least four times back without betting receipts. *If* we can influence certain outcomes everyone could make ten times the amount. The initial investment would buy everything we need: costumes, equipment, our registration with the organisers and a good cup of wine or two for the right people to get us in. And of course a little amount for some advertising to let people know we are in it to win it. After this there might be a little cash flow enhancement required from time to time for sundry expenses. Now, regarding the events themselves, I am pretty sure Decius could best most of the gladiators out there and

Kratos could out-box most boxers. Saxum can wrestle or box. Borras, you could wrestle or enter the beast hunts. Same with Corvus — we already know the beast hunts are your speciality," he said, nodding to the silent Corvus who sat on the end of the table sipping some water. Corvus lifted his cup in acknowledgment but seemed his usual indifferent self.

"As for you, Galba? Well, you used to drive a cart, right?"

The decanus looked up from his meal with a quizzical look. "Yeah, my father's, before the army. Why?"

Felix nodded. "Because you and I shall be in one of the main events! The Homeric chariot race! You ride five laps with me on board, then I jump off and run the last two laps as per the rules! Even if your driving is, as I suspect, fucking lousy and our chariot stops last I cannot see who would beat me over two laps in a Circus Maximus!" he said with enthusiasm.

Galba looked at Felix, pointing his table knife right at him. "You cheeky sod, my driving is fine but an ox cart is *not* a racing chariot," he said, knitting his bushy eyebrows together.

Felix sighed with exasperation. "That's exactly why I will be the one who will need to make up the time on my running! Besides, like I said, most of the investment would hire us a top line racing chariot for the events, especially one that is superior in design compared to those of the competition! I already met a man in Little Athens who knows another man who knows someone, who has a chariot like those they use in Britannia," he said, tapping his nose.

Kratos raised an eyebrow. "Britannia? Has any Roman even been there before? Sounds like a tall tale to me!" said the Greek through a mouthful of fruit salad.

Felix pinched the bridge of his nose again in exasperation. "Numidian, did I say the man was Roman? It's a Greek who knows one of the Hispania Celts, who knows a Gaul, who got it off a Briton! My plans are easier when I do not have to explain the minor details for the dim-witted!" he said, tapping himself on the forehead.

The section cackled with laughter and continued eating in good humour while a tavern slave refilled the cups before walking away to another table.

"Fuck it!" said Saxum with a belch and shoving away his empty plate he grinned at his peers, showing his filthy teeth still caked in his breakfast. "I have been a mighty hero of battle, why not a hero of the Arena! As long as I ain't gotta dance like a fucking catamite? Or do some bloody actin'? I'm in!"

Kratos looked thoughtful. "Greek-trained *Pankration*[90] fighters do have the edge over Roman wrestlers, generally. And my boxing is not too bad," he said, looking around the table.

Decius emptied his cup and clicked his tongue thoughtfully. "I want to see what gladiators they are bringing in first. I am not using their stupid theatrical weapons. If I can go onto the sand with my gladius and scutum then I could pull it off." He paused, looking at his empty plate and scratching the livid scar on his cheek before giving Felix a hard look. "I could pull it off... *If* the winning prize is worth the risk."

"I have hunted a fair bit and I am pretty good with a spear," said Borras "I... uh... don't think I will do too well at the technical stuff for the wrestling. Still learning, see," he said sheepishly, scratching his head and looking at Kratos, who nodded in polite

---

[90] Ancient version of mixed martial arts involving boxing, wrestling, submission grappling and other techniques. One of the original events in the first ever Olympic games in ancient Greece.

agreement knowing that despite Borras' great strength he lacked the technical ability for professional competition.

Felix looked at Ignavus who nodded enthusiastically as he noisily chewed on a mouthful of chicken. "If I get my cut and it's a fair split... yeah!"

Corvus remained coolly silent as always and just nodded. Felix knew that was enough as all eyes turned to Galba. The decanus was now spooning down some delicious fish broth and his suspicious eyes flicked back and forth, examining them all from under his bushy eyebrows. He set the spoon down and wiped his mouth with the back of his hand as he glared at Felix. "You are mad!" he gestured around the section. "And you are all mad for listening to him... but to be honest, when it comes to plunder you lot seem to be blessed by Fortuna. I have seen many sections with much more professional soldiers who never had half the luck or made a quarter the amount of coin. Besides, I'm getting old and the army has fucked me for promotion and pay for too long... so I guess I'm in!"

Felix hooted and slammed his palm on the table, causing the plates to jump. Saxum enthusiastically bettered him by smashing a huge fist down and causing one of the tabletop planks to snap, which had the innkeeper's wife scurrying from behind the counter, spitting oaths and demanding that they leave immediately.

"Out, you drunken savages! *Out*! This is not some infantry pisshole for you bastards to destroy!"

Felix stood and elegantly bowed to the woman and the alarmed customers who seemed exclusively from Tarraco's affluent upper classes. "My dear hostess," he said soothingly, "we are not merely 'infantry', we are now the famous entertainment company called 'The Brazen Bull'. Trainers, owners, competitors and winners of all the games we enter!"

The proud boast did not stop them being ejected or having to hurry away from the scene before the prefects arrived. The section ran away laughing, apart from Galba, who cursed them all as bastards. Felix laughed because he saw the plan coming together.

SPQR

Chapter 18

The final weeks leading up the Ludi Romani had gone gloriously for Felix. He had immediately bribed his way out of all duties and ingratiated himself with all levels of Tarraco's polite society. He organised the section into a 'theatre troupe' with a falsified background and list of fictional achievements. The whole affair was costly, as being a magnanimous socialite was absolutely necessary to get anywhere, even if it was ruinously expensive. His largesse, bribes and feasts soon made him the toast of the town and friends with equestrians and patricians alike, not to mention the magistrates and officials who ran Tarraco. However, once the actual Ludi started, the cracks in the plan began to appear.

Felix had spent the opening ceremony in the arena, sitting with all the other lanistas and managers next to the place of honour occupied by the magistrates and members of the Scipio family. The packed arena had cheered the competitors as they were paraded for the people to see. He had even seen several important officers from his own legion who had travelled up from Corduba to the event, often not realising some of the men under their own command were taking part, even though many of the off-duty soldiers did, which guaranteed a small but dedicated fan base. Despite the support of the 10th men, Felix had paid for professional crowd leaders to cheer and clap and gossip about his men, and the plan had worked wonderfully. The crowd had roared as Decius had stood in his glittering *Mirmillo*[91] armour. Corvus and Borras had attracted many cheers for their outlandish costumes and fearsome appearance. Kratos had paraded bare-chested with the other wrestlers and pugilati, and Felix made sure he was well oiled! Despite his smaller stature, the ladies had immediately made the Greek their favourite and the cheers when they announced Kratos had been noticeably higher-pitched in tone. Saxum in particular had plunged into the theatrical elements with such enthusiasm that he would not compete unless he was called 'The Kraken'. He even used up a huge amount of his own spoils from the Lusitania campaign for advertising and paying a large entourage of cronies to follow him wherever he went. The Kraken had made himself quite famous before he had even fought in his first bout. It *was* glorious, for a short time... But then it all fucked up.

The opening ceremony seemed a long way off now as the Ludi Romani festival had entered its last few days going into the finals. Felix sat in a dingy tavern called the *'Aureum Vellus'*,[92] which was locally known just as the *Vellus*. He mused how apt the name was as he looked around the deserted, grimy little drinking establishment. He looked at the stinking piss pot that had been brought in from the street; it was simply too dangerous to go outside for a piss these days. He listened to the sound of a noisy prostitute servicing an energetic patron up the stairs and looked around the empty tavern at the pot-bellied innkeeper whose thick eyebrows joined in the middle. He was known for badly watering down the wine, but now he stood absently digging around in his nose with one greasy finger as if he were trying to poke his own brain.

---

[91] Mirmillo - a heavily armoured type of gladiator, armed with a gladius and scutum.
[92] Latin: golden fleece.

"Micon! Tell that stupid bitch to suck instead of scream! I am trying to think!" snapped Felix angrily.

The innkeeper wiped his finger on his filthy apron and looked at Felix with indifference before calling to a large black man who stood in the shadow by the doorway that led out onto a now quiet street.

"Juba! Go tell Cordelia to keep it down," he said, scratching his mop of dark, curly hair before pushing his finger back up his nose.

The muscular African shot a white-toothed smirk at Felix, who sat with his head in his hands, before going up the rough concrete stairs to the location of the passionate screams. Felix looked at the myriad of wax tablets laid out before him that he had 'borrowed' from the legion stores and carefully examined the figures again. He had spent over four thousand denarii preparing everything for the section and building the theatrical troupe known as the Brazen Bull Company. Money had been spent in vast amounts very quickly for gladiator costumes, weapons, wild animals for the hunts, paying legion scribes to make hundreds of posters and flyers, a small parade through the town, wining and dining the local magistrates and in particular the fat and ever-hungry local official, Titus Vipsanius, who was in charge of the games. Zeno and his crew had stolen a racing chariot which they had hidden in a tent in 'Little Athens'. He had ordered several vicious bears from Narbo for the beast hunt. The whole section, despite their attributes had insisted on training for the various events. His own expenses had gone through the roof and now the Ludi had started everything was unravelling right before his eyes.

He sat back, looking into his own lap with a quiet sigh as a thunderous roar of a crowd could be heard in the distance. His expensive toga was dirty. He looked at a small brown smudge on the fabric in his lap. He vaguely remembered the cheap whore that he had last night. She had sat naked on his leg, wiggling her ass, while he was drinking. He lifted the dirtied fabric to his nose and sniffed. Wait? Is that...? Urgh, it *is*!

"That dirty fucking bitch," he said aloud in disgust and leaned forward with a sigh, concentrating once more on the tablets that covered the table. Three of them contained all the corruptions listed as 'beneficiaries'. These included bribes to several referees and judges of various events; payments to people who would lead the crowd in cheering *or* booing who Felix decided upon; payments for innkeepers, waitresses, prostitutes, town prefects, other soldiers from the 10th Legion on official duties, people who worked in the baths, who worked in the docks, who worked in the magistrate offices, etc., etc..

The list was long, everyone was in on the act and it *should* have been perfect. Even Petronax, the gang leader in charge of the local collegium, proved very helpful to the Brazen Bull. His thugs were lying low with the extra policing of the garrison based here and after Felix went to see them with Saxum, Corvus, Zeno and a few others in tow they became quite friendly and were happy to cooperate in return for a small share of the profits. But now, after some suspicious gambling issues and arguing, they too were turning against him.

He looked at one open tablet that was marked 'profit' at the top of the page. It had very few entries scratched into the wax.

"Profits," murmured Felix.

What poxy profits? he thought as another thunderous cheer went up in the distance.

Ignavus was a shrewd bookmaker and some money was coming back in the gambling receipts, but it wasn't enough. The chest was the main prize, but security in the arena had increased and the lure of the gambling had been a nasty sidetrack that had now left them without money for the original plan. Felix began to doubt it could even be pulled off.

Micon walked over with a jug of wine to refill Felix's cup. The screaming had stopped and Juba walked down the stairs. He looked out of the doorway and quickly up and down the deserted street before settling onto a stool near the door. He looked at Felix shaking his head and asking for water as he once again put his head in his hands.

"So, will I get paid today?" asked Juba coolly, his deep voice breaking the silence. His dark skin looked almost midnight black as he sat in the shadows by the door. Felix looked absently at him for a moment, then back to the tablets.

"It depends..." he murmured thoughtfully. "Kratos needs to lose his fight."

Juba gave a wry smile and scratched his freshly shaved head with scarred arms that had seen many street fights involving blades.

"He didn't go down last time though, did he?" said Juba absently with a yawn.

Felix scowled at his companion and looked once more at the tablets as the sound of running feet echoed down the empty street. Felix immediately stood up and reached under his toga to draw his gladius as Juba sprang off the stool and took up a long club that stood next to the doorway. Micon grabbed his spear down from the two nails that held it above his bar and rushed forward to defend the doorway. The group relaxed as they recognised the small, scruffy, pinch-faced man who ran breathlessly into the tavern and stopped in front of the table

286

where Felix had sat facing the door. The man was Felix's age but looked older. His lank hair was brown and long in the Celtic fashion, even though he wore a filthy Roman tunic and braccae. His eyes were too close together and made him look more rat-like than a human should.

"Serpo! You beautiful little cretin! Tell me there is good news!" barked Felix anxiously as he slid the gladius back in its sheath and arranged his toga to conceal it once more. The weasel face of Serpo puffed breathlessly, blinking and shaking and nodding his head all at once.

"The scar-faced one reached the final! He killed three wolves quicker than the champion *Venator*[93] from Carthago!" he gasped with a gap-toothed grin.

"Yes! You beautiful, scary fucking bastard!" shouted Felix, punching the air. "Thank you, Corvus! That's four hundred denarii back in the pot. What else?" he said, looking hopeful.

Serpo scratched under an armpit and stammered, "Umm... Petronax and his gang are outside the Arena looking for you! They grabbed me asking if I had seen you. He says he wants his money! He says he knows you made the 'Kraken' take a dive in the boxing and bet against him and everything!" he stammered nervously.

Saxum, or 'The Kraken' as he now wanted to be called, had been a pugilistic prodigy... up to a point. He was, in the words of Kratos, one of the least-skilled fighters he had ever seen in a professional bout, but he had a remarkable talent: he was virtually impossible to knock out. The famous Kraken had won all the early qualification bouts, but unlike the professional and enthusiastic Kratos, who was remaining sober, training, bathing and being massaged every day, Saxum had let his burst of fame

---

[93] A type of gladiator specialising in wild animal hunts.

get to his head and wandered the town from inn to inn with his entourage of whores and freeloaders. He had been throwing his own money everywhere, saying how rich he would be when he was the champion.

His first few days in the Ludi had been glorious and thanks to the advertising campaign the crowd loved the ugly, indestructible monster, but his last two fights were an absolute shambles. He was dead drunk at one and fell asleep after being punched, which went down on the scorecard as a knockout. Then in his bout to be the 'best of the losers', which still paid a prize, he did not turn up at all! Felix had run from the boos of the crowded Arena and eventually found him in a tent in 'Little Athens', stark naked in a pool of his own vomit after an all night orgy.

After Saxum's inglorious exit from the Ludi, the collegium had agreed to stage a little underground event of its own. The fight would be between the Kraken, who could still draw a crowd, versus a powerfully-built Celt with a big belly. The match took place in a warehouse down by the docks, that soon filled up, with late-night drinkers raucously calling for the fight to begin. Lots of money changed hands and Saxum was odds-on favourite to win. Felix immediately conspired to have Saxum go down within the first few punches totally against the odds, of course with a large amount riding on it. This ruse worked, as the Celt toppled the Kraken with a vicious punch, but it did not take long for the drunken crowd to notice the 'unconscious' Saxum taking quick peeks around before screwing his eyes up again as he lay on the floor of the makeshift ring.

Felix and Ignavus, who had organised the bet rigging, had escaped from a window with a thousand denarii that should have been much more, but the murderous crowd that had searched for him chanting *Cheat! Cheat! Cheat* had other ideas! In the end, the soldiers on the town watch duty broke up the angry, riotous mob with their clubs as the crowd were about to lynch Saxum. Thanks to their intervention the brute had just managed to escape with his life and came to hide at the Vellus. That was last night and they had been holed up there ever since.

"Those dumb *cunni* don't know I took a dive!" said Saxum who appeared at the top of the stairs, wrapped in a threadbare blanket, yawning. He walked down, snorting through a swollen, busted nose and spat at Serpo before sitting down on a stool at the same table as Felix.

"Water," he croaked to Micon, then prodded his bruised, swollen eyes before grinning at Felix.

"It's not funny, you idiot!" Felix said angrily. "Fucking lying there and peering around like a newborn lamb at everyone when you were fucking supposed to be knocked out! We could have made three thousand in that fight, but I barely got away with one! *And* the collegium want that back!"

Saxum blinked lazily and gazed absently at the writing tablets spread across the table before looking at Felix with a leer. "Balls! The Kraken fights! He does not act!" he said in a lofty manner showing his filthy teeth.

Felix snorted and pointed at him with a scowl. "'The Kraken' got kicked out of the Ludi! The Kraken is probably nearly out of money! And the Kraken has probably fucked up the plan to make any money!"

Saxum squinted at him and clutched the little leather bag on its string around his thick neck for a moment before replying. "Yeah... money? I want my money back I gave yer!" he said with a nod.

Felix slammed his hand on the table so hard the wax tablets clattered and Serpo jumped.

"*Your money*!?...How do you think you got entered into the Ludi? How, in the name of the furies, do you think you managed to compete? Did you not notice your name and face scribbled on the walls? The posters? The advertising? The announcers telling everyone your story? The crowds paid to cheer for you?" he cried, looking at the huge brute who grinned back at him.

"Yeah, they love me here!" Saxum said, lifting his ugly head with pride. "Like a proper hero from Rome, eh! Just as you said! A proper champion, eh!" he said, nodding enthusiastically.

Felix took a deep breath as he calmed himself. He looked at Saxum who clearly did not remember the anger of the townsfolk who were about to hang him and cursed him as a cheat. This agitation would not do, thought Felix, composing himself. He looked at the weasel features of Serpo who still stood fidgeting in front of the table, looking alternatively awestruck and terrified by Saxum. Felix felt a surge of calm and pointed at the squirrely man.

"Go see Zeno and Ignavus, and remind them we have money riding on it and we need Kratos to *lose* so we can recoup the losses on everything with a big bet. Make sure someone tells the Greek this time! As for the 'other thing', tell Zeno we might not have enough men winning laurels to pull it off. We still have men in the beast hunts and the chariot race will be easy enough, so that's a win," he said calmly.

"And Petronax?" asked Serpo, blinking unhappily.

Felix rubbed his forehead several times and looked thoughtfully at the wax tablets before nodding. "Tell him he will have his money on the final day of the games! That's only two days away, so he will have to deal with it!" he said smoothly, now back in control.

The sound of many running feet echoed in the empty street and the group instantly armed themselves once more as a gang of ruffians came piling in through the doorway. Felix recognised them as Zeno's men and sat back down with an irritated look.

"What is it, gentlemen?" said Felix as politely as he could.

The heavily breathing leader gulped before replying, "We just came from 'Little Athens' and someone has knifed our men on guard and pinched the racing chariot! Looked like Petronax's gang are openly against us," he said excitedly. "We are heading to the Arena to protect Zeno... Oh, we saw someone coming back from the Arena and we heard your Greek won!"

The group turned and ran off with Serpo in tow. Saxum looked bored and wandered over to the bar asking Micon what was in the kitchens while Juba looked sympathetically at Felix.

The cunning face looked thin, pale and exhausted under the shock of red hair. The usually sharp eyes that were full of mirth looked incredibly sad and watered a little as Felix stared blankly into space. He gently lowered his gaze to the brown smudge on the expensive toga and then laid his head on the cool table. Felix sighed as another thunderous cheer went up in the distance that, to him, sounded like the whole world celebrating his downfall.

SPQR

Chapter 19

Galba was furious. The section was silent as he kicked the wooden walls inside of the makeshift building until his foot went through a plank. They were in the backstage area of the arena that had spilled out beyond the entrance gateway. The fenced off enclosure was a warren of huts, tents and cages with wild animals, gladiators and acrobats all mingled together. There were also various huts for the athletes of other events who would troop out tomorrow after the grand finale. Next to the chariot park by the main entrance was a small wooden shed bearing the symbol of the Brazen Bull on the door. Inside the shed was already packed with a multitude of sporting equipment and now the entire section lined the walls. The sullen men sitting on the floor while Felix sat on a stool behind a tiny desk at the back of the room. He looked calmly at one of the wax tablets and ignored the furious decanus as he kicked the planked wall into splinters. Galba turned on him, red-faced with anger. The lumpy remains of his ear looked more livid than usual.

"How much have we lost?" he asked again with a growl, standing facing the desk with his legs splayed wide.

Felix sniffed and daintily scratched something on the wax tablet he was studying. Luckily for him Galba could not see he was drawing a pair of tits.

"Well, I will be frank," he said looking around the room at the men who sat on the floor. "It's grim. It's pretty much as grim as the cheapest whore in Corduba, to be honest. As we all know the

292

chariot we paid for was pinched by the collegium, so we had to withdraw from the event. To top that off we owe the collegium a couple of thousand denarii. Decius, you are injured and cannot fight, so we understand that you had to pull out," he said, nodding to the man who nursed a badly sprained shoulder in his sword arm.

"Corvus, you are still in for the win in the beast hunts, as are you, Borras, which makes two prizes, but the finale might not go as gloriously as I hoped, because one of the bears has died and the other has been sick for days and is getting worse. I have Zeno's people looking everywhere for replacement beasts, but there are no wild animals to buy for the finale tomorrow. Ignavus has run bets well enough, but we are not earning as we should from the betting because Kratos keeps winning," he said icily, looking at the Greek who immediately sat forward to defend himself.

"Felix! The idea *is* to win. That's been the plan from the start, hasn't it?" he questioned angrily.

Felix ignored him with an aloof glance at the tablet before drawing another, even larger pair of breasts.

"Anyways, as I was saying, we might have three prize winners and that might recoup some of the money from the initial investment, *and* the little financial boosts you have all given me since then to keep the enterprise running," Felix said, looking up from the tablet.

Borras narrowed his eyes. "'Financial boost', my ass. I gave you a loan!" he growled, which caused a flood of agreement from the gathered men.

Felix held up his hands to placate them. "Brothers, brothers, please settle down," he said in his best courtroom voice. "I would like to refer you to the initial meeting we had over breakfast where you agreed to the preliminary investment *and* the possibility of further 'cash flow enhancements' as the enterprise went forward!" he said, looking around. "Kratos, Decius? Surely you remember those words and agreeing to the terms? Corvus?" asked Felix with a raised eyebrow to which the whole room protested until Corvus cut in.

"He did say that. And you all agreed," said the scarred man indifferently.

"But I have literally lost everything!" wailed Ignavus. "You made me place the wrong fucking bets! I even put most of my own money down, too!" he cried bitterly, pointing at Felix.

Saxum threw an armoured gauntlet at him. "Pipe down, you rat faced bastard! Typical you, trying to make money on the side! You made money off The Kraken, didn't you, eh?" he grinned, looking pleased.

Kratos spat in disgust and nodded at Saxum. "Yeah, but that was from an illegal fight and you could not even pretend to be knocked out properly, you stupid great oaf!"

Saxum's piggy eyes screwed up. "Oaf, is I? You filthy Greek shit! I will knock you out!" he said, sitting bolt upright and brandishing a ham-like fist.

"Yeah, you can talk, Kratos! We bet a huge chunk of money on your last fight to lose, and you break that man's bloody arm!" said Decius bitterly.

Kratos threw his hands in the air. "In the name of Apollo!" he cried out in exasperation. "How many times do I have to tell you? I thought we were here to win! No one told me about the little schemes you came up with at your drunken parties! I have stayed at the inn near the baths the whole time! And you pissheads could not organise someone to tell me? No one told me!" he protested, looking around.

Borras, who sat next to him and had been tending the corner of Kratos during his events, growled at Decius in defense of his comrade, "At least he is not 'injured' and *can* fight!" he said with contempt.

Decius stared at him for a moment before he picked up the beautiful Hispanic-made gladius that he had recently bought for a huge sum of his own money and calmly unsheathed it. "What's that supposed to mean? You saying I am scared to fight? Well you try it! Any fucking time! I have skewered bigger bastards than you, fat boy!" he said viciously. Borras face reddened with anger and he leapt to his feet, as did Decius, followed by the whole section pointing and threatening each other with accusations.

"SILENCE, YOU *CUNNI!*" Galba roared in his centurion voice that seemed to shake the rickety wooden planks of the hut. He kicked a helmet that narrowly missed Ignavus before crashing into the wall and ordered everyone to sit down.

"Shut the fuck up! I am sick of this bickering!" He pointed towards Felix who had been sitting quietly and drawing on his tablet during the angry exchanges. "YOU! *You* got us into this mess! *You* get us out!" he said angrily.

Felix scratched yet another pair of even larger tits on the tablet and thought of an idea that just might work.

"Friends… I have a plan that might see us come out of this with coin and honour enough," he said evenly. "But I have to talk to you all individually and you must do exactly as I say!"

Kratos sat upright. "I am not losing the fight! I don't care if others take my cut of the winner's purse. I have worked too hard!" he protested, shaking his head, and Felix hushed him with a raised hand.

"You don't have to, Kratos. Look, let me talk to you all individually and we can come out of this on top," he said soothingly. "However, someone *will* have to lose in the main event," he said, looking at Corvus and Borras.

The scar-faced man shrugged while Borras wrinkled his forehead. "We don't have a main event, Felix. One sodding bear is half dead and the other one *is* dead," he groaned.

Felix smiled benevolently. "Even dead bears serve a purpose, my friend! Luckily, I am smart enough to see a way how!"

***

The sand of the arena was flattened and cleaned during the interval. The crowds cheered the troupe of midgets who fought a comical gladiator fight below them and marvelled at the athleticism of the acrobats whose bodies were a twirl of movement as they jumped and tumbled over the warm sand. The gang of arena slaves in their bright green tunics hurriedly cleared away the heavy ropes that had been laid into the sand to create the twin circular rings where the boxing and the wrestling finals had taken place moments ago. There was a hum of noise in the great amphitheatre as the crowds talked and laughed at the spectacle before them or momentarily left their seats on the wooden benches to visit the multitude of food and drink vendors that set up stalls under the arches near the many entrances of the southern side. Even outside the arena there were throngs of people visiting the piss pots to relieve themselves or making bets with the various bookkeepers who stood under the arches. The stone columns behind where they stood had the odds scrawled onto them in chalk and a few lucky gamblers were there collecting their winnings.

Felix was sat in the special seating area called the *podium* on the northern side. This enclosed section was right at the front of the arena and had been partitioned off to the rear with a fence of wooden boards, taller than a man and covered in gaudy cloth bearing the symbol of the Scipio family. There were only two entrances, one on either side of the central canopy that covered the seats of the most honoured guests, and these entrances were well guarded. Behind him, the first few rows of seating were empty due to this fence blocking the view. However, a multitude of vendors had set up stalls in this empty section.

The whole northern grandstand of the arena was built over a descending rocky slope of hillside that had once been a quarry. The southern side, facing away from the nearby sea, was a raised stone and timber affair that had recently been augmented with extra seating. Felix looked to his left, past the central canopy to the seating area that mirrored his own. This part of the arena had been designated to wealthy merchants who were sponsors of the games, high ranking military officials and other dignitaries. Felix could see Pug dressed in a military tunic and all his armillae. He could also see Tribune Considius and several other officers he recognised. *They could be problematic,* he thought and wondered if the entrance behind them was as secure as his own. Felix's portly companion had waddled out of the private entrance to the podium several times for a visit to the snack vendors. This entrance led up a stairway behind him, past many rows of spectators and out onto the level ground above. He heard an angry exchange and turned to see a town watchman punch a garishly dressed man and push him away from the entrance, while another grabbed him and dragged the man protesting up the stairway. The crowd behind them whose front rows consisted of the wealthier merchants and middle classes of Tarraco laughed and pointed at the sight of the local actor being dragged up the stairs.

The florid-looking man sat next to Felix saw this and chuckled. "Actors, eh! Those scum always forget they are banned from the games! Worse than slaves if you ask me!" The portly man's cheeks wobbled as he giggled in a childlike way that irritated Felix. "At least slaves know their place but actors always have such a high opinion of themselves! Always talking about politics as if they have actually studied the subject! I mean, really? Such honour for merely pretending to be someone else? For having the admiration of the plebs? Preposterous!" said the rotund man with his fat cheeks quivering indignantly.

Felix nodded, barely listening to his perspiring companion, and looked along the podium to the place of honour. There, under the elaborate canopy, various members of the Scipio family were relaxing in the shade. The three rows of seated patricians were being offered cool drinks and delicacies by a band of pretty serving girls. Normally, Felix would have felt entitled to walk over and immediately try and take up residence in the best possible company, but this time he wanted to lay low.

Once again his eyes flickered hungrily back to the wooden chest that sat open in front of the patricians. Even from the side, he could see a glint of gold in the sunlight under the half-open lid. Every day he had seen the four burly slaves carry the heavy bronze chest in on a litter and place it down in front of the guests of honour. The twenty guards who escorted the chest at all times then took up their places behind the rows of chairs belonging to the esteemed patrons. These guards were not soldiers from any of the Hispanic legions, certainly not the 10th, as they looked much better fed and equipped. Felix also noted these highly polished but soft-looking men gave arrogant smirks to the battle-hardened soldiers of the 10th Legion whenever they passed them.

"The 10th men will give you parade square bastards a leaving present soon enough!" he muttered under his breath.

There was a ripple of applause behind him as Kratos came walking down the steps carved into the rock face, escorted by another two guards. The Greek had many lumps and bruises on his face and looked every part the fighter. His olive complexion was still flushed from the exertions of his wrestling match, but he was now wearing a clean, white tunic and fresh green victory laurels on his head. He nodded and waved to the crowds left and right of the stairs as they rose to congratulate him. The Greek grinned as a pretty girl grabbed him around the neck and kissed him while her many friends squealed in delight at her daring. Another taller woman with broad shoulders did the same and Kratos stared in astonishment as he realised he had just been kissed by a transvestite. The laughing guards guided the stunned Greek down the last few step to the private entrance before 'her' other friends could try and kiss him too. He entered the podium area with a bow to the Scipii who turned to clap him with polite smiles on the faces of the men and much more suggestive ones on the women. Blushing, he walked to sit down next to Felix amidst the other victorious contestants, trainers and managers.

"It's a pity Galba is still angry and went back to camp. How could he not enjoy all this? It's been a glorious day! I certainly could get used to this!" Kratos commented, still grinning.

"Get used to what? Being kissed by men in women's clothes?" murmured Felix absently.

Kratos said something in reply, but Felix did not hear. He was looking past the fat man on his left, who was eating some nuts as noisily as any human possibly could, and stared at the chest of gold once more. Felix turned and looked rearwards again, up the stairs to the last rows of spectators up on the level ground at the top of the sloping grandstand. He checked once more that Serpo was there, wearing a bright red scarf on his head like a turban for identification. He turned back to look along the seating on his side of the podium and saw the games organiser who had dined out on his money many times.

The fat Titus Vipsanius was talking to the announcer dressed in purple whose immaculate grey coif was framed by golden laurels. They discussed details on the large wax tablet he held and the announcer pointed to various items and nodded. Despite the gentle offshore breeze, Vipsanius was sweating profusely. The preparations for and the whole period of the Ludi had been good to him. As organiser of the games he had drunk and eaten for free, lined his pockets and generally had a good time. He certainly looked fatter than the first time Felix met him and the red-haired man was irked, knowing he had most likely paid for some of the man's jiggling paunch.

Below them in the arena one of the wooden gates creaked open and a cart pulled by two oxen came trundling in. The large cart was low with wheels that sank in the sand as the powerful oxen dragged it along. The platform carried a square cage the size of a small hut and the whole thing was covered with a large piece of red cloth. The noise of the crowd changed instantly as people pointed and commented on the curious cart while the staff drove the item slowly once round the arena before stopping in front of the podium. Several ropes were quickly slung through the small gaps in the arena wall, some to remove the cloth and one to open the cage. The oxen were uncoupled and they quickly vacated the arena, along with all the midgets and acrobats who disappeared, twirling and dancing, through various gates in the wooden walls down in the arena. Only the cage remained, with its mysterious contents still hidden by the cloth, eliciting a hubbub of excited curiosity from the crowd. Vipsanius waddled over to Felix, grinning with crooked teeth that were stained from wine.

"I cannot wait to see your Chimera!" he said far too loudly into Felix's ear.

Vipsanius's stinking breath was only offset by the foul smell of this man's sweat. Felix smiled pleasantly and was about to reply, but Vipsanius had already turned and waddled back to his seat nearest the Scipios. Felix swore under his breath as he watched him go. The fat man was clearly drunk as he tottered a little, then settled himself down with a deep breath. He belched and nodded to the announcer as he wiped his dripping face with the hem of his expensive toga.

The announcer raised his hands and the grouped musicians who were stationed to the rear in the last rows near Serpo split the air with a piercing cry of horns. Felix had noted that many of the musicians were Aeneators from the 10th Legion earning a little extra coin. He was also glad of the many hundreds of other soldiers mixed into the huge crowd — it made him feel a little easier.

That's my backup plan right there! he thought.

He turned to check Juba was still close to the private entrance and looked higher up the packed rows of spectators to where Petronax was sitting. He was not sure how many were in this gang, but Felix could see at least ten men around the tall collegium leader. His stylish hair was oiled and arranged neatly and he wore gold chains hung outside his expensive grey tunic. The smooth, refined face glared at him with open hatred that was mirrored by his men. Felix also grimly noted that, despite the warm weather, many of his followers were wearing long togas that most likely concealed weapons. One of them looked at Felix with a grin and ran a finger across his own throat in a gesture that anyone could understand. Felix smiled and waved cheerfully at the man and turned back towards the arena as the blare of the trumpets died away.

"Citizens of Tarraco!" cried the announcer "By the auspicious blessings of Jupiter, Juno and Minerva, *and* our most generous

benefactors, the family Scipii! It is time for the final matches…
Venators, then Gladiators!"

The crowd cheered and in the arena several slaves in their green
tunics ran out carrying various colourful banners showing the
sponsors of the Ludi which they then walked quickly around in a
circle in the centre of the sand. The immaculately coifed
announcer let the cheering die down before looking at his wax
tablet and quickly continuing.

"This match is brought to you by the house of Vipsanius and his
honoured friends… The company of the Brazen Bull… Tarraco's
Guild of Metal Workers… Quintilius' Finest Togas... and the
Tarraco branch of Polydorus Slaves Massilia! If you want the
best and most beautiful slaves? Buy Polydorus!" cried the
announcer as the crowd let out a slightly less enthusiastic cheer.

The gaily dressed man with his purple toga and golden laurels
paused for a moment for theatrical effect as the advertising
slaves in the arena sprinted out through various little doors.

"AND NOW! The moment you have all been waiting for! IT'S…
TIME!" he roared as the crowd cheered and stamped its feet.

"ALL HAIL! VENATOR CORVUS!" he shouted as the
musicians added their weight to his voice.

As the instruments blasted their heroic salute the crowd stamped
its approval, causing the wooden parts of the arena to shake.
Corvus ran out onto the sand wearing his black theatrical
costume, armed with a long spear and hunting knife. His
charcoal black braccae had a belt with crow's feathers hanging
from it and two crow's wings were attached to a circlet he wore
on his head. One arm was covered in mail made from black iron
and the rest of his upper body was bare. His wiry strength was
apparent and the fans, especially the children, were fascinated by

or even terrified of him in the parade. Despite the beast hunts not being as popular as the gladiator matches, the crowd enjoyed Corvus for being nimble, skilled and clearly quite fearless.

The announcer raised his hand and the musicians sounded another shorter note. "HERE! for your very own amusement! The foulest beasts from darkest Africa and the far reaches of Asia!"

As two of the smaller doors opened in the arena wall, he cried, "*LEO! Et URSUS*[94]!"

The crowd peered into the black entrances that betrayed no movement. Then suddenly from one ran a lion growling onto the sand, obviously after taking a prod to get him going. The crowd cheered its approval as this was the biggest cat so far in these games. Corvus readied himself as the lion roared in anger and terror at the swelling noise around him. The animal ran wildly to another gate and clawed at it, trying to escape.

From the other darkened entrance a bear plodded out on wobbly legs before sitting on the sand, looking around lazily. The frustrated lion ran to another gate, scratching underneath at some unseen arena slave who yelled and beat the giant paw with a stick. The lion roared and sprang back in fury before noticing the bear. The huge cat puffed itself up before running over to circle the big brown beast while showing its white, dagger-like teeth. The bear, who was clearly under the weather, did not react at all to its ferocious adversary.

The crowd gasped as the lion jumped on the passive bear and immediately went for the throat while Corvus ran over to try and intervene. This was not good for a spectacle! Felix swore and sat bolt upright, looking sideways at Vipsanius. The games organiser was being lectured by a dissatisfied member of the

---

[94] Latin: lion and bear.

Scipio family who was gesturing at the events before him with some distaste.

The lion was now enraged that Corvus was seemingly trying to steal his kill and defended itself from the jabbing spear. Many of the crowd booed the lion as the bear weakly rolled sideways as if dead. This glorious battle was not going as intended. The announcer looked backwards at Vipsanius, whose bloated face had turned a deep scarlet in anger or shame, or both! The organiser looked worriedly at the bored faces of the Scipios and the jeering crowd. He nodded frantically to the announcer, who raised his arm again for the trumpets to sound.

"For this titanic struggle, we need a bear of our own! Let's fight strength with strength! *Our own Hercules! Borras!*" he cried hurriedly and the trumpets blasted the signal for the gate to open.

Borras ran onto the sand in his lumbering stride. He was wearing his costume of a lion skin and club, just like the legendary Hercules. The crowd alternatively cheered and booed as the lion ran from Corvus to try and escape once more and he in turn dutifully tried to make it look like much more of a battle than it actually was. Vipsanius strode down the podium to Felix and grabbed his shoulder angrily as he leaned down.

"What the fuck was that? Your bear was half dead or drunk! The crowd is laughing at me!" he hissed angrily, looking at the jeering audience behind the podium as Corvus and Borras now tried to chase the lion who was determined to get away. The beast jumped, clawing up the side of the walls, and tore down the wreaths and garlands that adorned the arena edge, causing those seated near the boundary to surge backwards in panic. Felix angrily shook off the podgy hand and glared into the face of Vipsanius.

"Get your filthy fucking hand off me, *cunnus*!" he said icily, uncovering one of the two swords he had under his toga in a motion that made sure his fat antagonist saw the weapon.

Vipsanius looked down at the hilt of the gladius and recoiled a little, then glared angrily at both Felix and Kratos.

"This is the end for you! I swear it, you little bastard!" he spat before hurrying back to whisper desperately in the announcer's ear.

The gaily clad man nodded and raised both hands as the trumpets erupted once more. "*AND NOW!* From ancient lands beyond the sea! A beast never seen before! A legendary CHIMERA!" cried the announcer to the crowd who did not hear a word above their own jeers and laughter.

With a tug of the ropes, the red cloth whipped away from the cage and its door sprang open. This revealed a curious sight that instantly made the entire raucous crowd hush. People gasped and craned their necks as they pointed and spoke quickly to each other, "Do you see that? What is it?" The creature was dark furred and tall with four legs and large feet. It had a misshapen lumpy head with white ears. It stood stock still in the cage.

The crowd barely noticed that against one wall the lion had pounced on 'Heracles' and sunk its claws into his shoulders. Borras yelled out in pain and barely avoided having his neck clamped in the snapping jaws. He only survived due to the expertise of Corvus who plunged his spear into the beast's chest, killing it instantly. The distracted spectators all caused a hubbub of noise now, murmuring and talking to each other in wonder at the strange sight that nodded its head but stood still in the enclosure with only a large round wicker basket in the corner of the cage for company.

Felix now urgently looked around up the sloped seating area. Even the collegium gang had temporarily forgotten they were waiting for him and strained to see the fantastical sight before them. He signalled to Serpo, who immediately took off his red turban and ran off out of sight.

"Now or never!" he said to himself, nodding through the private entrance at Juba who nodded back.

Down in the arena the beast stood still as the bloodied Borras and Corvus moved into the centre of the sand. Many thousands of pairs of eyes strained to see the nodding creature and they all saw the lid of the basket begin to move behind it. The lid lifted up and a hand snuck out, waving blindly around and trying to feel for the nearby creature before disappearing back into the basket. Then it appeared again, this time with a pugio in its hand. It began blindly waving around once more until it jabbed the creature in one of its rear legs. The crowd gasped as the beast burst into life and bucked its powerful back legs, destroying the basket with a shrill whinny as it propelled itself out of the cage.

The powerful kicks had thrown off two of its white fluffy 'feet' to reveal a set of hooves as it leapt down into the arena sand. The beast bucked and whinnied like a horse as its other white feet seemed to fall off. The white 'ears' that were the wings from a large white bird also came away with the bearskin that covered it. The bear's head mask that had been tied on the head flopped to the side and the whole bear skin, still tied with string, slid under the belly of the enraged, flea bitten cart horse that pranced around the arena as the stunned crowd went silent.

"Arghhhhh! You fucking bastard!" came the loud groan from the rubble of the basket in the cage and from under the destroyed wicker crawled Saxum. He stood and staggered from the cage covered in broken twigs, and seeing the horse, charged after it in a rage.

"You filthy, long-faced *cunnus*! You will pay for that!" he bellowed.

Someone in the still silent and stunned crowd shouted, "It's the Kraken! It's the cheat!"

The cry was taken up as the booing became universal. Food and drink, plates, cups and jugs now rained down into the arena with thousands of people trying to hit the hated Kraken. Saxum had caught up with the frenzied horse and hung from its neck as it bucked and tried to bite him. With every bucking jump you could hear him roar as he hung on to the frantic horse and tried to bite the enraged animal back.

Vipsanius ran with surprising speed to Felix, dodging the hail of food and missiles that now sailed down from the seating behind, and dragged him to the feet by his toga. His bright red face twisted with rage.

"What the fuck was *that*! Your 'Chimera' is a fucking carthorse! You have fucking ruined the Ludi!"

Felix quickly kneed him in the groin before springing behind the stunned Vipsanius and looping an arm under the fat chin to apply the choke hold Kratos had taught him. He dragged the resisting man onto his own seat as he felt him lose consciousness. Felix kept squeezing the arm under the fat man's neck with murmurs of "There, there... Hush, you will be fine" as the unconscious man flopped on the bench, unnoticed by the stunned, angry crowd throwing its missiles at the Kraken. Felix then looked back toward the western arena entrance just as the first puffs of smoke began to billow around the arches and the seating nearest the gate.

Some of the spectators in this area instantly forgot about the Kraken and screamed *"Fire! Fire!"* The crowd surged to get away as the first flames licked through the dry wooden beams and many in the packed tiered seating area tripped and fell or were trampled. Saxum, who had fallen from the bucking horse, was finding it hard to withstand the intense hail of projectiles that rained down on him. He forgot his four-legged enemy and was now roaring oaths and shaking fists at the crowd as he sprinted zig zagging around the sand at a terrific speed trying to avoid the barrage of missiles. A small jug hit him on the shoulder as he frantically tried to open a stout arena door that was designed to withstand bears. He immediately abandoned the door and headed to the cage, which was the only piece of cover available, and just before he made it he was struck with a stone on the back of the head. The brute staggered as he got to the cart and then for the first time in his life he passed out with his upper body slumped into the cage while his legs stood unfeeling in the sand.

The smoke billowed and now bright yellow flames licked the dried out wooden seating area and the western entrance. Many members of the crushed, panicked crowd were jumping down into the arena to avoid the fire and ran scrambling to the other side. Felix spotted some members of the collegium who had jumped down with drawn knives and were moving purposely to the unconscious Saxum. Corvus had already spotted them and nimbly sprinted behind one, plunging his spear into his back, then racing to the other man just before he was going to stab the helpless giant. The lightning-fast hunting knife of Corvus left a widening red line across this man's neck and he looked down in surprise to see his life blood splashing down his chest as he sank to his knees, frantically trying to hold the gaping flesh of his severed throat together.

Some of the crowd cheered at the unexpected drama unfolding below, but other collegium members roared in anger and jumped down onto the sand from all sides. These men drew their hidden weapons and hurried to attack Corvus, who was now next to the

308

cage calling to Borras for support as the gang members closed in. The whole eastern side of the crowd were on their feet as the spectacle unfolded. They were laughing and cheering as the enraged horse who had been the 'Chimera' now was in a clearly excited state. The amorous beast with its head inside the cage had mounted the unconscious body of Saxum and began thrusting its hips passionately to the delight of the spectators.

"*Felix!*" bellowed the surrounded Borras just below him "*Do something!*"

Felix turned to see Petronax and his whole gang jostling through the animated crowd to get to the private entrance. The food vendors' stalls were splintering to matchwood and their wares were stolen as people grabbed anything they could to throw into the arena. Many of the vendors were now fighting with the crowds that plundered them. The women of the Scipios screamed as one man jumped the fence, only to be stabbed by a nervous soldier. The death caused the crowd in the northern stand to become furious and immediately attack the soldiers at the gates who defended themselves frantically. The collegium members openly drew their weapons as they descended with the crowd and the fighting became almost like a real battle. The serving girls screamed and threw expensive wine cups at the men trying to scale the fence. All of the male members of the Scipii took up anything they could and along with Pug and the military officers began battling the crowd with all the rest of the competitors, trainers and guests of honour on the podium. The temporary fence now took up its unwanted role as a fortress wall under attack. Vipsanius had rolled off the bench and was now semi conscious and vomiting a great deal of red wine onto the floor.

As the western gate burned and the crowd in that section rioted, the eastern gate burst open and a team of horses pulling a chariot came thundering through the entrance, making the dozens of confused citizens now in the arena dive out of the way. Zeno stood in the basket whipping the horses while Decius, in full legionary battle dress, hung on for dear life. The crowds in most of the southern stand and all around the eastern gate were still on their feet, cheering and roaring their approval at the chaos before them. A great many were even wondering how much of the spectacle unfolding before them was part of the show.

In this scene of chaos and confusion the chariot sped through the scattering citizens of Tarraco to the embattled Borras and came to a halt. Several of Zeno's men were now jumping down to join them and began helping to secure the area just under the centre of the podium. Felix grinned as the smoke billowed across the arena, covering everything in a gloomy grey cloud that blocked out the sunlight. He tore off his toga and tunic, revealing his full battle uniform underneath, and handed a gladius to the shocked Kratos with a wink.

"Let's get rich, Numidian!" he said, speeding off along the podium to the unattended chest.

The treasure was completely forgotten by everyone on the podium as they desperately fought with the several thousand angry townsfolk in the north stand. The flimsy wooden fence was beginning to buckle under the pressure and it would soon give way. Missiles rained down and the elegant canopy sagged as someone jumped on it from above. The material ripped and a yelling man crashed down awkwardly onto the chairs before lying still. Felix reached the unattended chest and immediately tried to lift it. It would not budge. Gods! He frantically called to Kratos who stood still, completely aghast at what was happening.

"Kratos! *Kratos!*" he yelled frantically.

The shocked Greek blinked, then jumped into life and sprinted over with a furious look. "Wha...? Are we are stealing this? Are you fucking kidding me?!" he shouted incredulously.

"Shut up and push... We just need to push it... down there!" Felix spat, frantically trying to move the heavy chest.

Kratos cursed as he tried to close the lid, but the trinkets on top prevented him. He quickly scooped out the top layers of treasures and they fell jangling onto the wooden floor of the podium. Once these golden cups, plates and diadems were removed, leaving only the many small sacks inside, he easily slammed the lid shut and closed the latch with a curse before hooking his fingers under the bottom of the bronze plated chest. Felix saw what he was doing and joined him. With a mighty heave they rolled the chest forward and right off the edge with a thud.

The chest landed in the sand next to the chariot as more and more of the crowd attacked the group defending it. Felix and Kratos jumped down into the melee just as Petronax and the collegium tore down a section of the wall to surge through, attacking the Scipio guards from the flanks. The crowd in the eastern side laughed and cheered as the horse finished its lovemaking with the unmoving Saxum and cantered off happily through the rioting crowd. The whole northern side rioted and the south and western side surged to escape the growing flames. The billowing smoke now covered the entire arena and the air was full of shrill screams and shouts of both fighting and panic. The great beams that held up the western stands began to crack and split under the roaring flames. The wooden planks of the stepped seating and the arena floor were littered with corpses or groaning bodies of those trampled and injured. The chaos was not unlike the sacking of a fortress.

Felix clawed at the chest frantically as the cordon around him battled the growing crowd.

"Borras, Kratos, lift this chest! *Borras!*"

The big man swung his club at the three men who advanced at him and shot a backwards glance.

"*What?!*" he yelled angrily.

Felix turned to see a bleary eyed Saxum stagger towards him, the back of his tunic dripping with what looked like…

"Oi… Wha… What the fuck are you doing here?" said Saxum with dazed grin, patting Felix on the head.

The cunning man stood up, slapping him hard on the cheeks. "Wake up, oaf! I bet you a whore for the night you can't lift this chest!" He gave a sly grin. "You look too weak!"

Saxum blinked and shook his head, trying to clear the fog.

"What? Whassat?" his piggy eyes screwed up "*Weak,* is I? I will show you!"

With a howl of rage he bent down and grabbed the chest. The sinews of his thick arms stood up like the heavy ropes on ships, his body engaging its thick knots of muscle. Saxum's powerful legs pushed and amazingly he lifted it clear of the ground hugged to his belly. The blood that had oozed from the egg-shaped lump on his head now ran freely as his blood vessels pressurised under the huge feat of strength.

Felix jumped up and down with joy, egging him toward the chariot, and purple-faced Saxum set down the chest into the creaking chariot basket with a scraping thud. Zeno looked frantic as more and more of the crowd surged onto the sand, screaming and pointing at the hated Kraken.

"We have got to go *now*!" shouted the thief in panic.

Felix nodded and grabbed an item from the basket of the chariot. It was a crude vexillum bearing roughly sewn bull, the symbol of the 10th Legion. He jumped onto the chest and raised it above his head and began yelling wildly.

"10th MEN ON ME! 10th MEN ON ME!" he cried desperately as Petronax's gang jumped down to reinforce their friends attacking the already outnumbered section.

Legionaries in the crowd saw the uniformed Felix standing on the chariot surrounded by enemies. They saw Decius, too. They knew Kratos, Borras and Corvus were also in the games. They had seen them many times, had played dice or taken exercise on the sagularis with them. They were brothers by oath and the bonds of the Legion are sacrosanct. No man worth his salt would stand by while a brother was being attacked by piss-drinking civilians, street thugs and Greeks! With the honour of the 10th at stake, many soldiers in their off-white tunics yelled and signalled to each other. They immediately began jumping down into the arena with pugios drawn. The men of the collegium shouted in alarm and turned to face this deadly new threat in panic. The encircled band around the chariot had been given a little breathing space... for now.

"*Let's go*!" yelled Zeno frantically. His clean-shaven face looked white with fear.

Borras jumped onto the chariot along with Decius who became furious when he saw the chest.

"A heist? This whole fucking plan has been a heist?" he shouted incredulously.

Kratos jumped on one of the chariot horses and kicked a man in the face as the terrified horses strained and gathered momentum. Corvus sent another gang member screaming onto the sand with a spear thrust to the abdomen before running and jumping nimbly onto the yoke between the rear of the moving horses and the chariot basket. Saxum ran bellowing after them with a baying mob in tow.

"*Wait,* you bastards!" he yelled as the chariot sped up in a loop heading back for the eastern gate. He sprinted and with a mighty leap managed to get into the overly packed chariot. Felix, still balancing on the chest in the middle of the fleeing group, laughed gaily until a wheel bumped over a dead body. The vicious bump sent him flying down onto the sand. He landed hard and looked up, only to see the chariot leave the eastern gate just before several centuries of on-duty soldiers came storming in to quell the riot. Unfortunately for him, Petronax and the collegium were closer. The gang leader yelled and pointed as they all charged the lone man, so with a quick look around he decided on the one place no one would follow. Felix was fast, even in armour, and ran through the groups of civilians, soldiers and gang members who all fought in the smoke-filled chaos until he made it to the burning western side of the arena. The gate had collapsed and he saw a narrow gap in the raging fire. He looked rearwards into the smoke and he saw the dark figure of Juba just behind Petronax. Felix smiled quickly as he saw a dark-skinned arm bury its dagger into the leader's back. Even with the head of the gang killed, this would not save him from the ten or so gang members charging at him now. Gritting his teeth, he sprinted for the break in the fire, jumped straight into the wall of flames and was gone.

SPQR

Chapter 20

The chariot lost a wheel and scraped along for a few hundred more yards until they came to a small forest track next to the road. Zeno steered the exhausted horses into the track for a short distance until the strain was too much for them. The foam at their mouths dripped and spat as they gasped from exertion and one of the beasts tottered before sinking to the floor. Corvus hopped off the chariot and immediately ran back to the *Via Herculea* to check they were not being followed on the great paved road from the city. Looking back to Tarraco he could see the billowing smoke from the vicinity of the arena just on the shore to the south of the city. No one was on the road behind them. Kratos jumped off the horse and stalked to the back of the chariot where the men were untangling themselves.

"*Felix!* You utter bastard!" he growled full of venom, but there was no answer.

"Not here! Fell off, didn't he?" Saxum said, rubbing the lump on the back of his head. "Can't believe those piss drinkers pelted me! Felix said they would cheer for me after you killed the Chimera! Like a send off, you know, the Kraken saying bye to his loving fans!"

A pale Borras tore strips from his tattered costume and began tending to the oozing wounds in his shoulders caused by the lion.

"What 'fans', you idiot?" he muttered. "The whole town hates you and Felix damn well knew that!" He winced as he dabbed at a gash on the shoulder.

Saxum looked suspicious. "You think he *wanted* me to get pelted? I am the star of this merry little band!" he said, glaring at them with his thick arms folded across his chest defensively.

Decius snorted and pointed to Saxum's backside. "Well, you were a favourite of someone!" he said sarcastically before turning to Zeno. "*You!* What do you know about all this? I was told to meet you backstage with the chariot and that I might need to give some protection when the results did not go the way we wanted. I was told it was a betting scam, yet I rode into a fucking battle and got back here with a chest with the Scipio family seal on it!" he said angrily.

Borras peered at the chest and his mouth dropped open. "What the fuck? What the fuck is *that* doing here! I was told we would do the beast hunt with the bear and the lion, then the last beast would be a comical thing that the crowd would like!" he cried.

Kratos shook his head. "That lying bastard has tricked all of us!" he muttered, turning back to Zeno. "Well?" he said glowering at him.

The eyes of the thief flickered back and forth nervously at the group of angry soldiers. He stayed silent until Decius moved towards him and drew his bloody gladius with intent.

"Look, I thought everyone was in on it!" he explained, quickly backing away and holding his hands up defensively to Decius. "You met me backstage and I was there with the chariot! He told me that we would drive underneath the podium and get the money he tossed down. Apart from that I had to check with the scrawny one first... Ignavus, was it? I had to check he prepared the pitch to light the fire! Look, umm, we need to get going! My men are just a little further up this track! We have a place where we can eat and drink then get moving through the night," he said, looking agitated at the bloodstained sword in the hand of Decius.

"You mean he *planned* that fire?" groaned Borras, shaking his head in disbelief. "We are fucked! We are fucked! This is more than a flogging and missio ignominiosa. We will be executed for this! Crucified! We are so fucked! We are so fucked!" The big man sat down on the side of the dusty track and put his head in his hands.

Saxum snorted and grinned at everyone, flashing his filthy teeth. "You lot just don't understand show business! I took a bang on the head, but still the Kraken put on a good show!" His ugly face clouded over for a moment in thought. "Then again, I can't remember half of it!" He grinned once more. "But I remember the fucking crowd laughing and all! They loved it! They should give us medals for making the best show that shit pile arena has ever seen, I reckon! And we come out with gold, too!" he said with a nod.

Decius sighed and pointed once more to Saxum's tunic with its suspicious stains all over his lower back.

"Do you *know* why the crowd were laughing? Have you seen what's on your back? Do you even know what was happening? Can you remember what that horse was doing to you?" he said in exasperation.

Saxum felt behind him and pulled off the tunic, looking at the gooey mess that was starting to dry into a crust. He looked at Decius suspiciously, then slowly a look of horror crept over his face.

"It... It... looks like...?" His piggy eyes pleaded with Decius, who smirked.

"Sorry, friend, but it *is* what it looks like! Man juice! Well, horse juice, anyways! Yeah, that horse had you over the cart while you napped and yes... the whole crowd loved it!"

Saxum looked blinking at the tunic before bellowing in rage and grabbing it around the collar, ripping it cleanly in half. He ran bare-chested into the undergrowth, destroying all before him and roaring like an angry bear. Decius smirked at the shaking foliage as small trees and bushes were torn down and he squatted to tend to the injuries of Borras. The large man, who had clearly lost an amount of blood from the lacerations the lion gave him, had gone pale in shock. Corvus looked at the dense bushes, listening to the insane gurgling of the unseen Saxum. He flashed one of his rare and grotesque smiles in the direction of the noise.

"It *was* pretty funny," he said softly.

Kratos leaned against the chariot and looked sideways at Corvus. "What did you know?" he asked quietly.

Corvus looked around him at the expectant faces as all eyes were on him. "I knew everything that happened," he said indifferently. "I assumed everyone knew more or less the same."

Borras who had looked up with a face creased with anxiety now let his head sink into his hands once more. "We are fucked... We are so fucked..." he muttered quietly.

Suddenly there was a clatter of hoofs on the road. The whole section looked at each other in alarm. "Off the track!" barked Decius and they immediately scattered into the bushes.

Zeno desperately tried to drag the chest from the chariot. He looked around wildly at his fleeing companions. "We can't just leave it!" he cried.

Corvus ran back with his wicked hunting knife drawn and thrust his face close to Zeno. "Off the track...*now!*" he hissed and even the hardened criminal blanched and dove into the cover of the bushes.

All was quiet as a horse cantered close by. Even the crazed Saxum had given up on his rage and quietly wept, unseen by the others.

They heard voices and a single horse breathing heavily. It approached slowly up the track. Corvus readied his spear and tried to move into a position of ambush. Suddenly, a loud voice split the air as clear as could be.

"What do we have here? An abandoned chariot! Why, a couple of simple soldiers like ourselves should examine this! If it proves to be auspicious there may be a reward for finding it. Our Pilus Prior will be proud of us this day!" said Felix quite deliberately while he scanned the bushes for ambush, or more likely arrest.

"*You!*" cried Kratos, standing straight up in the undergrowth. "You have some fucking explaining to do!"

Everyone apart from Saxum left the bushes and came back onto the rough track to see Felix mounted on the flea bitten 'chimera' with a bruised and soot-smudged Ignavus sat behind him. The cunning swindler was wearing his scorched uniform and armour, and his arms and face were almost completely black. His head was totally bald apart from a patchy fuzz, his hair having been burnt off during his escape, and his blackened face made his white-toothed smile flash even brighter. Ignavus slid off the horse onto a clearly injured leg, wincing. Felix half turned the horse back down the track as Kratos, Borras and Decius advanced on him.

"Brothers, please!" he said loftily. "This is a moment for some rejoicing! Let us put anger to the flank where it belongs!" He spurred the horse away as they kept moving towards him with grim looks on their faces. "Brothers! You have lost your senses," he said evenly, his blue eyes flashing in the blackened face. "Juba will be here shortly with a cart full of civilian clothes for all of us who want to make an escape. We have a hiding place in the hills and contacts in all the ports from here to Massilia. Those who wish to continue with army life can do so and take their share as they wish."

Decius gripped the sword in his hand tightly and glared at him. "Get off the horse *now*!" he said, shaking with rage.

Felix lifted a hand to calm him. "Decius, please, calm yourself! Think about what we have in our possession, and what possibilities await us in the future!"

"The army *was* my future, you bastard!" spat Decius angrily. "I wanted to be a centurion one day! I wanted a career! *You* have made me a fucking criminal on the run!" His face began to crack a little.

Borras took up the argument "Same here, Felix! There is making money on the side, then there is planning a daylight robbery from patricians! I would have never got involved if I had known! What happened to winning a few coins by entering in the games, eh?" he said weakly, looking drained. "Now look at us... fucked! We will be crucified for this! They will send an army after us. It doesn't matter where we hide. We are so fucked!" he cried and tottered back towards the chariot, weakly kicking a clod of mud in anger.

Felix looked at them evenly from atop the fidgeting horse. Kratos and Decius stood still, one in a now dirty white toga, the other in full fighting attire, both angrily glaring up at him, Borras sat back down next to the chariot and put his head in his hands while Ignavus hobbled to stand with Zeno, both of them clearly anxious to open the chest, but nervous of Corvus who leaned against the broken chariot basket, staring back at them. Felix sighed and pinched the bridge of his nose.

"Right, we don't have much time and first things first... Corvus?"

The scarred man nodded and in a flash drew his razor-sharp hunting knife, plunged it into Zeno's neck and whipped it out, giving him a hard kick to the belly before coolly sliding the weapon back into its sheath. Zeno fell backwards from the blow and tried to sit up as the arterial blood spurted from the wound in his neck. He turned to Felix and mouthed gurgling words of hatred on lips that spewed blood before sinking backwards to the ground in front of his shocked audience.

Felix jumped down from the horse and strode over with a sneer at the dying thief. His teeth and eyes flashed white in his burnt and blackened face.

"The silly *cunnus* was going to have us all killed later today," he said quietly, watching the life fade from Zeno's hate-filled dark eyes. "A few miles up this track is a hut full of poisoned wine and those who wouldn't drink would be finished by some of his gang that is waiting there. Juba told me Zeno had asked him to go in on it and split our share with him. I do not think the stupid shit ever realized you never fuck with the 10th Legion."

He looked around the stunned group and sighed. "Right! Let's see what we have, then quickly make a decision. If you like I will take my share and be gone? If you lot want to return to town

321

with your shares to hand back in, I thought some of you might have a cry about it, so there *is* an option and it's up to you. You can say you jumped into the chariot to escape, then you say you realized it was Zeno, the famous thief of Massilia. You have the body right there to back your story," he said with a glance at the gladius in Decius' hand before looking into his face. "There is even a reward for his capture and that would look good amongst the Legions officers, neh? But first, let us see what we have."

He stepped over the lifeless body of Zeno, moving to the chariot basket where Corvus and Ignavus helped him flip the chest the right way up. Felix drew his pugio and hammered on the broken latch with the hilt until it came loose. He opened the warped chest to reveal many leather coin pouches, all securely tied. Felix did a little dance and cackled as he opened one and looked inside, before freezing like a statue. He snatched up another pouch and opened it, peering in, only to drop it on the floor. Then another and another. He fished deeper in the chest, pulled another pouch from the bottom and frantically checked it. His shoulders slumped and the coin pouch dropped from his fingers as he turned and walked on shaky legs to sit down wearily next to Borras with a dazed, drunken grin on his face.

"Hey, you big Teuton ox! What a day, eh?" he said and his eyes rolled in his head as he fell back, into the long grass by the track, unconscious.

Borras looked stunned for a moment, then jumped in astonishment as Ignavus sank to the floor with a sudden shrill wail, his skinny, blackened arms striking the ground as he wept bitterly. Corvus pick up a pouch and emptied a quantity of small, flat river pebbles into his hand. Decius and Kratos looked at each other, then took up another pouch and emptied it, then another. Pebbles... all of them, every bag! Suddenly, in the distance, they heard the sound of hobnailed footwear jogging on the great paved road, coupled with the jingle of equipment from many running soldiers getting closer.

"*Rapist!*" came a roar from the bushes and everyone jumped in fright. Saxum came crashing from the foliage with a tear-streaked face and chased after the panicked, flea-bitten horse. His old enemy gave a shrill whinny of fright and ran back down the track with the maddened brute sprinting after him, yelling furiously.

Ignavus cried bitterly, face down in the dirt, and Felix still lay on his back, unconscious. Kratos and Decius looked at each other, the pebbles and the body of Zeno with shock and disbelief. Corvus took in the scene around him and gave a smirk, which turned into a smile as he began to chuckle. Borras, Kratos and Decius all stared at him in horror as hollow laughter rang from his mouth. When he saw their shocked faces he laughed so hard that tears came from his eyes. He was still laughing when the arriving troops surrounded and arrested them.

SPQR

Chapter 21

The legendary arena riot of Tarraco was blamed on the collegium. The local magistrates needed heads to roll for this and the deceased Petronax and his men were clearly identified attacking the guards of the Scipios before gaining access to the podium. Fifteen remaining collegium members were hunted down and publicly executed. The games organiser, Titus Vipsanius, was told he would stand trial for the desecration of a religious ceremony, mismanagement of the games and for causing the fire through poor safety practices. He pretty much passed the blame down to everyone on his staff and the trial would be ongoing. Several soldiers had been seen involved in the fighting and illegally competing, but a Tribune Livius, who had been the senior officer present, chose loyalty towards his men over the accusations of the townsfolk and roundly chastised the local government for letting their own citizens ruin the Ludi. He was on the podium that day and after he had to arm himself and fight desperately alongside the Scipio guards he staunchly blamed the civilians for causing the riot. The taverns buzzed with gossip and rumour as many of the spectators claimed to have seen the 'Kraken' heave the treasure chest into the chariot that hurriedly disappeared before the garrison restored order.

Strangely, the treasure of the Scipii was not much of an issue in the allegations and finger-pointing after this event. The reason the chest appeared mostly full was because they merely wanted to appear wealthy for the sake of their own prestige in Tarraco. The senior members of the family in Rome who decided whom they would send to attend Tarraco each year would never let the junior relatives take such wealth by sea to a provincial town; the chest was a ruse for keeping up appearances. The actual wealth and prizes for the competitors had been scooped out onto the floor by Kratos and most were recovered by a Scipii family member who had secured them soon after the garrison had regained control. The chest was found, a mile out of town, with a section of men from the 2nd Century; however, because they clearly had none of the gold, the matter was not pressed. If anything, the contents of the chest were a source of minor embarrassment for the Scipios, so no case of prosecution for theft was brought and the chest was not even mentioned by anyone. It was almost as if it had never existed in the first place.

Due to this, the Army did not have the legal right to punish the men for anything to do with the chest. It seemed Felix talked his way out as well as he talked his way into things and managed to compile a fantastical story of bribery, theft and gang warfare between Petronax and Zeno. The performance company called 'The Brazen Bull' had merely been a few soldiers of the 10th trying to do their Legion proud and in the end even managing to kill a notorious thief for which they had the body as proof on arrest. The local magistrate had no jurisdiction over the army and Tribune Livius raised his eyebrow at every part of the story, but through lack of witnesses and evidence had no choice than to hand the section over to Pug for lesser punishments.

The praefectus castrorum, of course, thought differently. To him the incident was the worst thing ever to happen to the Legion. He had two soldiers dead from fighting and fifteen under the medicus from the arena incident. As for those several dozen that had been arrested, he wanted to have them all dismissed and their hands cut off. The new Legatus Labienus sent word through Tribune Livius that he did not want the legion so decimated, so Pug was refused his request. For our section it was due to the arguments of Tanicus and Falco, *and* the fact two of the men were personally decorated by Caesar that we were not given a worse punishment.

Galba came forward, spoke on everyone's behalf and listed the attributes of every man apart from Felix. Pug chastised him for being weak with the section and said seeing as he liked them so much he could 'oversee' the punishment of the men. So officially the charges for illegal entry into the Ludi, brawling and gambling irregularities were dismissed, yet a punishment still stood for bringing the Legion into disrepute. Each man would get ten lashes, go on half rations and *pecunaria multa*[95] for three months of road repair as far away as Pug could find.

Several other groups of soldiers were punished for various incidents that day as the chaos allowed for many opportunistic crimes both inside and outside the arena. The Riot of Tarraco became a 10th Legion legend and many would laugh about that day for a long time after. The instigating section, apart from their decanus, were flogged and given a week to heal, in the jail of course, before being sent out into the miserable wintery rains to begin their months of hard labour living next to remote pieces of road.

***

"Should have never got involved," muttered Galba once more, spitting into the rain as he sat on his stool under the makeshift shelter. He stared at the spitted chickens gloomily as Corvus turned them slowly with his good arm. The scarred man did not take his flogging well — not that he feared it, he just resented any man giving him punishment. After a huge fight with the men conducting the punishment parade Pug himself had smashed his arm with a club, right there in front of the assembled cohorts.

---

[95] Fines or deductions in pay.

The section had learned over the weeks how damaging it was for them, as his hunting skills were sorely missed.

Kratos sat silently looking into the burning embers while Ignavus ate noisily from his mess tin and stared at the sizzling chickens. Decius stalked over and took two bowls of gruel to the tent where he sat with the miserable Saxum, still covered head to toe in mud. Wincing, Corvus flexed the fingers on his damaged arm and muttered quietly to himself as he boiled eggs on one part of the fire. The rain now drummed on the already waterlogged awning and it would be dark soon.

"*See!* Always eating! Your fat friend is coming with *more* food as well!" came an angry voice from the road. An old man with a pointed hood and large, stout boots stood in the rain glaring at them, then walked around the gap in the road in disgust. As soon as he got back onto the pavement he hurried off with a final call back to the miserable soldiers. "You bloody lot need Sertorius as your commander!" he yelled before hurrying on with his staff clicking against the wet stones.

"What in Dis was that all about?" said Ignavus, shaking his head at the departing figure.

Kratos wound his cloak tighter around him to guard against the encroaching chill, glancing up at the old man hurrying off into the approaching gloom.

"Borras will be here soon," he said quietly moving his feet closer to the fire. "Then we can settle down for another night of shivering." The Greek not only looked thinner but much older these days as he gazed sadly into the orange flames.

"Still, we will have a full belly this time," said Ignavus cheerfully, slurping down another spoonful of the horrid-looking egg and porridge mixture.

The unseen winter sun that was muted by the rain-swept clouds sank below the hills and the sky began to darken quickly. Felix sat laughing under another makeshift shelter with Cassius and the men of the 7th Cohort around their own cook fire as Borras arrived. The large man had smelled the roasting chickens long before he had seen them. He tethered Marius to a nearby tree and quickly approached the awning to look at the assembled Kratos, Ignavus, Corvus and Galba, who were all silently looking at the birds. The skin on the chickens was crackling and browned, and the fat that dripped into the embers with a hiss sent delicious smells around the huddled group of famished soldiers.

"What in the name of…" Borras gasped. "Chickens!" He quickly squeezed in beside Ignavus and Kratos. His reddened cold face lit up like a happy child. "Where the fuck did they come from?!" he chuckled incredulously.

"One bloody guess," snapped Decius, who had come to stand near the shelter. The rain had stopped, the sky was clearing and the men knew the night would be freezing. They had seen it before. He stood looking unimpressed at the group. Borras looked around the impassive faces and back at Decius.

"Well? I give up!" he said with exasperation before grinning. "Not that I bloody care!" he said, rubbing his hands together in glee. Decius scowled and pointed over towards Felix.

"So you too are now 'friends' with that fox-haired bastard?" he asked with a sneer at the big Teuton.

Borras' eyes flashed to the chickens that seemed like the best he had ever seen or smelt in his life, then the sheepish face of Kratos who nodded and gave a slight shrug, almost in apology, before looking back at Decius.

"Felix got them?" Borras said with a worried look. The large man's face fell in realisation. "The bastard is bribing us," he moaned, shaking his head.

Decius sniffed and looked back at Felix with hatred. "You don't have to eat it... Me and Saxum won't!" he said, jutting his chin towards the tent where Saxum now slept soundly under a blanket, exhausted from weeping.

Borras looked at Decius, then towards the tent. He saw the guards with their own chicken and Felix with the 7th Cohort men about to eat theirs. He looked back towards the chickens on the spit and Corvus, who was readying everyone's mess tins for their portion. Ignavus bobbed up and down in the peculiar way he did when hungry and Kratos looked at the big man, seeing the torment in his eyes. He too had sworn he would never have anything to do with Felix again, but that was before he was weak with hunger and chilled to the bone.

"Look, we are all starving, Felix isn't going anywhere and neither are we. Hate him if you like, but eat the chicken, Borras. You need it," said the Greek sympathetically, looking around for support. "I know I need it! Gods! We *all* need it."

Corvus half shrugged, half nodded in his apathetic way while Ignavus vigorously nodded as he stared intently as the sizzling chickens. "Yeah... we do," he murmured as his mouth watered.

Decius folded his arms across his chest and opened his mouth to argue but Galba raised a hand.

"Quiet, Decius! Let him make up his own mind," he said, turning to the big man. "Borras, you can sleep in a cold tent with some gruel and a frozen onion in your gut if you like. Surely a bit of cooked chicken is better? I will *never* trust that red-haired swine again, but I won't waste chicken on a cold day like this. If

329

you want it, eat it," he said with a final look at the glowering Decius who spun on his heel and stalked back to the sleeping tent where he would spend the rest of the night.

Borras watched him go and felt a pang of betrayal for an instant before turning back to the chickens that Corvus now slid off the spit. There was a busy little exchange of knives and mess tins, and then lots of slurping and sucking on fingers and bones. Felix enjoyed his own chicken with Cassius and the other men from the 7th. The guard detachment laughed as an unlucky colleague finally won a bet at dice and punched the chilly air in triumph. Despite the cold and damp, the mood in the camp was good and Felix was absently listening to one of the 7th men telling a story about a midget prostitute he had in Gades.

"Honest, she could stand up straight and still suck your cock without you being stood on a stool or anything!"

Cassius, the veteran of the group, snorted as his teeth tore into a fat chicken leg. He gasped and huffed as the hot chicken burnt his tongue, trying to answer at the same time. "Are you sure you were not screwing some young pullus?" he said, eyeing his companion as he took another scalding bite.

"Cassius, I am telling you! It was a full grown woman! Well... sort of? Apart from the height. Kids ain't got tits and a big, hairy *cunnus*, have they?" said his companion, laughing.

Felix usually appreciated such conversations and would often tell a story to match, but he sat quietly eating his portion. He heard the commotion of mess tins and looked over at his section in the darkness. Felix smiled as he saw the happy face of Borras in the light of the flickering campfire and listened to the rest of his friends eating their delicious meal with gusto.

SPQR

Chapter 22

The horse laboured northward along the straight road with some difficulty. The slip had clearly caused some damage to the foreleg of the flagging steed. Sextus Pinarius Ocella cursed his luck once more and flicked the crop against the horse again to keep it going. The sun had now disappeared over the Ligurian sea, which was off to the east a mile or two away, and the distant hills and mountains to the north and west that had reflected the red, dying rays of sunlight now looked black and foreboding. The wet flagstones of the road that had caused his horse to lose its balance now looked like they would remain ever shining with moisture as the fine drizzle started coming down once more. Ocella shivered and hunched his shoulders into his wet travelling cloak as he urged the horse onward at a limping trot.

The fertile agricultural plains of Luna with its many productive farms were now dark and the road traffic on the *Via Aemilia Scauri* had been nonexistent for the last couple of hours as travellers settled down for the night. The twinkling lights of the town of Luna lay in the distance. Ocella was looking forward to getting to the way station and snatching some much needed food and rest. He once again checked the small satchel at his side for his own official pass, knowing he would not procure another horse from the station master without it. He fumbled under the cloak, ran a nervous finger inside the leather flap, felt the small sealed scroll and breathed a sigh of relief. He had not touched the satchel since the last check but he did this often and always had done.

His wife had laughingly said, "It's exactly because you worry so much that they give you important messages to carry! The way you panic? I am surprised they do not make you nanny for their children, too!"

The messenger smiled in the darkness and wondered what his wife Numeria would be doing right now. Probably humming to herself as always while tending the children and getting herself into bed. Never a care, that woman, he thought with a grin, so different from him. Probably why they made a good couple.

The puffing horse slowed from its trot into a limping walk once more and Ocella cursed. He saw a milestone in the gloom and drove the horse onward.

"Come on, boy! We are nearly there! We can soon rest!" he urged, flicking his riding stick against the horse's flank.

The creature neighed and shook its maned head in refusal until the rider struck it harder. Ocella knew a limping horse, once stopped, was hard to get started again. He flicked the flanks, squeezed with his legs and the horse sighed before taking up the trot once more and, despite the noticeable limp, carried the messenger toward the twinkling lights in the distant darkness.

The drizzle had not stopped by the time Ocella reached the large *mansio*[96]. The small rider could see lights flickering from a high window and breathed a sigh of relief. He had been here before, but it was more than a year or two ago and he could not remember who staffed the place. Occasionally, the less diligent workers of these mansios would lock up and go to a wine shop or home to their wives if no official travellers reached them before the dark watches of the night. Of course, this was a form of dereliction of duty and made Ocella furious when it happened

---

[96] Fully furnished way station / travelling house for officials and those on official business.

to him last summer, but during that incident the skinny mansio keeper insisted he had a fever and that message was particularly important, so Ocella did not have the time to report him anyway. The rider now dismounted the tired, injured horse with a grimace and banged on the large wooden gate to the courtyard. He waited for a long moment and heard nothing but the laboured breathing of his horse and the patter of the rain. The small man sighed impatiently and banged again, much harder.

"Yeah! Yeah! I am coming!" said a gruff voice from behind the doorway. A small, barred window snapped open in the gate and Ocella saw a sputtering oil lamp and some unidentified, lumpish character behind it.

"Stick yer head closer and state yer business!" snapped the husky voice with annoyance.

"I am Sextus Pinarius Ocella, a messenger on behalf of the office of the Consul Lucius Calpurnius Piso," he snapped back in his own official voice while fishing out the small sealed scroll. "Here is my pass and I ask you immediately to open up and assist," he said, offering the document through the tiny barred window. A hand grabbed it and he could see a tough-looking man swathed in cloth inspect the seal before pushing his face up to the bars to examine Ocella. The beady eye that glared at him flicked left and right, squinting into the gloom all around before the scroll was thrust back through the bars.

"Yer late!" the voice grumbled and the little window snapped shut, followed by the sound of scraping wood as the bar was raised. The rain-wet gates groaned open to reveal a large, high-walled courtyard with neat rows of stable stalls lining either side. Ocella led the injured horse by the reins onto the muddied flagstones of the courtyard past the squat gateman standing in sandals, tunic and part of a toga wrapped around his head and shoulders. The grumpy man immediately shut the gate, locking it with the bar, and turned away with his sputtering oil lamp before Ocella could get a look at his face.

"Stick yer horse in number two," said the retreating man, jerking a thumb over his shoulder in the direction of the numbered stalls before hopping over puddles as he hurried back to the lit up doorway under the eaves of the tiled sloping roof. Ocella's forehead wrinkled in irritation.

"This horse is injured. He took a slip on the road and..."

"Yeah, yeah!" said the squat shape as it reached the door. "We can sort this out tomorrow! Now I am getting cold and I have all sorts of guests to sort out tonight. Yer want me to show you to yer room or not? Stick the nag in number two and come inside before all the warm air is gone," he snapped.

The messenger sighed and squinted into the darkness to see the barely legible numerals on the individual stables. Once he identified door with number two painted on it, he led the limping beast into the empty stall before closing the wooden gate behind it. He felt a little surge of anxiety once more and double checked he had the messenger bag with its important contents before going over to the illuminated doorway. Ocella stepped into a small hallway that was lit by a glow coming from the room at the far end where a low hum of quiet conversation emanated. There were several open doors nearest him. One showed a darkened kitchen, with the other room opposite looking like the small bedroom of his unfriendly companion, who now shut and locked the courtyard door before pushing past him to put a large meat cleaver down next to a thick wooden chopping board on a table just inside the kitchen.

"Can't be too careful, eh?" grunted the stocky man when he noticed Ocella's look at the deadly tool. The host then threw the damp toga he had used for protection against the rain into the bedroom.

"Anyways, the name's Tuditanus but you can call me 'Tud'. Not sure if I have seen you here before? I have had lots of traffic lately. It seems everyone is on the move. Right, so follow me and we will get you settled. Kitchen is closed and the bath is cold. Luckily there is plenty of bread, fish and some stew left from supper, so I will get you some food in a bit. I have all sorts of patricians and equestrians in tonight and the upper class gents are all army officers, so keep yer trap shut if you know what's good for you! Regardless of them, this is my station and while you are here there are some rules!" said the man, stumping off down the corridor.

"Good! I have a message for an officer who might be here," said Ocella to his ignorant host who continued along the corridor rattling off a practiced monologue of various rules, dos and don'ts, and times for meals and baths. The rider followed, looking at the silhouette of the thick neck and shoulders of the man that clearly marked him as an ex-soldier.

The pair walked out into a spacious, warm room, lit with many lamps. The open area had many large but simple tables flanked by benches that were occupied by various groups of people all eating and talking quietly. Ocella nodded his hellos to the few people who looked up with a vague sense of interest and hurried after his cantankerous host who was warning him about drunkenness on his premises as he led the messenger down another, more narrow corridor with many curtained doorways, each with a neatly painted numeral above it.

"Right, this is you in number five," grunted Tud, opening the curtain to reveal a tiny but very clean room with a simple bed and stool that had a lamp sat upon it, which the host immediately went forward to light. In the glow of the lamp the rider could now see the furrowed lines of age on the station master and an eye that looked milky with some scarring around it. Ocella's memory now sparked into life and he smirked as he remembered this less than gracious host. Tud stood back up with his own lamp and nodded down to the other light source.

"That one's yours. If you need more oil, I keep a jar in the common room. If you need a piss pot, I keep it out the back door where you just come in. What do you want for food?" he said gruffly, looking at the tired rider.

"The bread and stew sounded good! And some water. Also, is there enough food for tomorrow's leg? I have to get my message to..."

Tud cut him off with a raised hand. "Look! We have a system here. Aculeo does the morning shift, see? The slave will light the fire and cook breakfast while Aculeo gives you a fresh nag and rations for the road. If you want water, it's in the jugs on the tables already. See you in a moment. I will bring your food out now," said the man, striding off with apparent indifference to his guest's questions.

Ocella smiled at the man's attention to detail as he took the lamp off the stool and placed it on the tiny shelf in the corner. The rider thought of all the other stations that were more friendly but much less organised as he stripped off his travelling cloak and spread it over the stool to dry. He sat on the bed, took out a set of worn slippers from his pack and wearily removed his damp sandals. He always travelled with a dry tunic and slippers to change into for days just like this, but this time he decided to take his supper in his damp clothes, as the common room was much warmer and so his clothes could dry off a little. The rider pulled on the slippers, set down his own personal travelling pack and took his small official satchel with his pass and the large messenger bag with its many documents with him as he walked back into the common room. Some messengers would leave these items in their rooms, but this was not in his nature. He felt a little panicked when they were out of sight.

As Ocella walked in the room, a group of common soldiers at a nearby table were quietly stacking their bowls and saying their goodnights to each other as they moved off down the narrow corridor. Another table at the other end of the room, partially blocked from his view by a column, had several occupants who were clearly the upper classes Tud had mentioned. All looked smudged from the road and had stripped down to their military tunics; only one stern-faced man still wore his breastplate.

Ocella walked to an empty bench and sat down, placing his messenger bag next to him and tucking the strap under his thigh in case of theft. Not that it would ever be stolen in this place, but he could not relax unless he did these little things that ensured his peace of mind. Another nearby man who appeared to be a dispatch rider finished a cup of water and yawned before getting up and leaving his empty plate. He headed towards the narrow corridor to the simple sleeping quarters. Ocella poured himself some water and nodded politely to the messenger who walked past to his own room.

Straight ahead from Ocella a larger and more decorative doorway led to the more sumptuous part of the mansio. He knew these parts were strictly reserved for senators, governors, tribunes, military officers, or indeed anyone with a high enough office or enough coin. Sometimes knowing the right person in the right position could get you a scroll that could make your journey a more comfortable experience. Ocella had stayed in the 'rich rooms' only three times before and that was thanks to a friend who ran a station down south, and only when the mansio was completely empty of other travellers.

"Here yer go!" said Tud, placing down a large wooden bowl full of warm stew with a clunk that startled Ocella. Next to the bowl, the grumpy man set down a big piece of bread and the spoon he had crooked in a finger. He then took out a wax tablet he had tucked in his belt and opened it with his thick tattooed hands while his good eye squinted in concentration as it scanned the neat handwriting on the tablet.

"Right. So, consular messenger from Rome, injured horse in number two possibly needs replacing, yer getting yer head down in room five," he grunted as he used a stylus to scratch the details into the wax. "If it's from the Consuls office, I am guessing you are heading northward with an urgent message and a classified destination?" asked Tud, sitting down on the opposite bench with a thoughtful frown on his wrinkled features. Ocella was taken aback by the details this station master required, but also felt Tud was now finally willing to listen to him and could help him with some of his messages.

"Actually, I have several messages for various places and people," he said vaguely. "But two are for officers that might be here. One was a 'Titus Labienus' and the other..." he trailed off, recalling only one by memory, and reached for his messenger bag. He opened it and carefully removed a small scroll, turning it to the lamplight as he peered at the neatly written name on the document. "Publius Licinius Crassus?" said Ocella quietly, looking up at Tud hopefully. The squat man nodded and licked his lips as he scanned his tablet with a furrowed forehead.

"T. Labienus... Horse in number ten, document case locked in the strong box and sleeping in patrician room one," he grunted, scanning further. "Ah yes, P. L. Crassus... Horse in number twelve, sleeping in patrician room three," he said nodding, looking up. "They didn't want the couches laid out on the good side, so they are eating back here with us. Yeah, yer Crassus message is for the youngest one sat over there! And the

Labienus fella is the big one still wearing his fighting kit," he motioned to the corner table where the officers sat deep in conversation.

Ocella nodded and immediately regretted changing into his slippers. He thought about getting back into his wet riding sandals, but decided quickest was best. *Besides, they have already seen me come in*! He cursed his own lack of professionalism. The dispatch rider thanked the station master, slung his messenger bag over his shoulder, got up and immediately went to the table that had four individuals sitting around it, finishing their meal.

"Excuse me, sirs! I am Sextus Pinarius Ocella, a messenger on behalf of the office of the Consul Lucius Calpurnius Piso. I have messages for Titus Labienus and Publius Licinius Crassus," he stated quietly in his official voice while bringing the dispatches from his messenger bag. All the while the small man was internally praying they would not look down at his slippers.

The officers stopped talking and looked at him. The large man in the breastplate immediately stood up and stretched his arm out over the table.

"I'm Labienus," he said flatly and promptly took the scroll from the rider before sitting down to read it.

The young man who sat closest to the messenger looked up with a smile and said pleasantly, "The other one is for me." He took the scroll from the dispatch rider who in turn removed a small tablet of his own, asking for a signature in receipt.

Publius Licinius Crassus nodded, took the tablet and laid it on the table near a flickering lamp to scrawl his name into the wax. Looking down, he noticed the dry slippers on this otherwise damp and road-dirty man.

"Are you coming from Rome or the north? When did you arrive?" he asked quietly as he signed the tablet and handed back to the messenger.

"From Rome, sir, and just a few moments ago, sir. I would have been here long before sunset, but my horse took a fall," replied the messenger nervously.

The young man nodded and immediately began to break the seal on the scroll. "I am guessing that this is a private message you have been given to augment your official duties?" he asked smoothly with a raised eyebrow.

The tired-looking rider blinked at him for a moment, then looked over Crassus' head in a soldierly fashion, almost standing to intente. "My journey manager works with the senatorial clerks and I just get a list of names and destinations, sir. I could not say who exactly sent the message, unless I am given it by a specific person," he said apologetically.

"Thank you," Crassus smiled. "If that is all you have for me then you may go and rest," he said politely. The relieved messenger scuttled around the table to get a signature from the man wearing the breastplate so he could leave. Crassus opened the tiny scroll under the eyes of his dining companions.

"Probably from your mother making sure you have enough underwear!" said the older, taller man across from him with a grin.

Servius Sulpicius Galba was a cheerful veteran officer and capable commander who had been in several engagements, noticeably the recent operations against the Allobroges tribe in Gaul. Crassus nodded politely to his brown-haired companion with a broken nose and smiled as he read the message from his father that reminded him of the important political union with

340

Caesar and, personally, how proud he was to know that his son was going to fight for Rome once more.

"Enough on teasing him! He has fought in wars, too!" sighed a young balding man named Quintus Pedius sitting next to him. "Anyway, Galba, what were you saying about the Dacians? Surely they differ in more ways than we can suspect?"

The tall Galba's smile dropped and he looked thoughtful. "Well, different in some ways, I suspect. But then generally I think all Celts are pretty similar, if not in tactics and dress then certainly in smell," he said with a smirk.

"The Dacians, or *Getae* as the Greeks called them, are more closely related to the Scythians, although admittedly they do have some amount of Celtic blood," said Crassus absently as he finished reading the note. The younger man looked up. "To assume they are the same in every aspect would be unwise. Surely, Galba, you are talking in jest and must have a huge respect for those who take the field against us. Did not Catugnatus, the chief of Allobroges, and all his men put up a brave fight at the Battle of Solonium where you were part of a great victory for our Republic?" said the young man, seeking to correct his companion but not to offend him.

Galba nodded at the intelligent young man with a guarded look, but smiled when he saw the man was apparently sincere.

Crassus continued, "In my own experience of the Lusitani and Gallaeci, peoples who share many similarities, I would say that comparing the Dacians to Gauls might be like comparing Roman to Greek," he mused to his thoughtful companions.

"Either way," said Galba with a mollified smile at the well-educated young man, "I suspect they shall be learning about our order of battle soon enough! Pannonia has good farmland, so I hear. I wonder if Dacia is the same? We have all heard of the Dacian King Burebista and his growing power and wealth. Imagine if he decides to head south? He has Greece on one side and Italy on the other," wondered the tall officer.

Labienus had finished reading the scroll and stuffed it behind his breastplate. His severe face had not changed as he read the missive, but he did not return to his half-eaten meal and pushed away the plate before looking around at his companions.

"Gentlemen, as I have stated from the start of our journey, we are not yet going to Dacia or Pannonia, or any of these other speculations. Why do you think Caesar asked for us all to come urgently? If we are heading to Pannonia, why are we on this road instead of heading up the *Via Flaminia*? We are going to Gaul!" he said in his curt tone that always made him appear rude.

Pedius scratched his balding head. "Yes, Labienus, you keep saying that, but the Legions are still in Aquileia," he said and sucked on a tooth as the stern-faced Titus Labienus turned on him.

"Yes, and Caesar is the overall commander of those Legions. And he has told us all to meet him in Gaul," he said abruptly. "You can ask him yourself in a few days' time. He said he is leaving Rome to catch up with us as soon as he has dealt with a few pressing matters that concern him. As you know, he can travel at a phenomenal speed and has asked us to press on and have the 10th Legion staged ready in Arausio. As I suspected, there *is* an issue with the Gauls. Perhaps the Allobroges again? Perhaps the rumour about the Helvetian tribes is true? Who knows? We will find out when we get there," he said curtly, standing up and calling to the messenger who had just finished his meal and was the only other person in the room.

"You there, fetch the station master!" he said, snapping his fingers at the small man who nodded and, clutching his messenger bag, scurried down the rear passageway. Crassus looked at the stern features of Labienus and tried to calculate what else had been in this man's note.

"Gaul it is, then. Did Caesar say anything else in his message?" the young man asked inquisitively.

Labienus fixed him with his unblinking stare for a moment.

"No, just that we should push on, as the situation seems a little more serious than he had originally heard," said the stern man as the stocky and clearly quite irritated station master hurried into the room.

"What will it be, sirs?" he said as politely as he could in his gruff voice.

"Apologies but your bed will have to wait" Labienus replied sarcastically, "We shall be leaving well before dawn! Probably after the third watch. I want *all* the men roused and *all* horses ready for the departure with food for the journey."

He nodded to the older mansio manager, who clearly looked even more sour at the prospect of very little sleep. As Tud scribbled in his wax tablet, Labienus saw the messenger creeping off down the narrow corridor towards the sleeping rooms.

"You there, messenger! Are you heading to Narbo and do you have any messages for the 10th Legion?" he barked.

Ocella froze, turned to the fearsome-looking officer and replied in a faltering voice, "Yes… Um, yes sir. The Legion in Narbo is on my list." He coughed, fishing around in his messenger bag. "I

343

have several messages, in fact, sir," he said, regaining some of his composure.

Labienus nodded and asked Tud to go and wake the clerk who travelled with them. The stout man checked his tablet under the light of a nearby lamp before he went off down the narrow corridor, muttering to himself, "Number nine... The clerk in number nine."

Labienus looked back at Ocella. "Get yourself ready! I shall have another message for you in a moment. You will need to ride immediately!" he said to the small rider, whose heart clearly sank a little.

All the officers except Labienus hurried off to snatch some sleep while he dictated to the sleepy clerk, who immediately wrote a quick message. Ocella sighed internally as he hurried to his room and donned the wet cloak and sandals, putting his slippers away in the bag. He came back to the common room to get the small scroll and swore an oath he deliver it as fast as he could. Tud then beckoned him down the back passage. The mansio keeper had a piece of bread, cheese and some dried fish that he bade Ocella stuff in his travel pack.

"Looks like yer shit out of luck! But me too, I reckon!" he grunted, wrapping the damp toga about his head again. He placed his lamp on the small shelf by the door, peered with his one good eye at the tablet, then stuffed it back in his belt. Tud cursed as he opened the door to see the drizzle still coming down. He snatched up the meat cleaver from the kitchen before he walked out into the fine rain.

"Number four... She is a good nag, in number four," Tud muttered.

Ocella was no longer smirking at his host's attention to detail as he mounted his horse and checked his satchels were secure. The dispatch rider hurried out of the mansio and with a last check on all the buckles of his messenger bag he spurred the horse northward into the darkness.

Chapter 23

The section stopped work in the bright morning sun and stood up squinting as the galloping rider approached. The clattering hooves on the flat flagstones of the road rang out from a distance in the still, cold air and Kratos waved his scarf to warn the dispatch rider that the section of road was dug up. An important message could be delayed by a horse with a broken leg, but often it was nice to flag them down just for some news. Sometimes the riders just went onto the earth either side and kept going with a shout of thanks for the warning, but today the rider did not and came to a skidding halt right by the workers. He blinked his teary eyes and unwound his scarf from a red, wind-chapped face as his horse breathed great clouds into the cold air from its labouring lungs. His kit and equipment told us he was military and as he revealed his face some of the section recognised him as a cavalryman from the 10th Legion.

"Here you are!" he said cheerfully. "I did not realise you had moved so far up country? You better get packing and heading back," he jerked his thumb back down the road as his horse snorted and lathered.

Galba and the commander of the guard detachment were both closing in and spoke at the same time. "What's going on?" they said almost in unison.

The young cavalryman leaned forward and patted the horse's heaving neck as it snorted and puffed, catching its breath.

"We got a dispatch rider in the middle of the night! The centurions have sent riders out to get all work parties in immediately. The cohorts in Tarraco joined up with the cohorts coming up the road and were moving north on the Via Herculea as I left. I suspect the 10th must be halfway to Narbo by now," he grinned and patted the horse again.

Galba sniffed and placed a hand on the horse's bridle while he tapped his thigh with his club.

"Narbo? That's in Gaul!? I will ask you again... what is going on? What were your orders? Why is the 10th marching to Gaul!" he said in a low but commanding voice.

The cavalryman sighed internally but eyed the club in the hand of the decanus and noticed the gaunt faces of these very impatient men who had suffered on the road for half of the winter. He sat upright in the saddle and looked the decanus square in the face.

"Apologies, I did not realise how remote you lot are out here. I am instructed to send word that all work parties are to rejoin the 10th immediately as they march towards Aquileia to form up with the rest of the legions gathered there. His honour the Proconsul Gaius Julius Caesar has requested the 10th Legion personally and will take command of the army as we move onwards," said the cavalryman smartly. He then leaned forward conspiratorially. "The way the officers received the messengers, it seems something pretty big is about to happen!" the young man said, nodding in earnest.

Felix pushed his way forward and eyed the man on the horse.

"Right! So *why* is all this going on?" he asked, irritated with the young messenger. "Why in the name of the fattest whore in Corduba are all the Legions forming up in Aquileia?"

The horseman started to smile once more, unable to hide his enthusiasm.

"Why do you think?" he said, tapping the long cavalry sword he had slung at his hip as he broke into another huge grin. "We are going to war!"

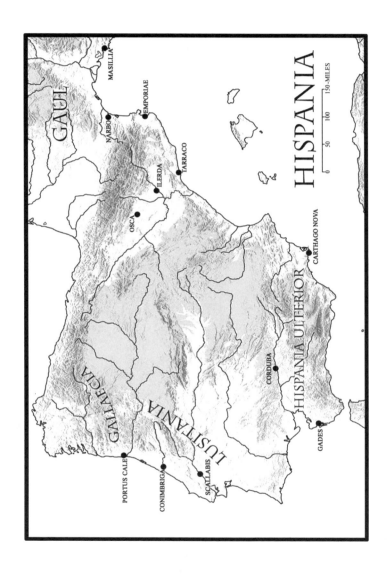

HISPANIA

0 50 100 150-MILES

GAUL

MASILLIA
EMPORIAE
NARBO
TARRACO
ILERDA
OSCA

CARTHAGO NOVA

HISPANIA ULTERIOR

CORDUBA

GALLAECIA

LUSITANIA

GADES

PORTUS CALE
CONIMBRIGA
SCALLABIS

349

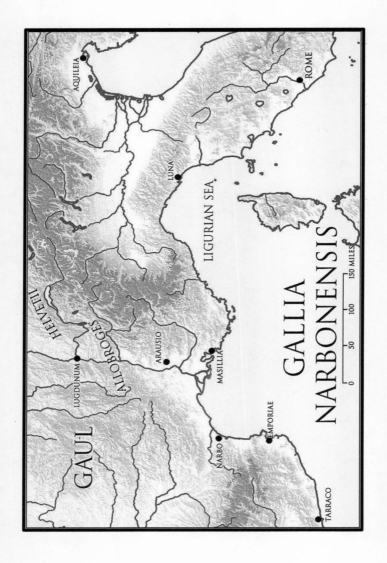

AQUILEIA

ROME

LUNA

LIGURIAN SEA

HELVETII

ALLOBROGES

ARAUSIO

MASILLIA

GAUL

LUGDUNUM

GALLIA
NARBONENSIS

EMPORIAE

NARBO

TARRACO

150 MILES

100

50

0